I0579721

Charm &
Strangeness

CHARM & STRANGENESS

Roc Sandford

Gometra 2018

Images by Robert Gibbings.
Frontispiece from *Sweet Thames Run Softly* © 1940
Title page and end-piece from
Marvels of the Insect World © 1938
Text © Roc Sandford 2018.   Set in 12 & 11 point
Golden Cockerel by Roc Sandford
This edition dated 27th July 2018.
Printed and bound by IngramSpark
Cloth ISBN 978-1-900389-01-3
Paperback ISBN 978-1-900389-09-9
This is number
of an edition of
copies

If you like this book, please
sign up for news of more at
rocsandford.com/list

Slim Truth dismissed without a character,
And gaga Falsehood highly recommended.

Greed showing shamelessly her naked money,
And all Love's wondering eloquence debased
To a collector's slang,
Smartness in furs,
And Beauty scratching miserably for food,
Honour self-sacrificed for calculation,
And Reason stoned by Mediocrity,
Freedom by Power shockingly maltreated,
And Justice exiled till Saint Geoffrey's Day.
(W. H. Auden, *Birthday Poem* (To Christopher Isherwood.)
Faber, *Collected Shorter Poems 1930-1944.*)

By night, mixed with fumes, the smell of latex.

And geranium.

A fizzling mosquito. You smack your face, silence, and then the noise fires up again. Insect music a sidelight on the future: reclining on your sweating mattress, seedy, beat-up, dazed, you are prepped for a death sticky, rank, and not that sad.

But a dream, recollection or presentiment: running up basalt steps of a grandiose, fuck-off museum in warm, splatting rain. Squirted, jetted, as in a car wash or a film, but no wind, just frying rain.

Inside, perfume of drenched animals. A mushy crowd, mussed hats and sodden anoraks, furling umbrellas and prodding dulled micaceous flags as their own steam floats towards wavering lights. Rolling my galoshes off, and pushing my shoes into a pair of grizzled over-slippers. Displaying my *Roneographed* permit and crossing wide galleries, under the belligerent gaze of guards. A gleaming light off the river, burning in the windows and on pale floors. And stopping at *Lust*, brought here by Catherine.

In love with her pasty face, bluish-violet eyes, corrupting, guiltless lips. Beauty is the promise of future pleasure sings Stendhal, when he means pain. Standing there a long time, lustful but loving, too late by several hundred years, yet framing plans.

Reclining on my mattress now, my heart drumming like a hostage in an auto trunk. Someone grazes my nether parts with lapis fingernails, vermillion lips. Under a sweaty shroud quite long enough to cover up my face.

But people flooding in, eyeing the pictures with suspicion whilst studying grateful Photostat notes. The galleries smelling less waxy than feculent. Advancing over brittle parquet with snow-like squeaks, moonwalking up an avenue of white-washed, aliasing Atlantids with mounting hysteria until, showing my permit again, I reach the library. My favourite desk. Going to the counter to collect the references.

Creeping back, insectile beneath a monumental barrel-vault in white and gilt, to read.

A marked shrinkage in the range ....

And looking up. At the book counter, a woman. The shape of her back as she waited, her thumbs hooked into the natal pockets of dark blue-jeans, her weight on one inflected leg, the other cocked loosely on a pointed toe, and swinging idly round. Striking in this drab place.

Her cool skin in darkness under the stiff cloth, and under that her meat, pelvis, spine. Navy-blue shoulders had twisted hair splayed out on them. Trying to hold it against her, this spray of greenish gold---the weird colours honey turns as you pasteurize and congeal it. But all the shallows, the routine factoid surfaces of nature, set against delight. Because something frothed and slushed and foamed in me. The room rather dark. Reminding myself of those occasions when, running straight down the street after the svelte answer, the auburn solution, you stop her, she turns, she has a beard.

... shrinkage in the range of ....

But I couldn't read. Could hardly see. Those lips, that twisted hair. Because though I'd never seen her face I put *Lust's* there. Here, in the heart of the State, this white Imperial library walled in pinkish, gold-tooled books was no more than a softened box prepared for the rarest artefact of all, the nicest work of art.

Someone beside me.

Off-gold hair vibrating with the movement of a pen. Thick loopy letters in green ink, the bitter taste of which got under my tongue.

She had taken the next chair. Needing to see her face. Her ear, propped on one hand, growing gradually pink. She knew everything. Beside myself, and needing to run.

By her elbow, a crooked tower of small white books, bound in vellum, with hand written black-letter titles, and also a few trade paperbacks with acetate jackets.

A twitch of her hair. Was she already cross with me for glaring at her? Before we'd met? It can and does happen.

She turned a page of her notebook, and again: writing. In both symbols and words---hieroglyphics, almost. Pictograms, glyphs. But first on the right-hand page, then on the left. Was she *trying* to be different?

What to do? My mind tornadic, but that was nothing to how it was when, having slowly laid down the pen, she turned her head, revolving it jerkily like a machine. And---forced a smile.

Scared.

She wasn't wearing a brace, but she smiled as if she was. And turned back. Went on writing. The red corruption of the lips, the bluish-violet innocence of her eyes.

Shit. Now she was copying something out.

> *... is because Arthur Schopenhauer believes the use of the word* logos *in the introduction to the gospel ascribed to John, 'so strange and mysterious and verging on the absurd' ...*

But what do I ask, what do I say?

> *... comes from the Pythagorean philosophy of numbers, and the word in its arithmetical sense of ratio ...*

We've never met, but ....

> *... which forms for the Pythagoreans the innermost, indestructible essence of being ...*

Guilty of offensive objectification, reduction to a body or to appearance, or worse (Langton, 2009) I yet found I was standing up, one hand on the back of my chair, ready to address the library at large. This is why she looked at me again, quizzical, her forehead temporarily corrugated into a sense organ. A red spot appeared on the front of her throat. The delirious scents of fresh alcohol and book dust; heaven a library, library a heaven, etc. Waiting for me to speak. Curious, at least, as to what I would say. A few stray fronds of greenish hair vined about her temples and her ears. Making my heart rattle, disturbing the other readers, scattered unevenly amongst the tables, whose rasping breath had fallen into unison, whose eyes had closed. As carefully as I could, I sat down. The sensation of when someone unknown takes away your chair.

Her forehead brittle, and her lips as if this same someone unknown, not hard, had hit her there. Their swollen colour changing steadily to a deeper red. The dark-blue strobing glitter through hair of half-open eyes, and the deepening red, opened over the dulled gleam of her opened teeth---well, fear. In sudden funk, terror, shifting away my chair, tightening my lips in an attempted smile which only made them bulge, I looked away.

I could hear her shuffling her things. Trying again to read.

A marked shrinkage in the range of ...

But on the white page amongst the black letters was an ornate insect in iridescent gold & green, imagic book-worm, shuddering its wing case and waving antennae finer than hairs. Understanding why it was here. So I could speak to her. Already pointing I turned towards her, my mouth brimming with teeth and words. She wasn't there.

The sky outside fetid and heaving; nauseous, drunk. The enormous square, with its off-centred, waggling column, deserted. Later, the Western hotels, the restaurants, the airport, even the railway station, its platform hollow as a stage and a night train cantering away. Not there.

Dank years later, face down now on a grey, wet sheet, my eyes, nose, even my frown of pain moulded into the perished rubber mattress underneath. Blisters all up my leg, and someone had been hacking at my tongue. As I reviewed these cringing mysteries: who on earth she was; and where was I?

I found her in a palace, on an island, in a reservoir. The rain, on the way over, crackling not on basalt steps but on the lacquered coach-roof of the Foundation's launch. Into the thickets on the island's shore, short waves of fresh green reservoir-water rolled and broke, jostling a soup of twigs, duck-weed, dead gulls, plastic bags and Styrofoam. It was noon, but the sky had gone so dim that the sodium lamps which lit the palace walls by night came on automatically and boiled the rain. Steam rose from each lamp, distended and fuming against torn clouds: trapped in this enchanted castle was a sleeping fairy tale.

By the time we reached harbour the storm had passed through. Everything white and smoking in an unexpected light, though the sky beyond the palace's grim, mediaeval keep was still writhing, flowing. On the quay the Belisha Foundation's fossil Rover, christened Auntie by the late Dotty Belisha, waited glossy as a prune with engine running and its single Cyclops headlamp lit. It carried away my bag as I followed on foot, dodging blinding puddles on the gravel.

Cutting through a farm-yard: deserted granaries, byres and stables, the remains of the rain still squirting off shallow tin roofs. Vacant windows, a blunt portico with a rusty tractor parked under it, and four eroded porphyry columns standing in an orange pool in which floated three white ducks.

I felt drunk, and sick. Something moving along a wall. Jeans stained by rain, rat-tailed hair stained too and dangling loosely down a hollow back. Her white shirt sticking to her chest so blackish nipples shone through. In one hand, half a loaf. She was staring seriously, steadily, at the ducks.

She came out of the shadow of the building. Each of the other colours- --face, hair, jeans---turned white. The over-exposed curve of her wet, disordered head and the line of her white forehead and white nose were haloed by a vague rainbow, set against slate green woods and slate green, flailing cloud. It was still raining there, but here ...

She turned her face back suddenly towards me---still moving, holding her bread---in an unexpected, returning flash of cream, raspberry and blue. Screwing up her eyes she vizored the side of her hand against her forehead because she saw me, or thought she did. All around us, white raindrops were falling slowly and steadily like seeds. The air smelt of rain on dust. As looking back she walked into the perishing vulcanised wheel of the tractor, pushed at it, dropped the loaf, and sat down in mud.

And smiled. The ducks, their wings open, ran away. Like me. I had seen nature bathing. And trembling. If tamed, then only just. Seated in an orange puddle not with a *splash* but a *plok*.

When I came back, followed in single file by three noisy, hurrying ducks, the water was still pulsing, its ripples hard, and I touched it to my lips. She of course had gone. I waited for her to change, dry her hair, check or reapply mascara and come back. She never did. And so, crying over spilt blood, heavy-spirited and very late, I climbed the squeaking paths towards the palace.

Dazzled, for a moment, by the opulence of the hall. Everything gilt and mirror except for what was malachite, ormolu and amber. On the floor a silky, faded Aubusson. And at the far end of an enfilade, the clamour of lunch.

At the threshold of the great salon---well, all these clattering strangers. Someone in green livery hurried me to a place which, thankfully, was between Kohlhaas and Cundy. At the head---Leicher, giving me a dirty look. Something peeled and stark about his eyes. Hard, hurt even.

The man who brought my *borscht* poured me wine. Then he took away Cundy's empty bowl. Hearing meanwhile, the far side of Kohlhaas, a voice I couldn't understand. And when Kohlhaas leant back to hand up his bowl to a footman, like a bruised Narcissus I gazed suddenly down into mine. She was there, beyond him. I saw her.

Glaring into my soup. Seeing my face reflected in glossy purple. The face of a beast. But looking at her again. The room darker than it had been. When she saw me, she shut up.

---'Go on,' Kohlhaas said.

Silence.

---'Go on, it's amusing.'

But she only closed her lips and shook her head. Without looking at him. Leaning so closely over her own soup that a stray strand of hair dipped in.

---'Can't be helped,' said Kohlhaas.

He cleaned it conscientiously with his napkin and up it came like battered gold. Meanwhile she was trying to dip her face in too. Or, from its colour, already had. A sudden glance my way. Confusion; speechlessness; sheepishness even.

I tried to say something---failed.

She wore fresh clothes. And the bread: she'd left that in the puddle, yet had a pile on her side plate. Her face was dry. But not her hair. As a hairclip she used an ear. That red too.

At each place, a bottle of fizzy water in a silver coaster. I drank mine. And glasses of different coloured wines. I drank all three. Kohlhaas was speaking, his voice droning like a voice in an aeroplane. She had laid her hands in her lap where, researching her own future, she stared at them. Her face making jerks as she tried to lift it.

But a commotion at the head of the table. Kohlhaas half-rising from his seat, napkin dangling from one hand like the handkerchief used to start a race. Johnston, Waddington and Sir Mel Pease gathered round Leicher. The great man had pushed back his chair and was gagging. The hurt eyes goggled. Then he flung his own napkin on the table and, raising his palms in front of his face, folding his fingers and extending his thumbs, grimly studied his nails.

---'What happened?' asked Kohlhaas

---'Search me,' she stuttered.

The others returning to their places. Leicher turned his face away as a man in a dinner jacket took away the crispy foil of a dead fish, sprinkled with chopped parsley. Then the word came down the line. Leicher had expressly informed them he couldn't eat garlic, but they'd put garlic in.

---'I would have had it,' she said. 'I love garlic.'

---'Really?' asked Kohlhaas.

She wasn't joking, and yet, her own fish lying there, round eyed, morose, untouched.

---'Have you remarked how power tends to corrupt,' asked Cundy, his mouth white with fish meat, tipping his fork back subtly towards Leicher.

---'Jim!' implored Kohlhaas.

---'Power doesn't corrupt, but discloses,' she said. 'As does its liquid phase, money. And its gaseous, fame.'

Cundy, craning to look at her, slightly aghast.

---'You dislike garlic,' said the man in a dinner jacket, taking away my fish before I'd even started. I was staring at a chocolate *soufflé* when it happened again. 'You dislike chocolate.'

Knocking back a coffee and a port, I figured what to say. Kohlhaas hadn't touched his port. Knocking that back too.

---'Excuse me?' I called across him. Kohlhaas looked surprised but leaned back.

She ignored me.

---'Excuse me, excuse me.'

Or she didn't hear. Leaning on the table, half-rising, I shouted:

---'Please!'

All down the table people looked on as she looked up. Her eyes making me tipsy; I'd drunk too much soup. She opened her lips questioningly over opened teeth, looked into my face, closed them again and smiled. Looking straight at me, brave. And then away. Uncertain, hesitant, dropping her smile and her eyes; before, more slowly, looking back and asking:

---'Yes?'

At which moment Leicher rang his spoon against a wineglass. We all rose. And went into the ballroom.

---'Who is she? What's her name?' I asked Cundy who had joined me in
the back row of seats.

---'She's a hellovagirl!' said Cundy. 'Boom-boom!'

---'Tell me, please. *Don't* point at her!'

---'Eugene Skippergate's only daughter. He owns Scandinavia? You must
 meet her.'

---'Yes,' said Kohlhaas, standing at the end of the row and looking on.
'Hey-nonny-no, as it were. Come hither, with a ring-a-ding, ding.'

---'No.'

Cundy looked at me sharply, then smiled, sweetly. And said:

---'O. I see. But you won't get her. Ha-ha.'

Then, gloomy, adding:

---'I've tried.'

---'Shhh,' said Kohlhaas.

Because she was sliding along the next row. A quick smile back at
Kohlhaas and one for Cundy as she sat down in front of us.

A lock of hair thick as a banana hung down the back of her chair. The
urge to hold and pull it. Up on the podium with Tod Waddington,
Leicher cleared his throat and opened his mouth. All fell silent and the
few still standing quickly found seats.

---'Who *are* you Dr Skippergate?'

This was Cundy into silence. The lock crept away. She looked slowly
round, forehead wrinkled, eyebrows raised.

---'Excuse me?' she asked.

---'Who *are* you?'

Kohlhaas flapping his hands.

---'No, Jim!' he said. 'Not like that!'

People began to turn. I was sweating. It was the stress of holding the future up. Always on the point of dropping it, especially with Cundy barging about. She, meanwhile, wondering how to take it. Her eyes, slightly crossed in her confusion, moved from Cundy across me to Kohlhaas, then back to me. As they did so, all around me, the room grew dark. Motorised curtains were sliding over the windows behind which, like the haw in the eye of a nestling, blackout blinds dropped. The lights glowed fitfully and went out. And crumpled over the gilt and mirrors of the ballroom wall, these words emerged:

A short herstory of SMM

Even as we watched, to a crackly snatch of spinet music, a screen slid from a slit in the coved ceiling and assumed them, ironed them out. Leicher, clearing his throat and goggling at us in the unnatural light of the overhead projector.

Then he began.

---'*SMM! Dream of young years, religion of my soul! I of course at once realised quite well how I had stumbled across a momentous revelation, if you like the* caput Nili *of sociometry* (vide *Leicher 1938, Leicher & Osbert 1940, Leicher et al. 1941*) ...'

His sonorous voice with its guttural twang, the sing-song intonation of a man pretending he isn't reading from notes, together with the overheated ballroom. Well: it was---even with her sitting just in front of me---well, very hard to stay awake. He'd only just started, but already my head kept lolling about. Kohlhaas was poking me helpfully, but with some alarm.

---'You're falling asleep,' he whispered.

---'Can't help it.'

---'You can.'

---'I can't.'

Hearing him she craned round to look at me, covered her mouth with her hand, and lengthening her eyes, made them wrap slightly round the sides of her head.

In order to keep going, I fixed my eyes on Leicher.

---'*Now* Webster's *defines 'science' as ...'*

She, meanwhile, put up her hair and pierced it with a yellow pencil
whose freshly shaven wood was the colour of her flesh. The strands
which hung against her neck had glints like the glints in the wings of a
clothes-moth.

---'*... by a multiple regression analysis of the data obtained revealed that ...'*

On the screen, a data cloud, and through it a thick red line. The next
thing I remembered was waking from a nightmare that I kept dropping
off in a boring but important lecture to find Kohlhaas prodding me
again. Leicher, already?, was preparing to sign off.

---'*... for this truly astonishing hypothesis and this truthfully wonderful result.'*

As soon as he closed his mouth and made, deliberately, the face of a frog,
there was an appreciative murmur followed by a roar of claps.

A moment's silence as the clapping died reluctantly. Kohlhaas still
clapping vigorously when all the rest had stopped. Sir Mel Pease quelling
him with a meaningful over-the-shoulder glare before rising from the
front row to say:

---'I think we call all sincerely say: thank you Professor Leicher. Now: have
we many questions please?'

I wanted to ask one, wanted to make my mark for her, but it was hard to
think what. Hard to think at all with her so close, her hair still bundled
up, though beginning to fray, perhaps because she'd taken out the
pencil and in the dimness, whilst smelling faintly sweet and fermented,
was writing something out. And well anyway, the air too hot. Heated
by the projectors, our bodies and beyond its nictating blinds, the sun.
Notebook keyboards fluttered. Through dazzling chinks came thyme,
rosemary, and the vague pulsing fizz of crickets. There was a weight
in the air, nothing was going to happen, but something should. Then
something did. Her voice, forced.

---'I'm sorry, Professor, but in your argument ...'

Shit.

---'... there is a potential fallacy.'

A moment's silence, then a shuffling as all turned to look. The word 'fallacy', potential or not, was tactless, mean. A Termagant, harpy, bluestocking?

---'Speak up, speak up' Leicher called.

---'I hate to say this, but there may be a flaw in your argument. I think.'

She stuttered now. Leicher, screwing up his eyes, lifted his glasses, the better to glare at her.

---'Can't see you. Stand up.'

She stood.

---'Lights!' commanded Leicher.

Tod Waddington pushed at a slide and lights came up. Cundy was disclosed in the act of praying, the tips of his fingers touching lips formed into an imbecilic grin.

---'Oh boy, oh boy,' he said, 'what fun it is to be an academic!'

Leicher's eyes withering him, so he slumped down with a winded:

---'Gosh!'

---'Curtains!' Leicher commanded.

Waddington prodded a button, but Cundy and Dr Skippergate didn't disappear down chutes opening in the rug. Watered silk curtains simply hummed and parted and simultaneously behind them the blackout blinds rode up. The room inflated with coloured sunlight as against a storm of bored sighs and pained exclamation, Dr Skippergate explained what the problem was.

---'You may not have sufficient degrees-of-freedom for the confidence levels you indicate.'

A further silence and then:

---'Who are you to say that?'

---'Excuse me?'

---'I said it clearly the first time. Who are you to say that.'

---'Well ... statistics ...'

And gently, slowly, in the presence of a dangerous beast, her jeaned knees together and buckling sideways, she sat down. But Leicher was shouting:

---'Stand up! Stand up!'

Flushing, she stood.

---'Name!'

---'---?'

---'What is your *name* please? I can't be much clearer than that' Leicher said.

---'Hella Skippergate.'

---'Well, Dr Skippergate, you might like to know this result has been based on a total of---yes!---twelve thousand data pairs and that this trial alone was one of seven such trials. The others we have rejected because yes indeed they have not been significant at 95% level. Degrees of Freedom! We have 7 times 11,999 of these.'

---'He's right, you know', affirmed Tod Waddington, nodding significantly.

Around the ballroom, the murmur of assent.

Hella using her tongue to push out her cheek. Then:

---'Professor, you have just identified a second potential source of spurious confidence.'

---'Yes, my dear?' asked Leicher, smiling, gracious. But his pale eyes, magnified by his glasses, were shifting uneasily, so that the brittle blue irises and yellowed corneas flowed and bulged and then seemed to melt and blend.

---'Out of seven trials, you chose the one which worked. If you went on long enough, you could obtain a spurious significant result for almost any hypothesis based on independent observations drawn from a population probability distribution like this.' She spoke gently, giving complex directions to a tourist lost. 'Even from a true random number generator, hypothetical of course.'

---'Of course', whispered Cundy.

Her colours: the blue of her face, of the forked veins under her pale
temples and neck, of her white shirt and blue-jeans, deepened and
became saturated, dripping from the strands of her hair and her finger
ends.

---'And I happen to know you are totally and utterly mistaken about that.'

---'It's a proof point. We don't need to argue, just work through the proof
from first principles.'

She looked at proof and we looked at her, just as by night we gazed at
the blushing harvest moon, tinted by the atmosphere, illuminated by
an invisible sun. Few understood what she was on about but then, the
charm of such cults as hers lies not in their clarity and not in their
obscurity, but in the intersection of these.

---'As the famous saying goes: You are entitled to your own opinions, but
not your own facts', whispered Kohlhaas.

---'Can we have one meeting please folks', said Sir Mel. 'You were saying,
Professor Kohlhaas?'

---'You are entitled to your own opinions, but not your own facts', gulped
Kohlhaas.

---'Beauty is proof, proof beauty', added Cundy, helpfully.

---'Ok?', asked Waddington slowly.

Waddington's new partner, Ms Modestine Auch, hailing from Paris, had a
question to ask.

---'What is it all this stuff and nonsense of 'degrees-of-freedom' please?
Since long time I have wondered this.'

Someone gasped, then whistled. It was Professor Johnstone. Then he
explained.

---'To tell you the honest truth, at first sight this concept often
seems almost mystical, with no practical meaning---this partly due
to simplifying explanations (like this one!), also counter-intuitive
properties of the concept itself, such as non-integer degrees of freedom.

But it is not at all hard to make mathematically precise given a bit of general knowledge of n-dimensional Euclidean geometry, subspaces and orthogonal projections.'

---'Yes,' Hella said. 'For instance, if you were to let P be an orthogonal projection from Rn to a p-dimensional subspace L and if x is any arbitrary n-vector then Px is in L, x–Px and Px are orthogonal and x–Px ⊠ L⊠ is in the orthogonal complement of L. The dimension of the orthogonal complement, L⊠, is n–p. So if x is free to vary in an n-dimensional space then x–Px is free to vary in an n–p dimensional space. Thus you can say that x–Px has n–p degrees of freedom.'

Keith Johnstone nodded as she spoke, using his fingers meanwhile to iron out his tie.

---'I haven't the foggiest what this has all got to do with SMM,' said Waddington.

Can't we just wash our hands of this and return to the germane.

---'Well,' she said, 'This is the thing because it is germane to your methodology because let's say X is an n-dimensional random vector and L is a model of its mean, i.e., the mean vector E(X) is in L, we can call X–PX the vector of residuals, and then we use the residuals to estimate the variance. The vector of residuals has n–p degrees of freedom, that is, it is constrained to a subspace of confined or constrained dimension n–p, like a perfect plane in a 3D Euclidian space for example. And so on for other statistical parameters, though slightly more involved. So the concept is relevant to statistics, and statistics is relevant to SMM because it forms the backbone of your methodology, at least as Professor Leicher has very kindly presented it today.'

---'May I raise another issue, Hella,' said Johnstone.

Several people called out:

---'Speak up!'

---'Address the chair!'

But Johnstone raised his issue without waiting for her permission, speaking up, or addressing the chair.

---'I think there is a certain amount of confusion here emanating
from the concept of independence. Which of course is one of the
assumptions for the proof.'

---'Yes, independence is a conceptually a little tricky because two
different yet related senses of *independent* are here germane. There is
independence of random variables and there is *functional* independence,'
she said. 'One of the many situations where conceptual distinctions are
masked, sometimes with almost a hint, a taste, a scent of conspiracy, by
the confusion introduced by the sharing of a natural language name.'

---'Functional independence?' asked Kohlhaas with what sounded like
genuine interest.

---'Well obviously,' she said with the gleam of a smile at Kohlhaas who
was clearly something of a teacher's pet w.r.t. Hella, 'as an example
(of functional independence), imagine we made morphometric
measurements of subjects □ say, for simplicity, in familiar 3D Euclidian
space, the three orthogonal dimensions X, Y, Z, surface areas
$S=2(XY+YZ+ZX)$, and volumes $V=XYZ$ of a set of real world cuboids-
--say a (non-empty) set of toy building blocks, brightly painted. The
three dimensions can for the purpose of argument be assumed to
be independent random variables, but all five variables are *dependent*
random variables because they depend on one another. The five are
also *functionally* dependent because the codomain (not the domain of
course!) ...

---'Of course,' said Kohlhaas.

---'Yes, yes, yes!' said Leicher. 'Get on with it.'

---'Thank you, yes, the codomain of the vector-valued random
variable (X,Y,Z,S,V) traces a three-dimensional manifold in R_5. Thus,
locally at any block □, there are two functions f□ and g□ for which
f□(X(□),...,V(□))=0 and g□(X(□),...,V(□))=0 for blocks □ 'near' □ and the
derivatives of f and g evaluated at □ are linearly independent. Now □
here's the thing □ for many probability measures on the blocks, subsets
of the variables such as (X,S,V) are dependent as random variables but
functionally independent.'

---'Owww!' It was Cundy howling, his eyes revolving in different senses
and omegas, his hands on the sides of his head, his mouth open.

---'This is just arcane jargon, said Waddington. 'Could we have an
explanation in queen's English if you please?'

---'Very roughly, in this context, the issue is how many observations
you've made, and how likely your confidence in your model is to have
been significant rather than arising by chance. The more observations,
the more confidence you have in your result, because the less likely
you are to have picked up random aberrations which are accidentally
skewing the result. If you're looking for a weak effect, you may need
many observations to have confidence that your sample parameter
estimate of any population parameters are within reasonable bounds or
the, that your result or hypothesis didn't merely arise by chance, rather
than identifying a repeatable regularity in nature. My concern is for
the assumptions you are making regarding independence of sample
variables, for the assumption of normality, and the for loss of degrees
of freedom when you estimate parameters as intermediate steps, part
of the procedure Professor Leicher used to calculate his statistical
coefficients. I'm not sure of this, the fallacy may in practice be harmless,
and it may not be a fallacy at all. But at the very least, the Professor may
be looking at the wrong column in the significance table. His results
may or may not be significant when the correct column is checked.'
Norbert Leicher meanwhile had got a grip on himself.

---'And what may I ask made you think up all of this?'

---'It was a little puzzling, how you arrived at your result, that's all. When
you think about it, its immediately obvious that something is not, may
not be, could not be, right.'

If good at statistics (we didn't yet know this yet), she was clearly bad
at politics---but perhaps it's always either/or, given the natures of the
beasts. Which could be why the world is a mess.

---'It's not just us who finds it puzzling,' said Johnstone, 'I think it's
fair to say, I find, that for the more attentive students, this a concept
which causes a lot of difficulty. You know it reminds me of the famous
anecdote I've always loved, which was the one about, about Russell
asking Moore what he thought of his new student, Wittgenstein. Moore
said he thought very highly of him, and when Russell asked why, he said
it was because he was the only one who looked puzzled in lectures.'

---'And?' asked Waddington, looking puzzled.

---'But, to return to Dr Skippergate's point please Professor Johnstone, and I am addressing Dr Skippergate now, why did the rest of us not conceive of it then, if so---*odious ...*'

General laughter. And from Leicher, a yellow smile.

---'---'

---'If it is so obvious?'

---'---'

---'Answer. No, do not sit down. Answer.'

He had a point. Perhaps she wasn't right at all. But wrong. She had to be. He couldn't have orchestrated a fallacious discipline over a period of fifty years without someone having picked this up. But: the two efficient market economists, the bank-note, the quad. Is that a bank note I see? asks one. Can't be, someone would already have picked it up. (Joke *a propos*, cited by Dr Cundy). Poor girl; her Quixotic folly. To alienate crude power by being mulishly and gloriously wrong: it's what's called walking into a buzz saw; it has been known, but it's unwise and it made me want to help her. Leicher was speaking still:

---'Very bad,' he said.

---'Excuse me?'

---'Bad!'

This pure value-judgement released the tension. A muttering began.

---'Degrees of boredom' said Professor McGovern.

---'Digression of boredom, it is more like,' said Ms Auch.

Leicher took more questions and now at last Hella, with a sigh whose wind I felt as she glanced back, was allowed to sink into her seat.

Then Sir Mel, retired diplomat and able chair as he was, sleek and perpetual behind the tinted pebble lenses of his spectacles, took them off---looking suddenly tired---and said with a sad look at Leicher:

---'I think we've reached the, em, natural break?'

---'Excuse me?' asked Leicher, also suddenly weary, grey.

---'Tea-time, don't you think?' said Sir Mel.

---'Yes, yes, yes,' said Leicher impatiently. Mel rang his pen gently against a glass:

---'The symposium is adjourned for tea.'

Laid out on silver trenchers in the drawing room were tiny tomato sandwiches on coarse rye bread. Tea---China and Indian---steamed in silver pots amidst pyramids of gull's eggs, dull as teeth. Chewing conscientiously and bearing a tea-cup, Tod Waddington came up to me.

---'Who are you? What's your connection with us?'

---'Anything for a Festschrift?'

---'Dr Cundy,' he said severely, 'I wasn't speaking to you.'

---'I'm interested in porting the methodologies of SMM into spatial biology. So my friend's mother, who's a friend of Leicher's, got me in,' I told him.

---'You're the one who steps out with Professor Ciama's daughter?' he said with some excitement. 'Is it true Orla's accepted the chair of FNCS? I'll tell you what ...'

He was rummaging in his brief-case and brought out an off-print which, crossing out his own name, printed at the top of it, he signed, dated and dedicated.

---'Would you bring this to her and say how much we are appreciating her over here in Europe?'

Norbert Leicher was watching us, and Waddington curled and uncurled his forefinger whilst grinning invitingly.

---'You were late for luncheon?' said Leicher, coming over. 'Where is your identity card?'

---'He's Dr Ciama junior's partner. I'll find it for him,' said Waddington helpfully, going over to the small green cloth on which the last few lay.

---'Ah yes,' said Leicher, sweetening instantly. 'Orla told me to look after you. It's a little known fact that her own department now commands in excess of a sixteen million dollar spend. Have you everything you need?'

Rescued by Waddington, returning with the card:

---'Here,' he said as he pinned it on. It bore in the centre of the ring of gold stars on a royal blue ground the italic legend *AQRONIM*---some wag, quite possibly Dr Cundy, who'd been deeply involved in the convoluted process of setting it up, had devised a self-referential acrostic for the institute.

---'What's it stand for?' I asked, but Waddington'd already turned away. An exultant, malicious hum of gossip, growing steadily louder, was silenced. Because she was coming in. Her blunt face a glowing pink and the strands of hair which framed it wet. She'd just washed her face.

---'Don't trouble your head,' Kohlhaas advised me from a sofa. 'It can't be helped. The world spins on.'

She took her tea. And stood alone. Sucking brown liquid from the cup without lifting it from its saucer, but lifting alternate feet instead from a burning carpet whilst looking out defiantly from under lowered, sun-bleached eyebrows which just hid the pupils of her eyes. This gave the impression of pure iris, of holy blindness.

No one spoke to her. But sensing me watching---she filled these blind eyes with life.

I looked away.

---'Sit here,' Kohlhaas was saying to me; 'sit with me.'

But I only wanted to sit with her.

Her damp hair, blondish brown now, done up into a gentle fountain half-way up the back of a shell-like skull, hung down in fronds. She saw me again, and smiled. And turned a darker shade of reddish brown.

I felt my way to the pot-bellied sofa in muddy-green watered-silk on the edge of which Kohlhaas perched, carrying my tea-cup, and a dish of eggs and sandwiches which had somehow got sodden with tea. And sat down beside him. Like a blind man. An old one. Slowly.

Through the windows, the purple sun.

---'What's she doing here? Where's she from?' asked someone.

---'She's from Aqronim.'

---'Aqronim?' said Cundy dismissively, having milled towards us; 'Of course she's not. I know the folk at Aqronim. I helped them get going. I made up the acronym. She's not one of them.'

---'I knew it,' I said.

---'At any rate, she's got it wrong. Herostratus,' said Kohlhaas. 'To make a name for yourself you burn down the local supermarket or academic discipline. Norbert Leicher's one of the greats. Look at his knock on impact on the history of ideas. She resembles those 'chavs' who assault famous cricketers in English public houses, just to be on the Home Service news. It shows courage, of course, to take him on. Courage, or stupidity. Herostratus was either courageous or stupid too. I forget what happened to him.'

Hella meanwhile, in a dark corner, was working through a pile of gull's eggs as he spoke. You could see her savouring their taste at the back of her mouth, absent, entranced. Nothing wrong with that. Body as well as spirit. Except that body wasn't what I wanted. This was far from what I wanted with her. Very far. So far that it was what I didn't want, even.

Yet it still looked good, her standing there in new blue-jeans, white trainers and a floppy white shirt with long pointed collar ends, feeding the white eggs through red lips to white teeth with her fingers, one hand held underneath her chin to catch dry yellow crumbs of yolk.

---'She's only doing it to draw attention to herself,' said Waddington.

---'Consuming gull's eggs?'

---'Cundy, please,' he implored. Kohlhaas meanwhile was trying to make an important point:

---'Listen to me,' he begged us.

---'Yes?'

---'Rather as Socrates only did it to draw attention? Galileo? Christ?'

Dressed unexpectedly in neon armour. Defending her.

---'Come again?'

---'What I mean is, should you abandon what you perceive as the truth just because it causes a fuss? Isn't that exactly when you should cling to it?'

---'Yes, but not if you are wrong. How does the saying go: it's a Jewish saying but so apt; anyway, I can't remember it', said Waddington.

---'Perhaps she's right.'

I had to say this; nobody else did.

---'Impossible', said Waddington, drained his tea, and stalked off.

---'So what if she is? Decency should come before mere slavish pedantry and servitude to facts. It's Norbert's baby, don't you see?' Kohlhaas torn, troubled.

---'No.'

---'Oh, but it is; it's Norbert's baby; she can't do this.'

Poor Kohlhaas. A war between two principles was taking place on his face. She meanwhile, defiant in her corner, eating the tomato sandwiches now, stood alone.

---'Oh dear! Can't be helped', he added.

---'What are you doing?'

---'I'm going to ask her to sit with us.'

And off he went; his courtly gestures and, clothed in lush blue corduroy, his enormous bum. When he brought her back with him she didn't look my way. The paisley silk hanky in the breast pocket of his corduroy jacket: this was the shade of her face.

They were sitting next to me now. It wasn't possible, or rather, wasn't realistic: Kohlhaas and beyond him, her.

---'What's your first name', she asked Kohlhaas; 'may I call you by your first name?'

But if she'd talk to Kohlhaas, wouldn't she also talk to me?

Kohlhaas was blushing.

---'What is it? I haven't offended you?'

---'My first name is Elric.'

---'Call him Elric if you *like*,' said Cundy, dubious. He was watching her lovingly, his eyes reflecting the green and yellow light from the long windows. I hated him. Then I realised Kohlhaas was prodding me.

---'Have you met Hella Skippergate?'

Gibbering slightly. I have rather would had---more time. But her lips were moving, she was looking at mine.

---'What?' I asked.

She turned her face away, so I couldn't hear; then looked back, awaiting with patience the answer to her question.

---'What,' I said again. 'What.'

---'I said I have studied in Manhattan.'

---'So what?'

---'But Professor Kohlhaas said Manhattan was where you took your first degree.'

---'So?'

---'I'm sorry?'

Her simple, unimaginable face, expressing confusion.

---'Manhattan: *transfer, island*,' said Kohlhaas by way of lubrication.

---'And project.'

Her voice warmer than it should be; and yet sweet; she swallowed back her words, or said them tentatively. But could she be saying such mundane things?

---'And Manhattan was where I learned the world was going to end. I was
 only five---too young. The lights came on, they had to stop the show.'

---'Don't make a habit of it,' said Cundy.

---"Don't worry,' said my poor old man, he's called Eugene, trying to
 comfort me. 'We'll be dead before then.' That was worse, of course. The
 sickness when you've finished nearly all the sweets; not only because
 the sweets have made you sick, but because they're nearly finished. This
 is how the world ends. And as he dragged me shrieking and convulsive
 through double doors which each had a wired glass porthole in —
 I sobbed all night, inconsolable — as they were dragging me away I
 remember seeing the lights dim as the stars came out on the dome again,
 after my interruption had been quelled. As they will too when the world
 should end.'

As she spoke, her eyes shone.

---'Man!' said Cundy.

---'We harden with time,' she said. 'I don't mind now.'

---'I don't believe this woman.'

---'I mean it. I really don't. But I majored in cosmogony, for a second
 degree, surveying candidates for the initial singularity, and examining
 (for aesthetic, at best heuristic motives, though you never know)
 Aristotle's conceptual unmoved mover of the *Metaphysics lambda*, its roots
 in the pre-Socratics (Socrates a pre-Socratic!), and the fascinating work
 Aquinas did with this -- Aquinas picked up the ball and ran. Because
 ho-ho I was going back like a superhero to change the laws of nature
 and cancel out the great disaster. But side-tracked by Kant's anticipation
 of aspects of Modern Physics especially w.r.t. field based conceptions,
 matter as energy, etc. etc., and Schopenhauer's self-consciously meta
 physics, contrasted e.g. with Nietzsche's to us questionable (absurd
 I would say if he didn't have a weakness for vindication) categorical
 rejection of the atomic hypothesis (Boscovich, Lavoisier, Proust, !) almost
 simultaneously (don't trust me, time in physics, as in philosophy, is
 imperfectly synchronous; always check dates) with Thomson's work
 on sub-atomics: everything has atoms, even atoms. So the reductionist
 project attacked and attacked with its own weapons — having reduced
 everything to electron, proton, neutron chemically proportioned like
 in a recipe, the ark opens, the menagerie escapes, and it is in the process

of acquiring — this is the illusion — as many degrees of freedom as the
world it supposedly simplifies — Russell's barber shaved by Occam's
razor, begging every question, so to speak, so the vast, pat reductionist
projects, the Principia Mathematica e.g., are likewise systemically
compromised, at least short term, by delirious results like Gödel's work
on incompleteness or Conway's hyperreal and surreal numbers.'

---'Of course.'

---'Man!'

---'It's a game. Snakes and ladders. The reductionist project is always
wildly successful, and founders. Thrilling from the history of ideas
perspective to what extent even (even!) the pre-Socratics were on the
right track w.r.t. our own conceptions, though maybe in their case simply
by covering all the logically possible bases. So as for the tinkering with
laws of nature, perfecting the universe, that will have to take care of
itself.'

---'And how!' said Cundy.

She spoke fast. It was hard to keep up.

---'Your current focus?' I asked her, almost to slow her down. Also this
seemed important at the time.

---'My mainstream physics interest now is QCD, confinement in
particular.'

---'Er ...?'

---'Quantum chromodynamics ... ?'

---'And what exactly?'

She looked at me almost fondly; by which I mean she stared, and I saw
her eyes water.

---'It's no good, you wouldn't understand.'

This was a way of teasing me---she could easily have explained. Perhaps
a Norwegian thing. But Kohlhaas had something to tell her, leaving me
staring at her along the back of the sofa with something of terror, horror.
My arm was resting behind him, and she didn't see this, because at that

moment, listening carefully to what he was saying, she put down her hand on mine. And snatched it away, as I did too, capsizing Kohlhaas's teacup which fell to the carpet and cracked as softly as an egg, releasing a pool of tea which, although deep, was somehow contained, dammed by the pile, and didn't spread far, but eventually seeped in.

Silence fell, and everyone looked sad. The sky was brimming, another rainstorm was coming, and the earth would fall into the sun. That was the first time I ever touched her body, but not the last. Then Cundy spoke.

---'Do you ever feel like something's going on behind your back Elric?'

But she was speaking again. To Kohlhaas. How could she speak?

---'... he made me realise the closeness of the water, the thinness of the ice. The ice holds us, but it is thin. You can see the water and the fishes underneath. And if you take a hammer and break the ice; well---then ...'

Scared she'd hear or see the thudding of my heart. But she wasn't looking at me, or Kohlhaas now; she was looking through the open windows at the woods, her mouth half open.

While she was speaking, Waddington had returned. He was becoming something of a physical constant, always hovering nearby, immanent.

---'I was always told it was extremely pretentious to speak about such things,' he said, wriggling his toes inside his shoes. At which she grinned, made her eyes sparkle, and raised them briefly towards Dotty Belisha's favourite Titian.

---'It would be---if you did. No, no; don't worry. No. I'm only kiddying you.'

Waddington's thundery face: he was not a man to be kiddied.

---'Why do---people like you make such poor scientists,' he hissed unexpectedly.

---'They don't,' she answered, 'but if they do, sometimes, make uncommitted ones, it's because they find it hard to rid themselves of the delusion that people are more important than ideas.'

---'You have to admit it, Waddington old boy. She's good,' said Cundy.

---'Stuff and nonsense. Like the one about a dog walking on its hind
legs. It's not that it's done well, but that it's done at all.' Waddington
was overheating. But surely he could do better than that. Or had she
not stung him hard enough. 'Just because daddy's rich she thinks she's
intelligent,' he added.

---'Smart as Croesus, I think you mean,' she answered.

---'Who's side you on?' Cundy asked her.

---'I haven't finished Dr Cundy if you please,' said Waddington. 'I know
for a fact that Blindern would only take her if Daddy endowed a chair.'

---'Miaou!' said Cundy, but then shut up.

---'Difficult to answer that one,' she said. Problem of counterfactuals, of
the hypothetical, even the hyperthetical. Themistocles to the heckler of
Seriphus.'

Perched on silk which was varnished and grained like the wood on
which my heart was knocking, she was drilling a hole in the carpet with
a pink rubber sneaker toe the colour of a white dog's nose as she waited
for Waddington and Mlle Auch to go away. But Waddington hadn't
finished yet.

---'And Dr Skippergate,' he added coldly. 'One more thing. I must also ask
you to display clearly your identity card.'

---'I'm sorry,' she said, 'but I have an aversion to them.'

---'A what?'

---'I don't like them. Bad associations.'

---'No, but I'm sorry,' he said in turn; 'you realise that there is a security
risk, Norbert's presence, etc., coupled with the presence of priceless
works of art ...'

---'Dr Waddington,' she said; 'I won't.'

Waddington with his mouth open for a second. Then he closed it. And
cleared his throat.

---'I see,' he said.

So did I.

It was too neat. Her system. She had it all worked out. She made the world seem easy. Cosy. Pat. It was so easy for her. For a while. And that's not fair on everybody else. Because it's hard. Waddington struggling to contain himself. He failed.

---'You're the same every time. I don't bloody believe it. Too clever by half. This afternoon, for instance. Norbert's an old man. Why be so bloody inflexible?'

---'Excuse me, but it's not me being inflexible, but statistics.'

---'Exactly,' shouted Waddington. 'And what's the point. What's the bloody point. What does it all matter, in the end. How shall I put it. Do you know how many stars there are in the heavens. Do you? Do you?'

---'Approximately.'

---'How many?'

---'On current estimates, of perhaps misleading precision, of the order of ten to the twenty-two to four.'

---'And you honestly think it's relevant if Norbert Leicher has sufficient degrees of freedom? Get a life won't you? Science isn't rigid, it's a human thing. Don't foul it up for us with misguided rigour. Be a little conciliating for once.'

---'Have you ever wondered how it felt as the Roman Empire crumbled and the dark ages began?' she asked. 'The great institutions falling apart?'

She was cross. Unexpected in someone who seemed to have a self-control verging on apathy. There was a new rigidity about her, a tightness of her own lips now. Her eyes even had something of Leicher's pained fixity of look. No longer inviting, tender, playful, serious and very deep, they had become shiny and hard.

---'Look, I shouldn't but I'm going to level with you,' said Waddington, glancing uneasily across the room at Keith Johnstone. 'We have an observer here from CAQ; this is a showpiece symposium and you are dickying with our funding. SMM currently generates a global-per-annum spend of at least fifty-seven million dollars. That's a significant amount by anyone's book. And you are dickying with it. *Capisce?*'

He watched for his words to sink in.

---'Integrity is a luxury I can afford', she said.

---'The insolence of money will out', said Cundy helpfully. 'Johnson, Dr Samuel, not Keith Johnstone. I mean. Whoops.'

---'Look; this can be sorted out later. Let's bury our differences for now, yes? Let's remember the meaning of the word courtesy? Yes? In private, I'm promising you now, you can be as insolent as you wish.'

Hella, as he spoke, turning red. And boring another hole in the carpet. As she bored, tea welled out. And when he'd finished she looked up at him, sideways, dark blue eyes in a dark red face, half covered by a jumbled fringe of dark blond hair, and said:

---'Okay.' Then turned a darker red.

---'Yes?'

---'I said okay.'

---'Good.' He couldn't resist a smile of triumph. Out it gleamed. 'You may not realise how you were playing with fire.'

His voice grated; it was a firm voice, strong, but harsh and somewhat sharp. Very occasionally it leapt up a register, to his shame and surprise, as it did now on the word '*long*':

---'It is a good way to make a name for yourself, in the short term, but the career of the iconoclast is not very *long*.'

---'I sometimes wonder whether it isn't over already, this career', she answered softly, no longer angry now, and her voice gentle after his. 'It's sweet, the academic life, steady, sane, rational and generous; one of humanity's great things. There is some corruption there, some rust, and this worsens slowly, but for the moment the machine still goes like a dream. And yet---in the end---it isn't me.'

---'Simple. You're not good enough', answered Waddington. 'Or else why would you be here? You'd be attending a symposium in your own discipline.'

---'Yes, sour grapes.' It was Leicher, who'd crept up.

Kohlhaas looking flustered and checking his parting.

---'You know the story?' Leicher asked. 'The fox and the grapes?'

She laughed gaily.

---'It's not like that. I'll suggest a paradox. In science you choose what to discover, in art you don't choose what to depict; science is free, art fixed, science subjective, art objective. I became a scientist for the freedom it entailed. And I tire of that freedom. I want to be told what to do. Beethoven's epigraph for *der schwer gefaßte Entschluß* movement.'

Waddington repeated himself:

---'You're not good enough.'

---'No, not good enough.' echoed Leicher.

She turned out her lips like a chimp and said:

---'Okay.'

One knee bent, drilling more holes in the carpet, waiting patiently, though with explicit indifference now, for them to leave.

And with their blunt spears buried in her steaming flank, neatly synchronised, almost coached, they turned on their heels together and did.

---'Silly farts,' said Cundy.

---"It's not me that's inflexible, but maths.' That's good,' said Kohlhaas kindly.

---'*Mais non, la mathématique, c'est moi!*' said Cundy, imitating Modestine Auch's voice. And then, with Waddington's squeak on the *bunk*: 'Math is *bunk.*'

---'No it isn't. It works,' she said. 'I don't know why, but it works. The aeroplane stays up. Usually.'

---'It only falls when mathematics tells us it should,' said Kohlhaas, earnestly.

---'Tells us---or tells it?' asked Cundy with a quizzical face.

---'No, what tells it is something else; mathematics is our model of what is happening, it isn't what is happening. But the nature of the beast which does tell it---nobody knows. Nobody knows.'

She looked sad.

---'Nobody knows.'

I shivered. And went on shivering.

---'Shit,' said Cundy. 'How does she do it.'

---'What?'

---'I don't know. Scare you like this. Something supernatural.'

Hella trying not to smile.

---'There is, isn't there. Admit it. Go on. She's a goddess in disguise, aren't you. I knew it.'

He knew she was flattered. Kohlhaas silent between us. I peeped round the back of him again; she looked up, and I looked quickly down. But my eyes went back there; dark blue eyes in a dark red face were looking steadily at me. With curiosity. Turning her face back to Cundy:

---'You have no need of that hypothesis,' she said.

Maybe. But before I knew what was happening, Kohlhaas had heaved himself up. He was tapping her shoulder and she was looking up questioningly. And with his gestures, he slid her along until she was sitting beside me. She'd looked doubtful for a moment, but she'd moved. Then he sat down beyond her, sealing her in, confining her. The sofa creaked.

---'There you are,' he said.

She, using her fingers, had covered up her nose and mouth and was snorting softly. The finger of her other hand was pointing so hard that it curved backwards; she moved it in circles in space, wondering where to point it, and ended by pointing at me. The saturated colour of her eyes, in a creamy face; she was also looking at me. And she was speaking but I couldn't hear her.

---'What?

---'---?'

---'Don't understand?'

---'I said 'Why are you here?"

---'What brings you to the Belisha Foundation's flagship institute?' translated Cundy.

---'They needed an Irish Citizen.'

---'From the States?'

---'It sometimes seems like most of us are. Either Britain or the States.'

---'Field?'

---'Spatial biology and classics. An interdisciplinary approach.'

---'What someone clever, I can't remember who right now, calls multi-disciplinary cross-sterilisation,' Cundy said.

---'Lepidoptera?' she asked.

---'Sorry?'

---'You'll do.'

---'You'll give nepotism a bad name,' Cundy interrupted. 'What about Orla Ciama.'

---'Jim!' squealed Kohlhaas.

---'Orla Ciama?' asked Hella, looking mystified.

---'Yes, tell her about Orla Ciama. And Orla Ciama's daughter,' said Cundy significantly. 'Orla Ciama's daughter Barbara. What about they?'

She looked at me.

I said nothing.

---'Barb Ciama,' repeated Cundy. 'Barbara Ciama. Lollapaloosa babe! Hot Eyetie totty, Ciama bomba! Mlle Charmer!'

---'Shut up Jim,' said Kohlhaas.

---'But mumma mia, that Bianca Castafiore type, her mother. I don't think
so!'

---'Jim!'

---'Madame Bruiser. A misogynist's wet dream.'

---'Jim ...'

---'And you?' I asked.

---'I came because I thought you'd be here.'

Silence.

---'I'm only joking,' she said. Weird joke. 'No, to be serious, it's called
doing the Dean a favour. Leicher e-mailed him to find *one good female of
Blindern to carry the light of tensor calculus unto the worthy multitudes of SMM.*'

---'Good old Leicher,' said Cundy.

---'Plus I'd never been to Italy. Then there are the moths, several strictly
local varieties in the sweet-chestnut woods along the shore. I have been
given permission to use the Foundation's racing skiff. So, several vectors
of differing magnitude all pointing the same way. It sometimes happens
and when it does I've learned to follow them. Something lies hidden
there, something important, even divine. Can you row?'

I'd never rowed in my life but the answer was staring me in the face.

---'Apparently.'

---'What do you mean, apparently?'

A flush of guilt. A flush of honesty:

---'I don't know, I've never tried.'

She smiled enough to show me her side teeth, and put her hand on her
mouth, turning her face away.

---'I can row,' Cundy said. Tired of standing, he tried to sit between us.

---'No, Jim,' she said firmly, pointing at a gilt armchair; 'you pull that up.
You sit there.'

---'Sorry I spoke,' he said.

She was racked already by guilt.

---'No, no, I'm sorry.' She wanted to make up. 'Tell me where you come
from Jim.'

---'Truth is my nation.'
---'Pass the sick bag, someone,' said Kohlhaas.

The characters emerge, like a group photograph in a dish of developer.
There was something necessary there; it was a photograph of a jigsaw
puzzle with no extra pieces and nothing missing; somehow they all
interlocked. Take away Cundy and there would have been a Cundy-
shaped hole; likewise Kohlhaas, and even Waddington, and especially
Leicher.

---'No, seriously, I had a letter from Norbert; *your stimulating paper etc. etc.;
symposium; etc.* I wasn't doing anything this summer; thought it might be
a lark ...'

She was laughing at his rendition of Leicher, and especially the frog-face,
stutter and the dribbles. Turning up the ends of her lips, then the ends of
her eyes in the same way. And Cundy, when he saw this: his own face lit
up.

---'But what really clinched it,' he went on, following the stream of smiles
to its source, 'was the photo-opportunity. I have it here.' And he pulled
out a crumpled photocopy and flattened it out to show us these words:
*During the symposium there will be an opportunity for each participant to be
photographed individually with the 'father of SMM', Professor Norbert Leicher ...'*

He laughed so much that tears came out on his face.

---'Grandfather, more like,' he was saying. 'Or great-grandfather. Or corpse.'

---'Exactly,' said Kohlhaas plaintively. 'That's the whole point. There may
not be another chance.'

Hella paused in her laughter to look at Kohlhaas fondly; I'd almost say
lovingly.

---'Isn't it cruel to kill moths?'

I felt provocative. Then I stared out Kohlhaas, then Cundy.

---'Time to dress for dinner, Jim,' Kohlhaas said.

---'If you say so,' said Cundy, grudgingly.

---'But I insist,' said Kohlhaas.

---'Sometimes you take the world too seriously,' she said, turning a saddening face to me when they'd gone. 'But then, if you don't take it seriously, it comes and gets you. And yet, again, a feeling that it comes and gets you anyway. I don't kill them. Before morning I let them go again. And who knows if the discovery and wooing and even possession of a trap-lamp isn't happiest experience in a moth's life. Unless your wings melt.'

As she spoke, a kind of moth-maiden herself, with her other-worldly forehead, thick, pale eyebrows tuned and fluffy as antennae and not blonde but palest sand. And her eyes, the blue, and green, of sand through deep water, and something in her face swept and soft; and her skin, no hard surface, precise boundary, but more a mere field. A moronic daemon was saying: 'Kiss her now.'

Socrates says it pays to take the daemon's advice.

The room almost silent.

---'Phototaxis in motile organisms, too,' she said.

Only Professor McGovern and Dr Vidal were left, conscientiously polishing off the last gulls' eggs. A clock ticked heavy as a metronome on the renaissance chimneypiece, the sundry holes and winders on its scored gilt back reflected in a blotched and tarnished looking-glass. And I was staring at her face. Her serenity, her slow, sad smile: she was half asleep. I tried to understand from where she drew her power.

---'You're funny,' she added.

A suction in her eyes and in her lips. But she must have seen something coming, because she turned her face aside unexpectedly and smiled.

---'Odd,' but her lips distorted by her smile so she found it hard to speak.

In her eyes, witchery. Not just her eyes, her lips, but also her hips. Angular, taut, girlish, unwomanly. And the crooked way she sat. On her hands. This made me want to stare at her hips, to understand them. If that was possible.

She looked down and covered her open mouth with spread fingers. Something erecting my trousers in the groin area. This made me sweat. Water, dribbling down my forehead and dripping onto the trousers only made it worse.

I reached for Waddington's autographed off-print, and put it in my lap.

The plunging drops of sweat smudging the signature.

She seemed happier, and if still calm, and languorous (stretching and shifting and wriggling in various ways), also very wide-awake.

---'Where have they all gone?' she asked.

McGovern and Vidal had melted away. The room was empty, the mahogany doors, ludicrously narrow, ludicrously tall, plastered in ludicrous ormolu, were shut.

Walking in that dangerous, unimaginable way, along a tightrope stretched beneath the carpet, but with no fear, ripe with elegance, she tried them. And turned back my way with a sleepy smile.

---'Locked.' Her voice quiet and hollow in the immense room. 'It's the Titians they're worried about.'

And she went to a window, which with a bit of rattling and the steady warning of her frown, came open in her hands, flooding her face with blood-orange evening light.

And stepping up on the sill and balancing there for long enough to smile invitingly at me, jumped. Fortunately, there was no moat.

---'Where are you going?'

She stopped at these words, tilting her head back towards the window through which I leaned. A strand of hair swung back and forth across her face and she clipped it impatiently behind her ear. Then, without answering, she walked on down the hill.

At a safe distance, I followed her. Her trousers too big for her. Stiff on her body. How could she walk like this? I was watching so hard I thought she'd fall down.

At the hill's foot woods began, which covered most of the rest of the island in an overgrown wilderness scarred with sandy tracks. Along the way in the woodland edges were stands of broom and tangled brambles, their tendrils streaming out across the sand, adorned with small pink flowers prettified with circles of black dots, and softened and browned by the bloated, sinking sun. The air was viscous.

---'Smell it,' she said, carefully plucking a spiked spray of gorse and, as she raised it to my face, holding her face too still, too close. Also holding her breath. Her water coloured eyes. Her voice, sticky with heat. I couldn't breathe. Then:

---'Do you mind?' she asked.

---'About what?'

And she tried to push me over with one hand.

She was undoing her laces to tip out sand. Her face, as she looked up at me.

And smiled. She sat down to put her shoes back on. Her forehead buckled up with concentration, almost with ferocity, but then taking on a strange texture, not entirely mammal, half gill, half alien, which pulled her hair forwards and her eyebrows up and, stretching the skin just above her eyes, made her noble, disinterested, spaced out, a sensuous angel just before lift-off.

She also had an air of having just left off growing very fast.

On her pinked cheeks, browned like the flowers by the late sunlight, a faint sheen.

She was already walking into the sunset again, and I was following her.

We came to a shed submerged in ivy. Bells tinkled lazily inside. Through the reeling door, a breath of goat. She cast a longing glance into the darkness before, in an unexpected burst of speed, she hurried past.

---'Hella ...' I said. She stopped, turned and made a strange, exalted chuckle.

---'What?'

The focus in her eyes altered a little, from my spirit to my lips.

---'What?' she whispered. 'Tell me. Talk.'

---'Don't be scared,' she whispered quickly, making her whisper somehow mythical. Her white teeth showing between the curved ends of her lips; the white end of each eye, shaded with lashes, showing between lids which had the same curve.

---'Sweet, dangerous.'

Is this how the magic was worked?

---'Go on, speak. Tell me.'

Burning.

---'Nothing,' I said.

Her pupils contracted, and the light in her eyes switched off.

And swinging her leg back, she kicked up a fountain of sand, a grain of which got in her eye.

Pause while we fished it out. Look up, look down, etc.

---'What time do you think it is?' I asked.

She was frowning. She looked at me in disbelief, one eye red and tearing, turned her face away, walked.

The intensity of her colours. Everything in saturated colours.

Crickets keeping time on the maracas; the air drugged with fig and pine and myrtle---it affected the imagination.

Then: unknown trees with lettuce coloured leaves. Between them the turf was cropped like a lawn. Across which ran the sandy track. She spoke, her voice slightly cloyed by a throatful of spit, her words cloyed by some Norwegian EFL teacher's dated colloquialisms:

---'Hello, hello, what's this?'

On the track was a hen tied up in a length of green hose-pipe.

Bending over it, she threw it into shadow, then shifted to let the sun redden it.

---'What is it?'

---'Someone's tied it up.'

As she reached her fingers down there was a hissing: a crested feathery head and open, yellow, beak.

She drew them back.

---'A rapture. Raptor I mean! Perhaps a buzzard, or a small eagle. Someone's tied it up. How strange. Some rite. Voodoo.'

She was whispering, alarmed by the noise of her voice.

As we watched the green pipe slid without moving.

Erect in the sky was a second hissing, crested beak. The blunt green beak of a slow-worm, scaled, flattened, set with glittery eyes.

If slow-worms hiss.

A flat black tongue flapped in air, and with a jolt the lipless little mouth lunged at her, so that she fell back hard, her legs outstretched on either side of it.

As she fell, the slow-worm, grass-snake, whatever it was, lost its hold on the buzzard, eagle, whatever that was. First one and then another wing was erected carefully like a tent, each wing as long as one of her legs. The lashing worm entangled itself in the sand-coloured hair blown by these wings across her face. All you could see was her nose and her hands, trying either to push it away or catch it. Even the buzzard had a fat gold curl in one claw along with the thick green body of the worm, but Hella didn't make a sound as she grabbed hold of this, too, fighting for her own hair with the enormous bird, which whether buzzard or eagle turned out to be not at all small. There was an instant of disgrace, of the ludicrous: all this, like the sand in her eye, was her fault. Reality,

even the modern, had caught up with her at last. But this was only my
cowardice, my own fault, mine.

As suddenly I figured I should help, get involved, that there was also
a part for me. I leant over them all and stretched out my hands palm
down as the buzzard rose beneath them, its wings like stiff brown quilts,
moving slowly away from her, the slow-worm whipping in its claws.
Mobbed by a manic black crow like the star that suddenly mobs the
moon at night, rocking stiffly it banked beyond an oak tree, out of sight,
leaving only a subsiding series of hanging pairs of rings of dust blown
up---all down the track---by its wings.

Her eyes fumed, smoked. The irises went darker, and in the dimness the
pupils disappeared. She said:

---'Shit!'

Because when reality turns symbolical, and if elliptical, still in such an
obvious way, it may be embarrassing, but it is elating. This sort of thing,
like sex perhaps, should not be talked about. And yet it was part of the
half-natural, half-supernatural air of the place. Or, as I discovered, of
her. Because this air followed her. Her surroundings, wherever she went,
played up.

Anyhow, there's nothing I can do except suppress reality, and we're not in
that business yet.

---'You see,' she added suddenly, and her lips flowered, visionary. 'You see?'
The tears were chasing a silver pattern, a tracery, into her dusty cheeks.

She touched her thigh. She seemed drunk.

---'*And* it's bit me.'

I checked her face: turned up towards me; the warm smell of the tears.
They looked cold but were warm. And the suction---strong. Her mouth
still tilted up to mine, but not her eyes now.

She'd closed those.

And opened her teeth.

Breathed unsteadily between them. Then unsteadily sighed. This sigh
alcoholic and sweet.

The faintest smile hovered in the shark-like dimples at the ends of her lips.

As she waited, eyes closed.

---'What is it?' I asked.

She opened her eyes with something of surprise. Shook her head. I lifted her chin to see her face. Carrot coloured, almost orange. Her eyes looked downwards into the sand, and wouldn't meet mine. Eventually, in a quiet voice:

---'Nothing. My shoes are full of sand again,' she said.

Undoing each plump white lace in turn I poured it out.

She wasn't wearing socks.

---'My feet are cold.'

I touched her feet.

---'Scared,' she said.

The light a brownish blue, the air hot and damp. Sweat, and herbs.

---'I'll look after you.'

---'That's what I'm scared of.'

And darting my face as unexpectedly as worm and buzzard had darted hers, she knocked her boiling mouth against my lips with enough force to bruise or burst them and opened her teeth to let my tongue inside.

And this is how she stole my sight. I couldn't see. However much I blinked and palmed my face I couldn't see.

She fell back on her elbows and sighed.

Reached up to pull me down to her, my head between her hands, her face still wet.

Her mouth hot and tasting of herbs.

She took her lips away to say:

---'We shouldn't do this.'

Then put them back.

Do what?

Until with her two hands she lifted my face again, looked at me, and smiled gently.

---'It sounds mad,' she said.

---'What?'

But as I answered I choked.

Something went down the wrong way.

Perhaps it was her spit.

She had a smile on as she waited for me to stop, saying:

---'Don't die.'

---'Why not?' I gasped.

---'Because I love you.'

A chilled bite of fear.

She laughed gaily:

---'Oh! He is so serious!'

And kissed me tenderly, drawing her tongue across my tongue. Mine.

Sitting up now, she was squeezing a fold of denim between her fingers. The cloth stained black. Then she started pulling down her zip.

Slowly. Too slowly.

---'Pull.'

When I did nothing she looked up.

---'I want to see where it bit me.'

So, the top of her jeans, coming over her hips, and suddenly loose and baggy between her legs.

Very close to her, feeling the heat and solidity of her body.

My fingers, hooked over the jeans' hem, brushing the plump white skin. Then tugging on the heels. Hella, her legs outstretched and slightly raised, pushing with her hands.

The colour of her legs; their shape. Their whiteness. But not as white as the pair of thick white undershorts, which moulded her shape, running a little down her legs.

On the front of her shin, where it was shiny over bone, two punctures, side by side.

Balanced on each, black and glowing, was blood.

Reminding me of something---what was it?---the two black eyes of the snake.

---'This is serious.'

---'He cares!'

---'How do you feel?'

---'Happy.'

She made her teeth and eyes gleam and looked at me sideways. Lying on her side, drawing her knees up, resting her head on her two hands. Still that smile.

---'Don't worry,' she said, her smile distorting the words. 'If it was poisonous it would have bitten the buzzard, and the buzzard looked alright ... It's cold. Lie beside me. Kiss me again.'

---'If it was a snake we should get an antidote.'

---'Time will tell.'

---'Hella ... '

---'Mmm,' she said. 'There's your antidote.'

Then she moved her knees apart.

A white band of underpant gleamed between them.

---'I've got no trousers on.'

Her spit, her tears; biting, fresh.

---'Ouch. My leg stings.'

---'How does it feel. Like venom?'

---'How would I know how venom feels? No, like nettles, or more like jellyfish. And anyway,' summoning all her emphasis, 'there is nothing I care about less.'

Something sickly about this. In her voice; such a yearning, such a painful, keening yearning. It promised so much, opened the world like a heated tin and uncovered fresh food inside, steaming but not too hot, blown on through her lips. It wasn't that she offered everything; but that she started up such currents that the questions she posed seemed insoluble, insatiable, exciting.

And then of course she answered them.

'Shall I put my jeans back on?' she asked. Stupid question.

'Yes.'

Walking back along the sandy track. We held hands and it wasn't enough. I couldn't get close enough. I wanted to be inside her, and not merely physically. I wanted to be her, but a different her looking in at her looking out. Nothing less was enough. The light nearly gone, but the landscape still brown and glowing with left-over heat. She stopped suddenly:

---'What's that?'

---'Again?'

A dark smudge lying on the track.

---'Hope it's not the buzzard,' she said.

And laughed.

---'Shit.'

It was.

We could just see yellow eyes screwed shut, a hooked yellow beak, and scaled yellow talons clasped on empty air like a dead chicken's feet. Its feathers were ruffled gently by the cold breeze rolling uphill from the reservoir.

She touched the talons and pulled on something invisible which lifted one of the buzzard's legs and turned the stiff bird over.

---'Look,' she said; 'a hank of my hair. How funny. And how small it looks---the bird I mean, not the hair.'

---'You might be poisoned too. Please take it seriously.'

---'We're all poisoned. You know that.' And letting the buzzard roll back she took me by the shoulders. 'No, listen to me now. Carefully. I take it very seriously indeed. Now I know you I should be proud to die. And I've never said this to anyone before. And never will. Whatever you and the world choose to do with me.'

Yearning for that lovely voice; each time it stopped, yearning for it to start. And yet also scared of it---she seemed too - intense?

---'Because the world is ending, but it had to end. We knew that anyway. So does it matter if we die?'

Yearning for more of it. Half whispering, whimpering almost, voiced.

---'And if it has to end,' she said; 'why be sad about being there? It won't be very nice. But you might as well see it, see what is happening, and even scream at the flames, at the fire, and not in terror but ecstasy.'

Near the buzzard, half a snake.

---'But perhaps that isn't possible. We, long before that, will have become extinct, leaving leafy motorways which will be assumed, perhaps rightly, to have had a religious significance. That doesn't matter: astrology will end, women's studies will end, literary criticism will end, even engineering and biology perhaps; but chemistry won't, nor will physics, cosmology, mathematics, logic, nor even metaphysics. Not for a while at least.'

And those white underpants, under her jeans, creased and rucked and slimy in a band between her legs. Like a dressing.

So: the strangeness of the differing textures offered by that day. Leicher's paper, or the opening lunch on its starched linen cloth, set against love on sand in a warm wood: her hot dry body, her wet mouth.

And yet: fighting the happiness, distrusting it, looking for the catch, the sentimental flaw, the deep and writhing embarrassment. Knowing it couldn't last. Saying: all the secrets are in this face alone. Which doesn't have to tell the truth because it isn't saying anything. I don't have to look into her soul as well. Making excuses out of fearfulness, superstition; keeping my fingers crossed. Because everything in her face was also in her soul. And I was terrified.

Tears ran out of her closed eyes and down the sides of her face. Her body, close on its bones: the stony ribs, the pebbled spine, and then the breasts, weird fruits, clothed not in skin but in mystery, veined, and in the darkness green.

---'What I mean is, I know the world's hard and is ending now,' she said, 'but whatever happens I'll look after you.'

Perhaps she was delirious. She had taken folds of my clothes in her fingers and tugged at them.

My shirt, my trousers. As I pulled them off, she sighed.

My heart, my lungs, which had been invisible, not-there, numb, felt mysteriously filled with fishes in a filmy, slopping sea.

My prick, like a windscreen wiper, scraping the sweat from her thighs. And then, oiled with sweat, sliding steadily in. And feeling everything: roughness, a smooth protruding bone, and something fluttery at the end, brushing about.

---'Don't,' she whispered, 'don't.'

She was grinding her head backwards on her neck, digging a hole in the sand with the crown of her skull.

---'Inside, I mean.'

But she could hardly speak.

She tried to push me away. But we were connected, fused, formed in warm marble, or warm lard, and yet she had to try to push me away, and had to fail.

She had brought her head back now, dangling it, however heavy, over the hole it had made, and was staring at me through round eyes, as if it wasn't me at all, and wasn't her; those eyes more than magnetic, grave, making me fall, so that my insides were tumbling and I was too and yet she was always there, looking into me with those round glowing eyes growing bigger; and her teeth too, the rim of them becoming more curved, tighter, the canines dropping further out til they looked like the were made of plastic, and her voice reluctant, pained not in pain but life, so that she was trying to recede, to go far but, still looking, to bring me too, and speaking not in language but in sound, and yet I knew what she meant, her hands round my neck now, bent forwards at the elbows just as the legs which gripped my waist were bent back at the knees, her eyes still on mine, holding them, with all the love and fear and tenderness imaginable. Until, still looking she tried to form her lips into a kiss and touch them on mine, but as she did so, her eyes closed, like someone in a movie dying.

Drawing herself up and back in the sand, her blonde hair black in the darkness, still wrapped round her neck, under her chin, a bottle green choker in this light. 'Look at me,' she said. 'Look.' And she was smiling, hungry, alight with her teeth and with her eyes, in the starlight. 'Look at me, look.' At the way her cheeks had formed on her cheekbones, the life in those cheeks, her forehead and the shapes of her eyes, life plastered onto a skull, in the faint light, and the dark hair, blackened with sweat, wrapped around her neck and falling down her chest but parting like a waterfall for her breasts, the dark nipples.

She was whispering.

---'What is it?'

To whisper better she held down my shoulders. I looked at her lips, then at her eyes, gleaming, excited, deep.

---'Go away now,' she said, and put one leg across mine.

Breathed in and held her breath, still looking at me.

---'Go away, go.'

Now she was sitting on top of me. So how could I. Her hair hanging down in front of her face in frayed ropes. Her mouth apart, black lips rimmed with white pieces of tooth. And her whole flushed body voice, so that wherever I touched her, if the touch was soft---she cried.

As she did so, I fell. Put out my hands to catch myself, but someone was holding them.

In the darkness, much later, Hella, lying on her naked front on sand, still holding both my hands. She was sleeping.

---'Wake up Hella. It's night.'

She opened her eyes and tried to sit up.

---'What are all those lights on in the sky?' she asked, half-dreaming, her voice still furred.

Then she closed her eyes again and went to sleep.

The sky had been holding its breath but had to let go; had been waiting, but had been prepared, made, especially for this: a slice of moon appeared, mineral, buoyant; first red, then yellow. Then green. And then snow-white. Huge and unfinished, fading away to one side.

When it rose, in amazement, all the crickets stopped.

---'Look,' I said, shaking her.
---'O,' she said.

The crickets starting up again.

---'Hard not to cry,' she said.

She was looking at me, but when I looked she looked away.

---'What are you saying?'

She was speaking but I couldn't hear.

---'Don't be scared,' she repeated for me.

---'I'm not.'

---'I wasn't speaking to you,' she said. 'I was speaking to me.'

And we tried to rid ourselves of all the sand which was even in our ears, and started back to the palace.

3

Well now, in the morning I heard there'd been shenanigans, apparently, last night, after a group photograph which we had missed. Everyone was now hung-over. Only a few of us made it to Modestine Auch's early-morning burnt-offering ⊠

Leicher and the politic of genius:

A forwards towards a meta-SMM

A hip and prolific writer, Modestine's prose was so ugly and her ideas so coarse that nobody with any delicacy could read more than a few of her pages. Which is why, given a dash of networking genius, she strode in unchallengeable triumph through the nine circles of the intellect.

She wasn't here yet. Strange---to love a stranger. To love her, to have had her squeeze her naked legs around your naked waist, knowing as she did so, however drugged with lust and air, exactly what you and she were doing. Exultant delight. Yet, for instance, her name. At this stage I couldn't remember that ⊠ someone was hiding it from me. And even her face had begun to disappear ...

---*'We gather here to revere this 'prince véritable', this 'poète véritable' of SMM ...'*

Up on the podium, a fragile Norbert couldn't repress a good-natured smile and started tilting his head about. But even as Modestine spoke, both leaves of the ballroom door opened slowly and all turned as Hella came through, hunched, slightly green, battling what looked like psychic flu. Slamming one leaf hard behind her, she left the other wide open and stalked moodily up to the front.

Remembering her name clearly now.

---'Hella,' I whispered as she went past.

She froze, one arm forward, the hand open.

And closed it slowly.

---'Hella!'

Slowly she exhaled.

Then, without turning, walked carefully on.

And sat beside Keith Johnstone.

Her lips had changed their shape, lost their double-inflexion, become long and thin. Sexless. Her eyes too. Bald. And her hair was wet.

But didn't look clean. It looked greasy.

And she'd changed her clothes. A short blue cotton dress, gathered just below her breasts, curtained a concave stomach. It was the colour of the sky in an illuminated manuscript. When she walked it swished about her upper thighs, which were a white through which you could see malachite.

Meanwhile:

---'*In phrase so memorable of Professor Norbert Leicher …*'

Ms Auch couldn't speak English, but I wasn't convinced she could even speak French.

---'*… the* caput Nili, *the holy grail, of sociometric thought, this SMM …*'

Yet Hella was already writing, head tilted low over the page.

---'*… this group intellectual which follow in the happy dance …*'

Perhaps she was doodling. As word followed word in Dotty Belisha's frescoed ballroom.

Then, in shifting her pad, she dropped everything with a tingling shuffle onto the varnished mosaic. Modestine Auch fell silent, and first looked pained and then looked up. But Professor Leicher rose majestically, descended the podium steps at a rapid shuffle, and going down on a knee which crackled a bit as he did so, gathered pad and pencil up. He handed them up to Hella with a bow and slight flourish, before Waddington took him under the arms from behind and hoisted him back up.

So as to say: wrong me now, cunt. Leicher to Hella, I mean.

Turning as she rose, tucking her chin into her chest and putting her palms to her forehead, she tottered out.

By tottered I mean went slowly, swinging from side to side.

Running down her face was the light in her eyes.

And as I caught up with her, she turned to slam the door on me. An ormolu swag dropped off and rattled about on the mosaic threshold.

She was on the terrace, perched on the rim of a lily-tank, her back against a high garden wall with a fig tree splayed across it, from which, pinned up like Christmas decorations, green and misted purple, ripe figs dangled. Each with a blob of white milk at the drain hole in its base. Crumbling a sugar lump she had found somewhere, perhaps in one of the two little pockets concealed in the waistband of her skirt, and feeding grains of sugar to the goldfish, grain by grain. She turned her face and smiled at me.

---'What's wrong?'

---'I've been washing.'

---'Washing what?'

---'My body. My hair, my clothes. Trainers. Everything. Even inside.'

---'Inside?'

---'Inside.'

---'Why?'

---'To wash you off.'

The skin beneath her one of her eyes fluttering.

---'Don't come near!'

The sensation of falling was so strong that I put my arms out and seeing this, imagining perhaps I was going to hit her, she moved her head back sharply and smacked it on the wall.

It sounded hollow. Her head, I mean.

Then she shook it about it a bit, put her hand there, and brought back blood.

---'Don't you dare!'

Her lips compressed and extruded.

---'Get away from me.'

Her cheeks and forehead with spreading red blotches. Her features ugly, ill-designed. And something tugging at the rims of her eyes, which had turned fluid. Her irises, soft and intense as egg yolks, though a different colour, seemed about to tumble over her eyelids and stain her dress.

---'Leave me alone. I don't love you. And I don't want you to touch me again, ever.'

Women as those little girls you are allowed to play with. Shouting at me now, her face dirtied by tears.

---'Not your mouth. Not your cheeks. Not your fingers. Ever.'

She looked down and away, but looked up suddenly.

---'And don't you look at me. Your eyes. Not ever again.'

A buzzer sounded.

It was Kohlhaas's paper.

She hurried in.

Following, I found a seat next to Cundy---mainly by feel.

And, blinded, sensed her in the poisoned light taking the place at the front which Johnstone had saved for her.

Her mask white with blue and pink smudges. She turned it to me, with her hands on her backside as she straightened her dress to sit down--- and sent me a beam of hate.

Meanwhile even Leicher had relented.

---'How are we feeling now my dear?' he asked from the podium.

---'And what have we done with our antlers?' punned Cundy.

A tired groan arose.

Leicher's olive branch:

---'This morning I have been e-mailing a research student to follow up your idea. If necessary, we rerun the significance tests. Ok my dear?'

She turned her eyes to him. What use were those disks of dull colour for seeing with? They looked more decorative than practical. Bathed in their mild blue light Leicher became slightly hysterical.

---'When I was your age I too used to dream of rocking the boat,' he said. 'This was not a wholly bad sign, in my case at least. Youth!' he added fondly. 'Who said 'youth is beauty, beauty youth'? Was it not Oscar Wilde?'

---'It was me!' said Cundy. 'Sorry, only larking about.'

Hella nodded grimly.

She was sitting next to Johnstone. Johnstone a physicist---seconded to the funding council and here to vet the academic antics ... and I was not. A physicist, I mean. Johnstone, patrician, functioning, soigné, with taupe chinos, penny loafers and a mauve polo-neck.

Kohlhaas began:

'Norbert Leicher's interdisciplinary approach is reminiscent of the rites of transposition of myth and sensation between the various faculties which we call synaesthesia ...'

Cundy cleared his throat and uncrossed his legs, re-crossing them the other way. Tightened the knot in his tie.

---'... *which Charles Baudelaire enacts in the privacy of that temple yclept Les Fleurs du Mal, Arthur Rimbaud in that piquant poesy ...*'

---'Excuse me, Kohlhaas, I have a question,' said Cundy.

Kohlhaas looking up. Putting his glasses on. Magnified by these glasses, serious eyes which flowed abruptly about.

---'Yes Jim?'

---'How long will this go on?'

What was sweet about Kohlhaas was that he saw the joke. As he continued he was afflicted by giggles:

---'*... resolved to embark on---embark---to embark on a numerical analysis of literature, that profiting from Professor Leicher's methodological advances, is an inter-subjective examination of literary value ...*'

Dabbing his handkerchief at his lips, he giggled and spoke.

But the slide projector clacking, and in its light, Hella---her head on Johnstone's shoulder.

---'Oh god! What is it?' said Cundy beside me.

---'Jim,' I managed to say, 'please don't look at me ...'

He looked away.

---'It's no good, he's lost me,' he said in his embarrassment.

---'Shush!'

---'Shhh!'

From the front, angry faces, craning back at us uncomfortably.

Wanting to kill him. Johnstone, that is. Standing up. But Cundy on my arms, pulling me down again. Shyly, he dared take another look at me.

---'Oh my!' he said.

Because: her head on Johnstone's shoulder. Oh his shoulder---her head. A sour, flaring hatred for Johnstone; hatred of physics, of insiders, of the successful, of the self-fulfilled, the intelligent, of those who know and who get what they want, everywhere.

---'Oh my!' said Cundy again.

When I slammed the door, I could hear the tinkling rattle as the same bit of Ormolu dropped off. In the long gallery, my eyes alight, needled by the garish daylight. Suffocating, blinded, bouncing down the front steps clinging to the balustrade, and tracing the edges of the island like the walls of a cluttered cell, this one with sad enormous pines and ilexes which only made me sob.

When I came back they were going in to lunch. Hella had taken the chair beside Johnstone. I should have stayed away from her. There's no doubt about that.

But on her other side was an empty place.

I sat down and she turned and looked at me before leaning past Johnstone to ask if Kohlhaas would exchange with her.

---'What's your problem?' she asked with ugly lips as she rose.

---'Don't abandon her,' rearrangement made, Kohlhaas said. Bringing his face close. 'She adores you.' He blushed. 'Don't walk away.' I felt his breath.

---'It's not---me ...'

---'You don't understand,' he said, with a glance over his shoulder at Johnstone and Hella. 'During my paper, when she had her head on Johnstone's shoulder---it was only because she was sleeping.'

Points of earnest light, focused by his glasses, moved across his face.

---'She loves you---I can *see*. And it will never come to pass again. Don't walk away; it's the only thing which will happen, the only thing; don't lose it, through pride, malice, sanity. This Johnstone thing; it's a joke, a delusion; it doesn't exist. Please don't screw up.'

Almost in tears. Him, not me.

---'She'll do what you want, you only have to wake her; you only have to say 'come away with me, I want you to bear our child'---no, I mean it, I mean it, that's your duty to nature, the future, the world; your only one, that's all you should---you have to do. Because she loves you. It's that simple.'

He looked at me as a dog does who's dropped a stone and is waiting for you to throw it. When I didn't he said:

---'She's the best---the most ...---and she loves you. What more do you ask? Can you ask? What else *is* there?'

His big nose red, and running. A coarse nose, for such a delicate man. Enlarged pores. His cheeks glistening.

---'In heaven's name, wake up. Because I sometimes---I sometimes worry---wonder---I---whether you are '*fucking*' good enough. For her, I mean.'

Pausing, to let his words sink in, before going on.

---'When she woke up during my paper, she turned round immediately, then kept asking Johnstone where you'd gone. We heard her from the podium. Then she went up to the windows, even while I was speaking, and drew the drapes aside. No one was listening to me. Everyone was looking at her. And she didn't even know.'

A fountain foaming away in my brain, some of which was leaking out my eyes. But I felt more like crying than chasing her.

So Kohlhaas did it for me. By taking my head in his hands, leaning back, and pointing my face her way.

---'Hella,' he said, 'Hella.'

All down the long table, silence fell.

Even the clinking of knives and forks was stilled. And people's mouths, like gargoyles, frozen in mid-chew.

She looked at me coldly, and also at him. Her face so white that it was green. I saw him shiver.

He was wrong.

She gritted her teeth and opened white lips, saying:

---'Would you mind not hassling me.'

And then, more loosely, more passionately:

---'Please?'

A mist of curious faces, pinkish, seen through smudges of blood, gathered behind her, looking fascinated, looking grim.

---'Leave me alone!'

As she started sobbing.

---'Why can't you leave me alone?'

And started barking. Or---it was retching?

---'You're alright,' said Johnstone, soothingly.

---'You too,' she said when she could. 'You're just as bad. Fuck off and leave me alone. All of you.'

Then she was sick. On her plate. Only a little splashed onto the table-cloth. Thick, like porridge, not runny at all. Round its edges it turned the linen grey.

The clinking of knives and forks and the hum of voices started up again, much louder than before.

Only Auch, Leicher and Waddington, compressed smiles, nodding at each other, their faces close.

4

Later, in the pained and painted ballroom, for the session after lunch which nobody wanted because the audience would fall asleep, it was Waddington who, evidently having drawn the short straw, mounted the podium to speak. He arranged his papers, cleared his throat.

The lights went down.

'*SMM: Explicandum and/or Explicate?*'

he asked in the half-light, and after solemnly panning his gaze about, began.

'Webster's *defines* 'manifold' *as ...*'

---'Waddington's drunk on jargon. He's positively intoxicated with it,' whispered Cundy.

'*... the texts, contexts, textures of sociometry,* ceteris paribus, *being uniquely defined by ...*'

---'Where does he think we are? Pompeii?'

Discovering the key: that Cundy couldn't help it.

---'*So the results I have to report are not in fact significant ...*'

His poor voice failed him here; you could see he was trying to talk on, to leave no pause, but something stronger than him knew there was one. So his lips moving but no sound there.

---'But they may be ...' Hella stuttered.

---'Speak up, I can't see you,' whispered Waddington. Hella stood to speak.

---'They may be significant after all---if you amended the means by which you estimate your parameters ...'

I could see Johnstone beside her, nodding seriously.

But Waddington was talking. Suddenly calm, suddenly majestic, he went on with his paper. Her words trailed off, she looked bewildered, and then sat down. Or tried to. Someone had shifted her chair away and she fell to the floor. General hooting and whistling. Johnstone looking down at her in surprise. Only Kohlhaas stooping over her, looking hurt himself, almost frantic. Modestine still holding the back of the chair. Waddington paused.

---'Pride before the fall,' he said. 'Hey?'

And couldn't resist a jolly good laugh.

---'Pardon?' asked Leicher.

Waddington explained the joke quietly, so that we had already moved on when Leicher astonished us all with a long, coarse bray.

---'Tragedy: the brilliance, the great height, the self-engendered fall. Not hubris, yet honesty,' explained Kohlhaas in a whisper. 'For the onlookers, catharsis. But if tragedy, who is chorus? Also, the institution of ostracism, of course. The clay shards, the scraped names, which can still be turned up now, even, I understand, in the gardens of Athens ...'

---'Dr Kohlhaas, please!' said Sir Mel in disbelief.

But Hella rose from the floor, standing stiffly now, the globes of her bottom patted with dust.

---'I still have a point to make, if I may, Dr Waddington.'

Everyone fell silent. But when she opened her mouth to go on, there was such a clatter, with shouts of 'Degrees of freedom!' that Sir Mel, languid, godlike, intervened.

Silence, again.

---'This problem of the loss of degrees of freedom ...'

---'Yes?' snapped Waddington.

---'How would you go about solving it?'

---'Assuming it was a problem, you mean?'

---'Assuming it was.'

---'Stupid question. By conducting more trials of course.'

---'That isn't necessary. There is a way of preserving the degrees of freedom intact from the original data pairs. The solution is trivial. If you were to calculate a population best-fit curve, the problem should be resolved.'

I looked at Leicher, who was studying the surface of his desk and nodding absently.

---'Proof?' he asked abruptly, slowly raising his face.

---'Proof?' echoed Cundy. 'Who needs proof when they've got conviction?'

But Hella held up a sheet of yellow paper. She was trembling so much that she was flapping it, deliberately, like someone trying to attract the attention of a bull.

---'It's like this.' And she explained.

---'Why do all the others not do it like this then? Answer me!' said Leicher.

---'I suppose they just didn't think about it.'

---'They did not think about it, did they?' Suddenly furious, he had long spools of spittle hanging and swinging from his lips. 'They did not think about it? And what have I been doing all my life? No,' he added more quietly, 'it cannot be. If you are right then all others are wrong.'

---'It has been known.'

---'Conceited,' said Cundy raising a finger. 'I like ☐ respect ☐ that.'

And yet her voice thick. Perhaps she'd caught a cold. Turning back to Leicher:

---'Would you mind checking it for me? You see---it's very simple.'

More laughter; every one smiling. In this ballroom on an island, so internationalised and so cut off, that if you didn't know already, you wouldn't even guess which country you were in. The future of Europe, perhaps: standardisation, metrification, the end of enlightenment---what we might term the *endarklement*. Cundy whispering to me:

---'Look, they're not fazed at all by this. They're smiling. They must know something she doesn't.'

But something wrong. It was tension, fear. They were the smiles of shock.

---'How do you do it?' asked Cundy eventually, breaking the silence.

---'It really just reduces to algebra?'

---'I know. But I know algebra, and I wouldn't have thought of it you little brute.'

Another silence. The future was wondering what to do.

---'Any more questions?' asked Sir Mel, raising his mono-brow and casting his eyes around the room. People were leaving, in a hurry; something was dangerous, or might become so; the air was compromised, smoking, green.

---'You got your math wrong,' said Waddington from the door.

Leicher had already gone.

---'Maybe. We don't need to argue. We can work it out.'

But even as she answered, Waddington turned away and left.

---'Words, words, words,' said Modestine slowly from just behind her ear, a rather grim smile on her face, one finger raised.

Hella getting tetchy now.

---'Yes, they are words, pretentious cow.'

Sexism; stereotyping; she was going too far again, putting herself in the wrong.

---'I'm listening,' said Kohlhaas rather desperately.

But it was too late. Sir Mel, glittering with enigma behind his spectacles, adjourned us yet again.

In the drawing room, an excited burble and clatter. But aware, suddenly, all around us, in the enormous room, that silence was falling like night.

She'd come in. Kohlhaas was panting.

Taking a cup and some biscuits into a corner she made her stand under two blotched and tarnished mirrors which rose up to the frothy gilded ceiling, far above her frothy, gilded head. A doughty girl, facing down the irresistible and boring forces of the universe. Her stand taken, not against Leicher, Waddington, Auch, or even dishonesty, sciolism and error, but entropy itself.

Leicher and Waddington, exchanging glances and striding forwards, side by side.

She smiled at them.

---'Dr Skippergate,' said Waddington reasonably, 'it doesn't have to be like this you know.'

---'I don't want this either.'

---'Of course not. Now sometimes you have to show a bit of solidarity,' he explained. 'Basically you have to decide which side are you are on. We all have to hang together, don't we, and not roam off on our own self-centred ego trips.'

---'I am hanging together; you're off on the trip. I'm trying to make you revert to the standard use of the statistical tools.'

---'You are trying to impose an intellectual straight-jacket.'

---'You've got your statistics wrong.'

---'There is no such thing. Everything is relative to its context.'

---'Okay. And relative to probability theory you are wrong.'

---'It is moments like this which make me doubt the effectiveness in our discipline at least, of stats and math,' said Leicher aside to Waddington. 'The wisdom of bringing them in.' But Waddington had his answer readied like a sword and was waiting impatiently to deliver his *coup de grâce:*

---'Precisely,' he answered her, as soon as Leicher had finished speaking. 'And relative to SMM it is you, not we, who are wrong.'

Various voices:

---'Yes.'

---'He has a point.'

---'Answer that one then.'

Hella shrugged her shoulders. Waddington, emboldened, standing straight. And in his voice was passion.

---'You talk the language of physics, but remember this isn't physics, O knowing one. Remember too how people like you gave us nuclear power, pollution, the electric chair, the atom bomb. You don't understand SMM, what it means, how it's done. And yet you have the arrogance to presume to correct us in our own discipline ...'

---'A discipline which, incidentally, I myself created ....'

Seeing the charm in Leicher too: Leicher as Toad.

---'... intellectual imperialism, if you like,' Waddington went on, 'as if we came into physics and started questioning Einstein's Law. Or went into another culture and had the insensitivity to go about saying ... I don't know .... but saying their customs are wrong.'

---'Own goal,' she said. 'In fact, two, I believe.'

---'What? What is she saying,' Leicher asked Waddington. 'Can she really be talking football? Strange, wayward child. Useless gifts, useless gifts.'

He shook his head sadly. Waddington, too, shaking his head and saying bitterly, a quaver in his voice:

---'I don't understand you. I really don't. Sometimes I wonder if I ever will.'

---'A hatcher of troubles, that is who she is,' hissed Modestine Auch.

---'Yes, but I don't understand the motivation. Why does she do it? Why?'

Is it surprising they hated her? What was surprising was how restrained, how civilised they were, in view of what she was doing. She'd turned over the hive, after all; was fouling the honey. But she seemed to expect not to get stung.

---'Let's assume, for the sake of argument, that the statistics is relevant,' said Leicher.

---'As the economist said to the archdeacon,' offered Cundy.

---'Thank you Dr Cundy for your valued contribution. Shut up now, if you please. How do you know you are right? How can you rely on your own judgement when everyone else sees so clearly how you are so wrong?'

Seeing what gave Leicher his greatness. This doggedness. Running through each conceivable permutation of argument. The way he disposed his resources, manned each successive wall and, as he watched it breached and fall, calmly retreated behind the next.

But also gave him his weakness; his genius was for special pleading. All the arguments were on one side. He was not trying to find the truth, but to defend his own position and destroy hers.

---'What is it they say about lying with statistics? Because that, when it boils down to is, is all she's doing,' said Waddington, his face white, his mouth so stiff he could hardly form the words.

Hella started each time one of them spoke, and kept looking from face to face of the ring which had gradually formed around her.

---'So, my child, I have a proposal to make. What if we accept the degrees of freedom point?' offered Leicher.

---'Is this what's called plea-bargaining?' she asked.

Leicher and Waddington genuinely mystified.

---'What on earth's she gabbling on about?' someone asked.

Leicher let it pass.

---'Would that satisfy you?' he continued, his voice softened with generosity. 'We'll do more trials. But on your part, we'd expect a greater degree of co-operation than hitherto.'

---'What do you mean?'

---'Less disruption; basically not to interfere with the smooth running of the symposium,' said Waddington.

---'In a word: keep your trap shut.'

---'Shut it, Cundy,' said Waddington, giving him the eye.

---'Gosh', said Cundy quietly.

---'Don't you understand?' she was saying. 'You don't have to. You only have to tinker with the mathematics of regression. No more trials, none of that; just re-run the significance tests. With any luck it'll come out right'.

---'Yes, yes, yes'.

Leicher, flapping his hand dismissively.

---'Be back where we started, in fact', said Waddington, gloomily.

---'But hang on a minute ...' she said.

She was looking up in the air.

---'Hang on?'

---'Shhh!' she said.

Leicher and Waddington exchanged furtive looks.

And started to back away.

---'We've got a problem', she said.

Leicher and Waddington, frozen in their retreat, side by side, too still. Their grey lips pursed, their eyes like small, popable balloons filled with tears. Waddington holding clenched fists carefully near his hips.

---'Speak for yourself', Waddington said.

She was silent; her corrugated forehead. Then asked:

---'Did you have a control?'

---'Please?' said Leicher, bitterly.

---'A control. What if your results were manufactured by the method?'

---'I am so sorry, but how could that be?'

He drew a grey handkerchief across his forehead. Then started giggling.

---'What is it Norbert?' asked Waddington in alarm.

---'Degrees of Freedom', said Leicher, tears on his cheeks.

---'You don't have to ask, I mean answer, that question; all you need is to run a parallel test as a control', she said.

---'And how would one effect that?' stuttered Waddington, his knees slightly bent.

---'I don't know; I'll think about it.'

---'Thank you very much indeed my dear. That would be most kind', said Leicher. 'Now: shall we return to the point?'

---'For instance', she interrupted, 'you are asking people to use numbers to express their perception of magnitude; but what do you know about their perception of numbers? Have you measured this?'

---'What complete and utter nonsense is this?' asked Leicher. And Waddington chipped in:

---'How can you measure numbers. Sometimes you talk very pure nonsense Dr Skippergate.'

---'Stick to what you know about and don't blunder about in things you do not', Leicher went on. 'You are making quite a fool of yourself, you see.'

---'That's okay.' In her voice the harshness of cold sarcasm. 'I enjoy the juvenile level at which this debate is conducted. People laugh at parliaments; but academic fora in the soft sciences seem just as unsophisticated, childish, base ...'

Her cool spite. A taunting, aggravating---serenity. She was hated for it, because by it she was placing herself above us. That instinct again, so strong in her: to put herself in the wrong. Unless she was. Above us, I mean. She was still speaking:

---'Show someone a piece of string; show them another twice as long. Ask what's happened. Maybe they say the length has doubled. Fine: but there is a missing link: what they mean when they say 'doubled' may not be what arithmetic means.'

Waddington had sweat on his face. His hollow cheeks and big sharp nose. And razor burns under the sea-blue stubble.

---'What on earth ... ?' he asked.

---'Listen to her,' said Johnstone.

---'Is there such a thing as pure psychological magnitude, devoid of any physical quality? And if so, what function is it of its physical---mathematical---logical---linear counterpart?'

---'Precious ... git,' said Waddington, so emphatically that even where I stood I felt the flecks of spittle.

---'Listen to her,' said Johnstone again.

---'Say I give someone a banana. Then give them another and ask how many more they have. The answer might not be twice as many. In this case they know; they have been taught; they hear the bell, salivate.'

---'What a prat!'

---'Did you know that the British word prat originally meant buttock?' Asked Kohlhaas, presumably as a diversionary ploy.

---'She reminds me,' said Cundy, 'of the little girl who knew how to spell banana but didn't know when to stop.'

And he was right. She didn't. You could jest of Cundy that many a true word was spoken in jest.

Leicher, meanwhile, with the face of a man who has had extra garlic put on his fish.

---'To use bananas isn't right either, because the quantity of bananas isn't a pure magnitude in the sense I am groping for ...'

Then she saw me. I was standing on the sofa to look over their heads. Her stony stare but at the same time a tint, a vague blue glow of warmth in it, a sense, perhaps only a hope, that she was fighting back a smile. As for her point, I couldn't get my own head round this. Icarus flew before he plunged; was Icarus already plunging?

---'What I am saying ... or what am I saying?' she asked, still looking sideways at me, '... yes, what I am saying is that psychological magnitude might be a nonlinear function of arithmetic magnitude. And while mathematics might say 2 is twice 1, our world, the world, might not. Now this may not seem particularly exciting, but it has implications. 'There are depths,' as James said. 'So that you could be forgiven for asking why there are depths.'

Leicher looked perplexed.

Waddington looked angry.

Cundy looked away.

But Kohlhaas hid a little smile.

And if there are depths, but ... there are also surfaces. Like that self-fulfilling prophecy, her face.

---'Anyway, I've said enough,' she was saying.

---'You sure have,' said Waddington.

---'Yes,' said Modestine. 'Keep taking the tablet.'

She turned her face my way. And curled up the ends of her lips faintly. This was all. Didn't smile.

---'She's just trying to be different,' Waddington explained.

---'Yes. I am trying to be different. What are you trying? To be the same?'

Waddington silent, his face in shadow.

---'Not always as dumb as they pretend, are they Mr Waddington?'

Almost deliberately, again and again, putting herself in the wrong. Arrogance? Stupidity?

---'She is just trying,' let's leave it at that, said Modestine. 'So trying, oh so trying.'

---'My patience is expiring,' Leicher warned her. 'You realise this pooh-poohing is how was treated Freud at first? And Marx? You realise that when it comes to importance SMM is of the first magnitude?'

Licking her finger and drawing lines in space:

---'Own goal, own goal, own goal.'

She knew how to be infuriating.

---'I beg to differ. Like me, great men both,' he explained, 'both achieved
fame, influence, and changed the history of the globe. Like me.'

---'Own goal.'

---'Stop saying this!' he ordered.

---'Own goal.'

---'What do you mean?'

Imploring.

---'Like Lenin, Stalin, Hitler,' she said. 'Because it is hard to build but easy
to destroy.'

Leicher formed raised hands into claws and asked:

---'Then why in heavens name are you taking it upon yourself to destroy
SMM?'

The trouble being, she was better than us. Higher. She had everything---
except a heart. Too delicate, too spoiled for that. But she had herself, was
herself; and this none of us could forgive. Her scientific and facial and
bodily riches, the way she made all want her without even meaning to,
and without any intention of gratifying the desires she provoked. What
could we do but despise her?

---'It is easy for her to make things difficult,' said Modestine. 'But what on
earth has she done?'

---'She's a conceited ass who doesn't know what she's talking about and
ought to learn from people who do,' Waddington observed.

---'However,' said Leicher, 'it does not disturb nor even surprise me when
third-rate people misunderstand something that is first-rate. This is
utterly consistent with my view that when it comes to thinking, many
people simply cannot do it.'

Hella blushed. But didn't speak.

---'No amount of physics and chemistry will help you here, my dear,
though a thorough knowledge of structuralism and of psychoanalysis

will be of some use along the difficult route to a full understanding of
SMM. It is rather as Nils (Nils Bohr do you know who I mean?) once said
to me: 'If you are not shocked by Quantum Theory Norbert then you
have not understood it.' Well: if you are not shocked by SMM, then you
have not understood it. Our fuzzy logics are not your 'hard' ones, your
rigid, classical logics, this is what you fail so utterly, so pathetically, so
miserably, even to grasp.'

And grimacing he clapped once, as if there was a fly between his hands.
As a kind of full-stop.

---'Tod?' he added.

---'Our logic, while not exactly fuzzy has elements of fuzziness. It bows
 to catastrophe, complexity and chaos theories. This is the essential fact
 which you have not appreciated.'

---'My view, for what it's worth ...' she started.

---'My dear, I couldn't be more disinterested. Shall we now move
 forwards from this sterile discourse?' said Leicher. Then whispered
 something acidic under his breath. Him and Waddington fell about
 laughing.

---'What did he say, what did he say?' people were asking.

---'I heard,' said Kohlhaas.

---'Do tell,' said McGovern.

---'He said 'I expect she is having her happy days."

---'Happy days?'

---'Her time of the month. Her curse.'

Waddington and Leicher, as he spoke, looking on expectantly, then
falling about again.

Hella, setting her lips together, almost in a subtle smile; and turning up
her voice, and beginning again to speak. To ask for it, in fact.

---'So; to recap ...'

And Leicher made a lunge. Not very far, only a little way towards her, but she stepped sharply back against a mirror, to back out, back through. As she did so her biscuit teetered on the edge of the saucer she still held, overbalanced, and fell turning slowly to the parquet where it spun briefly on its rim, before settling. Leicher, in his rage, got his toe to it and ground it exaggeratedly in. Meanwhile he cracked his knuckles and by grinding his teeth made them squeak.

It was a heavy moment. It was also ticklish, irritable. There was a ripple effect in our softened vision as crackling and squeaking he strode about while Waddington and Modestine seemed to drift on an undulant backcloth.

---'To recap ...'

For defence he went behind a table and braced his hands, cracked and veined and smudged with freckle, on the starched cloth.

---'... of degrees of freedom can be remedied simply, but the question of the perception of magnitude, if there is such an effect ...'

---'SHUT UP!'

Someone shouting.

It was Leicher.

Lips lifted from yellow teeth. Eyes screwed up. And a hollow mouth. He was leaning towards us. Two crystalline drools of spittle hung from the corners of his glossy, dangling lip.

The heat, pinning us down like insects in the midst of this reservoir, on top of this bluff. Slowly he opened pale eyes. His nose contracted, dark, frilled.

---'Thank you,' he said. In a pause, a pause almost in time, he took his glasses off and I thought I saw another pair underneath. With fine black rims. They were the circles round his eyes of course, sharp blackened furrows defining the glasslike flesh within. Over the heads he looked at me, standing up on my sofa behind the others, as if with the extra intuition of the blinded he knew my thoughts.

Then quickly fitted them back. Poor man, I imagined him sleeping later, naked in his bed, prized from his shell, all crooked, arms and legs thrown about, his white cock upwards on his belly---and his glasses on.

But suddenly, breathing heavily, he threw his papers on the floor.

And, in trembling hands, plucked McGovern's teacup from its saucer. Flung that into the empty fireplace. It bounced about in there then rolled slowly out.

Stopped.

Rolled back, unbroken. Stopped. Waddington, scrupulous acolyte, crushed it with his foot.

---'And we are expected to suspend this whole major symposium simply because last night Dr Skippergate got moist in the downstairs department and entered into a no-pants situation?' he asked.

His chest was pumping under his short-sleeved shirt.

And the tip of the biro in his breast pocket moved like a pointer steadily back and forth.

---'Careful old boy. You'll reach premature climax,' Cundy advised.

---'What she needs is a jolly good one. Up her back passage. She needs a fat dirty raghead to come up her rear end,' he said in Dutch.

---'There are few things less beautiful than the stupid insisting on their point-of-view,' she answered calmly, in Dutch too.

All his features moving independently.

---'Vicious! I just hope they've got no-on on the committee which decides your funding,' said Cundy.

---'What did they say?' asked Kohlhaas.

She translated. This struck me. She had time to translate for the bystanders. While red, trembling, and looking at the ground. But Leicher was speaking again:

---'You know, of course, we didn't want you here. It is simply that EC rules stipulate a certain quota of woman.'

---'True,' said Waddington.

---'I like it. Quota of woman. Can I quota you on that?' asked Cundy.

---'Affirmative action. Shut up Cundy'

---'Negative action, more like.'

---'Cundy, please don't talk, you're making it even worse' Hella said.

He looked suddenly hurt, went even a little pale.

---'Sorry.'

And he was. Sorrow: a sudden gale of it blowing through his skull and across his face.

---'No, no,' he was saying, 'she's right, she's right. Sometimes even I get excruciated by how awful I am; I see me doing it, and all I can do is look on helplessly and be ashamed. But then I realise; that's me, I have to accept it; so I learn to revel in it. I can't be anything else, I'm not anything else; I am excruciating. So I've come to terms with my soul. But I don't say it isn't tough.'

---'Don't worry about it, Jim,' said Kohlhaas. 'He shouldn't worry, should he, Modestine. Debonair, lovable Jim Cundy shouldn't worry about a thing.'

Modestine Auch looking mystified.

---'Say again please?'

---'It's true,' said Cundy miserably---or mock miserably perhaps. 'It's so true.'

---'Truth,' said Kohlhaas loudly, clearing a space for an aphorism, 'truth---listen to me---let me---truth, truth at a Symposium---*c'est comme un coup de pistolet au milieu d'un concert.*'

Kohlhaas becoming witty. Something of Cundy's influence in this. Bringing him out. So that now, as Cundy fell, carrying Cundy's baton he strode on.

---'Look at us!' continued Cundy. 'Squabbles, misunderstandings, bullying. An onrushing tyranny. And meanwhile a tempered free-trade in ideas.'

---'Science is universal; *lingua franca est*; the trade in ideas is always free,' said Leicher, loftily.

---'Not true,' said Cundy; 'There's Teutonic science, Frankish science, Castilian science, and so on. At least on the practical level. At the level of the ideal---true, on the assumption that there is only one reality there is only one science ...'

---'There is no reality,' Johnstone said.

Something of the shallow, garbled atmosphere of a phone-in.

---'Ladies, Gentlemen, Sir Pease, I have something to say. Let me speak,' Kohlhaas asked.

---'*Not* Sir Pease but Sir Mel I think you mean!' Modestine Auch corrected irritably.

All turned towards him. He cleared his throat.

---'Formal gardens, running down to Newton's beach. Ilex and pine woods, sacred to Artemis, and the field of ignorance and emotion which lies beyond. And us, marooned in this garden, trapped on this island, tamped in an ivory tower of Babel so to speak, wishing but not daring to let down our long hair, not understanding the sound of one another's voices, and not wishing to ...'

---'Steady on Professor Kohlhaas,' said Dr Waddington eventually. 'I can't take much more of this.'

---'Steady, steady now. He'll blow a fuse,' said Cundy.

---'What's he saying?' asked Leicher. 'I am not understanding a word.'

Kohlhaas paused with a pained expression which he turned towards Sir Mel. Sir Mel obliged him.

---'Ladies, Gentlemen, please,' he said.

This was the last I heard. With determination on a childish face she had bolted for the open window and without even touching the sill, hurdled right through.

Outside, sunlight falling heavily on the grass.

Above the demented noise of crickets, the sound of her clothes and her hair as she ran downhill. And hot rosemary, hot thyme, as I ran after her.

Where the lawns ended and the scrub began, she stopped.

And turning her face suddenly, chafed with tears, her eye-whites pink in a red face which made the eye-blues even bluer---stared at my lips. She was twirling a strand of her tawny hair into a paint-brush to paint her temple, the top edge of her cheek, and finally her own lips. I knew--- how?---it being so unlikely---that she also wanted to paint mine, and not with the brush but her tongue. Leaning, almost a stumbling forwards, knowing the action would be *not-to-kiss*, this would be the event, the thing, decision, surprise; kissing was so inevitable that it was nothing, or not inevitable, perhaps, but the way which lay *along* the road, as existence also does. Her eyes closed; lips parted, teeth whiter than her eyes had been, because untainted with pink, and lips much redder than her face. She was out of breath. Smelt vaguely of sick. A sense, under my two hands, of the thinness of her waist; the inflexion from ribcage to waist to hip; and her lips boiling, almost to hurt. And then a ragged cheer from the palace windows, a whistling, great hooting, stomping and a *hey-hey-hey!*

She looked back blankly, turned away---her back hollowed---and walked into the woods.

And amongst the scrubby hazels and pines, combing leaves and needles through my fingers, making the branches swish, I hobbled after her.

At the modernistic harbour, formed in flowing shapes of concrete, picking up the oars which were lying in the grass and throwing them at me.

Pulling roughly on the painter of the rowing boat.

Climbing in.

And, as I fitted the oars on their pegs, turning a red face down to the water, looking for her reflection, and dripping tears on it.

---'Where are we going?'

Without looking up, she pointed to the chestnut woods on the shore beyond Sfondrata, the local town.

---'I've got to get off this fucking island', she said. 'Before I go mad.'

---'Too late maybe.'

Her flesh, so hard under its clothes, was forbidden, distant.

---'So?' she asked. 'So?'

Afloat on the lake, now; something supernatural in the way the boat floated, was pushed up by the water. And this water so clear it seemed like we would fall.

---'You don't even listen to me', she said. 'You stupid fucker.'

I beckoned to her, and she put her ear gently to my mouth, to hear the sea.

---'Don't be like this.'

---'Why not.'

---'Don't be mean to me.'

She shifted suddenly back, making the water around us splash, and looking straight ahead of her, over my shoulder, set her lips and whitened her skin.

---'Bullshit', she screamed. 'Fucking bullshit. You don't even know what meanness means.' Something unconvincing about her rage; however well-acted, it was acted, as she stared at me with glowing eyes from her perch in the bow. I don't mean really that it was acted---just that it didn't fit her perfectly, a rejected hypothesis as to her feelings or how to transmit them.

Floating towards us was a beach of coarse, burning sand---dark, reddish, the colour of her hair.

A side glance flicked at me. She was almost trying not to smile.

And I knew, wrongly perhaps, it would come out right, had to; there was no way round. Goodness was compulsory and evil out-of-order in this new paradise.

---'The cat who's eaten the canary', she said. Compressed happiness.

---'I have.'

---'I can see.'

But put a cautionary hand on my wrist:

---'Only you haven't. You only think you have. Because it was all a mistake, of course, a one-off. We don't get caught out like that twice.'

She smiled again, sideways. The self-delusion of the sane.

---'My poor thing,' she added in an exultant voice, seeing my face. 'Have I done wrong?' And making her eyes go wider open: 'It wasn't meant to be, but happened anyway,' she said. 'There is nothing you can do but close your eyes in shame, cling on, and wait. It doesn't take long. But afterwards, something different in your relations. The question has been asked, twists and floats in air like cigarette smoke: should you be fucking not with your bodies now, but hearts. This by the way,' she said seriously, 'is you and me.'

Heavy.

---'Obviously.'

Set on the branches which hung over the beach, ingenious thick black salady leaves. And the air of an opera set. Of the calm before the overture. As the keel of the boat grated on sand and, making all the props rock, including the reservoir, the sand, the trees, the spiral nebulae, Hella clomped on stage.

On her face: yet more tears.

---'What is it now Hella?'

---'When I came here I ...' Her voice clogged.

---'Can't understand.'

---'... thought I was going to have a good time.'

The light already going, under the low branches. Her face like a clock, luminous, looking out from in there.

---'But the---well, the effort of making the future come ...'

---'What?'

---'Not happen, but come. The knots and tangles; the fairy-balls in your hair. Sometimes you have to snip bits off. Mare's nests---that's the idiom. And that's all.'

---'What do you mean?'

---'Snip-snip is what I mean.'

---'What?'

---'It's not right. We can't be doing this. I can't see you again.'

---'Johnstone?'

She looked at me in disbelief, didn't even answer that.

---'Sit in the roots,' she said. 'Move up. I have more to say.'

And sitting down beside me she fell silent.

---'I don't know how to ...'

She didn't mean to touch me. But her weight spread her prat, so that she did. I could feel the pressure and warmth through her skirt of skin.

---'... well, I like you very much,' she said, and my heart sank. 'You are a special person.' Sank more.

Across the water, silhouettes of cliff, palace, island, in various receding exotic blues.

---'But I didn't *want* to fuck with you!'

---'When?'

---'I never did!'

Both quiet.

---'Or I didn't mean to want to,' she added, in the softening tone of pity. And chuckled. And exhaled between her lips. You could see, or hear, the blue veins pulsing in her temples, where the damp skin sank in.

---'Plus---Haakon ... we've bought a house.'

---'I have a girlfriend too.'

For a second, the confused scuffle between jealousy and relief.

---'Is this Barb? She's very lucky,' she said earnestly, and rose, pulling the baby-doll skirt---its miraculous blue---out from where it had lodged in her natal crack and brushing off sand.

With an unnecessary clatter, she threw the oars into the bottom of the boat and started pushing it out.

It didn't move.

She grunted.

Gasped.

The boat motionless.

After a while, she gave up. Came back. Sat down.

---'So?' she said.

---'So what?'

Her tone business-like.

---'It's only because I was taken by surprise.'

---'What?'

---'That I let you ...'

She blinked as she spoke; more than hypocrisy, this was lie. And lying didn't become her. It does become some people, aesthetically, at least, if not morally, if these are not identical. Not her.

---'It wasn't meant to be. We were always meant to be more than lovers--- we were always meant to be friends.'

A falter in her voice, a pallor in her skin; was she really lying to me? She who was supposedly---officially---so into truth?

---'A brief fling. Purely physical. I was just having fun. Weren't you? I thought you were.'

Her message sinking in. I'd drunk that spit; sucked in that breath, smelling faintly of herbs. And while I lived, never would again.

---'Poor thing. I should have warned you, shouldn't have led you on. It wasn't fair on you---I realise that. Now.'

Unless by force.

A mottled song thrush singing a rambling, bubbling song. Through the swinging gaps in the branches, in a sky still a blue which was also miraculous, like her dress, were three or four stars.

---'What do you want me to do?'

Trying to keep my voice steady. But she heard.

---'Poor thing.'

She stroked my hair.

---'It not true,' she admitted, eventually. 'All I wanted in the world was you.'

Trying to speak. But I couldn't.

---'Last night---the hot air, the noise of crickets, the low sun half-blinding me so everything looked black, even the sky, even the sun. I was saying, secretly, without any intention of it happening, in fact with the intention of it not, never happening, 'Let's say something happened? Happened now. What would I do then?"

She sighed.

---'A sweet feeling, but pointless because it would lead to nothing, would leave ends untied. A dead end, even a bitter one. It would be too easy, and only enjoyable, only pleasant, and things must have austerity in them, wormwood, to be good. And so I knew I would fight with you when you tried to kiss me, on the lips at least.'

She sighed some more, and turned the pale facet of her dark head my way. I imagined her frowning wistfully.

---'Only with an unmistakable sign would I kiss you. And not something that could be pushed into reluctant service as a sign; and of course there wouldn't be such a thing. Because I was safe I could think, 'What next?,' in the hypothetical situation which would never arise. This might have been the mistake.'

---'What next?'

---'Yes; this interested me, too. Would I let you kiss me, but only kiss me, and not inside the lips, either? The crickets were too loud for me to hear the answer, and the resinous syrupy smell of wild rosemary and wild thyme became unbearable, like roasting meat. I could taste it all in my mouth, which had filled with spit. Then I saw the bundle, tied with green rope like a chicken ready to be plucked and cooked and asked 'What's that?''

---'I didn't think that this might be the very thing I wasn't expecting. When it bit me I was excited, moved, the kind of excitement and movement you feel if told you have a year to live. *A whole year?'* I still didn't know why. I still didn't realise it was what I wasn't expecting. Perhaps because it was so cheesy. This new religious sense---exaltation, fervour, belief, and not the mere sign itself of course---was what made me vulnerable. The feeling that the world is just a dream and one with a golden message which unlocks the hidden gates which lead up to the next level of the mystery, of the game.'

My head going round. But I saw what she was doing. Destroying by analysis the best thing ever. To build it up, but only in order to take it down, pull apart, release the ghost, the happy spirit.

---'And you got me when I was vulnerable, sitting there, my legs outstretched, after that bird had flown away with the worm. I was soaked in sweat and so turned on I kept wanting to touch myself---so slimy, so wet that my body had become a liquid, one you could dip your fingers in---thick, warm, slimy, and sugared and soapy as heaven itself...'

---'Willing you to kiss me I lay back; my closed eyes, under their lids, were floating in tears, and when I opened my them, rigid, staring at the sky, the tears came out, and trickled down the two sides of my face, and filled my ears, so that still, however much I shake my head, there's a crunching sound in there which drives me wild. Only, maybe that's sand ...'

What light there was gleamed on her wet teeth, and she took my hand and kept it in hers where it stayed, heavy with reluctance now, sweating slightly, until she let it go.

---'But no. No---in the end. Although it is good to do this sometimes, afterwards you must return to reality.'

And she shook her head.

---'Must?'

The breathless branches too, shook their heavy leaves.

---'Must.'

Leaning against chestnut bark.

---'Because it doesn't need to be physical. You know that.'

I didn't.

---'We can be above that. Above the sweat and dirt, the whiffs of---shit, the coarse, ugly hair, the aesthetically---limited---sexual organs.'

She twisted her mouth in an ugly way, became flimsy, skinny, weak. She was brittle anyway---and something cold about her, the coldness of physics and mathematics themselves perhaps; of statistics, even; even of money---and yet this was also attractive, and put a spin on the attraction which made it unique.

I slid my arm around her.

---'Don't do that,' she said. But her ear was pressed against my shoulder, listening.

She didn't move.

And in a rush, the tipsy scent of sex, making my heart thud until it nearly shattered; and her voice asking:

---'Do you still want me? If I had been available, I mean.'

---'Yes.'

---'It can never be; don't you understand?'

---'That was a wet dream: and now we draw back from the edge and climb the steep, dismal slope of turf. It's over---this is what you have to see. And what's so wonderful is that I'll be home early!'

Holding Haakon up before her in self- defence, like a crucifix.

---'I can't wait to see him. Because you must know I can't stay here.'

Now it was me who was livid. Her whole life, pat. The career, the boyfriend, the new house. Hating her. And in parallel an unexpected sympathy, almost a love, a gale of love, for Leicher. As much too early, in the darkness, almost before it had set, the sun showed signs of rising again.

---'You see, I'm right,' she said, pointing at the dawn. 'We've talked all night; we don't need to---fuck---one another.' She yawned, fanning her teeth.

---'We are way above all that.' She blinked a few times in her exhaustion.

---'I'll take you back. I think that's what you want,' I said.

---'There is much more to life than mere sex,' she added quickly, then paused. 'We are not animals,' she went on suddenly, 'driven by lust. Above all, we don't betray our trust. We don't have to, that is what makes us so different, what makes us so valuable, fidelity I mean, and we can be proud of that.'

---'We should sleep maybe.'

---'*If* you can be proud of the abstract,' she qualified. 'Perhaps not. Perhaps you can only be proud of choosing wrong, not right. Only then do you use the will the gods sent.'

And went silent again. We sat still. Moral exhaustion. I didn't want all this. In some ways, all I wanted was sleep. Kertész, on his liberation from Buchenwald, could only ask why they were late with the soup.

---'The paradox of sin is that sin is good which is why the shepherd cares more about the one lost lamb than all the other sheeps.'

Her intellectual intercourse; something of masturbation as substitute for sex.

The leaves on the trees rattling and crackling. The sound a fire makes. And a silent thunderstorm above the dam, far away in the south. The storm played on the dawning landscape in shuddering flashes and faint grumbling booms. Our bodies both shivering at once. And not with

cold. The sun really was coming up, and heating the breast of her sky
blue dress.

---'Life might not be all bad after all. Perhaps good things can happen.
Perhaps it might be good.'

And all the world coming luminous. Every fat bird that clattered through
the branches, shining orange in the new and unexpected light, had a
sudden heavy significance, meant something extra, over and above 'bird.'

And watery, low sunlight from the sliver of sun which had risen for
us came filtering through the dewy, cobwebbed wood, as a fine mist
rose slowly and slid down the beach and out across the silky, mirrored
surface of the reservoir.

---'I'm shattered,' she told me quietly. 'But we have overcome the earthly,
the bodily now. And it was worth it. We are safe.'

In a way, even I was pleased. I began to see her point. That you don't need
all that. That 'that,' though you think it is for yourself, is really for the
other, futurelings.

Such was her suggestive power.

And breathing in each other's faces, holding each other's hands, we went
to sleep.

Waking suddenly. She was yawning.

---'I'm tired,' she said.

---'Let's go back.'

---'Perhaps that's better.'

And quickly, to leave no doubts as to my strength of will, I rose and went
to the boat.

---'Come back,' she asked.

From where she lay, a heraldic charge, half on wet grass, half on wet sand,
she took the sides of my face in her hands and looked at me.

---'Why don't we sleep?' she whispered, her forehead gill-like, her eyes
very serious indeed.

I lay beside her. But we didn't sleep.

---'I can't bear this,' she said.

Then she put her arms round me stiffly, hugging someone she didn't want to hug.

---'I really can't. And yet, the damage is done. Is it worse to do the damage again?'

Her lips so red. Was it the light of the sun?

And she was buckling up.

---'Only cramp,' she said. 'My foot.'

Walking around, standing on it, and dipping the foot complete with shoe into the reservoir. When it was better, she came back. Again, the whiff of neat, wild alcohol as she knelt before me, sitting on her heels, knees wide apart, looking. Her glossy eyes, with a few dry feathers of yellow hair fanned across them, and her glossy lips, more inflected than before, and a silence in which she held her breath. So close I could feel the heat of her cheeks. Suddenly she spoke.

---'Are we going, then?'

And she rose, picked up the oars and threw them again in the boat.

---'Push,' she said, leaning against the bow and, with my help now, making it slide down the beach.

---'Harder.' A grating, and then a liquid silence. It was afloat.

---'Get in,' she said. 'Take the oars.'

A new energy to her; and a gleam in her face.

---'You're absolutely hopeless. Come on, give them to me.'

She took them, and sitting on the central bench, her knees together but her feet apart, one further out than the other, giving her a charming, asymmetrical lilt, she rowed us back towards the island.

From where I sat, trying to see her underpants. And also each time she leaned forwards for a stroke, trying to see her the tips of her breasts.

And as she rowed, she smiled ruefully and asked:

---'What have I done?'

And moved her knees apart. So surprised at this that I looked suddenly into the smiling, sulky, frowning face. Her skirt, as she rowed, rode up. Each time she leaned back a shaft of low yellow sunlight grazed the roughened front of her knickers.

Having to hook my hands on the rim and pull them down. Some force making me do this. I didn't though. Too much self-control, or self-delusion. But sat on my hands. Her face growing red with effort. Eventually she rested on the oars. The sound of ripples, caressing the sides of the boat. She was smiling: her lips apart.

---'What are you looking at?' she asked.

---'Your thighs.' Fatted by the bench. And between them: 'Your underpants.'

Moving her legs apart. Tease.

Lifting my fingers, reaching them out.

But she put on a stern expression, snapped shut her knees and immediately resumed rowing.

Heaving on the oars. Leaning back as she did so, far back, and looking sternly back at me.

Her golden hair, like light, getting in her eyes. Using her lips to blow it out.

And something in her motion---sexual. She had to lift her heavy pelvis with each stroke, glaring at me all the while, her face red with effort or emotion.

Her legs, open again. I touched her knee.

Looking cross, she said nothing. Moving my hand slowly up her inside leg, so soft it seemed dusted with graphite. She was rowing still; rolling her pelvis as she rowed. My fingers at the softest, fattest part of the thigh, and her staring at me. Then I felt the joints of my bent fingers brush between her legs. Still expressionless, still she stared. Again, brushing;

still she stared. Looking at me. But I could smell her, sweet, pure, strong.
And spreading as she leaned back to row, a wet patch, smelling like this,
smelling sweet. Still she stared, still she rowed.

Halfway back to the island now, the light growing bright.

And no sense of humour; no smile.

---'Stop rowing,' I asked.

She stopped, and rested on the oars.

---'We can't,' she said.

She was out of breath.

---'We don't have to. Let me touch you.'

Her legs wide apart, as wide as the ridden-up dress would go. Touching
her.

Pressing in to the wet. Then getting my fingers round the band between
her legs, and pulling it away from her so that suddenly my thumb,
moving up and down the oiled skin folds, slipped in.

She gasped. Biting her lips. Looking down at me, expressionless, stern,
but out of breath. Eyes a little rounded, face very straight. Making
another stroke with the oars, but a feeble one. Then slowly letting out
her breath.

I was pulling at the band between her legs. She lifted a little from the
bench, put a hand to each hip, and helped me pull it slowly down
between her thighs.

---'Not off,' she said. 'Not off. Touch me though. That's sweet.'

Opening her eyes and relenting slightly she added.

---'Look I'll---make you come.'

So: kneeling before me in the boat, her knickers still half-down.
Dangerous pose for someone who was supposed not to want sex. And
looking at me steady with bright, smoky eyes while she licked the palm
of her hand. When she touched me, I started.

---'Does it hurt?'

It was the sweetest thing on earth, touching her while she touched me, till she widened her legs and gasped.

Her red lips, open over her white teeth. Even her cheeks with blusher on. And her hair damp and flat. I pulled the pants off.

---'Turn round?'

She opened her eyes, but didn't close her mouth.

---'Over the bench?'

She nodded. Then she did.

Kneeling myself behind her, between her widened knees.

She had reached forward, and with white knuckles, was gripping the sides.

Her dress-covered bottom. Slowly drawing this up. Until I saw her sex, red, swollen, hairy, cracked, and smeared with slime. Distorted by the bench, lifted towards me. I touched against it, slid up, and down. With fingers widening her, opening her up. And on the threshold, ready to sink, pausing. She was whimpering, her juice flowing out and hanging down, and swinging against the plumpness of her thighs, where it gleamed and stuck. And then she reached one hand beneath the bench, and took my balls. Still, that sweet scent, ferocious, alcoholic, musty, but how sweet. And pulled them so I sank slowly in. Pulling me, so my balls touched her, and she pressed and rubbed them there, and groaned. And let me start sliding in and out, slow, but soon, hanging onto her hips, more bouncily. She was crawling away and I crawled after: her hips were on top of the bench and her head had got under the triangular bench in the bow. The boat meanwhile rocking and splashing, so that water even fell on us; and me still smacking down on her, until she groaned louder and in all the pure richness of her warm voice called out. And went on calling. Opening and closing her fists.

Then---she went out. Extinguished, totally still. Even her breathing gentle. Asleep. All I could see: her split white bum. Reddened by the marks of my hips. And her red crack. Pulling her out from where she'd got to, under the bench in the sharp bit to the front of the boat.

Turning her over, lying her down in the widest part, on her back, her legs cocked up, her belly flat, or even sunken, beneath the fullness, under the flimsy dress, of her tits, and the back of one hand covering her forehead and her closed eyes. Moving her knees apart for her, seeing the red and swollen part, ragged, open, wet, and coming down on top of her: sliding in, laying my lips on hers which opened when I touched them, as her legs had.

Her hips flexed. She put hands around my head and feet around my back, her eyes screwed up, kissing me gently, until she started breathing more heavily again, and started moving too, grinding her pelvis and turning her face aside, as I began to lose my grip, the world went black, then white, the hem of her bright blue dress getting tangled around us, until she pulled it up around her neck, and again her voice, her eyes open now, round, and her mouth round too, looking so deeply into me from so far away that I thought I would fall through her face into whatever was beyond. The world lost its balance as, in wave after wave of squirting lust I came, while the boat flipped---it had to come---and still clinging together, still squirting lyrically up inside her, so far inside that I saw or thought I saw it come out of her mouth, her naked legs still clinging round my naked waist, we sank.

But the reservoir cold as a drink with ice. We surfaced under the upturned boat. Her smile in the green light which shone up from the water. Shone too out of her eyes, as if they were something she'd found on the bottom.

---'What?' I asked.

---'I love you now and always will. That's what,' she said, before, closing first one nostril and then the other with a finger, she jetted out snot.

We came back to the news, delivered by a strangely ecstatic Kohlhaas, that they'd decided to throw her out. Hella: a smile of triumph curling up the ends of her lips. Disdain's victory.

'*It is not possible for a bad man to hurt a good*' says Socrates in a legalistic moment. But would he say it now? Since then the world has lurched downwards. Even the Forms---even the line, even the sphere---are distressed. Even the sun and the moon and the fire. As she answered:

---'I was going anyway.'

Waiting only for our sodden clothes and shoes to come out of the spin-dryer. Then: flight. The wreaths of cheap twisting smoke and the glass thimbles of grappa in the square at Sfondrata. In our excitement, almost without noticing, we finished off a whole jar of brandied plums they had on the zinc counter. The sexual textures of the plums inside: the soft, tough skin and, when you bit them, brandied juices, squirting out.

Hella was the toast of local men. I didn't like this, she did. Then: rumbling over a pass and down towards the city in a gas-fired taxi. Against a current of fluorescent green arrows nailed to rough wooden posts, hammered into the earth pointing back the way we had come. '*AQRONIM*' printed in smudged black type.

Escaping the Minotaur and his pathetic optimism. Or even Gabriel. For we knew now how Adam and Eve felt. And it wasn't all bad. A certain relief, a lifting of the spirits, a gathering and then a clearing of cloud, a squirt of joy. Something tame or even stuffed about the symposium; something free and eternal about our destiny in the world outside. It could be embarrassing, really embarrassing; but it could be great; and this 'could', even if unfulfilled, as she was determined it should be, was what was important---was all there was.

---'Mired in that symposium, as if it were the world, and we were anxious to leave the world. I'm glad we're out. And it was the world: impurity of principle, impurity of purpose, and for what? For acclaim, citations, a chair or readership. I don't hold it against them. They've got a living to make. But that's precisely it. So they drown themselves in intellectual garbage, for various good reasons, but they still drown. Growing bloated and corrupt, losing sight of the love of speculation for its own sake, the love of science for its own sake, the love, even, of ignorance for its own sake, of the passion of the reason, etc. Etc. This isn't anyone's fault, it is the world, is necessary even. But as academia begins to assume the role of the church, both in good senses and bad, maybe another reformation's due?' she asked.

Technically, perhaps even deliberately, by hanging around too long in Sfondrata eating our plums, we had already missed the train on which her sleeping berth had been booked by Natasha, Sir Mel's apologetic assistant. Ungainly in her fine blue-cotton dress and a perished leather coat, strapped into a red nylon back-pack piled high with clinking moth-trap, sleeping-bag, sleeping mat, and---mug?, she stumbled down the crowded platform, asking how long ago it had gone.

Her bare calves, knees, thighs.

No one knew.

---'It's not I'm in a hurry to leave you,' she said. But she was. She wanted me safely in the past where I belonged.

Her train was late, it turned out. Hadn't yet come. And I was in the future still.

---'I need a drink. I have to talk with you,' she suddenly said. My face: she was touching it.

The bar opened off the platform and opened on the far side onto the main coast-road, zigzagging down the line of the old town wall. Tables were set along the pavement, half-hidden in clouds of pale-blue diesel smoke. We drank cold beer from heavy, misted glasses at one of these.

---'It's the right thing to do.'

Her wheedling, moaning tone, over the voice of the traffic. Something of the mosquito there.

---'It maybe was even right to fuck, just in order to get that bit, the physical over and done with. The gross.'

---'It wasn't physical at all. It was chemical, biological, geological.'

---'So you like to think. And now it maybe is right to call it a day. We can be friends. I freely admit I tormented you by trying to be faithful to Haakon. I didn't realise the best way to get this purely physical attraction over and done with; which would have been to screw rigidly for a few days, and overdose. And now I have to go. I'm leaving, on a slow train ...'

---'Revulsion therapy. Then---station of the cross.' Finding no force in my voice.

---'Haakon would have understood.'

This restraint, meanwhile: nothing could be sexier, or better calculated to exalt lust to a beautiful illusion. What we thought poison was really medicine. Or was she wiser than this?

---'I hadn't known whether it was possible to stop, whether we hadn't already gone too far. You see it was possible after all, and we hadn't. It

is even possible that we have made things better, made ourselves closer
with that one---no, two---slips. And now, we know we don't have to
betray our lovers---you what's-her-name ...

---'Barbara ...'

---'Don't tell me, I don't want to hear---and me Haakon. We know our
own power of self-denial, for a greater, a better good. Even after that false
start it is possible to be friends.'

Her frail voice above the traffic. An exaltation there, morbid and static.

---'I thought, while the Symposium lasted, we could be happy. Then
we could separate, but even when we have suffered and died, no-one
would be able to take it away. Two---animals?---would have been perfectly
happy, deliriously, throughout cold time. While the past lasts; while
it continues to exist. To have existed. So: that's why I didn't say. About
Haakon. Before, I mean.'

---'Was I wrong? Yes; because you got 'involved', thought you could have
me. But was I really? Wouldn't it have been worse to deny that joy? To
deny the moth its lamp? Wouldn't such a crime have echoed through
history, revolting the souls of men? So I was selfish; and I'm sorry, and I'm
glad. And it's over now. It's over now. It has to be.'

Now she spoke as fondly, as warmly as she could whilst shouting down
traffic. Her sweetening voice, still naughty, I realised. With a tender
laughter coming back into it, she was talking herself into the reverse of
what she thought, half swallowing her words, but also slightly hoarse
with exhaust. As with its spiritual counterpart, hypocrisy.

---'And you have to let me go now; do you understand? Do you? Do you
understand?'

So that history isn't pre-ordained, but makes itself up as it goes along; so
it seemed at least from what was happening. There was a wild element
in it, a randomness, an unpredictability which was more than error-term.
An essential unpredictability, a will to go off the rails, perhaps as a way
to be taken firmly and put back on. This was what was happening to me,
and I wasn't old enough, and perhaps never will be, to handle it, I mean.

---'Because you have to.'

---'Let you go?'

---'Understand,' she said quickly.

So: this formality of speech. And it was charming; suggestive of the self-consciousness which always goes with depth.

---'Hella, don't.'

Her lips paused, just about to speak, and her eyes asked why.

---'I love you.'

This made them glisten and she tried not to smile, her whole face pushed upwards on its bones by this trial.

---'It isn't possible.'

---'Why?'

Why was I croaking?

---'If we can't be friends we can't be nothing. We can't be lovers, certainly.'

---'I love you.'

---'Stop! It isn't fair. If we can't be friends we can't be nothing.'

---'I'm not your friend.'

---'So: what I have to say then is this; have a nice life.'

Her reluctant, clumsy brutality. Then she turned her face aside.

And tears rolling out on their own. Then a slicing pain, delicately serrated, sawing away at my optic nerves. And wading away from her into waves of honking traffic, waist deep, willing it to submerge and drown me, hating it, yet daring it to hurt me more than she had. Cars and women screeching all around. The crump of crushed bodywork, but not mine. She was in there with me, battling away. She had my arm, and half shaking me, half dragging, got me through the surf of bonnets and glinting windscreens, each with a disembodied face inside, floating like a trapped balloon, back on the pavement.

---'Act your age,' she said. 'For once.' Tears on her cheeks too, and walked away.

Following her half-blinded, back into the darkness of the station. Just as I had followed into the trees. She trailed her backpack onto the platform and waited there, looking the other way.

A feral with a felted beard and felted hair was playing the bongos. On other platforms, with something elemental, patient about them, waited other trains. Like, if they weren't in the myths, they should have been. A signal clunked and with its lights on, even by daylight, a train rolled slowly in. Coming to get her. Dull-green. Numbers and letters. The word *Pariji* cut in sheets of tin like a stencil, one for each carriage.

I lifted up her things. She disappeared inside.

Following her struggle, from the platform, through a fatted, sweating torrent of humanity to her berth.

Seeing her evict a man from her bunk where he sat airing his feet. His white socks, stained brown on ball and heel and each distinct toe. This meant his shoes were new. And a butterfly trapped behind the greasy glass. He crushed it with a cigarette-pack, and offered her a smoke.

She didn't smoke but took one all the same. And came to the window and hung out her arms. To cool her hairy arm-pits, behind the wet round patches in her bright blue dress. Panting and saying something too quietly for me to hear over the rumbling of the engine, the steam hissing from its brakes, and the ding-dong-dang of the announcements.

Marco, her fellow-smoker, was tapping her shoulder from behind.

'Io sono Marco. Dove vai?'

She turned back to me without answering. The platforms too low, making me into a child, and as a man in an eye-blue suit and dove-pink homburg stooped under the coupling between two carriages and emerged with a grunt to ask me for a light, a cockerel cried out behind a wall, over which a thick green creeper was draped.

---'I don't know how it happened,' she repeated, more loudly, ignoring Marco and the Homburg man, who were now talking to each other with some excitement. 'I wasn't supposed to sleep with you. Ever. In the history of this world.'

Through the immense arch at the end of the dirty glass chamber lay the sea. Its colour so delicate and yet intense that, like someone who'd never seen it before, I couldn't look away. It made a physical sensation on my cheeks, a fizz, a buzz; but this was only her. With the tips of her fingers she could just reach down to me. When I looked at her she smiled, sad, shy. And yet, my own eyes turning back to the blue, deep, vibration of the sea.

On it, only visible after a time, hulks at anchor, built of rust. You couldn't see them move, yet they formed themselves slowly into different constellations. And, just as a dream sometimes contains the hint there is a message there, has written on its envelope 'I mean', these boats did too; this invisible movement, tiny with distance, faint and dusty against the sea, shifting and swinging diffidently; a sensation that these arrangements spelt things. Perhaps it was as simple as forming letters and spelling things.

---'Look at me. Please. I'm going soon. For ever. You don't seem to realise. You can't just look out to sea.'

As she spoke, a whistle blew, the locomotive gave a violently reluctant jolt and her carriage bounced about. Hella half lost her balance but righted herself again. Marco evaluating her tensed bottom in the gloom inside.

A hiss of escaping steam, which drowned a few words she told me.

A second jolt, more vicious, more successful. She half fell again, closing her eyes, frowning, and tapping the side of her face against chromed steel. The train began to roll. I was following it, trying to hear what she was telling me, walking without looking, except up at her frightened face, her pursed and stiffened lips, colourless, moving quickly. Until suddenly, struggling, she fell backwards into the darkness of the cabin. I stopped and, window by window as they passed like the frames of a film, I saw her stumble along the corridor over the fat lady, the Arab children and the mound of luggage, until she fetched up against the window of the carriage door.

Walking again now, faster, to keep up with her. She flitted around the edges, a sense of opened wings, her hands pressed there, whitened. An inverse of Marco's socks. Almost trying to come through like a bird that doesn't yet know about glass. Calling out to me, above the clanking and the hissing, the vicious, patternless jets of steam. And as the train began to go too fast, drawing ahead however fast I ran, she gave up, sank backwards slightly, and her face became dim and even calm; and at the same time the door swung open with her holding on; a brown squashy bag tumbled out and rolled along and burst, emitting flames of clothes, she herself was running with enormous flattened steps through space, faster than she could run, trying with her own weight to stop the train; until she let it go and slid down textured asphalt on outstretched knees and outspread hands as smoothly as if it was ice.

The door hissed shut. The train disappeared. Clanking and winding round a corner in a deep cutting, walled with red shadowed rocks and damp green fern, beneath the stinging expanse of sea.

Hella, her own eyes shut and her pale face green, opened her mouth to expel a mouthful of vomit. And opened her eyes, sea-coloured---nothing came out of them. Lifted her round head, draped with yellow hair. And spat out a few more whitish fragments that had lodged on the back of her tongue.

---'Poor hands, ' she said.

---'Why did you jump off the train?'

In the neonic ladies', cushioning her hands with toilet paper which went damp and pink. Cushioning her knees.

---'My backpack has gone away. It's gone back to Haakon.'

---'Why did you jump? What were you saying?'

She looked at me like I was mad and said:

---'I wanted to say goodbye.'

When I looked at her, her eyes swerved. And wouldn't meet mine.

---'But anyway ...'

---'What anyway?'

---'Maybe we should get it over with,' she said with forensic cunning. 'Give it what it wants and let it die.'

So: crossing the dual-carriageway into the city. The streets resembling
film-sets; too contrived, too artfully lit. And wandering down the hill
towards the harbour.

A circular bay, inflated with meaning. The sea down here dark grey, pink,
almost black; the hills a bright green close to yellow, close to red, lit by a
low and saturated sun. The illusion was of the sea rising in a hump in the
centre. Not flat at all, but humped. And behind the hills, above the sea, a
slowly turning wheel of ill-oiled gulls.

I already knew the place, already loved it. I'd never been here. Yet a deep
sense of seen-before: as with her. Some unravelling calculus whirring
out inevitabilities. Her profile, and beside it this scooped and perfect
bay, these pored ginger rocks on which a marble esplanade was set like
cream on brandy snaps, under shrubbed and steaming walls---what was
so suggestive?

About the scents, too, of rubber, figs, salt, sewerage?

Segments of balustrade, cordoned off with rusty chain-link wire, had
fallen in the water, where you could see them, coated in swilling
seaweed, as sloppy ripples popped and gurgled. The mouth of the bay
so narrow that even with a swell outside, the ripples were silky here,
tinted by a film of oil in jagged colours. Once the pleasure suburb, it had
become the red-light district. Nothing weird in that.

Then: *Pensione Otarí*---a pulsing sign in broken green neon. Inviting us
up a rat-infested alley. Pools of light, pools of darkness, pools of piss.
Steep mounds of black-plastic sacks, and grimy paladin bins. And
watching her walking before me, scaling the garbage mounds and with
delicacy squeezing amongst the bins: still this disbelief. At a tall girl with
inflected blue eyes, but also with a supernatural air, so that she had no
chance of fooling anyone; she was so obviously in disguise; so obviously
prime and formed of different things.

Her limits, her margins so sharp that she didn't, like others, blend into
the world. Disbelief in her existence, or that she was with me, she was
here. And with this disbelief, somehow a failure to rise, a brokenness
which stopped me rising, which didn't admit that this happy ending to
the great fairy tale, this treasure under the stump, this goose, could all be
mine.

All she had now was what she wore. A perished leather jacket, heavy, stiff, with some of the big leather buttons missing, and the threads that once held them sticking out like wires. Done up with a wide leather belt. A flimsy bright blue cotton dress which left her scuffed and weeping knees (still padded and trailing damp pink toilet paper) bare. Flat white sneakers with pink rubber noses, freaked with mud. And tied around her waist in a neat, flat band, a canary coloured cardigan with small black flowers on white knitted bands set down all the edges. And somehow brave to be like this; her body, her clothes, out---even abroad---in what she had called the cold, cold universe; this and nothing else. If a piece of music or a landscape can make you cry, what do you think a woman can make you do?

The *Pensione's* flaking arch was formed from the same ginger sandstone as the bay itself. The leprous walls had black electric wiring sagging across them, treacly as fly paper. And like fly paper, catching flies. The walls too: sticky, catching flies. By the pulsing light of the neon sign, reflected off the walls, we climbed a wide shallow staircase to reception on the second floor.

Mourning the nobility of academia. The spring-water bottle, the linen sheets, the small pile of bedside books chosen specially by Sir Mel. The price of integrity, or rather its cost. She meanwhile was looking round with an idiot delight.

Our room had two steel beds with stained quilts, between them a bidet, a sloping ceiling low as a forehead and several scraps of rank carpet. Two oblong windows at the level of her damaged knees gave onto the bay. Lying on the floor you could see the white spire, half-submerged, of a lighthouse.

---'We've walked into a myth, or brothel,' she said, suddenly wistful, closing the door on the enduring suspicions of the concierge. While through the open windows, much too loud, came the heavy breathing of the sea.

Irrationality, under science. The first thing she did was to look behind the mirror which hung above the basin. People watching us. Did she really imagine this? Then she lifted the pillow and brushed the bugs she found there onto the tiles.

---'At least there is a pillow,' she said.

The sheets an acid, human grey. The walls bruised. The white, wrought-iron lamp was in the form of an asphodel, with light bulb positioned to represent the mystic's blossom.

Her clothes all she had, and simply, almost drably, limply, she took them off. Her waist flimsy, far too narrow and weak for the rest of her body. And her seeping knees, her ankles, feet; too long and delicate.

Looking hard at me. A little scared. But then you have to be scared; scared or bored; this being all there is.

---'It doesn't matter what we say,' she said; 'it's like death; it happens anyway. Come here.'

She unbuckled my belt and boots. Taking them by the heels, pulled my trousers off.

And kissed my lips.

Her breath had something in it. Her spit had, too. Fine, sweet. And my prick, nosing out through the fly of white cotton underpants, became suddenly in its darkness on whorled white, the horn on the forehead of a unicorn. Painful, as I say, but there it is. Where this left the virgin---thirsty, too thirsty, sluttish now---rolling in sweat on a plastic bed wetter's under-sheet, because with her feet she'd paddled the grey nylon over-sheet away ...

---'Don't come, don't, don't ... , I want you to fuck me behind ...' she said, pushing brutally.

And drawing her long legs in to turn over and erect her bum (somehow just as the buzzard had erected its wing), marked and scored in red by rumpled plastic, she moved her knees as wide apart as they would go, stretching herself, splitting herself, so that her arsehole and her cunt opened and spoke to me like mouths.

Something vaguely wrong. Not necessarily with us. It may have been the city. Or the world. A mistake made, somewhere very deep. The great deep thuds that camouflaged her skin in cream and pink made her whole soft juddering body echo as wrapped around each other now we surged about.

Or worse: the serpent, having sold the apple, returning inside as worm. A moment's weird regret that she hadn't after all gone away by train. That this body, hot and sloppy and hollow mouthed, squirming face down on wet plastic and bound in spiralled nylon ropes, was hers. Was mine.

A little too much. Not enough of the televisual in it, of the artificial; too much of the real. To a squidgy, slopping noise, hypnotic, slapping, repetitive as the row of tungsten-halogen arc lamps outside the windows, and growing steadily loud.

Because it turned out this wasn't our room; wasn't ours alone at least. Marcello, his flip-flops squidging against sweaty feet, approached. Threw his duffle-bag upon his bed.

And undressed at the foot of ours. Splashed and then examined himself with some care astride the bidet. Used a square of bath mat for towel. And wrapping himself in his sheet, started snoring organically in time with the sea.

The burning asphodel, and his flip-flops perhaps, and his feet of course, attracted flotillas of mosquitoes, so the room went dim with smoke and our skin whined.

The closure of the future; the dullness of happiness, of every success. We don't want that; don't want what we want; we want to chase, to strive. Not to succeed, but to fail. This is our success, to fail. Succeeding means you didn't shoot high enough. And another thing. The city; not a good place to be in love. Unpropitious. Corrupt. For a little privacy I reached to turn out the asphodel. But a strange, trilling sensation in the hand I snatched away. It was live.

Still: a squidging not flip-flops now. Hella switching her head from side to side so as to dodge imaginary blows which had bloodied her lips and swollen the skin beneath her eyes. And crossing her once delicate ankles, already thickened with bites, behind my neck.

Having endured her trial. Because this was defeat. Understandably, she wanted to make the most of it. Eager, hurried, parched, wanting to betray Haakon. This had become the point. Now it was me holding back. It was too charged, too much.

Looking up at me, her chin doubled from this angle, the eyes she opened coming on, her mouth and legs also open, on her back on the bed in the naked light, lungs going like a pump and her jaw slack, she said:

---'We're going to kill ourselves ...'

Reaching out her arms gently, a ballerina imitating a swan. Her voice and lips smeared with spit. Sticky as honey. And her cheeks.

Later, woken by shouting. Only Marcello's dreams. Hella looked like a sleeping blaze-victim. Her face rebuilt from a snapshot, fuzzy, coarse. Her skin tacky and smelling of sour milk.

Moronic music, very loud, thumping in the next room. The yodelling of gulls, swooping out of darkness into the glare of the arc-lamps at the foot of our bed and coming on like lights. It should have made us love each other more but there wasn't room for that. Regretting, more even than Lear, the abdication scene. As Cordelia, her hot sweaty breasts pressed against mine, twitched her long bare legs and groaned and muttered in her sleep. And, without opening her eyes said:

---'Don't look at me like that.'

Sleep was out. We dressed. Down on the street: tarts, applying their icing in the wing-mirrors of a squad-car. The driver dangling his arm down the door, watching, chatting. The world chummy and clotted. The tarts had seen us coming out; one came running up and flobbed my bollocks asking for a light.

Trying to wank me even as I walked, even with Hella beside me. And when she figured I wasn't rising she frisked me for a wallet instead. Batting her roughly away. But even then, she ran after us, making her buttocks swing and slap, and hurriedly adjusted her stretchy cyclist's pants to show the slit of her cunt and told me:

---'You look, down here, you look ...'

Meanwhile a great proud African whose shades hid half his face, standing very straight, erect, slipped his arm round Hella so that she looked at him in surprise, not anger. He leered at me saying:

---'Fuck-off.'

Not a good place. Someone else was coming up, sad, cadaverous, his skin as white beneath his stubble as sweaty snow. Forming the fingers of each hand into cones, he fitted them to Hella's breasts, lifting these high so that she had to lean back slightly and stigmatic nipples pierced his palms.

---'She's too classy for you Ali,' he said lazily. He could hardly be bothered to speak. 'Beauty, you're with me now.'

---'Achille ... ! Fuck off.'

Ali's warning not lazy at all, but resonant. And sinister in its quietness. Unwise Achille didn't fuck off, but prodded the lion's eye with a stick by pursing his lips.

Hella very still. Her eye gleaming. Very still.

As Ali, his great hand still moulded to her hip, used his other arm to clear Achille away, sweeping him backwards as his heel caught the curb and he stumbled against the plate-glass window of a darkened cinema. I saw the glass bow. It creaked. But didn't break as he came back like a wrestler off ropes pulling a knife which he paused to show Ali. Ali had a bigger one of course, shining, blinding, and with it was beating Achille's chest, who leaped back again, swearing and calling down God as he somehow exploded the plate-glass and contrived, from his chest, a pulsing fountain, fine and black. The squad car starting up and squealing away. The stretchy-cunted tart too, her arms up, also squealing away, spread fingers fluttering and swimming buttocks flapping and splattering. The other tarts already gone, and Hella gone, too.

It took me a while to realise what was up.

Because Ali had rounded, the dangling knife already scabbed with rust. Through flat enormous shades appraising me. Meanwhile, Achille wriggling in glass which crunched and squeaked like snow. The hole he'd made; the texture of a hole in ice. His shins and his twittering feet, hanging down outside. Hella came back to find my hand and pulled it, roughly, so hard it hurt, just as she had amongst the cars. Was it simply because we ran that Ali followed us? Through the dark streets, his smile alight? Hella was in no danger; she was fast. But like the next man in the relay she hung back, trod ground, waiting for me.

When we stopped at last, we found her pockets packed with shivered glass. I made the flat tips of my fingers seep by picking it out.

---'An ambulance?'

---'The squad car. He's dead anyway. He has to be. Thanks to us.'

A sense of responsibility can be carried too far. Not quite understanding this, or her resentful calm; or the fact that, wanting simply to cream the walls of some tart's creamy cunt and clinch some powdery deal perhaps, Achille was dead. Pathos too can be carried too far. Following her meanwhile, back towards the hotel, street by street. The wooden cobbles, buffed by car tyres, gleaming feebly as the stars.

---'You sure we should go back?'

---'If we don't, they'll think we're running away.'

---'The squad car saw.'

---'Maybe; but maybe Ali is his pal.'

The esplanade deserted. Even Achille gone. No squad car, no ambulance, no one at all, except for someone sweeping glass, and someone else sprinkling sand on blood. As we watched, sweeper and sprinkler met to lift a square of stencilled chipboard over the hole and, moving their hammers far too quickly, out of sync with the soundtrack, nail it up. Otherwise everyone had disappeared.

Except for Ali, waiting coolly in the darkness under the keystone of the *Pensione's* arch. It was the light of a burning cigarette-end, flicked past us and exploding in tiny orange stars which suggested this.

Perhaps he wanted to apologise. Anyhow, we skipped the checking out.

It was hot, even by night, in a kind of half-hearted, sizzling rain now. We navigated rocks at the foot of pleated cliffs, following the edge of the sea. When we could we turned inland, struggling up the bed of a dry stream clogged with builders' rubble, garbage and dead cats. Eventually, battered and torn, we climbed onto the hard-shoulder of a motorway.

Nets of pinked drizzle hung quivering around each of a row of double-headed sodium lamps. The shooting red and yellow lights of cars were reflected in shiny tarmac. And no one stopped. Trying to remind myself that it wasn't so terrible, standing beside a hot wet road with a hot wet girl. The rain grew heavier. Hot rain, like falling sweat.

A lorry drew up at last and we sprinted after it. Its bodywork as fond and blunt as a face, with a canvas roof over a wooden clamp. Behind this was a large, squat trailer. The driver, with sweaty back and greasy arse, dropped heavily onto the tarmac.

---'*Non, non, non,*' he said. '*Fuck off.*'

Hella about to cry. This was how resolution looked.

---'Stupid fart,' she said, as his piss started to gush and splatter on his own front wheel.

We turned back towards our hitching station, but as we passed, Hella slipped behind the trailer and hoisted herself up to look over the tailgate.

---'It's full of sheep,' she said. 'Sheep,' she repeated when I looked blank.

It was true: above the distressed smells of exhaust and hot brakes, I could smell sheep.

Alighting on the earth only to leap higher, she rolled over the tailgate and disappeared with a heavy thud which made the trailer wheeze on its bearings and settle briefly.

Then I saw her face, one side printed with a greenish crescent of sheep-shit.

---'Quick.'

---'But what ...'

---'Quick!'

Already the cab-door had slammed. The lorry began to roll. I was hopping along behind, clinging on to an aluminium loop in the side and looking for somewhere to rest my feet. Just as she had hopped along behind the train. Reality as subtly repetitive, musical. This was its air; the air of someone pregnant with a mystery. Or someone putting this on.

Such were my thoughts as I hopped along. Should I let go? I couldn't. This wasn't possible. It wasn't in the future, wasn't in me. Besides, Hella was holding one of my wrists. And yet there was nowhere to stand.

Luckily we stopped. The hard-shoulder ended here for the road to cross a viaduct. Which, as a nearby sign advised us, was 343 metres up and

1127 metres long. We were awaiting a gap in the traffic before pulling out. With my own momentum I leapt up and rolled over and fell with a hollow thud on the shorn back of some poor ewe.

Who, with little dignity and a certain amount of unnecessary skeetering about, rose to her feet. Anger burning in her eyes, lit by the moving lights of cars reflected off the steamy aluminium roof. I hadn't known sheep got cross. Bony, noble, livid but yet resigned, and not in the least surprised. The other sheep, rocking knowledgeably as the trailer rocked (we had moved onto the carriageway) made us a space. Just as we---all of us, in our lurching, bouncing trailer---were made a space by the irritable traffic of the motorway. Nested structures---like repeated ones, becoming an obsession. Something to do with her perhaps.

The floor was slick with sheep-piss, sheep-shit. But not an element of the wholesome, as well as the unpleasant. Unless you wanted to keep clean. We made our way to the front-end of the trailer and sat down. Where, my head on her shoulder, her cheek in my hair, we feel asleep.

Barb Ciama followed the lorry, mounted on a charger. She wasn't sitting in the saddle but between its ears. Her bare white legs were ringed with tubes of fat, her ankles crossed. When I opened my eyes our lorry had stopped. I saw an old plastic Michelin-Man, lit from within, wearing his goggles and yellow beauty-sash, screwed to the crest of the lorry behind.

---'Border. I think.'

We crouched and looked woolly, and tried to find ewes willing to be clasped from beneath. Borders meant something then.

---'Mirror on a stick, a sharp one,' she whispered. 'Shining a torch at it.'

A broken beam of reflected torchlight moved over the steaming backs.

Until with a jolt which made us all sway, all open our eyes, and the ewes stop chewing, we rolled on.

Later she looked through an empty screw-hole.

Cold blue light shone onto her eye and the carefully moulded skin of her lids.

---'What is it?'

---'The sea.'

I looked out too: a dark, dusty plain, far beneath. We were climbing along the coast road. Hella's face was pinched and squeezed. Someone had been drawing on it with a blunt red pencil and dark green ink. Marked and dented, blotched and lumpy, it had even changed its shape. And each blotch had an amber zit. It was not so much the damage the mosquitoes did, as the damage they made her do with her sharp, dirty nails. Straggly blonde hair, also stained green. And yet the mosquitoes had given her face depth; too pure before, perhaps, air-brushed, too much the miraculous illustration, the fashion-shot, and not painterly enough, so that her beauty had been misleading, suggestive of surface, not depth. They---the mosquitoes---had also made her shy, unwilling to be kissed. But her eyes shining as we bumped and rattled, the ends of her lips drawn up. Her mouth open. And her knees. And between them, formed in white cotton and shadowed by her skirt, the occult shape, flat, creased, both sunken and lumped, where the tops of the insides of her thighs nearly met.

---'And what are you looking at?'

A fellow traveller bleated, then squatted down to relieve herself. Hella added:

---'I need this.'

But as she felt her way towards the back the trailer swerved, presumably to overtake. Anyhow, she slipped. Her hair rose up as she fell, and she touched the side of her forehead against one of the aluminium ribs. Then she disappeared under sheep.

She came out covered in muck. Blood seeped evenly out of the length of a slice in the rind of her forehead. One of her eyebrows a spongy red. The fall knocked her very slightly silly. She wanted to get her skirt off, green with muck as it was, so as not to get it stained with blood. I tried to stop her but she wouldn't hear me. Struggling with me as we surged and slipped along the *autoroute*.

Of course, the shape between her legs, as she sat down to lift it off, tuning me in, switching me on. The swelling and, as I say, the creased hollowness. I too wanted my trousers off.

---'I'm only using you; you realise that? You do don't you?' she asked.

She kissed me sweetly. In her lips, the smell of blood.

---'I only love you for your body. What's it like, to be loved for your body?'
she asked.

And cried out when I touched her. We didn't mean to fuck. We just
wanted to lie naked side by side in blood and sheep shit. And she
wouldn't take her knickers off: But these were too thin, too slippery.
Almost as thin and slippery as the world in which we lay. She gasped
when I touched her through them.

Was sex all there was? So it sometimes seemed. That the science, which
after all was why we'd come, was a mere pretext for sex. What about
that?

Because the science was important, of course, not so much in itself, as
for the light it cast on her mind. For the sensation of screwing someone
with a mind like this. Someone who knew and saw. Everything. All of it.
Rich and sad. And her intellect part of her, part of what made her soul
possible. Even her looks perhaps. And necessary for getting to the core,
through that of her body, of this spirit. The feeling of unknown bones
through unknown membranes of burning flesh, slick and soft as rotting
silk. Was part of her in essence.

Something in her face, reddened with lust and scratched mosquito welts
and blood, her bulging, staring eyes, her wide-apart lips and wide-apart
teeth did frighten me.

I'd changed her into an animal, for later sacrifice. And when I kissed her
lips and the insides of her mouth, the rough texture of her tongue on my
tongue was all I needed to make me choke and make me come. And as I
did she smiled, very tender, very gay, made the sweetest girly noise, and
pissed all over me.

What a mad thing. But it didn't strike us then. The air of the journey to a
concentration camp, for the animals at least. This didn't strike us either,
then.

Meanwhile we were getting there---somewhere. The roads smaller,
bendier, and climbing steadily enough to make our ears pop. Sunlit
sliding trees, over the tailgate. And a slot of sun moving about the inside
of the trailer above her head, as well as a moving constellation of bright
spots projected on the sheep and us by empty boltholes.

Often, presumably at junctions, we'd stop.

---'Do we jump?' I asked.

---'Too dangerous.'

---'He'll be cross.'

---'Too bad.'

---'We could put out his eye, and cling on under a sheep.'

---'You're just so funny.'

She wasn't being sarcastic. For her, language had not yet acquired its weary, ironical twist. Nor had thought. Scientists: young for their age. Like doctors. Like musicians. Or Scandinavians who are half-Swiss. Virtuosi with less time to live than work. She laughed, holding the sides, for now the trailer was bouncing and jumping over ruts. The sheep still swaying, all together, expertly. Vacant, woolly faces. Awaiting patiently the verdict of fate. And fate was looking good. Ruts on the way to a slaughterhouse? It didn't add up.

Unless it was potholes or a railway track.

But when the tailgate fell with a rattling of chains to form a battened ramp we saw a sunlit field, bright green, and a dark green beech wood, stained with the pale crowns of a few bright ashes, at the foot of a frosty crag, torn and veined like meat. The setting for a pastoral.

---'You see,' she whispered. 'You see!'

The driver hissing, whistling, and slapping the lorry with his hands.

The sheep, as they ran down the ramp, leaping high in the air.

It was infectious. We leapt high too. Hella bleating.

He didn't see the joke: shouting and cussing he ran at us.

I don't know what he wanted. To slaughter us, perhaps. There was no chance of that. He was too fat. There was no way he could keep up. He ran with his legs prized apart by the girth of his thighs.

When he ran, his arms stuck out.

Meanwhile the sheep, rippling out over the field, in the circular shape of a wave-front, already as they walked tearing out mouthfuls of grass.

Watching this from the sheltering shadows of a beech.

And wandering on when he wandered back.

The first thing she found was a telephone in a yellow-roofed stand by the road. In the shade of an oak. Mystifying, this proffering by reality of the elements needed to make the future come. These very elements, not others. I haven't put this well. But the future has a necessity of its own, and the world, independently, without this necessity, still proffers the necessary props.

Hella made a call.

I didn't want this. She wouldn't say who.

When I asked she crossed her eyes slightly, made the gesture of slapping at flies. Then continued to dial.

When I asked again she hit at me with the receiver, which was attached to a long silver tube like a shower tube. Not long enough, luckily.

I had forgotten about telephones. About the illusion that there are other places with people in which they create. A sense of the telephone as a blunt instrument. For bludgeoning the spirit. Wrong. Superficially helpful, but morally disorienting. Corrupt. Physically corrupt too. A bell or electronic cheeping cutting in on your intimacies and dreams. It's a cruelly sophisticated device. Symptom of an obsession with other times and other places at the expense of this.

Meanwhile, her gestures. Explaining, conciliating, declining blame and then accepting it.

In her mind, he could see her.

Her expressions. He could see her, holding the clotted hair from her eyes, under a small yellow roof, against a dark wall of oak-leaves. As if he existed, too. Eventually she got worked up. As far as I could tell, this calmed him. By the end she was smiling fondly.

This made me scared. Tears in her eyes as she put the receiver down. I didn't like that at all. Then she started giggling. She was holding her hand over her mouth. And as if someone heavy had fallen on me in the back of a lorry, I too felt cross.

---'What is it. What's so funny?'

---'They blew up the moth trap in a controlled explosion,' she said. 'Haakon got questioned when he went to ask. *Dupont et Dupond* thought he was a fundamentalist. 'But I've got green eyes,' he kept telling them. He's proud of his eyes, you see.'

---'What's so funny about that?'

---'Nothing, except that Haakon didn't see the joke.'

---'You were happy when you were speaking to him.'

---'You know what? This is the funniest part. They strip-searched him. I said That's what you call 'Haakon *exposé*'. He was too sore to see the joke.'

I didn't see it either.

---'Did you say you were with me.'

She looked serious, even sad.

---'No, I didn't say that.'

Why did I feel trapped and ecstatic?

---'I meaned to,' she said. 'But I couldn't. Say it, I mean. So I said I was with my mate Valentine. He's ridiculously jealous you see.'

A bitter-tasting pang of ice at the back of the throat. I was sucking chilled slug. Knowing, already, much too soon, how Haakon felt.

---'Valentine?'

She laughed. Hollow.

---'*Haakon* is ridiculously jealous. Anyway: 'Are you sleeping with her?' he said. 'Who, Valentine? Who do you think I am?' 'I know who you are,' he said.'

The frozen slug warming, and creeping about.

---'Lighten up. We have nothing, and no one even knows what state we are in. Including us. Isn't that interesting? Exciting, even?'

It was true. The sun warm. The oak leaves rustling. And a stream, crawling like a living thing amongst the stones.

---'There comes a point when there's no way round it,' she added. 'You have to live.'

She was right. This was where, as best we could, we washed. Hella, one black eyebrow caked with blood. And our clothes, printed and smudged with green. Lanolin, urine and sheep shit. And even a little ewe-milk. Something like that. But not just that. Also the full stench of sex.

Upstream was a village, half-hidden in dark green leaves. We found the bar. It wasn't hard; there were half a dozen houses here, wedged into the shadow of a cliff. Inside, above the stove, an orange fox sniffed the feathery vent of a white ptarmigan, stuffed and yet fuller of life than the men with dark blue coats, bony skulls and enormous ears who sat in a row on a bench. All staring at a patch of light on the varnished concrete floor.

The barman chased us out. We stank. And so ate bread and unripe cheese at a table beneath a plane-tree which, up to eye-level, had a white-washed trunk. When she touched this, she left a green mark.

The sun shone here, but in the shadow of the plane it was cool enough for her to borrow a roll-necked sweater from the barman, a moustachioed bachelor torn between beautiful lust and hygienic horror. As beauty sometimes does, it won. She pulled it on, trapping her hair all round her matted head. She was turning a water glass in her fingers in a ray of sunlight falling through the leaves.

---'Look at the colours,' she said.

But tilting it to splay the colours wider, she tipped the water out. A dark blue stain amongst dark green ones, on a dark white cloth. She was a like that. When she spoke she was disappointed:

---'The colours have gone out ...' And she refilled the glass from a glass jug which also cast a rainbow on white cloth.

Pretty. Too pretty, but this is what she was. I was more worried about the cloth. I could see the barman through the window, making a selection of the faces which mean your patience is running out. His red face, together with his red V-neck, made his moustache and eyebrows very black.

---'Oh him,' she said. 'It's the sad thing about the French. They don't like you being yourself. Unless being yourself is being French. Assuming, of course, this is France, which it has to be, given all the French. Don't worry. He's eating out of my hand.'

---'You speak as if you weren't.'

---'In France I'm Swiss, in Switzerland Norwegian. Only in Norway am I French.'

Hers was a mix of the tease's lukewarm blood with passionate cold--- her mother a Parisian, of French-Swiss origin. Chauvinistic, pretentious, arrogant, hypocritical, sensuous and extremely pretty, from what she said. And Hella, therefore half-Parisian herself, was caught out in her own games of hide and seek because, just when the game was becoming hysterical, she always gave herself away. But in place of her mother's hypocrisy (by Hella's account) was Eugene Skippergate's Nordic earnestness. The humourless Viking, carrying off the swooning flirt.

But she was playing with a place mat now. She was sawing it with a knife-point, and making two parallel slits.

---"Look, physics lesson," she said. "Young's slits."

Through the window, the barman.---

---"Just concentrate."

She held the mat in the light and shading the table-top with her arms and hands, turned it a little, back and forth, looking at it whilst I looked at her, and I saw her lips come open, and her mouth widen at either end, and turn suddenly up into a smile, and trying to hold it steady she looked quickly up at me.

---"Make a cup with your hands and look in here. That's quantum electrodynamics; look at it, look."

Because I, my mouth a little open, was still looking at her.

---"Is it safe?"

She made an irritable double-take, and I looked; and saw, in the dark compartment formed by our hands, a strange, barred, zebra pattern, hardly visible, but seeming to move, and grow, and shrink, in a disturbing, organic way.

---"QED."

She made me shiver.

---"It's disgusting."

---"And do you know what is so strange," she was asking, ignoring me. "That it is there, so clear, and yet so shallow. We don't need anything fancy to see this: just two slits and some monochromatic light: and look, there it is, we have torn its mask off, and it lay so shallowly, in all its purity, beneath the surface of things. The depths may be hard to find, but they are not deep." I shivered again.

Shivered.

And went on shivering.

---"What's interesting about the world is how-few states it can take, how predictable it is, how it has voluntarily---it seems at least---renounced most of reality, or possibility, in favour of what we've got. The world: very shallow and very wide. QED."
---"Quod erat demonstrandum," I said helpfully.
---"Quantum Electrodynamics. Silly. Weren't you listening?"

Subtly threatened, like I was wearing the wrong jacket and flared trousers.

And my teeth stuck out.

And my hair.

Because. Well---do we want our girls smart? Do we Really? Really smart?

Afterwards, sleeping it off in the grass at the foot of the whitewashed plane. The barman, his face clogged with fury, moustache and eyebrows beetling slowly about, kept waking us to ask if everything was alright. Hella seemed blind to this. Some kind of sturdy perception of her rights, amongst which was the right, still caked in sheep-shit, to sleep in scented grass. Trying to pacify him economically, we took another bottle of wine. So, with the barman coming in and out of focus, half drunk and still drinking, we slept and woke, slept and woke.

When we rose, the sun had set. The air was cool and full of a shining, indirect light. Crickets cheeping like birds. And swarms of jackdaws fluttering and squeaking in the ash-trees which grew from the face of a cliff. I knew this sound already: it was the sound she too made, sometimes, when I touched her through her clothes. She, meanwhile, used the bottle as a telescope to watch them with. Unfortunately the telescope was still half-full of wine. This sobered her up.

---'Come on,' she said, still blinking, her lower jaw slack. 'Let's walk.'

---'Where to?'

---'Don't care.'

In the dusk, the overgrown track and rotting sleepers of a little train. The air cold, and with a first breath of autumn, even as early as this. St Antonin's former station, now demolished, was used as a car park---but the signpost was still there---St Antonin. And we could just see the route of the abandoned railway, hugging the hill upstream and joining a still functioning line which crossed the valley on a sloping viaduct of dark blue bricks.

The glow of the sky changing all through the blues. Then a cold star. She smelt of wet wool. Sweet. Sheepish. The river stumbled towards us over wide, bright pebble beds, giving off its own light, a whitish black, and bursting amongst egg-white boulders, splintering into fractured braids and then subsiding, pooling, reflective, quiet.

Night fell, and so did rain. Black branches reached from the hedges which lined the railway track. The pale green grass, almost brown, almost white, in the meadows beyond. And then cattle, looming out of a powerfully rising mist, exhaling mist themselves like smoke machines. And snorting, looking in our direction, ears raised, reduced to silhouettes and pawing the ground superstitiously. And in the mist, something dark, enormous, crawling towards us along the ground. A bouncy tail. It stopped. Without having risen it was staring intently at something, its tail moving slow.

What was it staring at?

A stone.

---'Hmm,' she said.

The dog, still staring. She picked up the stone; the dog-head rising steadily, intently. And by moving the stone from side to side she made the dog-head wobble ludicrously like the head of a dog on the back shelf of a car.

---'Don't tease the thing.'

A brief look at me, black lips drawn back over spiny teeth. Then back to the stone.

She lobbed it and the dog was off, faster than he needed to, faster than the stone, so that he'd already overtaken it before it fell and snuffled pointlessly in the grass much too far away. Hella was pointing it out for him, saying: 'There, there;' but he didn't look where the finger pointed, he looked at the finger, his head tilted and his tail swinging in helpful perplexity.

Jumping on boulders, we crossed the river, the dog wading behind us and snapping at ripples. Tennis courts cluttered with weeds and sheep. A swimming-bath filled not with water but mud and last year's rotten leaves. And half-ruined bath-houses with oxidised counters and marble spigots clotted with minerals through which spring-water dribbled.

---'A deserted spa.'

---'Where are we going?'

---'I wonder,' was all she said.

An avenue of poplars had been planted to either side of a track, edged with white pebbles. It seemed to be leading somewhere---to rusty gates and twisted railings, a fallen lodge, an overgrown bandstand with a scaled green roof.

---'There's a light.'

Fixed to the wet ochre wall of a mill-like building. Dimly, more dogs barking, somewhere off. What looked in the moonlight like smoke issuing powerfully from each of the chimneys high above was birch, rowan, willow herb and buddleia, clinging to the teetering stacks. And the upper windows, which reflected so brightly the light of the stars, were empty, without glass. What we were seeing was no reflection but the stars themselves, gleaming and burning through the fallen ceilings of the rooms inside.

Fixed to the wall in mossy wooden letters: *Hôtel d'Europe.* She turned to me and smiled.

---'Promising,' she said.

---'They won't take us in, not with no luggage. No car. Covered in blood and shit.'

The French can be like this.

Through a window, and net curtains, beside the door, three people watching a television set.

Hella tugged the bell-pull. A distant jangling. A light in the vines just above the door came on, went off, came on again. Distant, muffled barking. Then the door opened, and a man wearing a tight beige truss over baggy trousers asked:

---'*Qui êtes-vous?*'

---'*Polly Maggoo. Je voudrai une chambre,*' said Hella.

He looked incredulous yet indifferent.

---'*Comment?*'

---'*Une chambre. Avec bain.*'

---'*Non, non, non. Nous sommes totalement complet.*'

Except when he said *totalement.* He liked saying that. Spittle came whizzing out.

Just then the dog goosed her with his nose. Hella leaped forward and squeaked. The dog wagging his tail. I could see he had half a mind to do it again.

---'*Mais nous n'avons pas de place.*'

But he shut the door in her face and went away. We watched him return to the television room. Much gesturing, and even hands cupped round tubed lips to shout.

Then he came back.

---'*Venez, venez,*' he said, impatiently. He held a large black key, with an enormous label tied to it on which was inscribed the number 1.

On her lips, a frothy smile. 'We're in!' As levering himself up by pushing with doubled palms against alternate knees, Albert climbed the stairs. I was too shattered to take much in, except a cool space where, however aggressively he threw the switch, no light shone, and the dog bounding about in the dark with a slithering of claws on marble and then, dog and Albert gone, sliding into a cold, damp bed and falling asleep, touched by her rapidly warming skin.

And waking next morning drugged with sleep in the dimness of the shuttered room. The smell of wet carpets and rotting wood, but also of pines, and on the shutters the rattling of a cricket. Hella was awake. She kissed me. As she walked naked to the window, a charming, high disdain made her ignore the chalky blossom which had flowered in the night on the carpet where, without waking us, part of the ceiling had come in.

---'It's a pity you can hear the motorway,' she said, clonking open the shutters. The noise became louder and the room filled with sunlight which rippled about on the stained and punctured ceiling and glowed in sheared brown squares on a worn red carpet. She meant the river.

---'But it'll do.'

She meant it was wonderful. Even from the bed I could see the water, viscous and black amongst white stones, its surface patterned like a rasp. And a line of black, burning cypresses. And the sun, shining horizontally across a wood beyond, which glowed a radiant, bottle-black. Craggy rocks, green with moss and grass and clumps of ash, making our blood bubble. Pointing through the window, one hand on a warmed iron balcony rail, yet looking back over her shoulder into the room, explaining the contents of a Poussin, Hella's lips came open, her eyes went bright, reflecting the clear green light from outside, and she stared straight at me.

---'The fat man with the truss is down in the garden, balancing on one leg
to stoop for broken twigs on the gravel walk,' she said. These were the
words she spoke. But in a tone of fond paradox, she used them to hint
at the provisional nature of the earth. And so at the underlying flesh of
God. I am not imagining this.

A muffled knock. Hella scampered back to bed and we turned two faces
to the door. It was breakfast---a choice of tea, coffee, and chocolate in
battered nickel-plated jugs; *croissants, pain-au-chocolat*. Le Monde wedged
sideways under one of the plates. It didn't matter that they were stale,
that it was yesterday's. Carried in by a small maid, coarse featured, a wide,
amorous, slightly idiot face, a *jolie laide*. On her upper lip, just below
her nose, were four or five juicy moles. Her hair, flattened on top and
spreading out to the level of her earlobes, where it had been shorn.

--- 'What does this remind you of?' Hella asked, her lips black with
chocolate.

The maid, having taken our stinking clothes, had gone.

---'What?'

---'Try to think.'

---'I don't know.'

---'Begins with an 'h.'

---'Tell me.'

---'The honeymoon,' she said. Then went red.

Late in the morning she filled a bath. The roaring of the water. And
steam billowing through the bathroom door, which gave our room the
atmosphere of a sight-seeing boat at the foot of waterfall. She came out,
dry, her skin matt, her feet big. As bowing her shoulders she squashed
her breasts with her arms. The triangle of hair between her legs brown
and soft as a sable watercolour brush.

---'I've left you the water,' she said. Left me her urine too which, when I
went in, was still lying in the toilet bowl, green as melted butter, with a
yellow scum.

Later still the clothes returned in a fleecy pile, still warm from dryer and iron. All the facilities & accessories of girls: the canary coloured cardigan, blue skirt, white underwear. And the blue of my blue-jeans, bright, almost violet, yet mixed in with white. At the foot of the bed, rolling them up her thighs one side at a time like stockings, she pulled these on.

Then socks. Then sneakers. Walked round the room. If she, like the jeans, had long legs, a bottom divided by a central seam, scuffed knees, etc., she, like the jeans, also had flies.

Which I wanted to undo by tugging steadily as each button came undone. This is not new; not even interesting perhaps. But I wanted to unlace her sneakers and, leaving the still-stained white knee-socks on, pull the jeans off. What is more interesting is that with these thoughts came such a delicate and powerful gust of love for her that I was thrown, until it unfolded into the vision of a toy frogman's outfit I'd once had. Grey plastic weights were threaded on a vinyl belt. A barbarous knife whose blade disappeared into the haft. Brittle flippers, flimsy air-bottles, a blinding mask, suffocating snorkel, and black PVC wetsuit---these trinkets had made my child's heart thud with its greatest joy yet. And now it thudded again with the same joy. As this doll with her own sparse trinkets, the contents of her pockets---clinometer, prismatic compass, scientific calculator and bright blue skirt, not to mention heavy, pink tipped breasts (the same pink as her lips - nature's parsimony, nature's thrift)---looked through the window because something was missing and she saw it there.

Being one of those fools who are ashamed to cry I was ashamed now. A bewildering tunnel had broken through from the past. The gush of tenderness and desire, pushing up and half-choking me, filling my lungs with un-gushed tears. The feeling, however frail or cheap it really was, gave a sense of the solid and the good, of the real, the not tiresome at all. Of turning away from the fire to look through the mouth of the cave at the tinny, sunlit landscape there.

So she undressed again.

Something ludicrous and trusting about her, poor little girl ▨ no one had told her she was going to die, and die relatively soon---made my pinched heart hurt. Her skin was palest whitish-brown except for the cut-out shape of a bikini bottom where it was pale green, the colour of skin through water. Her body flimsy, almost bony, and yet the fineness of her shape. Her breasts, though, were burning, and like her bottom somehow too heavy, too dense for their own weight. Between them, under a stretched flysheet of skin, distorted by her ribs, I saw the bumping of her heart.

Coming to the bed, she pulled the sheet up to her waist but it moulded itself carefully to the plumpness of the front of her thighs, to the sloping belly, to the texture of her hair and the liquid folds between her legs.

---'Don't' she said, as she lay down on her back, looking straight at me at a few inches range. Her voice with breath and low and high notes. Her chin doubled, her eyes rimmed and full, wide open. Her round, inflated tits, ripe, sweet and white as ice-cream, dipped in red-sauce. And her body, except for these breasts, unexpectedly flat. She lifted the sheet. She caught her breath.

And we fucked, heavily, in the sagging bed. And slept amongst sticky, drying juice, Hella slumped across me on her back, with her head jammed up against the wall.

As I watched, a tear came out of one eye, ran down beside her nose and in again at her mouth. Perhaps she wasn't sleeping after all.

Tears in my eyes too, and in my temples a drilling sweetness. Everything had too much meaning, everything was over-ripe. The world: its breasts too big. Exaltation, something inexpressible, a kind of fizzing in the heart, a sleepy happiness, but a sense, also, that it was too much. That I wasn't up to this. Not old enough perhaps, I mean in geological epochs, not years. As half-asleep, myself now, scrappy words and ideas streamed through my head.

So: excitement, urgency: there would be time to do what I wanted provided I did it quick. But what was it that was so urgent? Time itself was going slow. Lying on the bed, nearly asleep again, feeling her limbs--hot where they touched mine, cold where they didn't---soften and twitch, and hearing against the whirring of the river, an orchestra of song birds, lambs, and the braying of an outraged donkey, rising in slow crescendo to a sudden climax with a rolling bar of thunder, and then a silence, shocked, inept. And, as shocking, an organ note, almost cello, but too terrifying, too deep, and sweeter and more tearful than a bass. Played with a hacksaw rather than a bow, slicing the strings it skidded across: there was blood in the honey, in the sugar, in the cream. There

was a sense of the temporary, even the contingent, along with the secrets
of what must not exist and what must. If music is eternal, the music said,
then only in relation to itself. For the world, music would not be music
without being provisional, vague, suggestive, and intimate with death.
However much I loved her, however out of this world she was---and she
was---there was something in me too that was repulsed by her. Her body,
the body of an ideal woman, but also ancient, material, haired, coarse.

She couldn't help this. They can't. And crossing hot tarmac, leaving the
footprints I would leave in snow, I tripped and falling pushed out my
arms suddenly. And woke myself up.

Hella still lay across me, her temple flattened on the sheet, her cheeks
and the bridge of her nose red, her lips a quarter open. Her mussed
hair was white on her forehead, where the quills came out of her skin.
And transparent, when you looked close, like honey, or certain parts of
insects; and crystalline. Sometimes flashing sparkles of blue and green
fire in the light. And realising this is how it looked: sand. Sand from a
distance, pale yellow, but matt, heavy. And sand close up, translucent,
crystalline, and deep---with things in these depths.

I didn't move till she woke. In the afternoon, she went for a walk. This
was when Lorchen came back to make the bed. Pluffing the pillows,
stepping heavily over floorboards which creaked beneath the carpet,
bending to tuck, to straighten, pad and puff, to tug, to slide, to flatten,
and then returning to the other side to do the same.

But moving round the bed she got her feet trapped in the quilt which
had spread over the floor in a scuffed chintz pool, and fell, giggling, her
reddened face pressed into a pillow, her skirt flicked accidentally up
her back, her amorous bottom supported by the edge of the bed and
clothed in white woollen underpants.

Or not woollen, so much as knitted; crocheted in fact. Through the
white wool was white skin, and coarse black hair, silky, sheened. Also red
flesh. And black shadows. And the faintest tang of urine.

Giggling; these giggles made her bottom flick from side to side, or so she
wanted to pretend. Her eyes shut, mouth open, face turned away to the
side. This perhaps explained the mystery: the chocolate, coffee, tea. The
washed clothes. *Le Matin* of yesterday.

My penis heavy. It got the message.

As I touched her there. Sweet. Wet, already. Dirty. No-no.

As with the same fingers I touched my lips. Lorchen had stopped moving. She was very still. But I could hear her breath. Slowly, very slowly, she raised her bum higher and moved her knees apart. What was this?

Under the white crotchet-work, her sexual organs open, flobby, hanging between her legs. Like fruit. Almost like balls. Only over-ripe. Touching her again: rubbing her and gathering enough of the crotchet in my fingers to let my fingers sink through. It was---like---this urine thing. Girl frenzy. I tubed out my lips away from my teeth like a horse. Something else was sticking out, or trying to. Heavy, trapped, and very much alive.

She was whimpering. My fingertips widened a line of four holes in the crotchet. I could feel slime. More slippery than anything, this.

A flash of bright brown eyes from the bed. Checking up. Her lacy shirt hanging down. Under it: hanging white breasts. All the meat in them had sunk to the bottom. And a hand reaching back; it drew my hand forwards, and cupped it on a breast. A melon-rind smile back at me meant: yes.

Scary. Like a pumpkin on Halloween. Yes. And footsteps on the stairs. Hella coming back. That was scarier. Already, still kneeling on the bed with her bum in the air, Lorchen was reaching across for pillows to plump. Dropping her skirt around her hips like a counterpane. The hem weighted: it swung more slowly than it should. And me: my fingers stank of sexual juice. I sucked them clean.

Hella threw some books on the bed and went out on the balcony. Lorchen, taking the tray. And, with a pointed half-glare at me, half-smile, she closing the door. That crocheted bum, that silky black hair, that wet red sex haunting me later. Haunting me even now. Here. At a distance of ⊠ sixteen years? Why? In general, the sex we didn't have more powerful than that we did. This was me, flapping my wings madly to rise out of her reach. I imagined she couldn't---*wouldn't* follow me into the abstract ether where Hella hovered, looking sweetly down. Unfortunately, it didn't come to this. I didn't even lift off. Because it struck me that Lorchen, and Barbara Ciama, back in the States: these were the world. And hadn't we come to live in the world, and not in heaven? By heaven I mean the abstract, the angelic, the moral, the sphere of ideas. Even of ideals. Hella was beautiful; Barbara was beautiful, Lorchen was not.

There's no way round this, though maybe its impermissible to say or
even see this. And however sensitive I was to the beautiful, I was also
vulnerable to whatever Lorchen was. Was thirsting for it, it could be said.
Blood in the honey. This is what I mean. Blood in the cream. And not, I
begin to think, by mistake.

It has to be like this. There is no such thing as clean honey, clean cream.
Because it isn't what we want.

Albert, in the surgical truss, managed but did not own the hotel. It was
our new friend Antoine, the man who kept the bar, that evening, telling
us this. And when I say ours, it is Hella's I really mean. Antoine drove
a Maserati and wore a vermilion V-neck over a claret polo shirt with
a Western string tie with lapis clasp. His thick moustache crept and
bristled on its own as he spoke.

---'Perhaps you are not aware of this,' he told us, 'but I am the mayor of St
Antonin. Have you ever considered modelling for photographs?'

He looked not at me but at Hella.

I wanted the girl I loved, like the books, to have a beauty which only I
would recognise. I wanted her beauty to be an acquired taste: and Hella
did have this kind, the mysterious, not physical but supernatural kind-
--rich, *insolite*, vibrant---there aren't words. But she also had an obvious
witchy prettiness which made smoothies try their hand, everywhere,
all the time, and made the disingenuous (I include myself), much too
quickly and much too hard, fall in love. It's trying being with this sort
of girl. Too much going on. The air twanging with too many vibes, too
many bowstrings, too many blunt arrows, among them Antoine's.

The hotel, he told us, belonged to a retired politician. A big cheese in
the Socialist Party. Formerly a big cheese under Petain. And therefore
old. The bar, on the other hand, belonged to him, Antoine. Freehold.
Downstairs was the studio-cum-darkroom which he'd show her in due
course. Upstairs, a crisp white flat with blonde floors and furniture
in chrome and black. Matt black hi-fi and video recorder. Enormous
television set. Enormous bed. Nothing was even mortgaged: this was the
beauty of it.

This coming winter he would smarten up the bar. The reign of
ptarmigan and fox was ending. He had ideas. So did the retired politician
who took so little interest in his hotel. It was, as he saw it, a building

plot. The plan was for a complex of time-share apartments serving the burgeoning winter-sports market. The snowfields above were to be developed with *Category 1* funding and a gondola would lift countless sharers-of-time almost vertically up the cliff.

What would the jackdaws do then, poor things?

Meanwhile, Albert, Marise and Lorchen had to make their way. The intention, I suspect, was to pocket whatever we paid them for our room. Marise was a strange young woman with a severe brown skirt and matching tinted pebble specs. Albert might have called her his daughter had he wished. She went to Condom once a week for major items of shopping, and once monthly to Albi. Quarterly to Toulouse. And Paris once a year. She had picked up Lorchen hitching on the last-but-one Paris trip. Lorchen, who was Austrian, had been *EuroRailing* and her month was up. They had taken her in and never looked back. People's domestic arrangements often mystify me. What they, and even I, choose to do. Hella's theory was that the three of them were lovers.

---'All three?'

---'The women in particular.'

---'But you said that about Tod Waddington and Modestine and Leicher.,'

---'Them too,' she nodded. 'Yes.'

She made no allegations of this kind about Pluto, their dog. It wasn't that he was sexless, but his sexuality was still in the puppy stage. He came without realising and there was more in this coming of the on than the in. His preference was to masturbate. He had something of the dumb dislocation of the rat-headed dog in one of Gaugin's paintings. I can't remember which. Hella, predictably, had views on him:

---'I can see why they called him Pluto,' she said.

She didn't mean as in Neptune, Jove, etc., as Gods, or even as in planets, but as in Mickey Mouse. As (presumably) had they. It was the long nose and long body. The floppy black ears and the bendy tail. And the nose like two prunes.

He followed us later on a walk upriver, jumping from stone to stone. To him we must have been an improvement in the facilities of the universe.

He liked us. Especially Hella. Especially when she caressed his glossy, slightly greased belly, even touched his stiff black balls, no longer glossy but matt, dulled, coarse. And, like the immodest tow ball on a motorcar, sticking straight out the back.

So, banks of sunlit, tangled undergrowth. And Pluto trailing behind in the water, snapping carefully at ripples. We came to a wide black pool with white scum on it, turning slowly, at the foot of a deep circular pit. Above us a heavy bird drifting in tight circles. So big that it was frightening. Hella, corrugating her forehead and watching it.

---'Well I thought it was an aeroplane,' she said. 'Until it flapped its wings.'

We undressed here and, holding our clothes above our heads, swam--- all three of us---across the pool and round a corner, to where the river became shallow again. Dammed by a landslide, it sloshed around flat rocks in a meadow fringed with woods. Fringed too with a herd of orange deer who watched us intently before pogoing into the trees.

We didn't dress. The idea of clothes made me irritable. It would have felt better to follow this foiled, silvered stream naked to its source.

---'So clear, that pool we swam through,' she said, 'that I want to drink it, all of it.'

A transparent trembling plug of clear jelly; this was how it had looked when you looked down.

---'The man who drank the sea,' she said. 'I want to rub it in. This is what I want.'

---'Where?'

With two fingers she touched very gently her lips, a nipple, the space between her legs, saying:

---'Here, here. And here, of course.'

And then of course she did. And drank, squatting slightly sideways, from a cupped palm. Water splashing on her knees, her feet, white as paint in the sun. The rocks too warm, the sun too soft to stay awake in. And on a big flat rock she curled half-up and closed her eyes and laid her head on her hands. Pluto the Epicurean snuffling the lower end of her bottom; glossy black demon snuffling for a truffle-like soul. At which she wriggled, and smiled, her hands still folded under her ear and eyes still shut.

Going in the sun not brown but gold. The colour of her skin nearing the colour of her hair. There was also green there. And when she opened her eyes! She looked a Martian: disconcerting, worrying. Something different; different substance, different form. Unbetterable in this world, and therefore absolute. Looked also a child. The simplicity of her face, outside of her nose, her eyes, her mouth. There was nothing else, except sandy, mothlike eyebrows, and rich, smoothly changing tones of colour and shape. The effect, which should have been naïve, was very, very sophisticated.

It meant nothing to me of course, all this. Except that the universe, having put on a pretty body and a pretty face, was further made to throb and beat to its very roots by a knowing mind and an unknowing heart.

And yet. The awkward silence of the honeymoon, after the rattling clamour of wedding. Alone with ourselves and panic: what had we done?

There was something missing. What was missing? What was wrong? Unless something always is. Because we had what we wanted. And this was wrong. A child pulling on the toy. When you let go the child falls down. And, after a pause for shock, quietly at first but steadily changing up the gears, begins to cry. We fell down too. What I mean is perhaps happiness, like tomorrow, never comes. Or was always already over, yesterday.

The two of us, in this remote, decaying place buried in the depths of a hypocritical, merciless and chauvinistic state: we weren't enough. We couldn't keep it out: the misery seeped in and squirted over us.

Which is one reason why, perhaps, we were so pleased to see Tod Waddington, Ms Auch and Professor Norbert Leicher. In a bug-blue Polo rolling past Antoine's bar. It stopped, reversed, and stopped again, and unfolding through its doors like paper flowers they came, Leicher last.

Standing on the cobbles they examined postcards. Leicher took a sheaf of cards into the depths of the shop, and came out pocketing a wallet. Between snipped forefingers he gripped a flat white paper bag.

One by one, like umbrellas furling quickly, they folded themselves backwards into the car.

The engine whirred instead of starting, whirred again, whirred again. By this time Hella was close enough to run the few steps up to it, calling out Professor Leicher, Dr Waddington!

Then the engine fired. The car lurched off, its inmates staring doggedly through the windscreen.

---'Golly!' she said.

---'They didn't see us.'

---'Yes they did.'

And the face she turned to me was a new face, full of girly malice which made her soul withdraw amongst its mysteries, making her physical body, meanwhile, and her physical beauty very concrete, super real, occupying space in front of the landscape, occupying time.

---'Look.'

In the distance the fiat had stopped. It was rocking on its suspension. Rearrangements were being made within. Why did we want so much to see them? Why did we want them to stop? Also, why had they too left the Symposium. Or was the symposium already up?

A sense of failure, fear, loss, when in the end the car rolled on.

---'Gone?' she asked, turning the goofy, stranger's face on me.

Why we wanted them was that paradise is alarming. Too much to lose. I calmed myself by making clumsy pastel sketches of the river and the trees---River with girl and dog ⊠ so on. She could have made another moth trap, but chose to borrow Albert's spade instead, and do, as she called it, some work on the soils.

Beyond the black pool with its eternally rotating scum berg, just where the valley opened up, a landslide had revealed the profile of the underlying soil. She had been intrigued by this the day before; by the processes which had led to such sharp horizons in the earth. To me, dirt was dirt. But here we had something layered as cake, in clear colours, pretty ones, ochre, black, grey, chestnut and yellow. She had stood looking for a long time. So rearranging our economy, introducing hobbies, pastimes---a taste for model railways, or bondage, or pink and yellow roses, to take us out of paradise for a bit. She dug narrow pits right across the valley, measuring the depth in each pit of each layer and taking readings of aspect, inclination, position. She collected samples from each of the soil horizons, for later analysis, in around two hundred discarded film canisters donated by Antoine. The scientific instinct strong in her.

---'It's not as if you find truth by looking for it, now,' she said.

When it rained we hid under the trees while heavy white drops were passed carefully from leaf to leaf. And at noon we went to the steaming rocks and lay there, baking slowly like fish. We ate sandwiches and touched each other. When too hot, we swam.

And yet. This business of sex with deep and serious girls: it may be the biggest thing there is but you can't live as if it is. I'd soon had enough, and seated with Pluto by a waterfall beneath a wild fig read *Romeo et Juliet*:

> *Deux familles de la belle Vérone,*
> *Qui furent du même rang ...*

Hella meanwhile, a clinometer in her eye, paced the hill pausing only to make her notes on paper. She had folded down the top part of her dress, making it into a skirt by tying the arms round her waist, and scrambled bare and heavy-chested in her sneakers.

Once, climbing up to where she dug, I slid my arms around the skin of her waist. Her belly was convex, so there was a slit you could slip your hand in between her belly and her skirt. She had been sweating and the sweat had dried. And her waist narrower than it should have been, almost a wasp's waist. So that you wondered how it was done.

---'Leave me alone, let me finish,' she said without looking at me.

Her eyes, always uncertain in colour, were now, from the side, a pregnant cloudburst green.

---'This is good,' she said, having done so, and having put back her dress, chilly now.

She was down on her knees with the tape, measuring horizons.

---'So precise. Like someone's done it on purpose.'

---'Argument from design?'

Licking her lips unconsciously as she measured.

---'And what is interesting about the world is how much of it is like that.'

The bells of St Antonin clanging as we packed up. Wind. A stinging, gritty rain which caught us on the way back. So that the time we reached the hotel we were drenched. Hella's nipples and her pants showing through her wet skirt, her thighs and hair showing through her wet pants, and her hair plastered to her head so that you could see the exact shape, moulded in whorls of hair, of her ears. Her face freckled with gleaming drops which gave it the glistening, livid beauty of her eyes.

Inside our room, the velvet curtains were flicking and whirring like flames. The shutters rattled and swung, until I closed them. Through them we could hear the wheezing fury of the unexpected storm.

We stood in the middle of the bedroom scoring circles of wetness into the red carpet. Its colour was bleeding upwards into her skin, as Hella too went pink.

---'What are you thinking.'

---'Nothing. Except ...'

Now she was red, and turned her face down and away, holding her clothes out away from her body.

---'Except?'

---'What do we do now?' she asked.

---'What do you mean.'

---'No clothes I mean.'

I looked at the bed. Long glutinous drips were falling from the ceiling onto the carpet beside it with a slow, knitting sound.

---'The bed's still dry.'

Her nipples, stiff as fingers, were pointed at me. And if her body was cold, her mouth was hot. Her wet brown-yellow hair had tangled into ropes, and something---guilt, overflowing feeling, some fantasy she couldn't control, made her first sit and then fall back on the bed, her naked knees apart, without responding to me at all as like an undignified

necrophiliac a corpse, I fucked her cold lifeless body until, both
exhausted, bruised, we feel asleep.

We dined in towels in the peeling gaiety of an enormous room, lined
with red banquets and gilt pilasters, under a cracked, decaying ceiling.
Gilded bits of wood snaked up the walls or lay about on the floor under
the marks which showed where they had been attached. The velvet
curtains, once all red, and now red only in the folds, and otherwise
brown. The wet enriched colour of the dripping garden through
Edwardian plate-glass, in which was reflected the vicious glow of a
coal fire beside---almost underneath---our table. The grass strewn with
petals of laburnum, lilac, buddleia. The lights were out, the sconces
and chandeliers, moonlike, merely reflecting the dying daylight outside.
Slowly the colours deepened, our plates, the table-cloth, our eyes and
faces, turned a sharpening blue, until tentative, starting as a mere glow
and brightening and dimming unevenly, all the lights came up at once,
disclosing the peeling gaiety again.

In the distance the thudding of a generator. And also a haired, dried dog
mess beside our table on the dining-room floor. Pluto, pretending not to
notice it.

---'The behaviour of these soil systems is unexpectedly regular,' she said,
as if reading to me from a paper. 'Horizon depths can be expressed as a
linear function of aspect, inclination and distance from the centre of the
river, it seems. R squared around point seven or eight. It's a wonderful
system, fresher, in a sense, than physical systems. Physics is still, which
in human terms are showing signs of fatigue. The discretion has gone.
It has turned deterministic, it has that air, even in the moment when
the laws become indeterminate. Before you could choose them, frame
them yourself, even if they were deterministic ones. Now, though often
indeterministic, it seems more like they are being forced, proffered, that
we are being funnelled down into an ever tighter system of laws. But I
don't mean this, perhaps, so much as that the cast, the entities, however
coldly beautiful, are getting too abstract, too wanky?, wacky? almost.
Like conceptual art. We long for the figurative, a tree, some earth;
determinism in a field or a wood, as some kind of opposite of what we
see there, is still alluring.'

I was already drunk on her spit. She, it seemed, was getting drunk too.

---'So, probing for the laws tucked like Easter-eggs just under the grass,' she said. 'Excitement, joy---the words aren't there. Touching, with the human heart, mathematical beauty, or even God---at the same time calm and also passive---biting, intense, passive. Like music, only better. Science as another art and another religion. These means and standard deviations---playing a difficult piece of music you know well. Even writing it. If it had never happened, I would never have guessed it could. I would have been like someone who is not only colour blind, but doesn't know. And can't be told because she's deaf. And can't read.'

Stretching cat-like in her seat as she spoke, her arms hooped, somehow unconvincingly, like the arms of someone who doesn't know exactly what to do with them, behind her head. Self-conscious as the over-intelligent so often are, self-conscious and insecure, insecure and incorruptible, undeflectable. This was the surprise---you thought the insecure could be moulded, pushed around, and then you came up against her. Thinking he was summoned by her raised arms, Albert arrived. She looked surprised, but had a pudding anyway, while the dim, succulent light from the flooded garden shone in through the windows, ever fading, ever bright. Making me think: women like her as delicate instruments through which to view the truth.

---'You heard the tocsin?' grumbled Albert, banging down an ice-cream and apple tart, so that Pluto barked. 'Marie-Claire is dead.'

---'Science and nature,' I said when he was gone, 'the train timetable and the trains.'

She laughed at this. I could see why she liked me.

---'Science and nature,' she was saying, 'the weather forecast and the rain, the train times table and the train. Yes: nature as richer than science. But science isn't competing, it is worshipping. And like most beauties, nature has a lust for worship. And yet, it's hard to know where it all comes from, on what it's based. If you go down into the foundations, it's built on sand. We go on with science because it works; it gets results; but also because it conforms to some deep instinct. So it's a human activity, with human motives. We justify it with scientific reasons, really: science is simply another---the greatest---scientific hypothesis. Not yet falsified. It defines itself, like all great things; it sees with its own eyes, feels with its own heart, and unlike nature needs no audience for its own happiness. Perhaps this is why we like it enough to put up with it. Proust says that the search for happiness leads only to truth. It is the search for truth that leads to happiness. By that I mean Science. And its big sister, of course. Theology.'

Hella smiling, her chin propped in her hands, a little bug-eyed as if she'd hypnotised herself. Not all there. Her eyes filmy.

---'It is also anti-mystery.'

---'The skin is more beautiful than the meat,' she said softly; 'the iris than the retina. We dig too deep.'

She couldn't quite get back to earth. And her wet eyes, black in this dim dining room, now the garden had gone black, and softer and also more hurt, more scared, than I'd ever seen them yet, and therefore containing the softness they'd lacked, took me in, almost digested me. But something in me not liking all this, distrusting the sentiment, as it were, the phoney mysticism. The poseur's exaltation ⊠ she had a way of making me feel thick.

---'It isn't the knowledge, but the finding out and the working out which is so delightful. What you know is dead. So perhaps those who are snobbish about science are right, letting the rest of us sort it all out for them, without corrupting the primeval tranquillity of their minds. 'Living? Our servants do that for us,' says Villiers. Likewise, Science. Our servants do that. Lucky devils.'

---'And yet---Herzen says that without the intellectual rigour of the hard sciences, we can't know the world---we miss reality's own mysticism. The real, the scientific, is the true ineffable. Is this the word?', she asked, her forehead corrugated and her eyes round. 'If reality is God then science is religion. As a journalist, Herzen can't be trusted. He was lifted up by his Muscovite father to see Napoleon ride by. That was something. Perhaps he saw Stendhal ride by too, but he wouldn't know that, which is kind of the point. The great: they find each other. Stendhal found Napoleon, though admittedly Napoleon didn't find him. Boswell found not only Johnson, but Rousseau and Voltaire. And Rousseau's girlfriend, who Casanova also found.'

Resenting the Norwegians, also, or maybe the Swiss, for educating their little girls like this, for showing the rest of us up.

---'Waddington and Leicher and Modestine, is that what you're saying?'

---'No,' she said, 'Pluto and you. And the child Mozart proposing to
the child Marie-Antoinette, because she had picked him up when he
slipped on the polished marble palace floor, not being used to marble
floors or palaces. Neither had lived long, or was going to live much
longer. This place is strange, isn't it.'

---'This hotel?'

---'This universe.'

---'You fly too high.'

---'Why not? Icarus did. And why? It wasn't just for fun. No, he flew too
high because he needed to fall. He was searching for meaning and this
was it: to fly higher than anyone, ever, and fall. Like Villon, too. Gaugin.
Marlowe. There's plenty of time to look for trouble, and find it. If you
succeed on the other hand, it just means you didn't aim high.'

---'Besides, what else am I supposed to do.'

---'And anyway, Humpty fell too. We all fall. All of us. There is no choice.
Unless the choice is this: whether to be Humpty or Icarus.'

Lorchen was standing behind her, staring past Hella's ear at me. When
Hella fell silent, Lorchen spoke. She wanted our wet clothes.

And in the morning, wrapped in a bath towel, which chastely covered
my nipples, I was sent to get them.

---'You go,' she said. 'I can't. I hate that woman. She smiles too much. And
she smiles wrong. Short or not, ugly or not, I hate her. The body is the
soul,' she said. The cruelty of the rich, of the perfect. 'Anyway, she made a
pass at me. The way she looks at you, too. She's got no shame. She's on for
it. Hot for the trot, as the English like to say.'

Poor Lorchen. She wasn't beautiful. Physically or morally. But there
was no way round this. It was true. And if she had a nose like a claw
and muddy eyes and a face like a pumpkin, and a body like one too in
fact, she also had profound sexual power. The fairies had unexpectedly
brought the most precious gift of all to the Christening.

---'At least she knows what she wants.'

---'I know what I want too. We all know what we want. Don't you?'

---'No.'

Because I was wet---was this the problem? But if wet, why did she love
me?

Outside of Lorchen's laundry room the upstream wing of the hotel was
reverting to nature. Clouds were painted on the ceilings of damp rooms,
and speckled mirrors reflected opulent ferns. The floors were putrid.
Coated in a layer of juicy Day-Glo moss, they sagged like thick green
carpet between each joist. And the many doors which opened from the
corridors onto empty space were not even locked. Lorchen, Albert and
Marise, beating only a gradual retreat, reluctant to quantify their loss.

At the end, Lorchen's room.

I could see her form and colours through a glazed door, misted and
studded with transparent drops: forceful strokes of an iron and clouds
of steam. She had a pitched glass roof on which rain fell and a window
opening into the sodden blue crown of a cedar. Under a old polished
copper smouldered a handful of twigs. This was for heat; the copper had
no water in. She washed in a heavy-duty *Miele* washer/dryer. There were
white shelves and zinc-topped tables. And a blaring radio. The room
smelt damp and sweet.

She turned suddenly at the sound of the opening door, already smiling--
-wrong---and holding up the mirrored flat of the iron used it to beckon
me in. When I saw my own distorted face reflected there I drew back,
and she smiled more broadly still and beckoned again.

---'Please, come in?'

She invited me to sit in a mound of blankets while she finished her work.
Gave me a Ricard in a tiny glass. Added water to turn it to mist.

She believed I was sitting too stiffly and pushed me back, made me relax.
Then gave me a piece of heavy silk to tip from hand to hand while she
did more ironing. Looking back saucily, she rolled up her sleeve and
allowed the tip of the iron to touch flesh. It hissed as she turned to me
and laughed.

Then she took the silk and drew it across the welt on her arm saying:

---'Good!'

She had me worried. Especially when stooped over me to draw the silk softly back and forth under my armpit. Especially when it did feel good.

---'Silk,' she said. 'Good.'

---'Yes,' I answered, 'it is good.'

But keeping an eye on that iron.

She opened a high linen press and brought out a square of crêpe. Flannelled my face. Irresistible. It made me close my eyes, relax every muscle. Except the sphincters of course. With her fingers on the rim of the towel which was still hooked round my belly, I felt her drawing it softly over my skin. I held on to the towel.

---'Good,' she stated. 'Good.'

Then went to her cupboard and stalked back with a sheet draped over both arms and folded into delightful waves of shade and light. She lathered this sheet over me. I was being washed in milk. She turned me over, and did my back. A sense of lassitude, ease, of never wanting to move again. I even had an erection from the touch of old linen, which covered my whole body, including my face. I hadn't forgotten the crocheted knickers, either, as, rolling me onto my back again, she massaged my feet.

---'Physiotherapy,' she said. 'Good!'

---'You're a physiotherapist?'

---'Good!'

Unfortunately the massage---and its message---began to climb my legs. This was when I tried for out.

But to my horror the fingers with which I gripped her wrists, far from pulling her hands away, made them touch my balls first, and then the belly just above it, and only then my cock. She twirled it between oiled hands: rolling a *Plasticine* snake. I wanted it to stop, but it couldn't stop. The will was there, but it had no force at all. All I still controlled were my eyes, and these moved uneasily in flickering movements from side to side, under the sheet. And my tongue: that flicked too, back and forth along wet lips.

Otherwise, mutiny. Or some trans-national authority, intent on ever-closer mystic union. I was breathing heavily, almost blacking out, the sheet bunching over my nose and in my eyes, and felt a wet kiss on my thigh at the lifted edge of the sheet, and a sudden sliding warmth and beauty, a sudden half-religious light, as coarse buttocks ground against my hips and a tight and hairy perineum caressed my balls. I was inside. Hot, sweet. Plenty of room. And the sense of soft masses touching, bumping, sliding gently about.

Also the braying of an outraged donkey, and the violence of someone trying to crack my hips, too late for me to do anything but howl too, until a sudden coolness, and washed with hot flannels, and wound from head to foot in a winding sheet.

When I lifted my head the room was empty. On the table were our clothes, ironed into a fleecy cube. The radio blaring. I wanted to laugh. Until I remembered Hella.

Carrying the clothes down steadily dripping corridors, I felt like crying. When I came in, Hella was crying. She was hysterical, in fact.

---'What's wrong?'

I couldn't work it out. Meanwhile a horrible woo-eeeing outside. Too many inputs, all at once. Too much going on. The clattering of a helicopter. Voices, traffic. The hill crawling with people, amongst them many people carrying metal-detectors. In the river were rubber boats.

Orange ones. And black. With men in frog-suits in. Suddenly remembering Ali and Achille---could they be after us? Albert came in. It turned out she'd been seen digging her pits, and each made of it what he wished. Asking at first about us, he said, now they were asking for us, the treasure hunters, a journalist, and the police; just as Gabriel, arriving in Eden, must have asked.

---'Give us a moment to get dressed.'

But on a less obvious level, Gabriel was someone else, someone also taking a close and though innocent, a sinister interest in our story. Sinister in outcome at least, if innocent in intention. In the short-term. At least. We didn't know this yet.

But filching bread, cheese, wine, tea, chocolate from the larder and stuffing a black-plastic bag with these, we checked out. Albert and Marise out front with Antoine, fielding questions with a certain justified elation, their moment come. God knows where Lorchen was. Leaving cash we slipped through a breach in the wall of Lorchen's wing and began to climb, under cover of the wet laurels and brambles which clothed the slope. After an hour, ears popping, trees thinning out. On the edge of a plateau of rank, primeval grasses and hidden flowers, a stop to eat chocolate. Where, on his belly, penitent, sweeping his tail slowly over the grass, Pluto crawled up.

---'Go back, Pluto.'

---'Pluto, go home.'

Pluto stood up.

---'Home!'

He had a look at the view.

---'Pluto!' I screamed and he wandered vaguely off and disappeared amongst trees.

---'Poor thing.'

---'He can't have everything.'

---'He's like a baby,' she said, folding up the remains of the chocolate in its blue foil, and swinging the sleeping bag over her shoulder. 'Our baby. Ours.'

We crossed a brook. Here she drank. And reached the snowline in another hour. The snow grey and heavy, like wet sugar. And while I was savouring a leathery lump of bread and looking back the way we had come, Hella pushed a snowball down my neck. So, sitting on her gently upholstered backside, I ground her face in snow, which came up shining, burning, full of light. In the end she forgave me.

Things were looking up, until we heard a sharp, short bark. Pluto again. Barking, barking. Perhaps he'd never seen snow. Hella offered him a handful. Cautiously, he sniffed it. Then he sniffed the real stuff on the ground. Then he lay down and began chewing it with a tilted head.

Finally he ran about jerkily, his legs sinking up to the elbows and the knees, wagging and barking.

We climbed more.

Big birds circling slowly in close up. We could see the glitter of their eyes. A wind blowing white dust off the edge of a snow cliff. The snow pure now, fluffy, light. It wasn't really there. When you looked down it seemed to have no surface, no reality. Then, rising slowly on the horizon: the shark-fin peak from all the postcards.

Silence. The scene serene. Where there was a gap between two mountains it was filled with another. And on into the distance. The air with a bluish tint, not air but sky now. The sky itself, meanwhile, had been turning steadily more violet and was now a coppery black. And to the north, the horizon fuzzy and smooth. We thought we could see its curve.

Mountains? We looked down on them.

Pluto climbing steadily behind. With intense concentration he placed cold paws in our shallow footprints, tail clenched between his legs. And Hella in front. The snow complemented her. If she was browner, there was still a transparency to her skin which matched something in ice. Her face retained the lust for white. And while the snow all around us exaggerated the colour in her eyes, it also quite apart from this had something in common with them. As it danced under my feet, and I lost the sense of its level, of elementary distance. Meanwhile, I felt tipsy and found it almost too easy to laugh. And Pluto, normally so morose, so perfectly resigned to his doggy fate, not only the fate of a dog, but the fate of having been assigned that fate, was animated. Even gay. This was when she saw the Alpinists.

---'Not so peaceful after all', she said. 'Look.'

Because, lumbering painfully towards us was a party of those earnest types who put on red socks to go into the mountains. They were shouting and waving ice-picks in heavy, mittened hands. Hella, looking at me.

---'Perhaps they need help.'

And so, going down to them. Expressionless black goggles reflected tiny white suns which moved from side to side like eyes. When I saw this I wanted to laugh. And on their noses and their lips a kind of paste. Yellowed teeth, and breath flowing out over whitish tongues. Breathless from their climb, they were all chattering at once.

---'What is it?' asked Hella. 'One at a time. Are you all right?'

---'O, you fools,' shouted one, as others bitterly chorused:

---'Yes!'

---'Who do you think you are coming up here without guides and equipment. You'll get yourselves fucking killed.'

Hella, looking surprised. She tried to speak. No point. They wouldn't let her. They wanted us to be like them.

---'Where's your map?' one shouted.

---'Your ice-picks, crampons, ropes?'

---'And the girl, why has she no coat?'

---'She left it in the *Pensione*,' I told them.

---'And why do you only have one glove each?'

We didn't have a map but we had a postcard. If she didn't have a coat she had a dog. They were not to realise this. And besides, being half-Norwegian, half-Swiss, she was snow-wise. Knew all there was to know of blizzard, crevasse, snow-hole. Isn't this what Norwegians know? And the Swiss? With a bit about freedom thrown in too? Or was it fascism? Hazy about this.

She also had a compass, which worked as a clinometer. More charming than any doll's accessory. Painted in red and white and luminous green, it slid out of a small leather box, with a minute screwdriver in a drawer for compensating year by year for the drift in magnetic North, under the crust. And she had a green pen-knife.

Looking at me she lifted her bright hair out of her eyes, smiled, turned, and began to climb. Waving their ice-picks, still roped together, they fanned out across the ice and kicking steps, tried to chase us.

Pluto looking back fearfully, his tail between his legs.

---'Come back you bloody fools.'

---'Don't you know the mountain code?'

Their frosted beards moving as they shrieked now, and puffs of breath coming out like smoke:

---'Who do you fucking well think you are?'

We could have asked them that. Their anoraks a uniform blinding mauve. They glowed as white things glow in discotheques.

---'O, you fools!'

Very cross indeed. We were spoiling it for them perhaps. Bursting in on a masque, wearing street clothes.

But not for long. Soon we couldn't even hear them, although for a while we could still see the trudging specks, threaded like beads on their rope. She called them the rosaries. We lost them finally when the sunlit ice-path turned a corner round a rock, and we startled a goat and her kids. She came running out towards us shitting a solid black slug of droppings which snapped into mothballs as it rolled, gathering in our footprints in the way the little white ball is gathered by a numbered socket in roulette.

The ice-path ended. A twisted wooden ladder, tethered to a stanchion at its base, dangled from an invisible support above.

Pluto, his tongue lolling out, was looking up. Hella too, shading her eyes, looked up.

---'How do we get him up?'

---'What?'

---'How do we get Pluto up.'

---'Let's see what's up there first.'

Nasty. The ladder swung as you climbed. And when you were near the top it rolled inwards, so that its base hung out over empty space. The steps which had been cut in the rock at the end of the ladder were filled with ice.

Hella looked shocked as she rose over the rim behind me and crouching low, came up the steps. Her body trembling as she put her hands round my neck and, uncertain of her balance, squatted and looked back.

---'Bronco ladder,' she said.

Very faintly we heard a yelp.

---'What do we do?'

Yelp, yelp.

---'I'm thinking ...' I said.

---'What are you thinking?'

---'He might find his way back ...'

---'How dare you---jerk. We can't leave him. How would you feel if we left you?'

---'We didn't ask him to come.'

Her face was reddened. She began to shout.

---'No way ...'

But as she spoke, the ladder began to twist and bob. Long pauses, in which we imagined him clasping it to his birdlike breast and looking down in horror or disbelief, before the steady jerking began again.

Eventually he came into view, gripping a rung in a serrated mouth before hooking a foreleg over it. A trembling hindleg pushed against empty space until it found footing. Urine was dripping steadily off his balls and floating away on the wind. He wasn't heavy enough to make the ladder turn, but climbed on up. I had to pull him off by the scruff. Even as I pulled he was working all his legs and growling through a still gripping mouth. When we reached safety, he turned round, splayed his legs carefully, and barked. Then he looked up at Hella and with panting emotion wagged his bum.

---'Pluto,' she said.

There were tears in her eyes as she kissed his forehead and his ears. Pluto squirmed, and looked the other way. But when she let him go, he dashed about barking wildly before going down on his forelegs, looking back over his shoulder and showing her the hole beneath his rhythmically flicking tail. Also his balls.

The rest was easy. It wasn't as steep as it looked, and on dangerous bits there were iron ropes. At the top, a rusty cross set in the snow was tilted like a parasol. We lay down, grateful for the solidity of the snow, and for obliging gravity.

---'Very sore, under my chin,' she said. The underside of her chin and the underside of her nose were strawberry coloured. The sunlight, reflected off the snow, had burned her. She was caressing me, and looking straight at me out of a lowered face. Her shoulders twitched.

---'Don't look scared,' she said.

---'What will Pluto think?'

Pluto, hearing his name, beamed us love, slowly wagging his tail.

---'You can't shock a dog, can you, Pluto?' she asked and, pushing me down by the shoulders, laid her boiling lips on mine while Pluto, barking, flirtatious, skittered about.

Later she went quiet, and wouldn't answer questions, but let tears run down her face, while looking out into space over the hazy, copper-blue edge of the globe. However much Pluto tried to make her play, she couldn't. She didn't even notice hi, and the tears coming out through her eyes dripped from the end of her nose. This, and her eyelids, red.

---'I'm sorry,' she said.

---'What for?'

She turned her blotchy eyes and face my way. Trying to make herself ugly. Then she laid her ear against my chest and put her arms around my waist. She caught her breath a few times, and then, low but rising in pitch, she began to cry.

---'What is it?'

After a while, she lifted her face.

---'Nothing.'

And she hid it again.

---'What?'

---'It's only ...'

But she couldn't speak.

---'Only what?'

---'Nothing.'

And I felt coldness over my body, or rather a removal of warmth, like
when the sun goes in.

---'Why cry?'

---'I don't know. I don't cry usually.'

Palming her eyes under her hair. Her lips, which was all I could see, were
quavering.

---'It isn't such a climb,' she said, blinking when she took her hands away.

Her eyelashes matted and sticky. Rushy.

---'We're not very high. Looking down on humanity, its staggering
simplicity, not only in its disasters, but even in its successes.'

She was being brave.

---'Pitying it its Leichers and Waddingtons ...'

---'That's not why ...'

Through tears, she gurgled.

---'No! But ... you ... wonder why we bother to be human at all, because
it could be a bird singing on an aerial, just as much as a woman at
the washing line. And then, amongst these concrete things, sudden,
unexpected monuments, surrounded with formal gardens. And woods.
And lakes. And grassy rides.'

She spoke like this---was like this. This was part of the package. Most of
it was going on inside in a monologue, of which mystifying figments
came out. In a tone of mild embarrassment. The wind blew, throwing
the gritty ice-dust in our faces. The dog, waggling his backside, barked
sensuously into the moving air.

A flattish surface of cloud formed, through a gap in which sharp ribbons
of sunlight fanned out. It looked like the spreading spines in the hand-
like leaf of a dwarf palm. And an organ note sounded, deep, pure,
making the empty space around our heads rattle. And clambered up the
notes in an unreasonable temperament, and then fell an octave where it
grated, resonant, deep in our chests.

Only the fretted iron cross, moaning in the wind. But the effect was
supernatural, infrasonic, acted on the spirit, made her happy, made me
scared.

The last clear part of the quickly clouding sky was black, and against
it flashed a silver airliner, motionless, wings outstretched, but seeming
when the light glittered on its scales to twist in the air like a fish. With a
whistle and a howl a stronger gust of wind closed this last vision off, and
the moaning cross began to accompany itself in shocking *vox humana*.
Hella, shivering.

---'We'd better go down now. Awful if the mountaineers were right.'

---'Let's.'

A wider track on the far side sloped gently south. We both felt drunk
and there were blank forms in our eyes from the brightness of the snow.
It was evening already, the clouds coming lower. The wind began to blow
steady and determined, and with a chilled bite which made Hella cross
her arms on her breasts and lean forwards, while her hair streamed out
behind. The dog, who had been plodding along behind us, inserting
his legs carefully in our footprints, looked up, twinkled his nose and,
barking with wagging tail, bounced on ahead.

It was a man in cheap shoes and a cheap suit.

His mouth was open, over yellow teeth, one hand resting on his hip,
his chest rising and plunging as he drew breath. His trouser legs were
sodden; he had tucked them into his socks. His shoes, originally black,
were now the grey of distressed leather.

He was asking how far to the summit.

---'Does he mean to go up there tonight?' I asked in disbelief.

---'Yes.'

---'No, No, No,' I told him. 'You can't.' And turning to Hella: 'What's dangerous?'

---'*Peligroso.* Now, I think' she said.

---'*Peligroso,*' I told him. '*Peligroso.*'

---'¿*Peligroso?* Is dangerous?'

---'Yes.'

He closed his eyes a little and, settling the two wings of his moustache with trembling fingertips, scanned the distant summit, rounded from this side. He turned to us and tried to speak, gasping through his teeth.

---'*Que?*' asked Hella.

But he was coughing, and flapping his hand at the level of his forehead, he shook his head, his face now purple and congested with blood. And arm raised towards it, as if, receding, he was imploring it to wait, he staggered on.

---'You're as bad as the Alpinists, taking a moral line like that.'

She was quite right. Before we die we play every part.

In the dim light, irregular patches where the snow had melted, muddy, with clumps of grass, and still hot and scented from the day. Our feet squelched in the sodden soil, and we could hear the percolating melt-water underneath.

Pluto sniffing sensuously. Above him, clinging to the cliff face, just above the path ...

---'What's that?' I asked.

An American. This I knew from the voice:

---'You're dealing with an unstable woman,' she said to me. 'And I apologise in advance.'

Hella looking significantly at me.

---'Son of a bitch!' The woman was panting, and making noises strangely
suggestive of her plight. 'I can't continue this way, and I can't hang
around much longer. Oh please, please,' she called to some invisible
assistant up above, 'pick up the slack and hold tight. I'm going.'

A faint answering murmur from the top of the rock. But then, with a
new resolution:

---'I do not want to go on. I am so exhausted. I'm really trying very hard
but I'm absolutely exhausted and it's too late in the day. It's nearly dark.
I'm hungry and tired and I can't do it and I want to go back to the refuge.'
By now her voice was dissolving---'I'm so sorry'---into sniffs.

She let go, and swung slowly out into space on the end of a rope. Then
swung back. And rather heavily, with the side of her body, hit the rock.

---'What is this, Disneyland?' Hella asked.

---'I'm sorry?' asked the girl. She was swaying at face level, her feet a few
inches from our faces.

---'We climbed so high only to reach Disneyland?' she asked.

What she meant: here, as in life, every wood a nature trail, the water
sports potential of every river fully utilised. There are too many of us;
either we need a new morality, or else new virtual joys.

---'Isn't Europe a scream?' was the reply.

We followed the party to a refuge, candles in its tiny windows, perched
on a bleak snowbound saddle on the edge of a moving drop.

---'Don't you just love it?'

One gable-end was made from a cleft rock. The cleft just too small to
work your way through, but you could see inside. Old bottles and baked-
bean cans, some black earth, and a few leafy, dark-loving plants.

---'It sure is different from the States.'

Hella, drawing her face reluctantly from the cleft to say, under her
breath:

---'Thank God.'

---'Racist?' I asked her.

Later, as clustered round a hissing *Tilly* lamp we slurped packet soup
from chipped tin mugs, Jo-Anne relived.

---'We were in the clouds! It was great. No, it was. Fair stuff.'

Meanwhile seeing Hella through their eyes. She made them shy. Which
made my heart press on the nerves in my throat.

We slept in pigeonholes on bare wooden planks, an arrangement I had
seen before in a weed-blown concentration camp. Above and below
was gentle breathing, and from time to time a smudged, wavering form
climbed gently down to go outside. Lying naked in a single sleeping bag,
on her naked body: we ended up of course by fucking as silently and
effectively as possible, like a grub. Even the whispering of the sleeping
bag over rough wood seemed loud. And as for our breath. Afterwards
she seemed to swell with silence. There were heavy tears in the air. The
air smelt of them. Placing her lips against the folds of my ear, she was
whispering.

---'What?'

---'No, I mean the bodies get in the way of the fuck.'

---'That's not fucking.'

---'What is it then?'

A stirring and a pure, resonant moan from between the boards above
our heads, and we fell silent. It was only a sleeping dreamer. Then, Pluto
from the floor beneath the pigeonholes, growling and yelping quietly in
his sleep. Soon she was whispering again.

---'Pluto,' she said. 'Now ...'

---'Yes.'

---'I want to tell you something.'

---'Go on then.'

---'It's important.'

---'All ears.'

---'I love you.'

A silence.

---'You exaggerate.'

---'I love you.'

Fear.

We were away before the Americans, still on Eastern Standard Time, were up, leaving a temporary farewell note scrawled in her neat loopy script on the misted diamond of glass in the door.

The crisp air smelt of cordite. One wall of the refuge, as I have already said, was built into a split rock. This rock - creamy, rounded, with a black cleft which had ferns growing out if it, and inside, on the gritty black earth, a few old Pepsi cola bottles - gave me an erection. Bestiality, arborophilia, lithophilia. 'Life: to have erections,' says Flaubert, and if he is right then being with Hella was also life. It was as if, like the symposium, like all of this in fact, these rocks were another side-light on her. Because their form was her form. Almost exact. When bending over, naked, turned on. It would be fairer to say her form was theirs. There is also a painting by that old squanderer of genius *Avida Dollars*, of a girl leaning on a windowsill. *Stupet Arius*. This was her shape. Out of this world.

But then of course, behind these rocks, behind the refuge, that immense drop. Scary, inviting. Weird. And, because the sun was only just rising, pitch-dark in its depths ...

The way led up again. We had no choice. It was either back or up. We couldn't---didn't have it in us to---go back. So we climbed the summit to the left, as you looked at it, of the refuge: high, rounded, almost a mound, striking not in its shape but its enormity. This was when the postcard blew away. She had paused to pick ours out from the various peaks whose heights and names were stencilled on the sky when the wind snatched the creased and flimsy thing out of her fingers: some places don't like their names.

Running over the snow after the postcard, ungainly like a spaceman she pitched forwards and grazed her chin, which became red and varnished, just as had her knees and hands in the railway station; it was as if it was wet paint she had skidded across, not snow at all. In the sunlight her lips were burning, pale orange against this red. And her blue eyes mauve. And her bright-tipped nose already peeling: it looked like someone had coated it in melted wax. So kissing this face, and touching all parts of the clean, hard body.

At the top, wading through snow, Pluto bounding along in our footprints. Streamers of fog, aligning themselves to the shape of the summit. And, in a wavering, dappled patch of sunlight, a team of meteorologists and astronomers scattered about at the entrance to their snow-hole, breakfasting in snow-mitts, goggles, furs. We must have seemed, walking on in flimsy clothes and trailing a particularly dogged dog, like back-packers stumbling onto a film-set.

They were only too pleased to see us, laughing and bouncing about as they fried up kidneys and eggs and fed us Jägermeister straight from a bottle to which they'd attached a black rubber teat. Their hilarity and joy: it was their last day. Their replacements (our Alpinists) were already on their way. Far away, far beneath, through sliding, luminous rents in cloud, we watched them through a monocular, lumbering steadily upwards beaded on their rope.

Hella discovered an amateur mathematician amongst them and got into some kind of tipsy controversy. She accused him, and by implication maths, of having too little interest in its roots. Of being interested only in what it could do, in its immense power, in where it was going. By roots she meant what it thought it was; how it justified itself. 'Perhaps, as Popper says,' she said, 'such questions are sterile.' Hella was a Popperian.

---'Perhaps, okay!' said Odon, all significance.

---'But sterile things can be interesting. The world a poorer place without geldings, worker bees, castrati and mules. So what is it? A deductive structure, a set of rules for the manipulation of theorems. Plus of course a collection of the most interesting theorems and manipulations. But what relation to reality has this set of rules and theorems?'

---'It is reality, its deepest structure. Look at the music, look at the rainbow. Look at everything, in fact. Math. In structure. Math is, furthermore, a means of transporting from one bit of reality to the other. If you are knowing there are three bananas and four pears you are knowing (without looking) there are seven units of fruit.'

Odon's line, this. I tried to think of something to add.

---'No; it isn't reality,' Hella said, 'but a model of the truth, of the structure of reality. The maths we know, we have made, is a model of the real maths, the true maths, which probably resembles it, but not necessarily identically.'

So why did she love me. Not only wet, but I couldn't speak like this. Couldn't even think like this.

---'Ah, *truth*!' said Odon, histrionic now. 'Truth! She is believing in truth. And I was thinking she has been a physicist. Physics, you may be knowing, has no need of that concept!'

The exclamation contained in his smug and witty smile. He had a blonde beard and very bright lips. A wide forehead, and the insolence of money so far as I could judge.

Hella getting shirty. She could bear contradiction if she knew she was right. The vice of the intelligent---they don't like being wrong. Not used to it.

---'Yes, I believe in truth,' she said, too loudly and too fast. 'The cat neither alive nor dead, but no-one said it had to be. It is the 'neither' and the 'no-one' which I mean by 'truth'. And if there are multiple aspects to reality, fair enough, as long as some of possibility is excluded. In this case 'multiplicity' is the truth. Or no, not truth but a model of it. The truth itself invisible. We can only see the models, and match them up with what, assuming causality admittedly, we may call truth's consequences, or rather the models we make of these, which we can also see and call reality. And mathematical models (even primitive ones: '1', '+'), as all others, may well be imperfect, may well not match the models of the consequences in the world. And even if they do match, we have no way of knowing they always will. Problem of induction. Such imperfections sometimes show up as paradoxes and contradictions.'

Perhaps she wasn't wrong. She didn't sound it.

---'As?'

---'Well---don't hold me to this, but I'll give an example. If we look
carefully enough, our circles are really n-gons where n has tended to
infinity---no, this is simpler: if we look carefully enough, the lines from
which we make our triangles have jagged edges. We have this paradox: a
right-angled triangle ABC with two sides of unit length; the other side
by Pythagoras has length root 2. And yet, if you resolve this other side
into steps, it has length 2, and continues to have length 2 as the size of the
steps tends to zero. Something changes at the instant the steps disappear.
That suggests something is wrong. With a vital concept (tending to a
limit) if not with 'our' world, or even 'the' world.'

---'Well, yes,' he said, looking battered, 'but they don't make it any less
useful.'

---'Our positions reversed. Still useful, but less true.'

Hella had a reasonable joy in equations, at what they signified, at the
beauty of mathematics, but she also had an extra, mystical joy in the
pure symbolism itself, in the notation, in precise meaning, in the same
way as she might have taken joy both in reading and in listening to
a piece of music. She managed to bring various senses to bear. And
it wasn't only this, either; the notation, the structures of theorems
were toys, and like someone playing with a train set, she was playing
with them, and with the same lust for their miniature beauty, solidity,
character.

---'This is interesting me. In your universe picture then, is math being
empiric or analytic?'

A gust of hatred for him, this Odon, this so-called meteorologist. What
interest could he have in mathematics? No, his interest was in her.

---'Or both,' said Hella, blushing.

---'Yes, both.' he said sententiously.

---'Unless, perhaps, it is not maths but the world which is also analytic.'

---'Maths as empiric, the world as analytic. I like it, yes.'

He smiled, he laughed. I saw his alleged charm. And she was staring at
him with those inflected planet eyes which had so moved Johnstone.
Amongst others.

She spoke meanwhile as if not even maths was wholly right, was only a
model of reality, accurate as Newtonian Mechanics, perhaps, or even a
little more accurate, but not precise. And it was intoxicating to hear her
speak---even if I didn't understand her. Almost as intoxicating as when
she spoke Norwegian. (I can't do Norwegian.) All that occult meaning.
All those secrets hidden in strange sounds. Even the weird way it made
her move her lips and eyes and cheeks and hips, like an actress reading
a poem she has misunderstood. So: the romance of what you don't
understand; it was rather like science; the rainbow was weirder than the
prism, and made your heart boil in a way; the prism only kissed your
cold forehead. As Father Blanès said: '*What more do I know of the word
'equus' when I know it means 'horse'*. And yet, even as I saw this I was coming
to understand her, learning the meaning of her *word*, and learning too
that maybe there wasn't any way round such understanding except
(which was unthinkable) to run away from her, and suffer an eternal
remorse for the worst crime on earth, a crime far worse than the mass
murder of generations of progeny which is its subset: failing to breed
with a girl you could love, failing even to love her, failing even to give her
the chance to turn you away.

What does it mean to be unworthy of someone. Morally? Aesthetically?
Can anyone be unworthy of anyone else, if every human life is of
equal value? Could that mean that, as she seemed to imagine, I was not
unworthy of her?

---'And how is it you do make this model of reality I ask?' asked Odon.

---'In the same way I make any other; by trial and error. The infinitesimal
calculus worked. It successfully modelled aspects of reality. Dubious
(what was it with these infinitesimals?) but it worked; and was accepted
into maths. Later it was improved, and the infinitesimals done away with.
But originally the criterion was empirical. As are the axioms. Especially
(which has a sneaky air, I know) if you look out into your mind as you
look into the world. Because your mind is part of it, if not most or even
all. And then: how does this mind know what 5+7 equals? We do it on
our fingers, or on the fingers in our heads. This is empirical too.'

---'No. We have discovered the axioms in our own minds. They are
how the world has to be to be thinkable, expressed in parsimonious
form. Muß es sein? Es muß sein! (What a comfortable!) Mathematics
is deduced from these, deducible at least. We may be discovering our

proofs and theorems in very strange indeed ways, but what they are are deducible from our axioms.'

The streamers of cloud drifting past my face. I took a slug of *Jägermeister* and passed the bottle on. What a wanker. Just because he wants to look at her underpants we have to listen to this. 'Want some dick?' is all he was asking her. And yet listening to this made her underpants still more alluring. They burnt brightly, especially since they hung somewhat loose now between her legs. He, however, wasn't to know this.

---'All of them?'

---'True. Good friend Gödel,' he said.

---'True?' she asked. Because with a click slither click she was driving him up the stairs. Grasping a *chandelier*, he swung heavily over the room, rather as the American girl had swung. (Perhaps we could get them together. Stratagem of jealousy, this.) Then, like her, he swung back again. Now she had him.

And yet she looked worried.

---'What is it Hella?' I asked.

She started, looked at me, her face darkening slightly.

---'But then---I was thinking---the grammar of proof---I'm worried about mathematics.'

Oriane de Guermantes, at dinner: 'I'm worried about China.'

---'Who is going to be proving the proof,' chorused Odon. 'In the end, its only because it is looking right that we are accepting it. It is not that it is being true---but that it is being unambiguous---or not even that, but that it is being only so precise as it claims to be being.'

Hum.

She stomped around, stomping down snow.

---'Are you cold?'

---'Yes.'

And Odon gave her his fur coat. It was like her hair: yellow sand on the surface and black sand underneath.

---'The theorems of mathematics', she was saying as she slid her arms in, 'are no more than scientific theories; each child, as she learns to count, performs mathematical experiments on her fingers, just as chemistry students, as they learn chemistry, perform titrations. I don't see the difference. No, I don't.'

Her science combined the mystical beauty of strange languages only half-understood, with truth. It was mystical and true. Truth being not true, but mystical.

And yet, there was the blue-stocking side too. All this sounded strange and ill-at-ease in the mouth of a person I knew better naked than dressed, one whose beating heart made the skin vibrate from under the bars of her ribs. Intelligence the gambit of the plain, as heels the gambit of the horse. So what was Hella doing talking like this?

An ugly child perhaps---an ugly duckling? Or is the world less mechanical than we think?

---'*Ja!*, just another empiricist', Odon said. 'And empiricism, as we are all knowing, is now washed up.'

---'Pythagoras's triangles are the white swans---we haven't found a black one yet, in a hypothetical Euclidian universe I mean. What looks like necessity is the carefully engineered, but otherwise arbitrary conventions of proof. Kant's point perhaps.'

The bitter, smoky scent in the pure, blowing mist: someone had been letting off fireworks. And the operatic atmosphere: the sudden choruses. And something wrong with the light. Growing light and dark with no reason. Everything has a reason, doesn't it?

---'And perhaps we *can't*', she went on to say. 'Our minds won't let us. And if so, what do the black ones look like to us? Inconceivable, unpredictable, ineffable, mysterious. This is how they look. But they aren't supernatural.'

---'It is a language, a content-less language, but one being used not only by ourselves to be deciphering reality, but by reality to be expressing himself.'

---'Except language, too, contains its own meta-mathematics. We say *the* number nine, not *a* number nine' she said. 'No: sometimes we say: What's that? Answer: A number 9. Where's it going? Tromsø.'

---'Tromsø?'

---'Home town.'

Why did she have to tell him that. The provincial schoolgirl talking; the ugly duckling from the Norwegian backwoods, with for father a drop-out millionaire, a hip trendy raver with blonde curls, jeans, a white t-shirt; himself the child of missionaries to seamen. And a sensuous Parisian mother having nervous breakdowns on the cold shore, almost as she might have orgasms. To the shush of wavelets. This, probably, what gave her the air of sadness. If, when your mother is the world your mother is mad, well, that makes you sad.

---'And other times: the number nine is the square of the number three. Not: a number nine is the square of a number 3. Why should that be? Odd, isn't it. All the 'a' 9s are simply names for something underneath them, 'the' nine; and we acknowledge this in the way we speak: in the way we speak we are already presenting a metaphysically sophisticated theory of the foundations of mathematics, of the foundations of the world.'

---'Kiss me,' I said to her, interrupting all this. It seemed to me like mutual masturbation. 'I'm not interested in your ideas ...'

Odon glaring at me. Jaw locked and a sudden trembling in his tight blonde curls.

---'... but in you,' I went on, but looking not at her but at him. I meant her, of course. 'The ideas---they're too much. Too relentless. At least, I am interested, but only for what they say about you.'

She blushed. Then, bulky in furs which swung like a bell, she came and kissed me, walking on over-long clapper legs which hung out the bottom. How did she operate them so well? She probably wasn't so much taller or so much thinner than Barb. But how much proportion, how much elegance, formal correctness, even, was crushed in. She, Hella, had tainted Barb, not physically, yet not only spiritually either. Her, Barb's body was clean, was glamorous, was stunning even, but there was virtual dirt in the crevices---between her legs, under the rims of her buttocks or the toe-nails, and where the flesh was nipped into swags beneath the tuck of each shaved but shadowed armpit. Inversely supernatural, and derived, if not from Hella, then from childhood spoiling or trauma. One of those things you can't identify, but which is there, like having eaten a pomegranate in a bad place.

Hella meanwhile had placed her hands on my hips and kissed me. Her face was cold. So were the outsides of her lips. The inside of her mouth tasted warm and sweet.

Odon scowled. Then looked away. Because she was mine, mine, mine. Odon could have Lorchen and Barb.

We could see the weary Alpinists with the naked eye now, fluorescent and mauve on their red rope. Before we left, anxious to get away before this party arrived, we stuffed a white quilted sleeping bag with tinned pizza, tinned frankfurter, tinned cabbage and even tinned bread, and other scientific delicacies surplus to their needs. The sleeping bag was almost too heavy for us and the zip bulged.

And seeing Hella shivering as, having taken it off she held it out to him, Odon told her to keep the coat.

---'No, Hella, you can't,' I said.

---'You will be taking it from me Hella Skippergate. And here, what I shall also now be giving is my address.'

The other meteorologists winking at each other. They didn't wink at me.

---'No, Hella!'

But they didn't wink at Odon either. Hella was nodding manically as he wrote, with somewhat rounded, bright, acquisitive eyes. For the address or for the coat? Or both.

---'High,' she said, 'high. High not on drugs but the world.'

As having waved goodbye at last, we edged away along a slowly sinking snow-track.

On one side, far below us, the map of Spain, on the other the maps of Italy and France. The sky violet and the sun, tiny at this height, almost black. And much nearer, spreading away, but skewed at the wrong angle, as if we were banking steeply in an aeroplane, was a metallic lake.

---'You fancied him.'

---'Who?' She looked astonished.

---'Odon. And why all that pretentious gizzle about maths.'

---'I like it.'

---'Why?' This sounded aggressive. She looked scared. 'Why?'

---'Its mystery. The beauty of any unknown language, particularly a language of signs. You want to know what it says. And when you discover: then, in the eternity of the ideas represented: triangle, class, acceleration, truth, and even proof. And then maths, like music, is unkind to fools. This is why I like it too.'

She wanted to know what equus meant.

---'Music in general being frozen mathematics,' she said with something of Odon's perpetual I have no need of that concept smirk. 'We learn the rules, the operations, the functions; our mind runs a little ahead and we are pleased when the proof of the theorem, so elegantly, comes out right. We are edified, too, if it comes out differently to how we thought it would but (after Beethoven, at least) still correct, and we are wowed, sometimes when the consequences are astonishing, moving, wrong' she said. 'And besides, mathematics is clean physics. Physics is dirty maths. One of the deepest and most beautiful laws of physics is this: that 1+1=2. Beside this, QCD is nothing.'

She was palming her forehead as she spoke. She looked tired.

---'And yet, but that's not quite it. Of a given piece of work, we know immediately whether it is maths or physics. Or do we even know that? If someone was laboriously counting mounds of pebbles before uniting them and counting the result, would we say she was doing maths or physics.'

---'This isn't how we learned the axioms, but how we learned the true theorems to distil them from. So, maths as dirty physics. But that's still not it. Could we say physics is algebra in which some of the unknowns are measurable? And yet, pi was an unknown until we measured it---I guess the measurement came before the calculation. Did trigonometry start as physics and become maths? Algebra in which none of the unknowns are derivable from first principles? But these principles are changing all the time. All the time we learn to calculate things we used to measure. It is possible that physics and maths are the same subject, tunnelling towards each other in different directions. When they meet, offset by only a few inches, a white tie function in the breach. Royalty, diplomats. I would be prepared to go along with this; to tip physics into the black hole of reductionism; but I think I would be wrong. There are new phenomena here, perhaps not just emergent ones. There are things in physics which are in the world and aren't in mathematics. Between circularity and truism you don't get far. This is the fairy-tale world where all the straight paths lead in circles. If you want to get somewhere, you have to try to go in a circle, revolving on your own axis as you do so. Only then do you escape.'

---'Part of what I like about numbers is how quirky they are. The game starts out so simply. And very quickly, asymmetries and idiosyncrasies appear. It is like walking in a garden. Why do there have to be all these different kinds of flowers? Wouldn't one kind do? But it won't. There are hundreds and hundreds of them. So many that very soon you start to hate flowers. You start to pull them out by the roots and tear them up like paper. Ideas are different; you don't have them so you can't tear them up. You say 'whale', but it doesn't mean you have a whale; you say 'unicorn', but it doesn't mean you have one. You say 'infinity', or 'root two'; it doesn't mean we have these things, or can ever have them. Because 'root two' is not root two, but root two's name.'

Relatively simple ideas: but somehow, perhaps simply with the tone of her warm voice, she brought them alive. A scientist's limited, childish art. She pointed up their mystery. But she was still speaking.

---'What?'

---'Were you listening to me?'

After saying which she burned and reddened around her neck.

---'Root two is root two's name,' I said, and she looked at me expecting more. But beyond this I couldn't help. Not being a mathematician. Which may show. Because I am trying to reproduce her ideas not for their scientific content, which is probably contained in her papers

anyhow, but for what they say about her. Because her fascination was
for the extraction of some ideas from others, in which they are not
obviously contained, by means of mathematics. For this programme, but
also for where this program failed, and above all for where it had to fail.
The exhilaration, e.g., and paradoxes of the number line.

She had paused to think.

---'Russell's argument is probably right, which is a pity, because it's more
ingenious and pretty, but less beautiful than Frege's or Meinong's. He's
reduced not only mathematics, but mystery, to logic. And yet, strangely,
that's in line with his character: we discover the laws of nature which
confirm our prejudices, not because the laws we discover are not
objective, whatever that means, but because we are selective in which
laws we find. Unless our prejudices are right, that is. But I forget, you
don't know what I'm talking about.'

It made me cross when she spoke like this.

---'I'll explain,' she said. 'It's like this ...'

But I didn't want to learn from her. We'd passed that stage now. Besides,
even logic has its troubles and its doubts. I didn't need more troubles
and doubts.

By late afternoon we reached the lip of the tilted lake, and followed
it round until we found a place cropped and swollen as a lawn, with a
spring, a tree, the face of a rock---and spread out the sleeping bag and
coat to sit and eat. Opening the plastic stopper of a wine-bottle with a
pop! which made Pluto sit up and look about. He dined on corned beef
out of the tin. Our own private vista of mountains, framed by more trees,
immense but divorced from us, seen through a picture window. Lear's
palette: the violet of the mountains of Palestine or Thermopylae. And
also, the cross-hatching and shading of a sketch in steel-nibbed pen
& ink. They changed as the evening came in, rotated stiffly, enlarged,
distended, twisted.

In the smoking lake I pissed. The ripples radiating over shiny metal. She
was already bound in the sleeping bag, one end pointed as a larva, the
other blunt. She rolled it down for me around her hips, wriggling like
a mermaid peeling down her tail, and inside, willing me to part them,
were soft, warm legs. So, whipping and curling inside it, her legs as open
as they could be, her slender, pliant body stirruped on mine, amongst

the glaciers and the rocks. Long white tubes of breath from her mouth walking across the grass on their ends like snakes. And falling asleep while it was still light, on the edge of the lake, under the face of the rock, hearing her breathing fall into step with the transparent, invisible ripples on a gritty pink beach.

Woken in the darkness by a kiss, and heavy breathing. The rock still hot- -you could feel it from several feet away. She wanted to say again how much she loved me. A sloppy tongue, slid between my lips, investigating my gums. A burning, hairy body pressed close to mine. Pluto, fore paws wrapped round my neck, hind wrapped round my waist, was lying against me and humping. He opened his round eyes wide and held my gaze for a moment; closed them again, and sighed.

Everything has its purpose, if not its cause. (Science the childhood of mysticism, not the reverse). Above me, the rounded mountain, blood-dark and mysterious, something of an astonishing asteroid rising into a brownish sky powdered with stars. Hella, as I looked up at this, shrieked suddenly in her dream.

---'Hella, what is it?'

Her eyes closed, but tears seeping out, and snot bubbling gently in her nostrils. This instability wasn't new, but it was getting worse.

---'Wake up, what is it?' She opened drugged and stupid eyes and looked at me in silence as if I was a stranger. 'Don't frighten me.' My words sounding ugly, false.

---'The dream.'

---'What?'

---'An oily, grooved, black snake-tongue came sliding out through the hole at the end of your ... thing. It flicked some times before sliding back in.'

She closed her eyes to see it again, and shuddered with her teeth together.

---'I don't know. Something strange happened,' she said. 'The world has changed not at the level of nature, but logic.'

This wasn't her. Or was it? Her tits gave the game away, of course, too rich for her spare body. Too dense.

I couldn't sleep again, but lay pressed against her, my knees in the small of her knees, my stomach in the small of her back. I could smell her unwashed hair; the ferrety sweetness of damp wool. A watery mist seeped from the soil and unfurled across the lake. Without dimming the stars: the sky was full, no relief, except around the moon, bright as burning magnesium and blackening a flared corona of sky.

As I watched, it buckled, struck along one edge---silent, as great things are. The earth lurched.

---'Hella,' I was saying quietly, without taking my eyes off a black disk which slid slowly across it. 'Wake up Hella, an eclipse.'

---'What,' she asked sleepily, and turned her swollen face back on her neck, and opened and closed her eyes. 'Why are you whispering?'

---'An eclipse.'

---'Yes!' she whispered, and yawned, closing her mouth with a snap. 'The fullest the moon can get, passing through full and out the other side to nothingness. An eclipse of the moon by the earth,' and turning back again to kiss my nose, rested the side of her head on her hands and went to sleep.

I watched the disk slide away again, the stars dim, the moon and then the landscape grow bright.

---'I dreamed the sun went out, bitten by a snake,' she said, later in the night.

---'Don't you remember?'

---'What?'

---'The eclipse.' She looked blank. 'You don't?'

---'In the night?'

Pettish now:

---'Why 'the fuck' didn't you wake me ...?'

Stale idiom. Imagining some hip English teacher with a patched tweed jacket writing on the blackboard the word slang, and then walking round to the front of his desk and perching on it, his ankle, clasped in both hands, resting his knee while she, in the front row, looked on with serious eyes. And whether he existed or not, hating him.

A thrush was singing in the night. The mist had thickened. Less like water, more like milk. The outside of the sleeping bag was wet, and there was a star-like drop of milk on the end of each of the hairs of Pluto and Hella's coats. But the stars themselves were wavering and going out. She sighed, and then she said:

---'It's getting light.'

A few strips of cloud went pink, and then sudden, dramatic, on the hazy, mulled horizon, a buoyant spark of fire, spreading fast.

She rose too and sitting on a stone in her flimsy blue dress, bent down almost double between her open knees, almost more than she needed to bend, to thread the laces of her trainers. When she had finished she stood up and stamped on the ground a few times. Then looked at me full and holding out her closed fist with an abrupt gesture said:

---'This is for you.'

It was her compass in its black leather box.

---'Why.'

---'It's all I've got.'

When I tried to kiss her, and she turned her head aside, and I ended up kissing a strand of hair and through it the side of her smile.

She went down to the water and dipped some fingers in. She undressed again, lifting the yellow cardigan and dress over her head. Then sucked some water from her cupped hand, and then stepped in.

Shy before the delicate, menacing beauty of her shape. The water rising up her legs until it reached the pornographic level of a stocking-hem. And her back bowed and fragile with cold, so you could see the stumps where the wings had been.

Beyond her was an ultramarine glacier, half-submerged. A *plok* as she squatted. And then a sudden splash; she'd disappeared; and came up later far away, and beckoned. More klaxon than siren, she was splashing and kicking with the cold. A sense, as she stood up briefly on a ledge of ice, streaming water from her elbows and her nose, and waded slowly, heavily out of the water, of the simplicity of her body, of her body as lugged tube.

Knowingly unworthy, I was too shy to leave the modesty of the sleeping bag. She looked too good---her body did. I didn't need someone so perfect to see mine---perhaps how Cupid felt.

But in the end I followed her back in. The lake bedded with something bright blue-green: ice or sand. So clear you could see both the fish and their shadows, and they looked like birds. The chill, heavy bite of the water, an insult. You had to thrash to stay alive. And then, nearing her, her face pinched up, thrashing and splashing too, I had a sudden fear at the height, that I might fall. Unlike her, I didn't want to fall. As through these cold waters---threaded with fish, with two splashing, cooling bodies in them, cooling but still warm at core, thrashing and splashing towards one another, in a cold lake with pink and orange clouds reflected in it, glittering in the climbing sun, set like a stone in an enormous, amphitheatre scooped from the side of a tiny mountain moulded in the face of the rapidly spinning earth ...---we swam urgently to shore, and touched our feet on sand again, and ▢ heard the cry of a beast.

It rang across the lake and echoed off the concave snout of the glacier.

---'Bird?'

---'What bird?'

There, skipping sideways and throwing up his arms with each skip, a naked man, half laughing, half singing, making a fluty sound in a boy's soprano. In his arms a bundle; was it a child he carried? This is how he carried it, but shaking it too, as if to hear if it rattled. He changed legs, and skipped the other way. His heavy cock, as he skipped, flapped or better, flopped. Pluto following him, skipping too. But realising: the deep blue, of sky, only darker, more intense, of her dress, in his hands. With something wrapped in it.

His inhuman noise. A bite of supernatural fear. As naked we came up the pink beach.

Quite unnecessarily, he turned about and passed us again, very upright, legs and arms pumping, like a man with a rugby ball pimping for pursuit. And so silent now that we could hear his breathing; heavy, wheezy, puffy, and also the padding sound of his feet. Angular patches of blusher on his chest and cheeks, and very serious eyes. Pluto, no longer skipping, but aware that something was up, hiding behind Hella's legs, bare like the laws of nature, and looking round at him. And it's true: I too wanted to hide there, behind those curved legs, studded with gleaming drops, and look at him.

---'Like something in a fairy tale. Or out of Lear,' she said, teeth rattling, her cold body glistening. Brown hair was plastered and fanned across her back and threads of water still hung from the ends of her fingers. When he heard her voice he looked at her and tilted his head like a puppy, stopping very briefly to listen.

---'Edward, not King,' she went on. 'The landscape pure Lear too. Like fuck: he got my dress! Catch him.'

Naked, almost hollow, holding herself half-bent like an animal, her body studded with drops of white fire as she came slowly onto the grass.

---'I said get him,' she said through chattering teeth now and bluish lips.

His firm strong thighs and stiff heavy buttocks had something to them of the hinder parts of a bull, though without the bull's pelt---around thigh and buttock he was crinkly, blackish, furred. His heavy beard grew to the outer corners of his startled eyes. And the blue-white underside of his stiffened penis moving over his belly like a windscreen wiper as he ran---or more like a metronome, because counterweight balls slapped steadily away at his thighs. The build of a toddler, this was his secret, and the pumping arms and all the liquid passion of a toddler too. Such men are attractive---they excite the baby-lovers in all of us. Could that be why he was here? To escape the lovers-of-babies, I mean.

If he was simply a drop out, a rat-race refugee who'd smoked too much and, too stoned, shed too much of his material, moral, mental baggage---even his decency, language, and clothes---why did he want hers? Had he changed his mind? Had it been mistake? Was this the first step on the road to suburbia and a solid position in marketing or sales?

So: first the demented businessman, and now this human baboon.
The Americans, too. The meteorologists. And the Alpinists with their
hideous dress-code and unshakeable morals. There was a message
there, but it was beyond me to pry it out. Perhaps I should have asked
her. And perhaps she would have calmed me by telling me the message
was simply this: that we were in it with the rest of them. Eden as full as a
cinema on a wet Saturday night.

She meanwhile was laughing, her two hands covering chattering teeth
and the place between her legs.

---'But he's got your clothes.'

She began to move about, her bent legs clamped together as if she was
afraid she'd wet herself. This flimsy tube; and yet within it lay everything
there was. This was the paradox; more inside than was possible.

But something sexless, too, naked at least. Say sex needs clothes---skins,
furs---to obscure and darken things. And yet: her brave face above this
simple body. It was almost that the body was fancy dress.

---'After giving you the compass, the clothes were all I had,' she said. 'We
bring nothing with us when born, either, except a certain amount of
gunge and blood. And a gust of love. If I wanted to leave the past behind
and embrace the future with all I ever really had: body, spirit, heart, then
he's helped. It's like an hourglass, through which we take nothing.'

She was being stripped down, losing each unnecessary thing. And this
brought all she really had out into sharper relief; made it more visible
and perhaps more real: a cool body, warm heart, hot mind.

---'Put on your coat before he gets that.'

By spirit she meant intelligence I think. Whether it was really so or
not, she saw the world as suggestive, romantic, deep. Watching her was
like watching a film. If the stars are beautiful and the film good. Same
exaltation, same rush, same hinting at, pimping of, truth. Whether or
not it is there.

---'Sad about the yellow cardigan, though. I loved that,' she added as with
one look back and one last frolicsome skip, a saucy curled pink tongue
stuck out, the thief disappeared round the hill's warm, green steaming
breast.

First I gave her my jeans, and wore my cashmere jersey upside down. But my machinery, such as it was, hung out.

---'Tie a knot in it,' she said.

Painful idea. So she took the jeans off again, and put the cashmere jersey on instead, feeding her long legs down the arms. She claimed that the zephyrs were sweet on her bruised lips, and told me I could take that how I would. She wore the pair of gloves on her feet like claws, and smiled at me as, slipping her arms round my neck, she first studied then kissed my lips.

Cold swollen tits, just inside the fur of her coat.

Wishing that I too had swollen tits, to brush against hers.

I hadn't got the jeans on yet. We lay down.

The claws, wrapped so tight around my back that I could see them from the corners of my eyes, even as I kissed her. Sex with a furry beast with cashmere legs. Violet eyes. Raspberry lips. And also a cashmere cunt. It was the singing thief who had brought us this. And yet.

It wasn't necessarily enough. Nothing was restful, nowhere was right. Mountains, wilderness; we thought these would soothe us. And were wrong. Filled with weirdoes and tourists who defied sense. Their behaviour was not law-like. There was no order, no scheme. And, because order or scheme was what she'd taught me to want. Unless those days are over now, those desires misplaced. And while the Americans had been welcoming and the meteorologists affectionate, and even the beast-thief charming in his own private way, and certainly fruity in effect, they tangled the nerves.

So: rolling the sleeping bag tight and rinsing the knife in a stream, which we then followed. Almost at once it joined the river which issued from the lake, improbably enormous, powerful, struggling. A kind of river I'd never seen.

We trailed it amongst stones, over turf embroidered with flowers. Until, after a time of calmness, flowing smooth and black over a wide, flat rock, leaving the safety of the earth it leaped fizzing into space, where swags of ruched foam fell in an endless bride-white scum, and in the depths of uproar strange jets and fuming, streaming fogs drifted eternally about.

---'Not too close.'

Hella, cool tease that she was, had gone far too close to the lip of the cliff. Still wearing the black leather gloves on her feet.

She had to swim in the glacial lake, and now she had to perch, swaying in the fuming mists, on the edge of a cliff. In the shadowy depths beneath, filled with a rising, sunlit smoke, the frothy pool lurched and roared about.

---'Come back, please!'

She turned her head and smiled at me and she stepped backwards now up the smooth rock, muddied by the damp. But her gloved feet were sucked gently towards the edge by the mere wind of the waterfall and the scale of its drop. Her steps took her nowhere; after each step she'd moonwalk back. I couldn't tell if she was hamming it up.

It didn't look so dangerous, partly because it happened so slow. But there was something unattractive in this stationary movement. As unattractive as the stationary movement of a mime artist, or the stationary movement of the waterfall itself.

Something pretentious, grim. Meanwhile her gloved, claw-feet were polishing the rock, kneading the faint trickle which flowed down it into the sweating mud so that now, even as she walked backwards, she was moving towards the drop.

This wasn't funny. And I didn't seem to be able to go to her. This would have been to go with her, but I wasn't thinking about that. There was something in me that needed to carry the news of this dreadful thing, if news there should be, as far as I could into the future. I saved myself in order to remember her.

Anyway, it was obvious that if I went I would only (in my rotating, clumsy slide) push her off. So I spoke.

---'Don't!'

This was all I could think as her heels moved steadily over the muddy surface towards the lip. She was smiling at me. Foolishly.

---'I love you,' she said, with her arms half out, elbows, wrists and fingers elegantly bent.

---'Stop!'

She stopped. For a time, at least.

---'I didn't mean it about the dream,' she said.

She was sliding all the same, imperceptibly, then slowly; and now she began to pick up speed, suddenly half crouched on bent knees like something on a surf-board, as I tried 'Don't!' again and she turned back a sheepish, smiling, consciously loving face as her claws went over the lip, and she crashed on her cashmere backside and sat there, on the muddy rock, her back too straight, a shocked and painful frown on the side I could see of her face.

---'Whoops,' she said, after a bit.

---'Why are you doing that?' she asked. Real curiosity in her voice.

I took my fingers from my cheeks. There was blood on them.

---'Shush Pluto. Leave him be.'

Pluto, squealing and barking, was trying to hang from my elbows.

---'I'm not doing it on purpose,' she added, with a dangerous complacency in her tone---too clever by half, as it were.

---'Hella. It's not funny. Don't.'

She was trying to turn herself round.

---'I've got to, somehow.'

Now she was lying flat on her belly, her legs outstretched over the drop.

Holding two tufts of grass. One for each hand. The gloves on her feet dropped and fell together, spinning as rapidly as cogs.

Would she?

---'Don't move. I'll find something.'

---'Don't be stupid. What are you going to find?'

---'My trousers.' Taking them half down. Then: ... 'A stick!'

Waddling urgently towards it, I snapped it off.

But she was panting as, by the means of grass, and her fingers spiked into mud, and the pressure of her bare toes, each working independently, once they found a purchase, she worked her way up.

---'Wait for the stick!'

She was already standing there, looking down at her body, the muddied cashmere, down about her ankles, the mud pasted in her sexual hair and the muddy feet.

---'That was close. Am I an accident 'waiting to happen', or what?'

I was already pulling her up the hill towards a tree. I clung to it and her, and wanted to cry. All she wanted to do was laugh. I was beginning to realise the obvious - that abstract intelligence was a two-edged sword. Hella falling, but Hella, adorable. Pluto, sorry I mean Plato, says you can't see when you come back into the cave. And the cave has dangerous things in it, like waterfalls. But some people---very few---love you more for what you have seen.

---'Never a dull moment. We're having 'a scream'!'

And yet, too, the strange thing is, there was. This wasn't dull, but happiness was. Eden as nice to visit but a hard place to live. If only one pomegranate tree, there were too many figs.

Anyhow, this was where the trees began. Mine had been the first. Its bark silver, flecked with marks, almost scaled. Finned, almost. We looked down on a sea of cloud in which floated blue wooded islands, some with the gleam of tiny waterfalls hidden in the trees. In reality, of course, these were not islands at all, but peaks. As we looked the sun, levering itself up over the higher mountains, reached the cloud and in a rapidly running wave of light turned it gold, and the wooded islands brown. But each island still had a far blue side and, like us, cast a long blue shadow over the curved and wrinkled clouded skin of earth.

And out into the universe.

---'Happy valley, lost world,' she said; 'Eden; promised land. Here we will love each other until you die, when I won't understand, but howl all night, lying on your cold, still, and very straight-faced body, and then before it rots bury it in a hole dug with fingernails and covered up with stones. No cross; we are before the cross; we don't need suffering and evil here.'

---'I die first?'

---'Oh, but you do, my child,' she said.

I was pained, sometimes, by this way of laying not only all her cards on the table, but all mine. She really knew, and it spoiled the game, revealed the plot. Sometimes she was too clear, too good; not dirty, evil, twisted enough. Some things which shouldn't be said.

---'How come?'

---'It isn't true. You know that, don't you,' she said, looking sadly at me. 'Will you be okay? Without me, I mean.'

This worse! My tongue crawling to the back of my throat like someone else's finger. But when she said she loved me: there too, fear.

Nothing was right. *Could* be right. As we turned and watched the sun, buoyant in the liquid sky. The mist beginning to melt. Whispery strings of it, hooked, notched, rose up and disappeared. A whiff of resin. Pluto, on his bum, his forelegs straight and his head erect and proud as any cat's was looking at us for a sign of what was expected of him. When Hella smiled and laid a cupped hand on his skull, he softened his face and panted. When she frowned and looked back down on the dispersing mist, he stood suddenly, wagging a stiff bouncy tail, and began to bark.

That dog barked too much. Then, dancing around, catching his breath, and going down on the flex of his forelegs, he laid his chin on the ground between them, and looking up at us, his wagging bum still held high, and the effort of turning his eyes skyward wrinkling the soft black fur of his face.

And suddenly frisking off; jumping up and twisting like a fish, barking, throwing himself about. We were his parents, he our child. And this made him jubilant. But a twittering, the sound of feathers from under our feet, and a blackbird he'd disturbed fluttering away with a long earthworm, knobbed towards the middle, twisting and whipping in its frogged yellow beak.

Hella looking suddenly at me.

A sense of the bird holding the worm gently so as not to sever it, and lose the halves in the grass. From which its wings had brushed the dew so you could see the marks like footprints. And Pluto chasing after them, barking, snapping, and jumping up. Until he ambled back, nonchalantly snapping at flies. He hadn't meant to catch the blackbird anyway. Reality playing it cheap again. Flooding us with meaning, or the appearance of it.

---'That's it perhaps,' she said. 'Allegory, and what's that other thing that Dante is supposed to use, antiphony? Analogical meaning? No. Being the structure of the world. Romanticism is realism. Etc.'

Loving her in all the ways: the way my heart kept beating---scared of her, yet also able to see her beauty in the way you look at a picture; but that really only after both before and after coming inside her. And--- reasoning passion. And---sexual passion. All of them pointing the same way, like vector multiplication as she would have said. And yet too tired to ask her what she meant. Because of something resembling another organ note, or even the foghorn of a steamer, silent yet filling the whole atmosphere, giving me a fright, making my lips taste bad.

Was it friendship, perhaps?

---'Ouch,' she too said.

---'What now?' Fighting back my own tears. Trying to talk with a steady voice, to walk with steady feet and knees.

---'That feeling. Like music. And what it does. Tickling the temples. From inside. Sucking out tears.'

I didn't want to let her see my tears. We spent the morning climbing down.

5

It was sweeter here. Even in her iris coloured eyes, cold blues and cold whites were replaced by warm yellows and greens. The river settling down, calm and sluggish, on a bed of eggy rocks which wound amongst pines. And the sun so hot that it dried the black mark of each tiny ripple instantly in a small puff of steam. An overgrown mule-track followed the river. Where the bank was gnawed away it had fallen in. We travelled slowly---she had bare feet.

Then there was a railway, coming unexpectedly from a tunnel. One of the two lines unused. Small pines and spiny shrubs had grown up between the cracked wooden sleepers, and the rails themselves had turned ginger. On them, palest green imaginable against the ginger, crickets whirring away, stalked by green lizards.

The other track still carried traffic. Although there were tufts of dry, cricket-coloured grass on the sleepers, and also in the gravel roadbed, the polished top of each rail shone.

Soon the path we had followed down from the mountain abandoned us altogether, doubling back to climb a tributary---or perhaps simply going on by train. We followed the railway, something unpleasant in the spacing of the sleepers making us take mincing steps, or giant, pacing ones. The gravel track-bed was too sharp for her. The best way was to walk along the polished lines, holding hands. This soothed her feet. Until with a screech of rage a train rolled up behind us, scattering us down the embankment and chattering past, its empty carriages made of varnished matchboards, with balconies at each end panelled in wickerwork, like a wild-west train.

Something else was happening. A further shift in landscape, another modulation in field and hill. It was a history lesson, following after the metaphysics, geology and geography: barren snows, primeval woodland, and now the first hints of the human arts: agriculture, architecture, even engineering. But still with the steady, unconscious purpose of web or aphis farm; doubtless, faithful. The valley opened reluctantly into pastures, cropped tight as lawn. And above us when we came round a bend, crowning a round hill, nipple-like and rosy in the sun, a rambling half-fortified farmstead with yellow walls and peeling green shutters, some closed, some dangling. At our feet as we looked up, the river hissed and rumbled through the stones. And Pluto, suddenly: the way he stood. Looking on. A bolt of fear at this. The world as language, saying garbled things.

In the garden: gooseberries, apples, blackcurrants and redcurrants. The grass here rank and overgrown. The sky so dark a blue that I thought it was going to rain. But all colours apart from this were bleached. Even the colours of her eyes, her lips, as she shook wasps from the holes in half-fermented peaches. She had fruit juice coming down her chin. When I kissed her, she smelt of peach. Tasted of it.

But we ate so much we gave ourselves diarrhoea. The colour of the unused rails.

Drunk on all this, I stepped in hers. She thought this very, very funny. So funny she couldn't speak, her nose ran, and tears flowed out of her reddening eyes.

In the ground nearby, feral onions and potatoes. But all overgrown, tangled in strings of honeysuckle and sweet-pea. Pinned up everywhere, lobed and fingered honeysuckle flowers. Blindly she took down a flower, her face still wet with tears and snot, and put it in her hair. The ear and the flower: lobed, fleshy, sucking in the light; and then the grained sheen of her hair. In this strangely bleached light, like waxed beech. And beneath it, her skin, swimming, inviting eyes. And pursed red mouth.

Exploring the empty rooms. Dusty floors, dusty furniture. Inexplicable objects: shaped woods, iron bands, leather pads and pouches leaking horsehair and wool. And in the cellars, cut from living rock, four wooden tuns the size of garden sheds, their staves shuffled and hoops loosened by drought. Reminding me of the catch in the story of Diogenes---not remembering what the catch was, but remembering there was a catch. It was cool, even cold down here. The smell of earth. Going back outside was like coming out of an air-conditioned cinema into the sun. A warm curtain, the crickets, the smell. Coming to rest in a garden gone wild; exotic beauties choked and screaming in an undergrowth of thistles and nettles. Where, her pupils unnaturally large and, teeth nearly closed, an unconscious expression on her face, as if to suggest deliberately to me, self-consciously, that it wasn't me she was

staring at so hard, but the future of the universe she drew me down
beside her and wriggled underneath.

Waking towards evening. Exploring the grounds. On the far side of
the deserted farmhouse a stream flowed into the river, and up it was a
tinkling pool, glimmering under leaves. The flat rocks which edged the
stream had the slightest gradient, so that the pool was hot as a bath at
the edges where it was only a few inches deep.

There had been no reason to climb the muscular, tendony trunk of an
enormous overhanging beech. Pluto looking up as we receded, panting,
showing us his black lips, yellow teeth; swinging his tail. The beech-bark
as finely pored and slippery as skin. I remember her whitish limbs (while
they were still that) clinging to one of these branches: her legs and arms
wrapped round, tight, distorted, her tits displaced, her white bottom
with its dark notch exposed, offered to the tree's massive trunk, and a
clanging sting of jealousy for the tree---way off the scale of the ludicrous,
but felt.

What we found near the top of this beanstalk amazed even us. Because
working our way out along a spar, our feet on one branch and our arms
round another, we alighted on an overheated lawn, wedged against a
lichen covered cliff. In it---the blued round entrance of a cave. With
tints of green, brown, black in it, like steel which has been overheated.
And this lawn: paved with both grass and herbs, and walled with hazel,
bramble, broom and gorse. Strangely inviting place. Something of the
nesting box: the plywood platform and the neat round hole. From it, safe
at last, and somehow very proud, we looked out over a wood---a world---
steadily turning orange. Not in the autumn---yet---but in the evening.

The trees mainly ash, hornbeam and beech, with leaves so perfectly
notched and scalloped that they seemed moulded out of chocolate and
wrapped in shiny-green foil. Their branches hanging in such a way that
they formed a gentle tent to one side of our platform, and when the sun
was too hot and yet the cave too cool, offered an ideal shade.

Vaguely, above the flickering crickets and through the trees, once or
twice a day, with the screech of a hysterical bird, the steady canter of a
train.

---'Everyone wants this,' she said. 'Everyone wants to be in love and live in
a cave.'

Someone had lived here before us. At the cave's mouth, a ring of white stones around old blue ashes, pierced with sprouts of grass. The skeleton of a brolly. And inside, a bed of dry bracken edged with stones. Pluto emerging proudly from the brambles onto the lawn, with burr-filled ears and trouting about. Snorting, snuffling. Lifting one forepaw, staring into the darkness, he barked.

The ashes of the fire said 'light me', and we did. The bracken bed said 'make me', and we did---burning the old bedding and making new. Hella in the twilight, playing not at houses but at caves, gathered ears of wheat and barley, crushing them on a flat rock with a rounded stone which lay beside it, and made one small biscuit---crunchy, damp.

While just above the long blue hills the sun like a wasp in marmalade struggled to escape from stringy, orange, wadded clouds, and having done so shone directly through the leaves, making the flames transparent and ashes bright.

Drinking rosemary tea from a half-crushed aluminium pan found in the farmhouse. And dreaming, meanwhile, of a lambskin wedding-dress for her, closed on the breasts but open over a flat brown belly, soft thighs and tight, short, lambskin draws. And for me, rabbit skin chaps and a deerskin cloak with antlers on, and then, through the eye-holes in the deer's flopping face ...

The glitter of my eyes.

And of course, a flint razor and all the comforts of freedom. The dream of a free future; because we too, in our cages, wanted out. We are cruel to all animals, including ourselves. To recover the animal, and to reintroduce a breeding pair into the wild: this a valid career. Not just in sex, in everything.

So we stayed. Day after day with nothing happening, until there were enough of them to become indistinct, more a rhythm of states of the light than days. On one, in the pool at the foot of the beech tree, a pair of swans, with all the drab grey cygnets looking out at us like toy ostriches from their perch between the cob's arched wings. On another, a shed antler. On a third, a Land Rover in a clearing with saplings growing through its open bonnet---and on a fourth a dead donkey with, beside her, a dead foal. And once, hidden in the bushes not very far away a secret cataract, with a beach of green pebbles and a potholed rock under a fan of hazel leaves on which she lay, true child of the arctic-circle, knees hugged, eyes shut, outstaring the sun through fretted leaves.

She won; it was the sun who looked away - each day, as she lay there, it grew dark.

As did she, until her face was darker than her eyebrows and her hair, and her body smelt alien, sweet, healthy, and fermenting. And when she spoke, a heavy beauty in her inconsequence, so that when she said *'Shall we go for a walk?'* she meant *'I want a child now.'* But carrying her in the opposite direction was another force, which made the eyes shine in the darkening face and which made her soppy, clinging, and eager to cry. And my heart beating, as she cried. In the darkness, hitting the edge of your head on the absolute: it hurts. And there isn't a rational answer; no one knows what is happening. Words can't describe nor explain. The bubbling froth of excitement, having caught hold of her tail, and being determined never ever to let go, however fast she moved, or changed. Turning back towards me, still so doggedly hanging on, she tried to cling to me, to hold my tail.

Which wasn't right, but wrong. What was wrong? Nothing was. If your life, your history, is merely the by-product of your search for it. Why, on meeting the snake, was Eve turned so ferociously on? Why did she snatch at and share the pomegranate? To get out of Eden, of course. To grow up, leave home, go away. To fuck off, to fuck and to bear. So that if, by some trick of fate we found ourselves returned here, and without a real snake this time (the buzzard/eagle/blackbird combo having seen to that), there was still something, mindless, boring, serpentine about it; it didn't seem the answer after all. Too corrupted for that. Us, I mean. Or me, at least. Because things are different now. The same truths don't work. Cocteau says: *We know more than the ancients. They are what we know.* Our position being still worse. We know Cocteau too. So that the problems we thirsted for, keeping dry, gathering food and wood, and going across to a slimy trickle off a moss-deep rock, garnished with ferns, to fill a half-crushed aluminium pan with water---these were not the right ones after all. The tax-return and the bank manager, the employer and the landlord had been maligned. We---I---needed them. Perhaps needed even Waddington. And Leicher. And Modestine Auch, is what I mean.

---'You know,' she said seriously, shaking me from my thoughts; 'There won't be any going back for me now.'

Again the chill bite of fear. These things too big, too fast. You fool.

Still, she was happy here, day after day, coiled on her rock, under her fan of hazel leaves, strands of gilding hair spread across her darkening face, the sun's warm hand through leaves on her belly, as if turning yellow and brown was a valid act in itself.

After gorging myself on a breakfast of peaches, nipped and guttered by the wasps, and then, half-drunk with half-fermented peach juice, having parted her legs and lips and nipped in turn and fucked her, becoming one animal, with the same reflexes, silk then ratchety movement; breath and even voice, first gentle, then harsh---there seemed nothing else to do. She, who drew pictures on my face first with peach and then her own juice, and finally with mine, would lie there, still sticky, her only further gesture a coil (in the green darkness of our laurel toilet) of resinous, ginger shit, and seem easy, calm, at rest. 'Slow down,' she told me, several times. She didn't understand my unease, disease, even, and restlessness.

Nothing is unmixed: this is what I am trying to say. Pluto was happy. Hella was happy. And I was bored. New troubles rise like moons, behind the mountains we have climbed.

Or every bed has peas. What next? Something had to give. I started by building a dam. The pool didn't need deepening but I deepened it, and changed the noise we lived with from a steady tinkling warble to more of a greedy rush. Then, with a pine brand I explored the cave. No good; it was floored in water, deepening at the same steady angle as the pool outside---the same stratification to the rocks. I had time to see that the long thin leaves which had settled all over this inner pool's floor in a strangely regular, geometrical pattern were really cream coloured fish. Pure cream, like cream paper, stained orange by the failing light, and with blackish smudges for eyes.

And then the brand went out. The sense in the dark was that the mouth of the cave was where the roots were, that in some strange way I had got inside the beech tree I had been so irrationally jealous of. The cave branched like the tree: twirling passages like nasal passages. Anyway, what was interesting here was that, if the cave was the inside of the tree, in any sense, it was still the tree she loved, climbing about in it naked, and getting the insides of her bare arms and thighs dusted with green.

For obvious reasons perhaps. The horsewoman in her, the rich man's daughter. Or the girl. I was into the cave.

---'What next?' I asked, coming out blinking and rubbing my eyes Platonically. 'What shall I do now?'

She had no answer, lying on her rock. She opened her eyes briefly, then closed them again, indifferent.

---'And how can you lie there like that?'

Pluto, beside her, opening an eye and looking pained.

---'By dreaming', she said, the back of her hand on her own eyes. One leg was cocked up, and its knee leant inwards over the other. A black crack, of varying thickness, where the backs of her thighs touched.

---'What of?'

---'All there is. The world. Universe.' Only her lips moved when she spoke.

---'What about it?'

---'Working it out.'

Some of the forced serenity of someone asked the time while doing a sum.

---'Working out the universe?'

---'Working it out.'

From anyone else this would have been a joke. Oriane de Guermantes again, still worrying about China. But Hella was the world, and like the world she had her own ontology. And like the world she had her ludicrous side. Her foolish poise, her un-self-critical earnestness. And I was bored of it. I'd had enough. As quietly as I could I went away. She heard me step into the water and asked:

---'Where are you going?'

---'Don't know.'

---'Don't go', she said.

---'What shall I do then?'

---'Talk to me.'

We sat in silence. Pluto sighed.

---'What do we do with ourselves?' she asked eventually. 'We're not here long.'

---'That's what I keep asking.'

---'I want to know what kind of chilly universe we two warm animals are running through.'

---'What are you talking about?'

She, too, sighed and said:

---'So that we'll love each other more.'

She achieved her aim, though not in this way. I was less interested in her ideas than in their strange effect coming through the swollen lips of a noble, shy, and pretty girl.

---'I'm worried about what our theories mean, beyond what they say they mean. I was taught that any 'why?' beyond perfect predictive ability is meaningless. For instance, in QED we have probability amplitudes, which can be represented by imaginary numbers, and it all works perfectly in those situations simple enough to do the sum. But what is going on? The question is formally meaningless. Primitive constructs like causation fall apart. And yet I want to make a picture, to ask why---'in human terms'---the system behaves so. Really I'm asking what's in it for me. I admit this. Physics is inhuman, and I am not. And I don't want to be.'

I screamed. Which is to say, I said:

---'Grotesque fallacy. The mathematics is a description of what has happened and a prediction of what perhaps will happen. It's not for you to go on adding entities you have no evidence for in pursuit of a fairy tale.'

---'That's the standard view. The dendrologists leave out the dryads. But provided we admit we're over the border into metaphysics, there's no harm in dryads. There may even be good.'

---'And we have to, anyway,' she went on. 'As the English poet Auden
said: 'Look if you like but you have to leap'. We have to look, even if its
dangerous. Perhaps we look because it's dangerous. So we have laws; they
exist, nature obeys them, or they obey her. In one sense, they are simply
another angle on the same phenomena: they are nature. And we can
ask, not only what do they mean, but what is beyond this? Am I really
expected to believe that nothing is?'

Sitting up, she withdrew the hand from her eyes. She clasped her knees,
distorting her breasts. Each nipple just missed, just kissed, the outside of
each knee. Her blunt, soft face looked at me somewhat seriously. Did she
really imagine that, naked, to the sound of a river, on rocks almost too
hot in the sun, with the smell of the sun on her skin---even under her
arms, between her buttocks---she could get away with this?

---'And I'm interested not only in whatever is behind what is expressed by
the laws. I want to go further. I want to look at what is behind law itself,
behind the existence of law. My interest being in the details of physics
not only for what they reveal about the structure of the world but that
of existence. I want to rip off the mask of the infinite regress and peer
into the undying eyes of God.'

Pluto getting up wearily, yawning, disturbed by her passionate tone.

---'Why do our laws have this characteristic beauty and simplicity,' she
said more soberly. 'Why is the world so simple? Apparently so complex,
actually so simple. Unless this simplicity is another level of appearance
above a writhing reality. But I don't think so. It is just as when you are
learning calculus, say, and someone sets you a difficult differentiation--
-you know you are right when the answer starts to come out neatly, and
all the terms cancel. It is as if someone has done this for us,' she said, 'has
set us a complex problem---complex but just within our reach---and
hidden within the problem the very information that our solution,
when we find it, is right; there is a tick, or a golden star, a v. good in red
pencil hidden beside the answer. Why, she asked, is physical law like
this?'

---'I haven't the foggiest.'

The serious face turned my way, uncomprehending. She went on.

---'It's not quite in the spirit of the production, is it, to go up on stage
and poke around behind the scenery. We are supposed to stay in the

stalls until we hear clapping, and then clap too. But it doesn't last long, this performance, and there is no evidence to suggest an encore, not to speak of a very long run. So I want, while I have the chance, to find out if I can how it's done. Or put another way, why mathematics is so good at describing the universe. Why its descriptions are so simple, so powerful. Of course, if it wasn't, there wouldn't be a mathematics, which I think is called begging the question, but it's still worth asking. It still has something to say about the world. Mathematics has evolved to describe the world; but the world must have certain structural characteristics to be amenable to such description. Why? Why does it have these characteristics, and what are they. This last is an old question, of course.'

She looked like she was about to cry.

---'Careful.'

---'What?'

---'You'll go mad.'

Her eyes: they had turned right round in their sockets and were looking inside.

---'I won't get anywhere of course---I'm a physicist not a charlatan. These questions are formally meaningless, or at least have no empirical content. They are not falsifiable, to use Popper's word. This is moonlighting on my own behalf. I need to work it through. Unfortunately, I'm like Popper, writing his great book anti-Marx and anti-Plato without access to their works. That goes for me: I too am marooned, though not in New Zealand, but physics. If he didn't have a copy of *The Republic*, I don't have metaphysics. Of course, he did better than me. But that doesn't matter. You can't go wrong when you do things for their own sake: cookery because you are hungry; metaphysics, curious; sex because you are in love.'

She reddened.

---'Otherwise, and it happens, the world dies on the branch, before the serpent even gets to stiffen, and penetrate cloven Eve.'

As she spoke, moving her own lips, sensuous, serious, looking out at me through her water-coloured eyes---and making my heart reel and clutch and lurch.

---'There are various possibilities visible even to us. That our laws are accidental statistical regularities for instance. Any bounded segment of space-time will have law-like regularities---they are statistically inevitable. In other words, given any world, you would find regularities which you would identify as laws; there are redundancies even in the random number table. Don't look alarmed. I don't believe this.'

She softened her nose and her eyes.

---'It's only an idea, but I don't like it, it's repellent. And somehow related to the idea that creation violated the second law of thermodynamics, which is really no more than a probability law, by chance alone, and thereby 'wound up' the world and made us possible.'

---'Questions like these lead very quickly to the question 'is the world real or ideal' or, if you prefer, 'is it there at all and if so, is it how it looks or not.' Because a law is either approximating a regularity in nature or one imposed by ourselves. Any instrument for inspecting reality will impose systematic distortions; some of these we may mistake for laws. And they will be laws, laws not of nature but perception. Even the laws of mathematics and of logic perhaps being precisely those laws capable of expression by a calculus of interconnected nodes---neurons, or viewed logically, bunches of axons which all go live at once. What kind of calculus is this? There is something arithmetical about it; about the summation of incoming signals needed to achieve the threshold to fire the next neurone. But it is more than a clock arithmetic, or muddled range of clock-arithmetics modulo the various thresholds, because you go on counting up to the threshold and then you stop, and also you need time to reset; and there are chemical effects to be modelled. The threshold is a function of time. But beneath this arithmetic is a simple on/off logic, with a modified form of implication: if (> t elements of the class p), then q, where p is the class of predecessors of the neurone q, that is of neurones with axons feeding neurone q. There is more to it than this; for instance, neuronal implication, unlike the familiar logical one which is faster than light, takes place in time.'

---'I catch the drift,' I said, intelligently. Why did I feel this white lie somehow made my teeth protrude?

---'Do you?' she asked, vague. Because she was speaking for herself, she didn't care. 'It is unlikely, of course, that the logical operation of the brain is summed up by a sentential calculus based on nodes and nets of trees (this is an empirical question which may already have been answered), but even this is an interesting start: it suggests some of the kinds of things we might be able to record on this kind of instrument. There is circularity here: we use the instrument to investigate itself, to make these reflections, we use the calculus to describe itself. There is no meta-language. Hence the paradoxes in which we get entangle---get entangle---get entangle ourselves,' she said. 'Strictly speaking, we should not be doing this. A notation or a logic cannot be described within itself; to try to do so will lead to contradictions; such, perhaps, as the tension between determinism and free-will. We need a meta-instrument to examine the mind; a meta-language, as it were, to avoid violating Tarski.'

'Poor Tarski!'

Was there scorn in the blankness with which she looked at me? No, I was paranoid.

---'Since this is not available, as far as I know at least---probably it is - we involve ourselves in paradox and self-contradiction. These are necessary failures, but there may also be unnecessary failures of our own logic and mathematics to precisely model the structure of the mind as reflected in the phenomenal world. These have the same status in the logical domain as what Popper clumsily calls 'falsifications' in the empirical. They are falsifications of our theories as to the *mathematics* of nature and its *logical* structure. All this may account for certain mysteries.'

---'Such as?' When I spoke, I croaked. My throat was dry. Could I see the comic side? Was there a comic side to her earnestness---could it be she was hamming it up? No, it couldn't. She was so much smarter than me, it made me love her and despise her. Also, the unattractiveness of the blue stocking (stroke blue sock). But if she wore blue stockings, they were bright blue, eye blue---and ended at the plumpest part of her thigh, well clear of the central, the essential, the iterative mysteries, and were suspended from a webby, leaf green girdle. And apart from her stockings and her girdle, she wore nothing else---except perhaps a short jacket in fine glossy reddish fox or rabbit or cat fur. In other words---the spanking wet dream of a whip fetishist---intellectually, I mean.

---'As I said, free will and determinism. Inconsistencies which burst our logic: they are the wrong shape; they won't go through the slots. We can't think them,' she said. 'The official line is deterministic, of course. Or probabilistic, dispositional, propensual, which to me have similar status. Physics and biology have still not made space for freedom.'

---'They may be right. It may be an illusion.'

---'Why such an illusion?'

---'It could be what a sum looks like which is too hard for us to calculate. What looks to us like us-deciding is really the sum being done. So if you asked someone doing 5 + 7 what the answer was going to be, he'd say he hadn't decided yet. And in the end he'd come up with his decision: 12. He could have chosen something else; only he chose 12. It's like the point that the only machine powerful enough to calculate what will happen next is the universe.'

She should have said don't try to show off---but she was kind---and there was also, in her---as perhaps in anyone who truly understands something, any poet of nature as opposed to feeling, a natural, instinctive, even lustful teacher.

---'And if you asked the white iris in a stand of yellow why he was white, would he say because he liked the colour?'

---'If I asked you why your eyes were a blue which somehow managed to be both dark, pregnant, saturated, and yet glowing, light, violet or mauve, and had twists of---orange peel floating in it like goldfish---zests I think they're called, and were scorched around the rims of the pupils by the heat of the drill which drilled without boring them---you would say because you chose this. And your hair, how it managed to be blond, and brown, and red ...'

She got cross. When she got cross she got breathless.

---'Eugh,' she said. 'And the baldness, and the cancer, and the squirming, shrieking, unconsolable death?' she asked. 'Ramon Llull in the church with his horse. It doesn't distinguish what we know we don't choose from what we think we do.'

---'It may then be a necessary fiction, advantageously selective, to steer us away from an apathetic fatalism. Determinism wasn't supposed to occur to us; and to snuffle about in it, and see things we shouldn't isn't playing the game. It's like opening your presents before Christmas. The passion for being right is a dangerous one, less dangerous than that for

being wrong, and also less common, but dangerous still. A bit of angelic
humility is in order sometimes.'

---'The freedom of the will; a fiction to stop us walking under cars. No,
that doesn't work either. And anyhow, even free-willers walk under cars.'

Long ago, outside the buffet of the station---she'd rescued me from a sea
of them, each with a burnished bonnet.

---'The will is free,' she said. 'This great programme of physics and
mathematics towards the axiomatization of nature will fail at the limit,
aping an ontological failure of the law-laden model. There'll be a law
of diminishing returns. Just as mass grows asymptotically as velocity
approaches c, we grow thicker as our knowledge approaches total.
And if I'm wrong it doesn't matter much. If free will is an illusion, it's a
pleasant one. I keep the illusion and say: fuck the reality. It's not a bad
deal. It's almost as good to see as to act. I am watching a fascinating
play; it makes my heart beat, it plays me like a piano. And,' awarding
a warmed & scented, soggy kiss, 'the leading actor, the pin-up, the
heart-throb, comes home with me. So it doesn't matter. It's enough to
watch the pageant. All the sweetness of life is in observing, in feeling,
in remembering: things like that; and all the pain in deciding where to
go and what to do, who to date, in being unable to be everywhere and
everything. To be prevented from doing what you want; that is painful;
but to be prevented from wanting to do it? You don't even notice. It
doesn't stop you reading books, that not only the ending but every word,
every letter, every riser and serif is fixed in advance.'

---'That's what you think!'

---'You still love Albertine, her sleepy naked body; you are still sad in case
Fabrizio escapes. You will even read these books again and again, despite
knowing what happens and how they end.'

---'So you are a determinist.'

---'I believe in freedom. This is plan B.'

---'How does freedom work?'

---'How does determinism work. Especially if causation is no more
than constant conjunction or a category imposed on reality. Nature is
ideal, in my view; but it is an imperfect model of a hypothetical reality

which has at least as much structural articulation, although it may be simpler. Paradox. And this is why we are both free and determined. Our model is deterministic, what we see is deterministic, nature is deterministic, but it doesn't matter; it is also unreal and the real-thing (which we can only see bubbling up inside of us) is free. You can see free will as an evolutionary approach to the disasters of central planning, of totalitarianism, of the welfare state. And to grant free will, you have to grant consciousness. Where's the selective advantage of that without free-will. Would self-consciousness have evolved in a deterministic universe?'

---'You're assuming Darwin.' I was pleased. On home ground, at last.

---'Darwin's theory is logic plus time---almost the existential quantifier--- qualifier---what's it called, I can't remember, plus time. That has its place.'

Oh.

---'This says why, but it doesn't say how it's done.'

---'That's difficult. I'll give you my best argument. How do I put it---let's see---yes: believe in free will; then, either you're right or you didn't have a choice.'

---'You've ducked the question. And that calculation doesn't sit very well with the priority of truth.'

---'Truth may not be prior; I don't believe that; it's just that the things which are prior are dependent on truth; it's a necessary condition of the good. That's the way the world is constituted, at least, construed; I don't know why.'

---'So why abandon this in the case of freewill?'

---'You're right; and although I still think it settles the question there is something uncomfortable about these tired ideas, just as there is about the anthropic principle. There's an air of sophism and circularity which ought to be interesting, but isn't---am I boring you?' she asked, and looked small.

She'd seen my face. Tolstoy describes a legal process as like those dreams where you can't move your limbs. This was like that too. A nausea, too, a sick scent, as in the grove of death which said; stay away from here, for God's sake stay away. Sam Coleridge's quicksilver mines. But she---or something in her at least, perhaps her training rather than her---Sam Johnson's bitch up on her hind legs, so to speak - couldn't.

---'The best hypothesis is that the laws of nature, to the extent that they are deterministic (and in turn, determined?), are the laws of perception. These are not free, but what is beyond may be, and this is us. All it is, is us. The paradox is this: the world cavorts about on a flimsy stage built inside our heads; all that is real encloses this; it is the possibility of such a stage, and this possibility has another name; it is ourselves. Because it isn't me you see when you look at me, but your picture of me; it isn't my voice you hear, but your image of it; all these things are inside of you. All admit this. It isn't in dispute. But more than this, when we talk about looking out or looking in, about perception and introspection, is there really a difference? A small scared beast in a dark hole looks out not only on the rolling sea, the torn clouds, but on these arms and legs which wave about, this weariness, misery, desire. All these things are in nature; only the animal is out. The thing which sees what is seen, hears what is heard. Where is it?'

Sitting on a hot green rock, rounded in form as if it had been melted, and looking at the black and white river, the yellow and green trees, the throbbing crickets, the smell of wild figs, and even the dark blue sky with a few white clouds in, and suddenly seeing: these are inside of me. It's no good reaching my hands out towards them---the hands are also inside.

Nausea, pleura-shock. Immense darkened shapes. Moving very slowly, and revolving slowly as they moved. And scaring me.

---'What we think of as the world is not the world at all, but a picture, the theory goes. But,' she asked significantly, tapping her temple and crossing her eyes as if to admit now she was mad - 'what is it a picture of?'

I'd slumped forwards and my chin was digging into my chest. I looked up at her. She'd taken the world away. I'd never thought of this. It may be ridiculous, but there it is. If she was also something of an intellectual wanker, the damage was done.

---'Why are you with me, if the world does not exist?'

---'I told you - truth isn't everything.'

An Inuk, after a terrible gale, was once found paddling a sealskin kayak through Liverpool. A small face, hidden in furs, and a half-eaten walrus lashed on front. When they brought him ashore he died, like a small animal, of fright. I.e. the world didn't look the same any more. It looked different. Very. This sounds stupid---but that's how it was.

---'Stop it.'

It looked like the after-world. His kayak, incidentally, sans walrus, was preserved for many years in a back passage of that Vernesque, Doylic institution, the Royal Geographical Society of London.

---'What's wrong?' She sounded alarmed. At least, my picture of her voice did.

---'It isn't true that the world does not exist?'

---'Are you making fun of me?'

I wasn't. She'd scared me. Ludicrous, but she had.

---'No, I don't believe that,' she said. 'Don't worry. Okay?'

Her warm voice. But: an illusion. I wailed.

---'Okay? Are you okay?'

I think my face was grey. Naïf perhaps, but this particular crisis came late to me.

---'What is it? What's wrong?'

But my heart was bleeding away. I'd gone hypotonic, flaccid, floppy. I felt it, in my limbs. They felt like warmed up *Plasticine*. And she looked sideways, my way, with a smile, and said:

---'Don't worry. There is a world.'

I had to see the funny side---through horror & misery. Even the lovely side. We were---serious. Sitting on a sunlit rock in a river in a wood, somewhere on the surface of a spinning globe. Somewhere in the universe. Somewhere in her mind. Worrying about China.

---'Even when sad, like a rat in the wall, happiness is near,' I said. She didn't hear.

---'Kant's famous view, of course, was that while space and time and causation were merely categories imposed on the world by us, there was also a real-world of things-in-themselves. His things in-themselves partook of the 'divine', moral order, rather as Plato's did. I tread with caution because his prose is so thick, his rigor so---so---well, not-there. There-does-not-exist. Like Marx in this, the prose and the rigour, although Kant had something interesting to say---Marx had mainly addictive lies, sugared lies, though a rich and fascinating procedure. But I wouldn't necessarily follow him, Kant. Why limit reality to the divine? Unless by divination, i.e. definition. I'd say we have things which we suppose to be real; we have an instrument for observing them, which we call the senses and the mind; we concede this instrument has ideas of its own and may not give an accurate picture, and we call this questionable picture nature, included in which is our questionable picture of the structure of the instrument itself, and our questionable belief that there was some kind of selective advantage in its evolution. And incidentally, springing up apparently from within this instrument are various little squirting fountains of will or desire, like hunger, fear, love, ...'

She had gone red. She always did.

---'Yes?'

She was looking the other way. When she looked back, she had drawn her hair across her face; through it her eyes shone.

---'Go on.'

---'Sorry,' she said through hair. 'And what does all this tell us? Plenty---about circularity at least. By this view natural laws are laws of perception, a mesh which minces reality, making the pig the sausage long before we get to eat it, long before we become conscious of it? But there is a pig. And we are townies. We know all about sausages and 'f all' about pigs. *But there is a pig.* And this is what interests me now, not the bright surface but the dark bed of science. Not sausages, but pigs.'

She tipped her face far back and rucked her forehead, and looked down at me out of eyes which were able to look straight down her cheeks, and had the expression in them of a horse which is rearing, as if she imagined she was saying something terrifying and significant, when what she said was harsh, grating---sharp and sterile, rationalist and unsenusual---against a backdrop of fizzy mineral water pulsing from a spring, visited by mesmerising swallows, and the vegetable leaves of a lime tree.

---'So, the structure of the real-thing is constrained by what can be expressed within the structure of mind & senses; but the very possibility of thought says something about the real-thing; this is Kant. The real-thing: even if we can't see it there are still words we can say about it, effects it could not have on our perceptive apparatus if it was not a certain way. Some rudiments of structure have to be transmitted to us. We need to explore the laws of the conditioning of messages, the warping of messages. So that information theory, if illusory, constrains the *Ding-an-sich*.'

---'This *Ding-an-sich*: it sounds like the future.'

---'What do you mean?'

---'What is irresistible; what are we desperately trying to understand, in order to dodge the cholesterol and the knife, what can we see, but only in a shimmering, shadowy state.'

---'Interesting.'

---'How about this, then. In objectivising the will into what provokes it; can I say that the true things-in-themselves are girls. Like you, for instance.'

---'I don't think I like your greasy side. No, with Popper I think I see the real-thing as something capable of being modelled---however imperfectly, which after all is what we are up to---in terms of the perceived universe; I see perception and thought and all the rest of nature not as the truth but as a model of the truth, as well, of course as being an aspect of the truth. And I see science, mathematics, logic as a model in turn of this. But there is a vicious, double circularity there. Nature is a model of the real thing, but is also part of it; science is a model of nature, but is also part of it. So that, incidentally, what we call truth, real-truth would be a picture of the real-thing. But if this truth also exists, the real-thing would have to contain a picture of itself, and the only things that can, given our imperfect arithmetic, are transfinite. So the real-thing, if truth is possible and our arithmetic is accurate in this respect, is transfinite ...'

---'I don't think I want to have to think anymore,' I said.

---'*Lazy* bones.' She kissed me on the nose. Smiled. And said:---'What do you want to do?'

What was there to do? What did I want to do? To breed? And manufacture beauty? Out in the chemical world. But it wasn't so easy to stop her as this---like music she liked to restate and vary her theme.

---'As I said I believe the idealist's regularities, created by our minds and imposed, if it exists, on the real-thing, are models in themselves of its structure, of which we in turn make models called maths, logic, laws. Now, if our models are models of nature which in turn is a model of reality, there are certain implications.'

---'Drop it, Hella.'

---'For instance, our logic, physics, mathematics, seem to organise themselves along axiomatic lines. We use proof and deductive inference. Are we suggesting that the real-thing has a similar structure? And if so, is nature manufactured like true theorems out of a set of axiomatic and probabilistic real-thing laws? This would not have surprised me once. The dream is implicit in physics, isn't it? But then, along comes Gödel, illuminating Hume, if it is true to say that implication is a sublimated form of cause, or cause a matter of identity or definition.'

She spoke as if it was the wolf which came along.

---'Old ground, like the *Quattro Stagioni;* beautiful stuff, but hackneyed, slackened on its frame through imperfect understanding and over-use, a beauty spot too near a station on a suburban railway, its spirit stolen by means of photographs. Gödel finished that dream: the world, unless finite, is either inconsistent, in which case anything and everything goes, or it cannot be obtained from a finite system of axiomatic laws of nature. Unless his proof would not apply to 'propensity' 'axioms'---I'd have to work it though. Or unless there is an error in it, which is not so much less interesting. How do you prove the solidity of your proof, without involving yourself in an infinite regress. And otherwise, taking Popper's route, everything is informal and indefinite, provisional, until further notice, which is not what we hoped.'

---'Anyway, in this case, either these laws are exhaustive, in which case there are areas in nature of inconsistency, where logic breaks down, and therefore in logical terms everything is true, because if a contradiction is true it is but a few steps of proof to everything being true, or, because we are compelled to accept that everything is not true, there are areas which are not covered by the laws of nature, where the laws of nature, like Heisenberg's uncertain observer, do not penetrate, and perhaps the deterministically unpredictable elements in QED (setting aside the probabilistic laws---I am referring to the area beyond the reach of these probabilistic laws) are in just such an area, a kind of singularity, to which the axiomatic nature of reality has to bow to raw, unprincipled, nature.'

---'There is an alternative.'

---'What?'

---'That the world is a finite system of facts, which could therefore be explained by a finite system of axioms.'

---'Well, that too is interesting. We are faced by a kind of dilemma in reverse, where both the choices are ravishing.'

---'What's interesting about Gödel is that the idea seems to be implied that the world is not just a set of axiom-a-likes and rules of inference---which is what you might suspect, given its susceptibility to axiomatic modelling. But no; the world isn't like this; in any complete system there are true theorems you cannot get to from your axioms. So he is a mathematical echo of Heisenberg. And in a very deep way I am pleased. The traitor. The fool. Who is paid in molten gold, poured down her throat. The world is not after all a scientific world; mathematics, science, are more than accidentally inaccurate, they are necessarily inaccurate; e is more than mere error, it is the whole point: and I, a physicist, am pleased. Is that sick?'

---'No. A physicist perhaps, but a woman first.'

Like Cundy, I sometimes say things which make me cringe. "Sir, a woman's preaching is like a dog's walking on his hind legs. It is not done well; but you are surprised to find it done at all,' says Johnson. She shamed me in my tinny, quadruped intellect, looking down on me as she might on a small maze in someone's garden from the moon.

---'Dinosaur. That's sicker,' she said. 'So, if the world is not a system of axioms, then what 'the fuck' is it?'

Inferior again. Or not exactly inferior: more jealous, and shy. Hella
was unifying worlds which perhaps should not be unified: beauty, sex,
mathematics. I envied her her future.

---'Yes?' I said at last.

---'If no finite set of axioms will supply every true theorem, then no finite
set of laws will either, and the laws become as numerous (assuming
an infinity of facts) as facts. There are paradoxes here, pregnant ones
for understanding the world. The sense in which some things are of
such complexity that we are not able to understand them. Excepting
significant redundancy, redundancy at the level of law as well of instance,
only a system of equivalent complexity could understand then, and
there are none of those. Meanwhile, quantum electro-dynamics and
general relativity theory are astonishing not for their complexity but
their simplicity. There is something fishy going on.'

---'Change the record. You're losing me.'

---'Am I?'

And she looked at me with happy malice, as if I was a bottled moth.

---'I'm losing myself. But only because reality does. Because interested for
the sake of reality, some of whose beauty it succeeds in expressing with
such necessity. Mathematics isn't nature, which in turn is not reality by
any subtle metaphysics; but it's the nearest we get. You are looking at a
picture of a picture of the roots of the world---doesn't that make your
scalp, creep? Physics is simply a contingent representation, painted with
the paints we have manufactured to mimic those world itself paints with
(Nabokov's moth wing with a painted droplet which *refracts* the painted
backdrop) ⊠ mathematics. I am interested in the destructive testing of
language, of thought. Trying to crash them, like a programme or a plane.
As I said before, paradoxes may come from the category mistake of using
the mind to understand itself. But if we believe the real thing exists, we
can also see paradoxes, self-contradictions, untenable but necessary
assumptions, as falsifying instances for our theories, embodied in
our mathematics, our logic and the structure of our minds, about the
structure of nature and of reality. Either the theory or the experiment
is wrong in some way. Either our logic, or the way we have applied it, is
wrong.'

---'Yes?'

---'Something draws me to the edges of mathematics, the frayed edges;
you don't have to be drawn to the edge of physics: somehow it's all edge.
And what, then, are the edges frayed by? Metaphysics? Of course not. So
what?'

---'What?'

---'Dissatisfied with all the prosy patterns on the carpet, and lifting its
edge to see what is underneath. Only, there is nothing underneath; not
for us at least. There's nothing underneath. Nothing at all. Where there
should be a dusty floor, pocked with oil marks and wax.'

---'Like the man who cut open his girlfriend to see what was inside?'

---'Nothing. There's nothing underneath. Just a square of space where the
floorboards should be.'

---'Through which we fall?'

She looked at me, and smiled. I was exhausted. Winded, even.

---'Let's go back down,' she said.

---'To the cave?'

---'We need other people.'

Packing didn't take long. On the way:

---'Look.'

---'A glove.'

It had swollen up like a hand and was turning in a black, slow pool
patterned with fallen leaves. Some of the stuffing was leaking out.
She swam to it, parting the cool water, and brought it back. Then she
shivered. The sun had gone. That fatal waterfall.

---'What would have happened had there been nobody there to see all
this?' Melancholy. 'These planets spinning slowly on, until one by one,
starting with the innermost, with a little pop, ploughing a fiery furrow,
they sank into the sun.' China. 'What would have happened? It would
have been sad. This reminds me how weird it is. It could so easily have
been otherwise: it was so hard for this to happen, for this to be. So how
come? And yet, of course, the question is fruitless, sterile; for me to ask

the question in the first place, it had to be, so there is no doubt about the answer, for now at least, and yet, how come. Sometimes it makes me afraid. It is a poetic raft we are floating on, and all we do is writhe across each other, make funny mouths and lean backwards under the water. That we exist should be enough, it is so astonishing, such a happy accident, once we have enough to eat, shelter, a balance of solitude and someone to love. But somehow it all goes wrong. We have to answer for that. That is something we do. Not the earth, not the world. We do it ourselves. Primates. (And religion!---its not for nothing they call bishops that.) And yet, why does it go wrong? It's a bit like the woman selling the house---each time she has a deal she thinks she must be selling if for too little, pulls out, and puts the price up.'

---'The economists, the 5 dollar bill, the quad. 'It can't be, someone would already have picked it up."

What we had been looking for was a place where nothing happened. While we were at the cave nothing happened. Time stopped, because each day followed exactly the same course. One day, tinned pizza and lime leaves, the next corned beef, but the other differences were subtle as the ageing of our faces. We could have stayed forever, only realising that real time had passed when we turned each other leathery, quizzical faces on hearing the parched scream of the first grandchild, if something hadn't driven us out, which is that this ideal can't be described, it can't be lived. It can only be remembered.

---'Romanticism is realism, remembered,' she said. 'It's also as lady John Russell once said to her grandson, the logical reductionist: *What is mind? No matter. What is matter? Never mind*. Infuriating. Because she had a point. They are not good for you, these ideas. Not only hackneyed, trivial and distasteful, they are also not necessarily real; like someone who cares more for quarks than boys, there is something anti-religious there, something anti-life. There is a sense in which I've wasted the last few years, spent on Krylov and before that on hyper-fine lines. What are we for? For embodying selective advantage; breeding, replicating our culture and our genes. Does the world exist? Are we free? It's chasing your own tail. You go mad and you bore and disgust people. So you make it exist, call it into being, and give up your freedom, by having a child.' The air was growing chilled. 'But when you step outside of this, you see amazing things, the kinds of things Icarus and Dumpty saw. You take back a garden, a sacred grove, from philosophy, which has filled it with arid, charmless, useless structures, into art again, and set out one or two straggly plants, in the hope of re-attracting the moving and the beautiful beasts who used to roam in jungles here. The relation is that between fiddling with yourself ...'

---'While Rome burns!'

---'... and love. And yet it isn't good, it isn't for us, it isn't where we should be. All they are is beautiful problems; hyper-fine cracks in reality; you put your eye to them and see---not the answer, but dark red space, dynamic, in the manner of Rothko, that consummate kineticist, viewed at dusk. The buck---the iteration, regress---stops here. These problems are there to exist: that is their function; they do it well. We haven't scratched their surface in two divine days. And just as we don't ask for a solution to Lust---have you seen her?---in the State Museum?---'

---'You always making me shiver, and my hair creep. Call me *le frisson dans le dos*, that's what should be tattooed all over your lips.'

---'Lust: it's enough to look at her and get moved and get scared, just so we expect no answer to these questions. *Pi* is more beautiful than its expansion to *n* terms. Even as *n* tends to infinity. It's like the systematic hypocrisy of our societies: our senses are systematic hypocrites too; but there is a truth, even for them.'

---'I mean the State Museum.'
---'Just as you read between the lines of the newspapers, you read between the lines of your own eyes, of your own heart.'
---'You've been to the State Museum?'
---'Don't worry. I'm teasing you again. It's not fair, is it. Yes; and you have too. I met you there.'

A bright and dirty---witchy---smile, slowly breaking as she watched my face.

When I didn't speak, she went on.

---'Well: not exactly; but I sat next to you. Each day for three days. It took three days for you to even notice me.'

---'It was you ...'

---'And when I came back from checking my hair and my face yet again in the tiny musty mirror in the musty toilets, to see what was wrong with them, you'd gone, you jerk.'

---'But I went to look for you ...'

The history of the world.

---'I looked too. I looked all day. That night I was leaving for Moscow to meet up with Haakon. And as the train began to roll I leant out from the window to say bye to the city where you walked or slept or ate or even screwed and saw you there, standing on the platform under the lights, steam rising from your shoulders and your mouth---your mouth rounded and water on your face, and my heart went out. And I was happy, very lonely, very happy, because I made-believe that you were looking for me. And that therefore you were meant for me. I had found you. Why else would you have been brought there? I knew that somehow, however imperfectly, you'd taken me in, that you would wait for me. But terribly lonely, terribly sad. And when I said 'never mind', and even fell asleep on the top bunk as the ran drummed and spattered on the roof of the carriage a few inches from my face, I knew I'd find you again, and I was right.'

---'Why didn't you tell me?'
---'If you tell your wishes they don't come true.'

---'It's strange. She looks like you.'

---'I know. She's not as pretty though.'

So, white lights downriver. Turning a bend, we arrived in the steep, arcaded square of a mountain village. With, as centrepiece, a long steaming barrow of straw and dung.

The arches which lined the square on all four sides were rendered and whitewashed, but bits of whitewash had flaked off, revealing various other pigments---ochre, green, blue. Plates of the rendering had also fallen off, revealing the soft red sandstone beneath. Panes of blue wood-smoke snaked slowly through the red freestone piers. A crowd of children making the noise of an aviary. A cloud of starlings too, twittering deafeningly. And a mule train coming in, laden with brushwood and fodder, led by silent men, very short, with stubborn, solemn faces, and mule-coloured clothes.

We asked an old woman where we were. She looked at us in despair. When we spoke again she shouted a warning, and wriggled a crooked finger deep into her ear. When we asked a third time, sweaty by now, she crossed herself, threw up her arms, screaming, and ran away.

We found the fonda without her---it turned out we had been standing outside it all along. The word in rain-washed powder-blue was painted on the wall beside a balcony, just above our heads. And carved on the keystone of the fonda's arch was a date:

16 + 92.

Through this arch came shouts and knocks and a piteous bleating. A brown and white ewe was being swung around by her back legs by a man with a stiff grey brush of hair and gold pince-nez; a dull pink sack hanging out of her, studded with pulsing, fleshy blossoms. A man and a woman were chattering excitedly while struggling to stuff this sack into the revolving ewe. I make it sound easy. There was plenty of lurching, plenty of shrieking. But with the suddenness of a red mess disappearing down an unblocked drain, the whole lot sank suddenly back out of sight into her innards and was secured with safety pins. It was a good omen that the sheep bolted away, only a dull pink smudge on her wool to tell of her ordeal, her owner stumping after her on short legs, swearing and waving a stick and leaving us to a blubbery welcome from Encarnación, the fonda's owner. The rapture, almost the lust with which she greeted us, was disconcerting at first.

---'Such a handsome brother and sister; your mother so lucky!' she wailed.

We weren't brother and sister at all.

---'Married! But where are the children?'

---'We don't have none.'

---'What handsome children they will be! When your first arrives, telegram for Encarnación, yes? Look at your forehead; what a lovely skull,' she said, lifting Hella's hair. 'But where are your shoes? What a disaster. You can't wear those clothes. What is this? Have you nothing else? Eat now; later we fix these clothes. It is incorrect, a handsome wife like you to wear such rags and immodesties.'

Inside, the whitewashed rooms seemed subtly melted, all their edges warped and dulled. Encarnación laid a small scrubbed wooden table beside the fire. Through a home-made casement-window we saw bantams scratching at a dung heap in the twilight, the roofs and clock-tower of the church, and an enormous blue-green valley, painted and vague. The hands of the church clock painted too; the painted time was always a quarter to three. Just then a bell clanged out the true hour, waking all the geese in the village, who started clanging too.

The river meandered away beyond, a cut-out through to the sky. Across it was a rival village on a reddish bluff, with an ivy castle up above. A few poetic spindly trees. And the sun setting miles and miles away, beyond a brownish flood-plain studded with minute violet hamlets from each of which rose smoke.

Pluto stayed downstairs with some other dogs. A row of white pigeons lined the windowsill, moaning like springs or people in a bed. Hella flung them crumbs, which scared them off in a clatter of wings. Together they spiralled upwards until, almost invisible, they stalled and tumbled in balls of rattling, guttering feather. Just above the ground they spread their short stiff wings and sheared off. Spiralled up. And down again, rattling and tumbling, to perch on the kitchen chimney, roo-cooing breathlessly away. Encarnación rose with a sigh to go and shut them in.

We ate cheese, salty as tears. Fried eggs, fried garlic cloves, smoked peppers in thick oil, black wine and white bread. Encarnación, frowning on a tiny, straw-bottomed chair by the fire, sucked threads and sewed, her eyeballs magnified by a heavy pair of glasses.

Our bedroom was above the kitchen. There was a cross was on the whitewashed wall at the head of a steel bed piled up with fleecy bolsters and quilts which smelt of smoke and milk. A marble-topped dressing table, a mildewed mirror. A naked light-bulb on a long buckled wire. Raising her elbows and catching the back of the collar, Hella lifted her shirt over her head. Her ribcage, with a hollow stomach underneath it, like a greyhound's, or a side of pork. Soon I was sliding a wooden cock through warm ecstatic slime between her legs. After which we slept.

Colour in her face as she lay sleeping in a bed which sagged deeply as a hammock, her hair bright against the milky bolster and milky sheet.

---'Hella.'

But even so, her skin so fine you could see the smudge of each iris through closed eyes.

---'Wake up.'

She stirred, but didn't wake.

Leaning through the window I turned away from her to smell the cold air---wood smoke, sweet dung, a whiff of burning plastic, and resin from the pinewoods. In the yard below was Pluto, sniffing cautiously at the buttocks of an enormous sow. I went back to the hot bed and slept more.

Then, beside a creaking, hissing fire we breakfasted on bread, garlic, and coffee laced with cognac, watching the smoke flow powerfully up into the light which came down the chimney. The skirl and roo-cooing of the pigeons perched up there came down too, and every so often a bird's shit fell on the ashes where it sizzled like an egg.

Encarnación came in with an air of mystery, and fresh in her arms a bundle of foamy cotton.

---'Look!' she said.

She held it gently against Hella's shoulders and shook it out. White, gathered and pleated tightly underneath the bodice, some kind of communion dress, totally impractical, yet making her fresh and edible, a warm and scented landscape on which cold snow has fallen.

It fitted her body uneasily, too big, too stiff; it wasn't even really touching her---would be easy to open all down its length, or in its stiffness, lift off. And so there was a sense, strong, that she was still naked inside it; that it stood out from her body, and even shone a golden white light, faintly green, faintly striped, on the hidden skin. So that her breasts and the lower under-slope of her lamb's belly, pelted with fur as soft as a sable water-colour brush and creased and lipped and folded like a mouth---all this was flooded and cleaned in the same gentle submarine light. She was being set up as Snow-White. Polished, scented, powdered everywhere---under the nails and between the legs. Cleaned up even there for the sticky lusts of some ghastly prince. This is what was wrong. She would have looked much better in black. The paleness of her hair, the greenness under dark gold of her skin, too much the same tone as this white cotton. There was something anaemic, even scary here.

Except her hair was blonde; clinging to this. The hair of such girls is black. Blonde and white was ecstatic, the golden pollen on the pallid lily, as golden as money and as white as death ☒ but it was still wrong. The dress should have been blac, it should have been. Not pale, bloodless, perfect. She was asking for trouble, even from me. Even in me something wanted to make fun of her; something else to jeer at her. And something worse to hurt, break, destroy her. Who did she think she was? With a ludicrously straight back and moronic shy smile and a stupid, steady kindness in her eyes. All around famine, pestilence and war while she went steadily onwards, journeying by fairy-tale. As if she was proving our suffering unnecessary---she'd made all the right moves purely to wind us up. And it had been so easy for her. Her daddy rich and herself good-looking, and well-bred, and intelligent. So easy; was this what made me furious? Because she was unreal, she didn't have a clue; she was healthy to the hot core of her warm body, and health has no place in this diseased wonderland. Does it?

The time for health is over now, and I knew this and she didn't. It didn't make it any easier for me, splashing on through the mists and muds of my sad crappy seeping life. There was a sense that this excellence had been stolen from me, that it was unclean, provocative of the gods as much as of me, that it must be destroyed, the pride humbled, the nobility corrupted and the innocence dirtied, willingly, thirstily. That before she died she should get a face full of sun-dried shit, and those lips, and that tongue, still gooey with it, should admit that she was wrong. Had been all along.

This was Tod Waddington's POV, I now saw; this was Leicher's.

And sometimes I felt it was mine. She should be taught that her world had not been the world at all but a wet dream, a corny, mushy, naff one at that, a dream of kings of reason, palaces of desire in a wakeful if dog-tired, malevolent and democratic age. Taught above all, that the free lunch will be paid for, that the reckoning is on its way. That though this lunch if excellent is light, the waiter will be graceless, the waitress tart and the bill astronomical ...

---'What's that?'

The squealing of a murder.

It stopped.

But Encarnación emerged unexpectedly from a home-made cupboard beside the fire and rounded us up and herded us in. Stone steps inside. Leading downwards.

---... because, and this was the real problem, she imagined she was better than the rest, imagined not with her mind but with her being. In other words, she had the nerve to be better; she so dared. She rubbed *my nose* in it, *mine*. I of course imagined, even knew, that she was not. Nobody was. But this squealing again, terrible, terrible, crackled through the sheets of brittle bone stretched across my temples ...

---'*Hoy, matanzas,*' Encarnación said, pushing us down the stone steps. This means 'Killings today,' in Castillian I think. Hella opened another small door onto a barnful of billowing smoke in which a thick crowd of small men swayed and pushed and shouted round a trestle table. Her placid look turned to fear. Her bare foot instead of reaching downwards for the next step, reached back up. Encarnación blocking our way with a smile.

When the crowd saw us all fell silent, all looked up. Even the sow on the trestle table stopped wriggling and screaming and her eyes fell on us. Enchanted moment, as the unwinged fairy came down the stone stairs, bare-footed and robed in white. Even the wreathing, swelling smoke hung frozen in the low weak sunlight which was shining through a hole in the wall.

It didn't last long. The sow on her back (the flabby blue stomach, the double row of teats) was squealing again, cantering in space, and in the shouting, lurching crowd of men, one had a knife. He brought it to her, turning it to catch strips of white fire from the sun, falling through broken tiles high above. Hella's lust for knowledge failed her; she didn't want to see for once and here, at the top of the steps we could see all. She hurried on down and walked gently over the flags to a second long table draped with thick white polythene. Here, half-hidden by the glazed pots and jars standing ready for the pulsing, steaming innards of the living pig, she sat down abruptly, facing the wall, beside an elderly beau at the table's head.

I can't account for this man's beauty. His skin and lips were good, his eyebrows thick, his hair silver and eyes sharp blue. The offspring of a union between a demon and an angel: this was his look; soft innocence and brazen experience mix'd. With bared yellow teeth he chewed a cigar; in his fingers he turned a glass of green wine. With the other hand he played with a hat made of straw exactly the shade of her hair. White socks, polished black shoes, white shirt, black string tie, and a pressed, sharp grey suit whose trousers were shorts which ended in turn-ups just above the knee. The group around the sow, meanwhile: shouting, grunting, lurching about. And the screaming---scalded, human. She was telling them with all the expressive passion available that she didn't want death, this sow, didn't even want to be a sow. Trying to get this terrible message across. And doing well. It worked. We heard what she was saying - but far too late: a fine arc of pumped steady blood wrote something in curly letters across Hella's gold hair and white back.

---'Hella!'

She turned as a thicker gout climbed and then slid down the arc of blood and splashed the side of her face.

She spat, and by reflex, raised a panel of white cotton to clean it off. Seeing her knees together, her long legs, greenish-brown, swelled into thigh and hitting up against loose, creased underpant. And seeing the ancient angelic demon also looking there.

The sow silent at last. The tension in the crowd around her was softening; people standing further apart as they scooped out guts in both hands and with their fists punched off the bristly half-human skin. Fadrique pulled on a rope and she rose above the table and swung gently around the room, head down, with open mouth and open belly. It both was and wasn't her, this dangling corpse. Someone else with a carpenters saw had already started sawing off legs. An orange handle, sliding back and forth, a rusty blade, and blood. And something of the magician's illusion. Sawing the lovely lady up. Her head---the sow's I mean - moving as they sawed: how was this? How Hella's head moved, her eyes wide open too, as we fucked. Not now: her eyes, Hella's, were shut. And the glazed earthenware dishes, each three feet across, filled steadily with varying textures of organ and gut.

Boiling vats of unknown things stirred by Encarnación's mother. The two huge hams were pasted with salt. Pinned up on a washing line weird innards, slimy ropes and glassy cloths, the things we also have inside of us. Deafened by sounds of sawing, grating, gurgling, bubbling, and the shouts and cackles (it was true, this language was shouted, not spoken) we sat half-blinded by the glare of low, early sunlight from the plastic table-cloth, watching Pluto panting in the dust outside, attached to a communal chain with all the other dogs.

Soon nothing but a damp pig-shaped mark remained. The earthenware dishes were carried away and we all lunched on first-fruits round the long table. Home-made wine, red, but tasting of *retsina*. All, as they ate, stared intently at the food as if there was nothing else in the world.

---'Finish this dish', Encarnación said; 'there isn't much'. And we finished it, and when we thought it was all over, were ambushed by another course carried in the with the air of showmen, of magicians.

This happened not once, but several times.

Meanwhile, getting drunker. Cesár, my neighbour, hitting me hard on the arm every time he wanted to shout something at me. Just where the muscle lies above the bone. The air of Brueghel, Memling or Bosch.

---'These are the middle-ages. They've lasted this long', Hella said. 'I never dreamed I'd see it', she added, hitting me on the arm to get my attention back. She was right, but not only that, she fitted here. The kind of girl with whom to trap a unicorn. A white dress, sticky with blackening blood, and gold hair, matted and gummed with it, and dreamy lips. 'It's over now of course. All of it will go. This what the EU was been created for: to destroy all this'.

Uncharacteristic bitterness. And unusual to hear her talk politics. But she figured the way it has of ambushing those who don't talk it. Hitting my arm again:

---'So much to be destroyed', she shouted at me, 'but then there always has been, and there's always more. We hope'. But a punch on my arm from the other side. Cesár underlining her point; he wanted to tell me about the new road. Financed, as had been the symposium, by EU cohesion funds.

---'We are now among the last places in the Sierra without a trunk road. That's being remedied even as we speak'. Even as we shout. 'Yes, it's on its way. On a quiet day you can hear the earth-movers. Sometimes there's blasting only half-a-league away. And if you go up the hill near the mill amongst the vines you'll see the little white crosses which look like graves, but which mark the route it will take. It will be eight lanes wide; we know this because it is already in use up to Orguel. Fadrique was taken to see it'.

---'I was'.

---'So was the Mayor'.

---'Completely true.'

---'When the road comes our problems will be at an end. When the road comes!'

Cesár and the Mayor nodding as they chewed with open mouths. Willing the future.

This willing being the fuel that drives the present along. Brave, optimistic, willing it to come, willing time onwards. The road would drain the town; would lance it, would let it flow away. Like building a bridge to an island, it was a sinning against God.

---'It won't be the same.'

When I said this the Mayor snarled and pulled with a finger at the end of his mouth. He was digging away at a strand of muscle fibre caught in his teeth. Spitting it out onto the table beside his plate, he hit my arm and answered:

---'Thank God. Because you understand we need work. When the road comes we can drive as far as Orguel in half an hour. Now we have to go by Land Rover and it takes two hours. In Orguel there is plenty of work. Life is nothing without work. Also, we have no cinema here, and no discotheque. The young are restless and bored and as soon as they can they leave.'

Everything they had: their little utopia. And what they were busily doing to it. A microcosm of the earth. Anlo, the town was called.

---'Hasn't it always been like this? Or has it?' said an anachronistic dapper swell, an angelic demon, in a deep dixieland lisp. 'There are times when things improve. The *pax Augusta*? The end of almost every civil war. But even if the world gets better, even as the world gets better, you and I get worse. The teeth go, the looks, the honour, the hair. The desire, the boys, the girls. So: the road will come; it has to come. And it will be a one-way road. They will drive into Orguel but won't drive back. This is how the naïve, even the good: invite our fate. How else are we to learn?'

But the man beyond Cesár on my other side; he too had reached across to hit me on the arm.

---'What's he saying,' I asked Hella who was falling deep into conversation with the demon, who had a mesmeric thrill to his scary blue eyes.

---'He's telling you this is one of the last towns in the cordillera without a road,' he said, slow, laconic, Southern. Then he smiled and winked at me.

---'Yes, yes, I know,' I told the man beyond the mayor, turning back to him. 'They've already told me.'

Gregorio, the patrician Dixielander---guest of honour, civil-war-hero (Spanish) on the rebel side, and local curiosity, took us back to his place afterwards, our bellies stiff as drums. It was a grand old generous farm-house, up above the village in the centre of a geometric grove of palms. Inside it resembled something out of *Interiors*. Coir matting on the floors, and on this scatter rugs. And deep and lovely sofas piled high with minute embroidered cushions. He gave me a folio edition of *The Faerie Queene* to read, bound in fragile red Morocco tooled with flowers. It had been lying open on an upholstered coffee-table before a brisk olive-wood fire, amongst the latest magazines: *Vanity Fair, Hello!, Vogue …*

---'Library's upstairs. You'll be undisturbed. Don't want to see your face again until the end of Book I. Want to hear what you figure Spenser intends.'

So: the donging as I climbed them of the spiral stairs.

The library windows looked up into the white mountains from which we'd come. Above, formed of the same white substance, in the sinking daylight was a watery moon. A *chaise longue* under a picture-window surveyed this sombre, chilly world. Beside it a chrome-plated stove. I read the opening lines, but almost immediately Hella came up, breathless, joyous, making the staircase ring like a steel band.

---'He took his trousers down. Said he only wanted to look at my legs.'

---'What's he doing now?'

My question answered by the mournful, solitary wailing of the old man. After a time, with musical steps, he too came upstairs.

Breathless, his shirt-tail nosing out of his flies, he managed to ask:

---'What do you think?'

Hella who was standing reading the titles of books, turned to say seriously:

---'Yes.'

---'Not there,' he said rapidly, 'you'll get blood on it. Sit on this.'

---'Stay on with me, the both of you. You'd be happy here for a year or two. On these shelves are Homer, Dante, Montaigne, Balzac, Mann (remind me to introduce you to Golo someday), Melville, a few bits of Camus (the late thirties and early forties *Carnets*), and poor Federico---I knew some of the boys in the firing squad. They told me where they buried him, but that news will go with my to my grave:

Then I realized I had been murdered.

They looked for me in cafes, cemeteries and churches

.... but they did not find me.

They never found me?

No. They never found me.

Then: Lowry, Frisch, Shulz, Gombrovicz, Longus, Apuleius. And next door, residing (as they will) on another planet, the Russians from Pushkin to Pasternak, Nabokov, Bulgakov (who by, had also, the way, a Hella). No one could do that now. The stuffing's gone in the sofa of their race. They don't make repressive regimes as they used to. Slackened springs, even in ours. Saul touches the mystery; but even he touches it in an apologetic way.'

---'Saul?'

---'Because we have lost our fire, and while once you didn't even need to pretend, it is now not even possible to do that. It's over.'

---'And Stendhal?'

---'A Beylist. I see. And what's wrong with Balzac?'

---'Stendhal's problem is that he is better than Balzac, and therefore his characters are less imperfect. He writes not novels but reality. That's what's wrong with Balzac. Which is why perhaps, all genius is equal; there is a point beyond which it does not matter how far they go.'

---'There is a coldness in perfection that repels us: Vivaldi, Mozart, Pope;
so that we have to destroy it, we have to break our toys, dirty our water--
-we have to go deaf.'

---'Beethoven doesn't have what you call coldness and I call simplicity,
gaiety, sadness. Nor do Chopin, or Stendhal. You are talking not genius
but classical genius.'

---'True---Beethoven's quartets, especially the late ones on sexual
intercourse.'

---'Who says that?'

---'No one has to. You can *smell* it as they said about *Gerontius*,' he said. 'Its
reminds me of what I told Vladimir when he published his masterpiece:
'You can smell the incest.' He promised he'd use that, but didn't have time.

---'It's like Balbi's *Lust*, said Hella. You don't need anyone to tell you what
she's about. You can smell her.'

---'And boy does she smell good!' said Gregory. 'I don't know Beethoven
knew what he was doing. God sometimes gives the artist a sealed letter
to post. But Balbi sure did---you've read the *Confessions* of course? And so
did Catherine the great wh-re and carnal epicure. It struck me as soon as
I saw you at the top of those steps: *Lust* is a study for you.'

She was always pleased to hear this, and it was a pleasing thing to hear.
Lust was amazing, almost as amazing as her.

---'You know her? You really do? In the flesh? I'm rather taken aback.
Stalin kept her at his dacha; he stole her from Beria. After Stalin died,
Beria got her back again. For a moment. Until Andropov put her briefly
into the State, no-one had seen her since the storming of the Winter
Palace. Now she's in the Kremlin. But this is all part of Balbi's scheme.
The mystery & horror only strengthens Lust. You know what they
say about familiarity. Some artists build this in. Discriminating about
their public---hence the shark repellent and the poison pill. Because
popularity destroys beauty. The slack heart and slack thighs or eyes
of the hyper-model. A masterpiece runs on mystery; this is a part of
the mechanism. Using it to advertise motor cars twists and breaks the
mechanism. A concerto can be flattened like a battery or snapped like a
mirror ...'

---'A theory can too. Newton: we are tired of Newton. Einstein: we are
almost tired of him. Quantum electro-dynamics: we like that still; but
only because it is more sophisticated, decadent almost, represents
a deeper, more corrupt stage in the development of the art than
Newtonian optics does ...'

---'And hence the *difficulty*, not because the same thing cannot be done
easily, although this too is possible, but like a hedge of flowering
hawthorn, to exclude the herd.'

---'This is why I abhor pop science.'

---'Hella, where did you learn English?'

---'Some things are indestructible.'

---'Yes, but not logic, not physics, not maths.'

---'Some things are eternal.'

---'Nothing is eternal. So you hide, you mask, your beauty---if you have
some.'

---'Unfortunately, it's often vacancy which is masked. Hegel, Marx, Fichte,
Freud, etc.'

---'Those who write as if they have nothing to hide.'

---'Or evil. Nietzsche.'

---'People have always complained about the morality of art, and
always will. And it's always the same people; they used to be called the
bourgeoisie; now they are called right-on. *Maintenant*,' he said in his Dixie
lisp, '*il faut épater les bohèmes.*'

That made her giggle.

---'No,' he said. 'There is no such thing as morality. It is an illusion, a ghost.
The cat's paw in the fable and the Landseer; this is morality.'

He was playing with fire. Talking abstract with her was like talking dirty
with a tart. She stretched her arms up in a tapering helix, twisting her
body sensuously, and couldn't resist rotating on the spot. Then she dove
straight in:

---'No.'

---'You believe in goodness? With an intellect like yours. I don't believe this child.'

---'The grounds of virtue are instinct and expedience. The virtue based on instinct is absolute; but we will never know our models of this are perfect; we do our best. A changing situation draws out fresh instincts, and the instincts themselves and their corresponding absolute evolve very slowly. But this is tempered by expedience: society's lunacies have to be accommodated or things get worse. It is an artificial conscience, which has evolved to make modern societies work in the same way as the real one did. You play the idiot game; this is compulsory. Otherwise they hit you in the face. The choirs of fools, that is. They hit you anyway, of course, but not so hard. And this expedience is relative, being defined by a changing legal and social situation---the existence or otherwise of a legal age of consent, of fanatical pro-lifers or anti-hangers---as opposed to a changing reality: birth-control, syphilis, penicillin, AIDS (interesting, those capitals, as if the sole vile motive of this latest pathogen is to draw attention to itself.)'

---'This may be how it works; but it suggests complexities. Somehow I prefer "Thou shalt not' writ over the door.' You know where you stand.'

---'Difficult, isn't it. The system is non-linear. It seems to refresh itself with new depths each time you reach the depth before. It is beyond us, outside of us. It appears to be coming from somewhere. How about this as a criterion: that an act is morally permissible provided that ... no it doesn't work.'

---'There is no objective moral imperative,' said Gregory. 'I do what I like, or rather, what I can get away with.' He winked at me. 'And it's no good making excuses for your unhappiness because there's no-one to make them to. Throw a one-person pity party if that's your kick; otherwise work out what does make you happy, and freaking do it. Do it before you die.'

---'I disagree again. The criterion is this: does what makes you happy make others unhappy even if they don't know what you are doing. If you want to seduce girls like me this will make some people---my father, my boyfriend, him---unhappy, unless they don't know. But if you want to rape girls, this has to make people unhappy because they have to know. This is the criterion of what is permissible in a civil society. Do not

misunderstand me: I am not arguing for lying. I argue for truth---perhaps
too forcibly. Perhaps I lack tact. I am saying if, which you shouldn't,
because it severs, as it were, your own vocal chords in corroding your
ability to communicate, you were to lie, what would happen then
should be the criterion of what is permissible.'

---'The problem is defining yourself, because this is what you have to do.
The problem is halting the infinite regress and saying: here is value. You
are hungry: food is good; you are thirsty: water is good; you are bored:
evil is good,' said Gregory. 'Or it would be, if God wasn't such a wet. Don't
you love the argument from design,' he went on; 'It's a joke in such poor
taste. What is interesting, though, is that things like this are given any
credence. That the choirs of fools as you call us so neatly are so nearly
there, so nearly intelligent, but the last tiny drop of wisdom which
opens up the universe to, as you would have it, introspection, eludes us.'

---'Is there some selective limit on intelligence perhaps? That once you
see how the whole thing is done, you step out of the game and cease to
breed?'

---'I don't believe this girl. Don't she ever give in?'
---'But that would be ...'

The child plays in the garden. She doesn't keep asking why it's there.'
---'Asking why *is* playing.'

Sometimes, like Leicher, all I wanted was to grip the edges of a table,
dribble a bit, and scream. She could be trying, but this was part of
the picture. And Gregory saw this. He appreciated her. Enough of a
connoisseur. I forgave him his lusts.

---'To wear the intellect on the tip of the senses, which is Eliot on Donne
I think,' he was saying. 'The tip of the dongle he meant---that's the idea;
the fullest, most complete life possible; but also fullest, most complete
appreciation of it.'

The sexiness of someone with an intellect. This one's subject being not
science itself, nor metaphysics, but the delirium of not being scared
to think. Jowett's passion of the reason, Auden's hermit's carnal ecstasy,
were also hers. Physics, maths, metaphysics were ⊠ had been conjured by
⊠ her yearning for the ring-a-ding, *Ding-an-sich*, for the Forms of heavenly
perfection. And she was my yearning---she was mine. She was what I
now loved about the world; she-in-herself; not the frail bones, the gentle

skin, the sulky dark blue eyes and yellow hair, but her. Squatting amongst
nettles and forming a coprolite or, wearing a headband of alpine flowers,
edging shoulder-deep sideways through gorse towards some interesting
lepidopteron---these helped, but it wasn't these but her.

---'The Jews,' she was telling Gregory; 'the rediscovery of the idea that
there is only one God. Unless you credit the Greeks. I don't know the
provenance of this revival stroke survival. Anyway, the holy trinity
is clearly an attempt to roll back this trend. Christians are the Jews'
decadence. And it gets worse. Despite what the scriptures recommend,
the saints are lesser deities and their images are worshipped too. The
irony is that the charmless spirit of Puritanism and its descendant,
abstract art, are probably closer to the austere aesthetic of Christ than
the Roman Catholic church---luxurious, oriental, despotic. As for the
holy trinity: clover as a bad image: they are not the three parts of a larger
thing, but three aspects of the same thing: its greenness, its inviting
bitterness, its form.'

---'And the clover flower?' he asked.

---'The mysteries.'

But she had stopped; she was gazing through the mica windows of the
chromed stove, her face orange, mottled, flickering, as if from within.
Eventually she moved her eyes slowly from the flames to mine, but she
scared me; she was looking at me like a thing. And then at him.

---'What is it Hella?
---'Proust.'

Did she have no sense of humour? Or was it a subtle one?

I think she had none. The snake who cannot laugh. She thought too
much, saw too much, was too conscious. Love of science, art, and
of me perhaps, for her being similar sensations, the same burning
impatience, hypothetical jealousy, joy and will-to-be; complete calmness,
and a confidence that this was the centre of the universe, a lack of any
dilemma, any doubt, the loss or resignation of freedom, a passivity
without alternatives, coupled with the most precious energy, fizzing,
uncontainable, so that it seemed as if her skin would burst in several
places at once and squirt out flames.

---'I'd forgotten him. But he is the world; he isn't art. Perhaps, like Kafka, he comes at the point, the very rich point, where your heart jumps as having reached the summit, you see where the descent starts. Rousseau was feeling for it; Byron got closer; Stendhal was there, as there as it is possible to be: he was the first point on the flat, snowy summit of which Proust was the end.'

There was more, of course. But I don't have the heart to put it down.

The stage with a lover when you discover you have started again at the beginning of the tape. That the same ideas, the same observations, even with identical gestures and faces, are coming round again. So that the film unseen, the girl unknown, the book unread is far more beautiful than the film or girl or book could ever be, and this is an argument for fixing yourself up to be an outsider. Some things look better without glasses, more like a poem, less like a photograph.

Not her. And yet, trying. Too rich.

Walking back down the hill from Gregory's towards Anlo. When she looked at me she looked sad. She slid her arms around me, in her awkward, compelling way, and holding her neck a little crooked, laid salty lips a little crookedly on mine. Between our two wills a third will, the will of an unconceived child.

---'A marriage of equals,' she said as we stopped underneath the arch which led into the top of the square. 'That's all I ask.'

Making my mouth, which had her tongue in it, go cold.

Cesár's shop was here and the boots he had promised to make her a few hours earlier were done. We could see them through the window. Made of sheepskin, with the wool turned to the inside, except around the rim where it was folded down over the ankles. They were soled with a piece cut out of a balding moped tyre.

---'Strange to wear shoes again,' she said as he knelt like a prince and she slid her blackened feet in. 'It feels sweet.'

Meanwhile, through the flimsy glazed door, Pluto barking in the square outside. He had seen his own reflection in a mossy trough and was biting and splashing at it, then waiting in silence with a cocked head and pricked ears for the water to calm down enough for the reflection to reappear, and then snapping and barking wildly again. Suddenly he stopped to listen to the echo of his own barks, and in a frenzy now, he twisted around in the air as he lunged at the now ferocious face in the water.

---'Echo and Narcissus,' she said, 'wrapped in a glossy black cloak. I am Pluto. I see my own reflection, call it world, and fall in love with it. I say: 'I love you,' and hear it say 'I love you,' back. Trough, square, dog. But one dog, only one. The doggy face in the puddle is my own face. The doggy barks are mine. I am alone. And tempted to quote Kurtz.'

---'Thanks.'

She seemed to be looking to see if there was somebody behind me through eyes which glistened blindly.

---'No; you're right. I am Bucephalus except: I sometimes wonder if you know you're Alexander. And except: perhaps I am right to be scared.'

By now all the dogs in the town were barking sensuously too. Uproar. Through the glazed door of the bar we could see people emerging from under all the arches to see what was up. And windows swinging open, people leaning out. Crowds were even gathering on the roofs. Some, shielding their eyes with their hands, were looking at the sky and pointing up at where huge flocks of starlings turned and twisted and formed weird, inviting and repulsive shell-like flowers, passing across the bright face, even in this blue twilight, of the moon.

Down at the bar, Hella warming her backside at the stove. I could see she wanted to lift the rear panel of the blood-stained dress to take the heat better on her goose-pimpled bum. And I wanted that too; I wanted the panel lifted. I wanted to see. Still. Again.

The Mayor was calling for calm over the town-wide PA and had put on a soothing soundtrack of jingles and nursery rhymes. We went outside with a bottle of wine and sat on a stone bench against one of the piers of the town's arcade. The air cold and smelling of smoke and chestnut. Hella crossed her ankles, her feet, encased in her new boots, up on a chair.

She was looking into space where the flocks of starlings described their moving forms, suggesting ideas ambiguous, disturbing to the point of nausea, and physically impossible. And she took up the bottle, unpeeled the lead-foil cap, flipped off the rubber stopper with her thumbnail, and raised it up, so her throat pulsed and the liquid in the bottle bubbled and frothed.

---'What about glasses,' I said.

And when I took a glass and filled it, she looked at me. Her voice very slightly slurred, as if drunk in advance.

---'Don't use a glass,' she said. Something imperfect in the air. As usual.

---'And another thing:' she looked down, looked sunken, looked suddenly up to me. 'One day, we'll have to go home.'

Pluto, having shook himself and sprayed us with muddy water, lodged under the table between our feet, wagging his tail but in need of reassurance.

We finished the bottle and took another. Hella, unpeeling it like fruit and flipping the plastic stopper off. And swigging greedily. The mayor sent with it a vinegary dish of minute silver fish. She turned her face up to the sky and holding each by its tail, let it fall into her open mouth and crunched it up. Her eyes, blind, wide, staring at the starlings turning and skimming and unfolding in space. Taking up the bottle again, she washed away the taste of fish. Until, struck by insight, she clopped it down on the scrubbed white wood, and watched a pinkish fountain squirt from its neck.

She giggled, and red wine fell from her giggling lips like blood, and curved from either end of her lips to her chin, which she held up high, and wiped with the back of a long brown hand.

The side of her face was on the table now, and she was looking at me sweetly, sideways. But I'd clicked out. I couldn't remember where I was in my life, what page I was on, and who was still alive and who was already born and who was not yet dead. And it didn't matter. Looking down on the whole of it, rather than being in it, this was the sensation. The mind disconnected, the illusions, but what replaced them far sweeter and more magical. An acceptance of, a love for, everything that happens. Seeing its divinity, accepting it, warmly, calmly. A feeling of no problems, ever again. Nothing mattered, all was good. Whether this in turn was an illusion or was true, time would tell, possibly with some brutality, viciousness.

Above us the moon floated upwards, the evening sky darkened and the starlings swirled. And all the dogs in Anlo roared.

Hella was beside herself. Her mouth open in shrieks of silent laughter, her eyes shut tight, suffering a fit. She struggled and battled for air. And raising her head, sighting it, taking the bottle as firmly by its neck as if it were a living chicken, she turned her eyes sweetly, trustingly, to mine, and lifted it carefully towards me.

As I took it she closed her lips, ballooned her cheeks, and allowed a mouthful of yellow sick to splodge upon the table. I put the bottle down. She smiled. The brightness of her teeth, flocked with shreds of sick, set in wine-stained gums. As I watched, her lips began to move, the teeth parted, and I saw a blackened tongue dart and flip about.

---'What you looking at,' it said, and the lips became enormous, and kissed the lashes and closing lids of my eye. A hot and biting whiff of sick.

Then there was a noise: Pop!

She drew her face back in surprise. Purple wine was flowing from the base of the bottle and streaming off the table and onto the flags. Finding a crack between two flags, it flowed along. Finding a hole it disappeared. She lifted the bottle by its neck, and it seemed to rise; but its base stayed on the table; briefly a bottle-shaped jelly of liquid wine seemed to sway and quiver above this base---and then collapsed, splashing across the table onto our knees and the floor.

It had cracked---cleanly, perfectly, in a circular hairline - on its own. As mysteriously as if both bottle and its contents had turned to fire.

---'Weird.' She slurred the word. Waving the neck of the bottle in her hand like a weapon, and accidentally brushing the soft underside of her wrist as she did so, so that in one of those confusing episodes of repetition which seem to cross the eyes of your mind---eagle and snake, blackbird and worm - a hairline crack appeared there too---in the bluish, greenish, white underside skin, and like wine, out seeped blood, blackish but turning quickly scarlet.

The world is hard to change; you think you've changed it, made it a new dress; but then the world is sick down the front of it, it gets stained with black blood and black wine. Things go wrong. Things go bad.

Coming back to the fonda, Hella's neat wound wrapped in one of those small, sodden squares of towelling, with the name of a beer shaved out of the pile, usually used to adorn the zinc lids of bars, we found the washing line hung with drying salamis. Tended by Encarnación who, seeing Hella's dress stained black with blood and pink with wine and grey with sick, formed the side of her hand into a chopper and hacked at the side of her, Hella's, neck.

Hella, her arm round my neck, could hardly stand. She kept going loose at the knees and trying to pull me over.

---'I'll kill her, I will', Encarnación warned, bundling Fadrique and me back out into the square and stripping Hella naked before sluicing her sticky body down with tongues of iced water from a galvanised bucket.

This sobered her up a bit. So that later, once in bed:

---'I love you', she said.

---'I'm glad you're beautiful'. Weak, but there it is.

And from looking self-possessed she looked small, young, scared. Then, kissing me over-passionately, her breath still scented with sick, and speaking loudly in my ear so it hurt, she said:

---'Fuck me then'.

Her warm bum in my hands heavy, blunt, there, yet not going beyond its ideal form; no heavier than it should be but as heavy, even the black line which split it---the bottle, the wrist, the spectra again - necessary, ideal. As I craned to watch a moth bounced off the light bulb and onto her back. And got itself entangled in a stray gold hair which looked more like a line of light than a hair. Struggling, trying to disentangle itself with its own hairy legs but only making things worse. As the line of light began to cut notches in its damp, dusty wings.

---'Hey don't, it tickles?'

---'It's only a moth'.

She felt for it, and tipped it about in the palm of her hand, spreading the wings gently like a bird's. She suddenly looked my way with an open mouth, as I suddenly closed my eyes. Why? It was too much. Too rich. Too relentless. I wasn't up to it.

---'I can't identify this.'

---'Wait till you get your books.'

---'It's got the wrong mottles, the wrong marks.'

---'Burned by the bulb.'

---'They're symmetrical,' she said.

And hid it under an empty glass.

Then she gasped.

---'What now?'

She pressed her skin against me all the way down. Her hair, in one twisted sheaf or mop, coiled across the crumpled sheet above her head: she was on her back, her head twisted round, mouth open, arms hooped up. I kissed her forehead, which was damp. Her nipples, burnt by the sun at the cave, had turned from brown to strawberry.

She went quiet, and I thought she'd gone to sleep until she said:

---'Hey ...'

---'What now.'

---'Open the window.'

---'What about the mosquitoes.'

---'I'm hot.'

---'Hey ...'

---'I don't want to be talked to anymore.'

---'I'm sorry.'

---'But, I can't sleep.'

---'Why not?' I asked eventually. No answer.

---'Why not?'

But her breathing, steady, slow. She had blunted her nose against my side. And looking down at her, afraid to move in case she woke, I had a subtle roaring in my chest, and I loved more sharply than I ever did awake. She stopped. This was why. No longer a moving target. Or if still moving, not moving so fast. Because even in her sleep she followed me across to my side of the sagging bed. Sweaty, hot. The air was cold but she was hot. And when I climbed out, and went round to the other side, she followed me there too. So that throughout the night I was balanced on an edge, on one side or the other.

And in the darkness, the mosquitoes began to roar. I could feel them landing on my face.

But I too slept. Disordered dreams. Hella was travelling by balloon. I was to follow in a canoe.

And I discovered that Hella and Pluto were sleeping together. Fucking each other.

May sound funny, but was terrible. Hella, knees apart and bum in the air, was making a voiced whistle as Pluto, glossy, black, passed his tail between his legs and slid it into her. Some of the hairs on this tail, bristling, slimed, out of place. I woke trembling and drugged, my mouth furred up.

Only the moon had moved. Through the window at the foot of the bed, a bright star shone like a compass prick at the exact centre of the sickle, which is impossible, so perhaps it was a satellite.

While above us in the darkness bats, having taken over from the starlings, flittered and turned and whirled.

6

It was the flies now who whirled and danced, and the sun burned through the thin, sprigged curtain. When I woke, Hella was scribbling in the marbled notebook she'd bought the day before in the square.

---'What are you writing?' Drawing myself up.

The page was filled with long equations in numbers and Greek. She was writing very fast and hard, as if trying to dig through the paper, and she turned the pages in a strange way, writing on the right-hand side before the left.

---'Shh.'

---'And why do you do it in that order?'

---'Please?'

Her hair had gone flat; and two white-tipped pimples had sprouted at one end of her mouth. Her skin dry, and her eyes too; they'd lost their lustre; the whites dull as the whites of hard-boiled eggs. I knew she'd slept but it looked as if she hadn't slept at all. Pale and guilty. The air saturated with remorse.

By speaking about leaving, the day before, by deciding to leave, we had already gone. I saw us dismantling our time together, fanatics breaking an idol or a skull to scoop out its power.

---'Shall we go today? Now?' she asked, suddenly turning her tired face to me as greenish tears started dripping onto the upper surfaces of her breasts. A drop formed on each bare nipple and jiggled as she spoke. Then she slid down and dried them on my bare chest.

Downstairs, the kitchen deserted. But hanging on a chair set with its back to the fire, was Hella's dress. Warm as milk. It had snowdrops newly embroidered on the bodice, in green and white thread. And somehow brought down, made figurative, earthed, its mystery lost.

She wanted me to sit next to her while we ate, and held my eyes so long it was embarrassing. Also she wanted to be touched all the time---she wanted my hand round her back and pulling gently at her waist. Casting heavy eyes about, a hand on my knee. Meanwhile her breasts, besides having sprouted sprigs of snowdrops, had become bigger, heavier. Even her hair had changed, taken a maturer light. Instead of hanging down her back, sheened, fine, straightened by its own weight and with only the gentlest of curls, it had arranged itself into thick spumy locks, which made it yellower, more creamy, something you could touch, live with, suck, pull her head about with when you fucked. A metamorphosis. As if what would crawl out at the end, if still an angel, would be one with the wings of a moth. Was this what they call marriage? At least, to use her language, what marriage is an imperfect model of? Because her thighs, also had a greater weight; no longer the lithe girl in the race but the young woman with, as body, an ideal. Before there had been something untouchable to her; something too fast and light to catch, something to yearn for but never quite to have; but there wasn't now. Now she was the woman who has been caught at last and, both hands clasped between her open legs, is turning back her swollen lips to kiss.

Out in the square a whiff of mountains, sulphurous and inorganic, and coldness like a physical force. And nothing else, except perhaps the sweet damp smell of wool. She went straight to a yellow post-box which was painted with red lines to resemble the folds of an envelope.

---'What's that letter?' I said.

She closed her lips tight and looked stubborn. Struggling with it, so the corner came off. That's all I could got before she slipped it into the box. I looked in the slit and tried to see who it was addressed to. I tried to get my hand in after it.

---'Is it to Haakon?'

---'No.'

A pang of jealousy, bitter as diarrhoea. Not even Haakon!

I pushed my hand harder but it wouldn't go through.

---'Who, then?'

---'You'll get it stuck.'

---'A lover?'

---'I hate that word.'

---'Answer me.'

---'Yes.'

---'Who?'

---'I can't say.'

---'Do you love him?'

---'Yes.'

---'A lot?'

---'More than I can say.'

I sat down on a bit of tarmac.

The obvious question: 'more than me?'

Ask the question.

But I didn't dare. Cold.

---'More than me?'

Tensing the muscles in my stomach like Houdini as she smiled.

---'About the same.'

Even worse. This was unbearable. Distrusting her. Even cutting myself off from her. Trying to get out of her who it had been.

Pluto gormless following us abound. I wanted to kick him.

So I did. The yelp came not from him but her. He looked guilty and slunk away. He knew what he'd done. We're all sinners.

---'You shit,' she said. 'I'm only teasing you. It's to my dad.'

Later, we carried his lunch up through the trees to where Fadrique worked.

Passing Gregory's on the way.

Hella walked with her shoulders rounded and her spine held slack.

Following the valley, we looked out for the smoke from Fadrique's fire. The landscape spreading out behind us as we climbed. Anlo, from up here, no more than a single square, with some whitish ribbon-development on the track to Orguel. And suddenly, going up like rockets, four white pigeons; and swooping down again.

A cold wind and sudden spitty rain as we waited for them to rise again. When they didn't, we walked on.

Erotic possibilities in a black plastic sackful of clothes, ripped open and scattered across the dust. She, with the rapid movements of someone at a jumble sale, selected an olive green jumper, shook it open, and wedged it under her arm.

---'I've just doubled my wardrobe,' she said.

Fadrique was at the far end of a terraced meadow sown with fresh green winter wheat, brighter than grass and already a few inches deep. Between each row glowed the shit-coloured earth, and the field had the same, pregnant belly on it as the sea had from the windows of the *Pensione Otarí* a century or so ago. The sense again that everything was the same thing, coming back to haunt or even tease us, in differing guises. The sense, even, that we were at a fancy dress party with one multitudinous guest.

Fadrique was sawing away at a great aromatic bush. Our job was to drag the black spiny branches out and throw them onto the fire. A blackbird was calling. And we were dragging braches. I still remember the pale disks of the sawn ends, gleaming with pure yellow light, and the filmy orange fabric of the flames.

---'Did it have to be you?' she said as we dragged.

---'Such a fucking chatterbox.'

---'Chatterbox?' She looked mystified, but chattered on. 'Or was it more to do with the state we were in than with you and me? I don't think so; it wasn't that it was pre-ordained that we should meet, but it was ordained that we should love each other if we should, whatever state you were in, whatever state I was.'

---'Stop ...'

---'Even if I was pregnant with someone else's child I should have loved
you. No, I want you to know this. You have to know. So: in that sense,
people are absolute, not relative. Which is why, when I was still just
about a child myself, I used to lie in bed at night, hearing the footsteps
pass along the icy, gritty boardwalk underneath my windows, and
suddenly get up and look out, in case it was already you; you won't
believe it, but it's true. Anyway, it never was; and then it was, but I lost
you; so that when Haakon having courted me was generally sweet, well:
I said I'd buy a flat with him. Perhaps there was an element of death-
wish in this, an element of sharing the common fate of the world. And
anyway, you took too long about it, you took too long ...'

This was when Encarnación came stumbling up, wheezing and gasping.
Her face white as the dove she held in her hands, except for the fine
purple sprigs of broken vein in her cheeks. The dove's eyes and wings
were closed. A thread of blood swung from each of the minute nostrils
pricked in its beak. She was spreading its wings, showing it to us:

---'When I let them out ....'

---'Yes?' said Fadrique.

---'They mounted very high ....'

---'Yes?'

---'And closed their wings, and tumbled and fell, tumbling over and over,
 until ...'

---'Yes?'

---'They encountered the ground.'

---'All four?'

---'All!'

---'What a shame.'

Hella was trying not to giggle, as at a funeral. Not entirely successfully.
Tears running down Encarnación's face.

---'Poor little things ...'

---'What a way to go!' said Hella. 'This has to be comforting. Like Shelley. Or more obviously, Saint-Exupéry. Or, of course, like Dumpty and like Icarus.'

---'Shelley? Saint-Exupéry?' Encarnación asked, her blinking eyes sticky. Before Hella could explain, a clattering came abruptly, no warning, and terrible. I remember the different resonances of a bush, swinging in the wind, which seemed to move in waves and eddies as the flock of starlings had. She looked up sharply and gripped my arm as the dark bulk of a helicopter leaped like a beast from the crown of a pine and hung over us. The flames in Fadrique's fire crouched along the ground and the sun went out---that was the effect, the machine so close. Gusts and flurries of brown sand and white ash whirled around and Hella's skirt snapped and rattled like the thick white sail of a sailing boat, pregnant with wind.

---'He's trying to frighten us,' she shouted, as it made as if to squat upon us.

---'Like Ali,' I shouted back. Fadrique and Encarnación had already disappeared.

Her small bare knees, reddened by the cold and by the sun, and her dress, inflated, fluttering, burning in the wind like a flame. We ran.

It followed. Danced along on a tail like an ice cream cone, its bubble up. Performing tricks. Surrounded by a carpet of twisting rabbits, we doubled and ran back, leaping the fire; it overshot us, turned on its side and drifted back.

Spraying a white dust from a nozzle in the engine, apparently onto the pines.

---'He's spraying the pines,' she shouted, 'try not to breathe.'

She was wrong. It wasn't just white dust now, as the helicopter bounced and rattled in the sky. Orange vines with jagged yellow leaves were creeping up the rotor shaft and dancing at the still centre of the blades.

---'What's he doing? The fool.'

Someone in camouflage dress was hanging from a landing skid; he suddenly dropped, landed on his feet, and coiled into a tiny pile like a turd. And another. A third. The helicopter, meanwhile, wanting to go backwards, and down, pivoting over its tail which dangled only a few feet above the earth, and over, and pointing its rotor at last at the ground, so that we could see the fear in the face of the pilot hanging inside his bubble, his lips opened wide over closed teeth. Close enough to meet and hold our eyes---first mine, then Hella's.

---'This way,' she was shouting---and I figured what was so spooky: the helicopter was dancing, to some devilish music, but very sweetly, courtly, stately: until it delicately buried its tail in the wheat, dislodging a few rocks. The blades nipped off and spun boomeranging through the scrub, scoring canary-coloured trails of shattered woodwork and shorn bark in which severed leaves and sawdust first hung, and then slowly sank, followed by slowly toppling trees; and little white squirts and jets of powdery smoke emerged through a glowing black cloud which now half hid the sinking machine. We could see enough to watch it lay itself down, gently, on its side, shattered: and then the rattling of someone desperate to get out of a bathroom, and a thundery detonation which stopped all that.

---'Don't look,' she was saying, 'just run.' And not for the first time she pulled my arm so hard it hurt. We ran. Stones flying past us; also things with trails of thick blue smoke spuming out. A pine, dislodged from its roots, pogoed beside us before tilting and settling softly into a bed of branches to one side; and white tracer, spewing rocket-trails of steam, moving unrealistically fast, so that even as we ran we felt we were going backwards in a comically accelerated film,.overtaken by the world and by a turning, rolling shaft which dug each vicious shattered spinning end into the shallow earth, splashing dust and pebbles as it span beside her us and span on---and all in silence until I heard her say, 'Lie down;' and then hot air behind us, a fart and a harsh hollow belch like the bursting of a heart, and her hair came up over her head and danced above it with drifting leaves, but that was nothing to the noise there was. There was nothing to do; reason couldn't help, it was fear; you had to run again; I pulled her up by the arm and we ran on until we came to the edge of the precipice, where the gully was filled with myrtle and *encina* and spread-hand-palm and sharp green thorns and with the blitheness of people on the edge of a dark green swimming pool, leaping as high and as far as we could, we jumped in.

There was silence at last, then.

The blackbird stopped. The crickets stopped. It was strangely hot.

She was lying across me.

---'Alright?'

Her face green. When she opened her mouth to speak, blood came out.

---'Fuck!'

---'It's only my shoulder I think,' she burbled through blood.

So that, above us the new successive booms and cracks of the helicopter didn't matter that much.

I could see the crown of a pine burning and crackling; every golden burning needle visible, even from our gully. Turning back to face her; she opened her mouth again; more blood came out. Strange: her lips and nose white as the whites of her eyes, in a green face with a red chin.

---'Shit!'

---'It hurts. My shoulder.'

Drawing down the white bodice with the reverse of sensuality. Underneath, smudged and printed with red.

And what looked like bloody, shattered chicken bones sticking out through skin.

---'Fuck it, fuck.'

The sense that having got in we couldn't out; the cat up the tree, the dog down the hole. Headfirst. Stuck.

She looked at me gently, steadily, calmly, out of those eyes, but she didn't look down. But smiled.

---'I doubt it's mortal,' she mumbled. 'Venial perhaps, not mortal.'

She spoke like someone coming out of the dentist's.

---'Keep your mouth shut. There's blood coming out.'

She sucked the air sharply, several times and said:

---'I know, I bit my tongue.'

On the edge of the gully above us, the airmen stood like two out of three graces, their arms around one another's necks, their faces buried in one another's shoulders, and they were bawling. Only Fadrique, holding his hat at his rump in the heat, his face and bald head glazed with sweat, was calm as if this happened often. He took out a handkerchief and scrubbed his wet face. Then, thinking he had stuffed it in his pocket, he let it fall, opening like a parachute and gliding sideways as it did so, to the ground.

---'It's Hella.' When turned and saw my face he moved.

Looking down at her.

---'Don't worry, it's snapped,' she said.

---'Did anything hit you?'

---'Are the others alright? Can we get out of here?'

---'Don't shout. It's over now.'

---'I'm not.'

And closed her eyes.

---'Stay here, stay here,' he shouted, hitting my arm and barely refraining from hitting hers.

---'I'm not going anywhere,' she said, but so quietly only I could hear.

And he ran away towards Anlo, shouting and waving his arms, a man imitating a chopper.

Very slowly, Hella cradling her arm like a bird, we climbed out.

Encarnación talking very fast and very loud, still holding the dove. The two graces cuddling, silent and white; the third still coiled on the ground. Black smoke pumping out from the tiny boned wreckage of the helicopter, visible now, emerged from its modest cloud, so you didn't understand how so much smoke could come from such a tiny thing, and in the heart of the smoke, were white, magnesium gleams, ruptures to another universe.

I too wanted to cry. Gregory arrived.

---'Jesus Bloody Christ!' he said.

And the Mayor in a *Land Rover*, with Cesár. Encarnación was led away, still talking very loudly and very fast, still holding the dead bird.

The external shock which restores a state of disequilibrium.

I kissed her forehead, but she raised her boiling, salty lips to meet mine with a gasp as she disturbed her arm, and then she laughed. The sexiness of her fragility---of the body defined as something material, animal, and this sharpening up, pointing up her soul until it was almost painful to look at her, made my eyes smart.

---'You ...'

---'Yes.'

---'Kiss me,' she said. 'No, not my lips, my collarbone. Kiss it better.' And in my clumsiness I did and made her shriek with pain. 'Better not perhaps,' she said, as soon as she could talk. Her arm was completely loose, and I threaded it slowly into the neck-hole of her dress, which sagged, revealing one hemispherical breast. 'I'm cold,' she said.

And then, a goofy face.

---'Hella,' sternly.

---'Yes,' all innocence.

---'What is it now?'

---'Icarus,' she said. 'He wants to fall. He makes himself wings so he can fall.' As she spoke, more blood gobbling out. 'They have touched it all. They have touched the mystery with their dirty hands. They have touched the swan.'

---'Shhh. No poetry.'

She sounded drunk . In her pain she'd licked all the colour from her lips, and also licked the blood away. Lying like a limp doll now at the foot of a tree, waiting for whatever. People standing around her, staring, particularly at one naked breast, which the collar bone made hang wrong.

---'The swan's feathers are black; you can see it, beneath the white, like the black soil beneath the melting snow. You can see the blackness hidden in the white.'

Serious or delirious? An element of each, perhaps. The anagogical mystery, the celestial fire she lit beneath her words. A parallel, essential spirit-world which she tried at least to summon up, kind of.

---'Shh, Hella! No poetry.'

---'No poetry after Adorno.'

It was a horrible pun, especially in the presence of violent death and flames, but she was in shock.

---'And this mystery: it is more than just the limit of our understanding. It is something about the world, something in the world, and something essential, important, more important than all our reason, more elemental characteristic of the world. This thing we cannot catch, this thing we cannot reach, this is the bone of the fruit. But should we be trying to reach it? Are we not here to be happy, and does this not make us sad?'

In these states, the world seems to be helping you, prompting you, giving you clues. All the mysteries link arms, dance, pout and point. But what is it they are pointing at? However hard you stare, you still can't make it out.

---'The golden age, and its loss; why? Deliberate: eating the tree of knowledge: you always will; and you'll always regret it. In each successive Eden, the first thing to look for is that tree.'

What I thought she meant: this time Gabriel came by helicopter. Ejecting us from Eden again. From the groves of olives, almonds, oranges, etc. But above all that we had invited this. No rationally, causally, but spiritually. Our guilt. Knowledge perhaps.

And again: the literal nature of the world's symbols. The world a naïve, if rich artist: something of a *Douanier* Rousseau, a Blake. For instance, these beings raining down on us from the sky: the white pigeons and this machine. The same structure endlessly repeated until, fed up with the heavy-handed hints, you devise a meaning for them at last.

Or there was a causal connection, as in one of the white pigeons getting into the engine, or the approach of the helicopter had scared them so much that they fell from the sky. Or both.

It was as if the blackbird with its worm had seen the buzzard, seen the snake. And the white dress spattered with blood again. And something else; specks of green.

---'Icarus flutters too high and then, poor earth and poor mankind.'

---'What do you mean?'

The pilot himself, the fourth man, lay carelessly amongst the wreckage, visible now the fire was nearly burned out. He was more recognisable and less damaged than his machine, his beloved device, with his oily, glistening limbs, blunt hands and feet, neutered body, and with pinks and roses in pink and white mincemeat flowering from his popped wet brow.

---'What the heck?' Gregory asked.

---'He went too near the sun.'

---'No, Hella,' he said earnestly. 'Hell, the man's dead.'

---'I'm not joking, I'm serious: we owe it him to see the poetry: it's all he has left, and there is some. He has left it to us. At least we saw: that should make him less lonely.'

---'Jesus, she's wasted in physical sciences,' he said.

---'It depends on your priorities. At least I have something to be wasted in.'

Faintly tetchy. Broken chords, harmonics, the way everything resonates, quite apart from her bones. The crumbs she threw the dead white pigeon, for instance, scaring it away, and the crumbs she threw me, scaring me. That these are the threads that bind the world; these are its nature. Without its resonances it would fall apart, would not stop being, but would start to not have been.

Pluto was trying to lick her eyes. His tail wagging, he was licking the tears away. Then, sniffing the wound, the blood, the shattered bone, superstitiously. And licking it too. Pre-Hippocratic medicine this. Unless it was more, unless it was Pluto's Christianity, because there was no doubt in his mind that she was divine. I had to pull him away by his tail, and even as I did so he stretched in the middle, and his long tongue grew longer and went on licking.

---'No Pluto, no.'

---'Let him be,' she said with her eyes screwed up.

---'What is good about the world,' she went on, 'is the way it evades analysis---at least the way it both accepts and evades analysis.'

---'Hella, can't you stop talking for a bit. Stop thinking.'

---'Our models work for a while, but in the end they always fail, even the most successful: arithmetic and logic. Rickety structures which sway when you move. This is one of the things we mean by God. God, among other things, is what we call the blind spots of our logic. Not God of gaps, I don't mean that, but God of mysteries.'

This was like a legacy, a testament.

---'You're not dying?'

She looked sad, but suddenly a smile gleamed.

---'We all are,' she said. 'And ...'

---'And what?'

Her qualities sometimes were not in her but in me; a fairy godmother at a Christening it was for me to choose not only which qualities--- prettiness, seductiveness, sensuality, charm, sexiness---to see in her, but also which bad fairies not to ask.

Being faced with her depth, of spirit, heart, corpse, made me understand that unlike her I must only consume: I could be human; I could fuck, eat and shit, I could make girls happy or unhappy, I could have children, perhaps. But in the domain of ideas, the domain-beyond-life, I could do nothing. I couldn't shout loud enough to be heard once dead; I couldn't see over the edge of my grave. And I wasn't good enough for her, would never be, unless like the people hanging on to the ropes of an aeronaut's balloon, I could bring her down.

And strangely, savagely happy, as if released from responsibility.

---'We look for the depth and mystery in the world,' she said. 'Bored of
the natural; it is the supernatural we want now. But every time we think
we have it by the tail, it slips away; it didn't have a tail, it turns out, or
it did but we didn't have it by it. And this too is a characteristic of the
world---perhaps a necessary characteristic, of any world which is to have
power and mystery, of any world in which we are to be curious. You
have to be able to reduce mathematics to logic---nearly; the world has to
have order---nearly; if mathematics was logic, if the world was order, the
world would be a machine; if mathematics was irrational, if the world
was random, we could never know it. So: this hard thing, if you press
too hard, flips away; you can know---a bit; but there is a principle of the
conservation of mystery who, if you move in with her, moves out that
night and goes to live someplace else.'

---'So how do you account for this?'

Showing her pine woods, wet with fresh rain and shimmering in
thousands of points of red, blue, violet, yellow in the shallow sunlight.
And chestnut woods, their leaves already banana yellow with brown
spots like the spots on bruised bananas. Her too: her face, body, mind,
heart.

---'This!' she said dismissively. 'You'll see. Too soon. It won't last long.'
White steam came out of her mouth as she spoke. Someone was offering
her coffee from a steel flask. And I felt my bones cool and shrink in the
padded, blood-wet slots inside my limbs.

The surgeon arrived on a mule, already, as it struggled across the field,
shaking his head. A handsome old fool, smug, vain. Gold pince-nez and
stiff grey hair. It was the vet we'd seen on our first night swinging the
prolapsed ewe about in the hall of the fonda. Now, his upper lip lifted
from his teeth, and his eyebrows from his eyes, wrinkling his forehead,
he looked down through half-moon pince-nez at her shoulder.

---'Ah! Aha! A collar bone!' he said. 'Clean snap.' He tore off a strip of the
hem of her dress and tied a sling. 'It's nothing to worry about. Nothing at
all. We'll send her down to Orguel. She'll be better in a week or two.'

Later another helicopter came, and took away the aircrew, both living
and dead, the dead in thick, black, oily-plastic sacks, and also Hella. No
room for me or Pluto.

---'Will they look after you?'

---'It is how religions start.'

Pluto running after it, as if it could be scared-away, made to drop her
before it was too late. His long, bandy shadow, too, running over baked
lumpy earth, tinted orange by the failing sun. He didn't look up---that
didn't occur to him. What he was trying to bite and harry was the
helicopter's shadow, with, presumably, in its belly, hers - moving over the
ground in a bitter, whirling wind. He was opening and closing his mouth.
Without the sound of barking; this looked strange.

---'Pluto!'

It was no good.

So I too ran as it rose---blowing me with its wind, blinding with its dust
and grit---and turned and thudded off. Very quickly it grew blue and
shrank, and disappeared behind a wooded slope. Only to appear again,
a little higher up, much smaller, following the side of the enormous,
wooded mountain; until I lost it, couldn't see it anymore, and tears on
my face, turned back.

The Mayor put his arm around my shoulder. I didn't like this.

---'The *Land Rover*---too humpy. You see what I mean? A road? You see
now? What I mean?'

The inconveniences of paradise, is what he meant. That's over now. Dead.

I was to follow her by *Land Rover*. And here it was, waiting, its engine
revving.

Pluto still not back.

---'We'll look after him,' said Encarnación, still holding that dead dove,
her eyes screwed up.

I was trying meanwhile to picture Hella's face, her body, under the white
dress. But I couldn't. My heart plucked out, and eaten, on a spine. All I
could see were patches of sprouting winter wheat, dusted with white
ashes, amongst moulded, flattish brown rock. And quartz, lying about,
broken into lumps like coconut meat.

Arriving at the hospital in Orguel: a sinking feeling. The smell of people's deaths, creeping, slinking all through the wards. Something ontologically frightening about it, something to make you hopeless. To remind you what life is for, but only once it's too late. And yet, if you think too much it all rots and melts, nothing holds; you wade through a stinking red & green sludge. With bones in it. And scraps of cloth.

Her mishap took a while to fix. She was in the hospital for a fortnight, while it was rebroken and reknit, and a seeping infection dosed with IV penicillin. Waiting for her in a sweaty apartment block. Like waiting outside the garage for your car to be fixed. Each day sitting on her bed, trying to feed her figs and pomegranates; each day going out of the room with the doctor:

---'Not yet. Tomorrow. Perhaps.'

When tomorrow came we left by train, Hella's nose and eyes red, her greenish hair flat on her head, and her arm resting in a sling half straight-jacket half folded wing. The carriages were built of fretted wood, with open balconies at each end. We rode in the last, and from its balloon-like balcony, lined in wickerwork, watched the landscape recede at a walking pace. As we travelled back, unpicking our work, making a request halt in the valley beneath the walls of Anlo where Encarnación, blubbering, and Fadrique, stern, returned Pluto to us, the glossy tube of his lithe body twisting like a fish, and on (with the shriek of some hysterical bird) up-river, passing the abandoned farmhouse on its hill and even the beech thicket which concealed the cave. Watching a calf run bucking and kicking away with a stiff kinked ropey tail, and a foal stream away too, with a stiff tail of made of brown candy floss. We, who naked from a thicket had watched so many trains pass, were now carried past our own thicket on a train ⊠ before the play ends, you play every part. Then: into a tunnel, cold, scented of clean mould, and a sudden rebirth into colder, bluer light. A further climb, in open air, to a pass. Wet, grey snow.

And a trumpeting, a kind of compressed or concertinaed fanfare when, with the air of the roller coaster having come almost to a standstill at the summit of the pass the train began, very slowly, to roll down the far slope. As we rolled, her eyes were flicking from side to side. She was counting the telegraph poles.

Also, licking her lips with quick, quick flickers.

A thunderstorm looming and the air growing ever more cold. We went inside and Hella, lying across the fretted wooden seats in the empty carriage, fell asleep. Her raucous breathing. The sound of a concertina, even a fanfare. Too much duplication, sending me loopy---unless it was just a symptom of loopiness. Her hair rayed and spreading with static, and snagging on the coarse upholstery of the backrests.

Now the train was climbing again.

A miniature storm, flashing with an unsteady but repetitive beat, like a neon sign, as if to mark the spot, to lead us on, to show us where we would at last be happy. The storm broke, rattling the windows of our carriage, and Hella's rasping breath softened, became inaudible. Leaving Pluto, licking his own black lips, and trembling under her seat, I went out on the balcony to watch.

The train was still climbing through intermittent darkness, whipped by rhythmical waves of rain. Something dirty about this thunderstorm, impure, unnatural, like a big-city storm in the course of an epidemic.

Going back inside. Waking her. Sex on the fretted seat; as if with a stranger. Moving with my movement, she looked at me, wide-eyed; pride, scorn. Distance. Somehow even hate.

And of course pain.

The train still climbing.

Guards with automatic weapons woke us, and soon discovered we had no identification of any kind. I explained that this placed us above suspicion, that no terrorist or drug-runner would present himself without papers like this, but heard Hella saying:

---'Come on, Pluto, let's get off.'

She led us round the back of the frontier post where we stumbled through a flooded gutter and past a row of whitewashed stones to board the front of the same train.

The rain had dyed her hair dark, and glued it in tangled strands across her wet face making her look, as she gazed blankly up at me once more before she boarded, like a mermaid caught in a net. The same face of passive tragedy.

Come dawn we were rolling down the dark-blue viaduct which passes over St Antonin.

---'Jump Pluto. It isn't far. Jump.'

Not from the viaduct itself; simply onto the track. She wanted him to find his own way home. But Pluto looked lovingly up into her face, and slowly wagged his tail.

---'Jump,' she said urgently.

Pluto looking on, patiently. She pointed out the hotel and St Antonin, revolving steadily with our movement like models on a turntable, and jolting with the jolting of the train, far beneath. And in the end, turning him bodily round, she put her shoe between his legs, dividing his black protuberant bollocks, and shoved him overboard. A railway is a rosary on which episodes from your history are strung. Pluto yelping as he rolled in the gravel, and then up and after the train, running as fast as he could, body doubled with speed, forelegs sticking out between the back, snapping at the red wheels and their white rims.

Eventually he stopped, and stood with his forefeet on a rail looking after us, growing rapidly smaller, tail at half-mast. And when I looked at Hella, her face wet; and as I watched, it crumpled up in ugliness and turned red.

---'That felt a bit like an abortion,' she said.

Reaching the terminus. And walking in the park while we waited for her train. A large orange sun sinking amongst plane trees. On an equestrian monument a little girl cooking up some dope; blunt face, the lower part coming further out than the upper; one of Renoir's strawberry-blondes; and a hard, boyish body; black jeans and a German army-surplus coat, and a strand of her hair bound up in coloured threads; and such a sudden, unexpected yearning for her, that I thought I'd never be happy; in my whole life never happy. She was hanging out with African kids. Rough ones; dealers. They wanted Hella to stay with them. And they wanted to sell me hash.

Climbing through a wooden paling, clearing the orange leaves from a stone bench. Winter, coming too soon. The bench, it turned out, was the lid of a sarcophagus, propped like a wheel-less car on bricks. Reality, sugary and cheap. Her face, and under it her skull. Nearby, in a muddy pit, a stone trough trembling with clear water, and clean bones with broken ostrich shells resting peacefully in it. Unable to escape forever from the academic vision, the academic take, we had climbed into a dig.

---'It doesn't have to be, you know,' she said.

Meanwhile, her hair, somewhere between pink, orange and blonde: crushed lips, swollen, sensuous cheeks and a way of staring without flinching when your eyes came round to hers, still staring, until reluctantly, slowly, starting to smile.

---'I don't want to go,' she said.

Her legs were crossed, and her hands on her knees, and she was leaning forwards over the well so formed---I don't know what it was: there was something there, in the cylinder of hollow space half-enclosed by her body.

Too half-hearted to have sex. So climbing out again and going for a coffee in the station buffet. And saying, thrilled as we crossed the road, as if this was a very good sign indeed:

---'Careful, you know you're fucking hopeless with traffic.'

History as farce. Here, a madman grunting and groaning, and there a party of ancient ladies uncertain what to have. Our duty to the old and to the mad, to live. Which means to love. Our duty even to the starving: to live. Which means to love.

---'What do you want?' I asked her.

---'Hey?'

---'Yes?'

---'Will I see you again?'

The question mad, out of place, unreasonable. A bad question to ask, because it didn't have an answer which could sound right.

The first tears running out now, finding their way down her face, over dry skin. As, finding its own way along the polished rails, her train rolled in.

We found the carriage, and she went inside to claim her bunk. I saw she had her fingers crossed as she disappeared. On both hands. Before she came back the train started off.

Waiting for her to jump, at least to wave, but she didn't. Couldn't get the window down, perhaps. And I imagined her still fluttering feebly up against the glass, as if this train would roll her down its shining rails and through a wood to Birkenau, and on in, under the pretty arch. And it was just about okay by her.

Back in the buffet: the pretty girl, now without the Africans, looking at me, and smiling, so that I could see the spittle on her brace; she kept turning back her head, looking, smiling. Her eyes gleaming. As unconscious, stolid, Northern, true and too romantic, Hella was rattled away.

The girl was tapping the end of an unlit cigarette on the bar.

---'*Tienes Fuego?*' she asked.

But I shook my head and walked out, full of rage at leaving her---and not out of loyalty to Hella, but in case I missed my flight.

I made the same journey by air as Hella made by rail, leaving after her, swooping and frolicking above her, and arriving in Paris long before. While I, at the airport, was hunting for the international departure lounge and flirting almost naturally, like someone who isn't after all in shock, with the apple-cheeked hazel-eyed girl at the transit desk, Hella was still journeying towards me, helpless, unconscious, ludicrously stolid, on her train.

On the way to gate 27, a bent old man in black saying 'Thank you' as it opened to an automatic door. But he was so light, or moved so slowly, that it closed on him before he was through. He dropped his duty-free. Alcohol seeping out of a yellow plastic bag. Slipping in gin he fell on the bag, and rose to his feet yallering, with blood dripping off his cuffs.

There were lots of clocks, but they all said different times.

I bought a sandwich. The cheese tasted of petrol; the tea of grease. What was wrong?

Something was. Something very wrong; beneath the polished plastic floors, muttering voices conspiring misery. And what for? The same old crime. Aeneas, on the rolling, hopping sea, looking back on smoke. Nothing was clear to me, nothing even is. I didn't know why my eyes were stinging, why I couldn't see, yet why the air smelt clinging, sweet.

Are airports always like this? Or is grief?

Somehow we got aloft. For a moment I was scared; the image was so familiar that I thought we had flown too high, burnt our wings, were out in space. For like the web between an outstretched finger and thumb, I could see the long, sandy roll of France, wrinkled with rivers, fronting on Biscay, the long steady curve all the way up from the Pyrenees to the notched and weary cape of *Finistère*. Aviator, looking down from my porthole in pride, alarm, past my burnished wings---on dark blue water engraved with waves and miniature super-tankers, and on the dusty sprinkled earth---wondering, would we ever land, would this flight not go on for ever, go too high, too far, while behind me in the cabin a neat and docile Arab in a djellaba, having removed his shoes, squatted in a wider part of the aisle, near the emergency exit, blocking the passage of the scuffed aluminium trolley which had our lunches in, and I smelt his feet. And in all the rage of pain a baby screamed, roared, and made noises without name, noises half-electronic, which got inside your mind and made you mad.

I upgraded.

Then: the monotonous droning of the flight. The very front seat, so through twin portholes, I could see the clouds dividing to either side of the nosecone, as if for me, as if for me. And upstairs in the bar, chatting, sipping Champagne; leaning back like an angel on a barstool and exhaling such bonhomie as I was wafted homewards that aircrew and passengers clustered round me to clink glasses and laugh.

They didn't know.

Later I adhered a do not disturb sticker to my shoulder and took a snooze. Next thing I knew was the bump! of the runway.

There was some hold-up with my connecting flight. Freak snow-storms in the North. Slightly deranged, almost relieved, but not looking forward at all to Barb as I ate my complimentary meals and made my complimentary calls. To admit or to conceal what had happened? To admit anything would be to admit it all; she'd worm it out of me. And yet, the instinct of secrecy, not through fear of Barb, though there, too, was that, but through love for her.

I couldn't even say her name, not even to myself.

After many hours, we took off. Coming in over New Cardiff in the small plane, rocking and bumping stiffly like a car crossing a railway track. A deliquescent orange sun was settling on the horizon, and underneath us, as we sank, a rusty orange gasworks, larger than the sun, dulled and tinted with blue by evening light; and all the shrubby waste grounds and empty lots, littered with garbage and melting snow, turned black and green by onrushing night. A few scattered lights.

On the way from the airstrip to Campus, a storm of minute ice-flakes, so light that they came in round the edges of the closed windows of the cab and flurried inside. Harsh spurts of wind making us swerve and rock.

What in my childlike arrogance I thought a fault, I was already realising was power, Hella's womanliness suddenly burning out too brightly from the husk of a girl. She flowered early, but only because the seasons themselves were wrong: the winter too mild, the summer too short; it threw us. And the sight of the rich new flower hanging there, petal-lips, leaf-hips, was too much for me, made me almost nauseous, certainly afraid. It was like being in a car-crash, I couldn't handle it. And already, borne towards Barb's body, her face, her soul, I was starting to realise and starting to wish that I could have handled it, had handled it. So far I'd known Hella for twenty-one days, this time round at least.

Buzzing Barb's entry-phone, humping my bag up to her apartment.

Barb disinterested to see me.

Her kissable lips, in fact her face like a kiss ⊠ cute, but a shallowness to it, now. Her eyes looked only painted on. Her features half-submerged and softened, as if by a flood. Her bum, its shape defined by the shape alone of her underwear through creased beige or was it mushroom linen pants. As she stared sideways out through the window at fine, whirling, tornadic flakes of ice lit up like stars in the night.

The right marriage, to the wrong bride. The substitution at the altar of a morally diseased cutie for the girl with gold hair and jewelled eyes. So that when you lift the veil for the kiss you get a sickening shock. How was it done? And why?

Barb was doing her doctorate in grief-counselling.

Her step-sister Darla Moore, based in SoHo, was successful as an art critic. I was weekly shown her by-line in the New York Times, and also occasional and syndicated pieces in many other periodicals. Somewhat bewildering, they were always a struggle to understand, confirming me in what was called 'art' was something beyond understanding, mine at least, something only the happy initiate would 'get' at the time, the rest of us having to wait a generation before we, too, were let in the joke. I had the misfortune to have been cast in life as a sad reactionary, a bourgeois to be *épaté*, the kind of man who preferred all along what was hung in the *Salon des Acceptés*, was appropriately shocked by *Entartete Kunst*. Anyhow, she must have understood exactly what she was talking of because she was very widely read. Often appearing on magazine shows, and especially the news bulletins, she commented on art-related news as it broke---such as the outrageous on-going cuts in Federal funding for arts administration programs., or, only three or four years ago now, the latest attempt on the life of a work by Hirst while that artist was still in the conceptual phase and before he turned to the academic still-lives and pet-portraiture; that kind of thing.

She was currently finalizing her own magazine series, working *entitled Hi Art! Lo Art!* and scheduled for broadcast one hour on one of the networks third quarter Sunday nights. No one understood why Barb didn't follow her step-sister's successful lead and go into journalism, television, or the arts. The arts in particular were crying out for efficient people like her, and it would have been truly easy to make her way, given her sister's reputation, contacts, genius & expertise. Barb's line was that she wanted to do something more constructive, concrete, creative for the society in which she lived; and as for making her way, people were crying out for grief counselling also, especially in this crazed epoch of car smash, cancer and heart disease, terrorist putsch, and that it was likely to be able to support a quite acceptable standard of living, a high one even, all things considered, and perhaps more reliable than media or artistic success, however well-earned and justified.

Darla, however, was imploring Barb to give up. Undisputed mistress of the fields of criticism, she had spied a fresh market and decided to mount an art show herself. She wanted Barb to curate. To give her credit where credit's due, she was a genius. Her art was conceptual, and consisted of very exact replicas of other works of art; pieces from shows only just closed. Meanwhile, she bought and destroyed the 'originals', themselves appropriated of course from someplace else. 'Art is advert' was the exhibition's title. One of her critics accused her of being derivative, and to be fair to Darla this was to miss the point. Darla, anyhow, landed with her ample, creased bum in the honey; she sued the hapless critic and *Time*; refused the submissive apology, and settled for $5.7 million U.S. in aggravated and punitive damages just before the case came to court. Coverage moved from the art to the legal pages, and thence to the gossip columns. Also, Darla wrote *Throwing paint*, based loosely round the law-suit and her celebrity life-style, in which media names were dropped like pants. *In the Eyes*, a full-length feature based loosely in turn on the novel grossed one hundred and twenty-five million dollars US. Darla had 0.5 % of gross, not insignificant, except perhaps in the context of her amazing good fortune in the libel case. Her critic, meanwhile, after a particularly harrowing demonstration mounted by *The Sisters of Action* umbrella group, sat in a car and, rather like our society, allowed himself to be poisoned by its exhaust. He was found in a long-term parking lot at Newark, N.J., blue and somewhat bloated, but still firmly gripping the wheel and gazing through cock-eyes at his closed-off future. His car radio had been whispering disco music: *I'm feeling so real*; that kind of stuff.

---'You're late.'

Barb still gazing out of the window as she said this.

---'Planes can be late.'

---'Don't you have something to tell me?'

---'Like what?'

---'I think you owe it me.'

---'What?'

She turned to me. I could see the strip lighting reflected in her eyes.

---'I've read the letter.'

---'What letter.'

---'This.'

She lifted it from where it had been positioned, on the breakfast peninsula, and waved it gently. I felt the waft of air, bitter, on my face.

---'What is it?'

---'I think you should be telling me that.'

---'?'

---'We knew already you see. Leicher e-mailed us.'

---'You're opening my mail?'

---'I didn't open it.'

---'You said you did.'

---'No I didn't. The corner was torn off. The letter came out through the hole.'

Despair at this flaky, legalistic defence. Before I had a chance to speak, with a short grunt of righteous indignation, she went on:

---'And besides, I was right to read it. You dirty fucker, you don't half pick them!'

She put her tin-rimmed reading-glasses on, and leaning her face back slightly, looking downwards, read:

---''*I love you like I love the sun.*' Christ. '*You've given life meaning; you've made me understand the universe.*' What is this gunge? '*I know I'll lose you now and it shouldn't matter. It shouldn't!*' Corny, or what? '*But I don't want to lose you. I don't know if I'm strong enough for that.*' What a load of crap.'

The suggestiveness of Barb's words, drowning the suggestiveness of Hella's. I could see Barb's: firm, lumped and glistening, with a strange, deep, jellied texture.

---'And anyhow, you have no right; you owe me. Orla having gotten you the place on the symposium's the way you got to do Europe. Oh yes, you take our help when you need it, and then look what you do! Crap on us. You turd.' She smacked me in the face.

---'I can tell you just this one thing,' she added with rather a bitter laugh, 'she's got a stinking bottom and a stinking twat! And her nose runs.'

The room resonating as a lorry rolled past.

Working slowly through the snow.

Struggling feebly, weakly to stand up for Hella. But too craven, or too generous to the relative, to the prior, putting it above the absolute. The absolute, after all, can look after herself. If she'd been with me it would have been different. But Barb, tears in her violet eyes now, flowing so freely that one eye had turned brown and a violet contact lens adhered to her cheek, had drawn my face to hers and was breathing on my lips. Her sudden tenderness. What had she been eating? Something spicy. She drew us down. Then, grunting slightly, pushed down her pants and revealed her underwear, black, lacy, threaded with red ribbons and split-crotch, so I saw her cunt there, open and damp in readiness, flaring, angry, like a man's damp mouth in his beard.

---'You like them, don't you,' she said. 'I knew you would.'

Could I say No? I am not defending myself.

---'Yes.'

Her bum smelt of cat shit. Mixed with dog shit in a paste. Only worse.

---'I'm sweating like a pig,' she said afterwards. 'We'll shower. Then we're going round to chez Orla ...'

Even her vaginal juices were sticky and stale; something wrong with the smell. What was it; was she seeing someone else?

---'Which skirt is better, here, look at me, which skirt ...'

But in turning to face the mirror she (in gesturing) accidentally nicked out a small chunk of my cornea with the end of her little fingernail.

---'Did I get your eye? Sorry. Is this skirt better or worse?'

I lay on my back on the kilim, eyes closed, ears buzzing, and water flowing out under one eyelid.

---'Answer me,' she said. 'What do think? Brown or black? Which is better.'

Barb's body was too long for her legs. And her two buttocks were not distinct. The crease between them was sketched on the surface, and the buttocks themselves hung down behind her. When she cleaned her teeth the whole thing quivered as one and it took me a while to figure out that what it twanged at so subtly was the revolving, convolute starlings of course. Not deep, mystical, fervent, and beautiful, but of equal magnitude but reversed sign: tragical, sad, base.

Such thoughts were my revenge. The little ant its spark of fire, as some poet, maybe Emily Dickinson, I don't remember, sings.

---'Look at me. I'm a putti. I'm a fucking putti.' Hysteria in her voice as she examined herself.

---'Putto', I said.

---'What?'

---'No you're not', I said, my eyes still closed, and tears flowing out of one of them and down my temple.

---'Look at my bum the way it swings and wobbles ...'

---'You're fine.'

'Just fine?' And she really was fine; if not the current ideal, it was incredible, her shape.

'You have a beautiful body.'

Just as Orlanda had been in her physical prime (she was only now entering her intellectual), Barb was a stunning animal, with even, brilliant teeth, and a strong upper body---she worked out most mornings.

---'You're lying. Oh I hate you so much. If you knew how I hated you ...

Like her mother, she wore her bottle-black hair in a crew cut. Her regular, brilliant teeth were the teeth of a star. She was a blowsy girl, with firm, weighty breasts hidden just inside a cream silk shirt which had just come out of a cellophane package from Saks mail-order. They (her breasts) asked to be lifted out and sucked, and her lips were a little like fruit, canned fruit, and her hair-care products gave her hair real body and shine. Men and women turned to look at her in the street, and even

to follow her holding out their business cards, but only because they
didn't know what the world was for---they knew what it was — an ugly,
selfish, grasping place where people used what tinny power they had
to manufacture evil — but no idea what it was for. And if Cocteau is not
exactly right when he says that the body is the soul---there's something
there. The cute girl with a corrupt heart.

---'Penny for your thoughts?' Barb asked, before adding: 'Get your skates
on, will ya? Orla's wangled us a table at Wully'z for a quarter after ten,
sharp. But we're meeting at chez hers first.'

So: drinking olive flavoured vodka from a block of ice cast in the form
of a bottle.

Chez Orla's apartment.

And snacking on vegetable chips and Macadamia nuts.

Orla Ciama — *what have I become?* — was a tottering jellyfish, her body
given structure by its clothes. Her thighs and bum poured in her jeans
like liquid in a flask. Anyway, she became an entirely different shape,
almost a different person when, because preferable during the day, as
being less constricting, more free, she wore some kind of muddy green
fuzzy-felt tent. The copious roll of her breasts, dwarfed by the lower
copious rolls of her belly and her abdomen. Despite myself I often
visualised what she looked like naked and whether, lying back on a
double bed, she would spread like a chunky jelly right over it. A jelly
with bones in.

Or stay intact. And her face was like those composed by ingenious
artists out of other things. Her nose a pored and fleshy segment of
orange-skin, her lower lip a pink ribbed worm. Her upper lip: no
substance or vermilion border or philtrum (implying she remembered
back before her own birth), but only finely creased skin, with an
exaggerated lip-stuck cupid's bow. The air of beak, not lip, of parrot or
octopus. Her skin itself had the creased yet swollen, old yet new look of
scar tissue.

Orla bore the guilt for Barb, which is why I linger here, bilious, spiteful,
mean, and doing myself no favours, as the well-worn cliché would have
me have it. Putting myself in the wrong, being unjust, bitter, chippy. In
reality, she was highly, but *highly* intelligent, and had replaced a fugitive
physical beauty with a compelling moral beauty. And she, Orla, was

Barb, Barb revealed, Barb-in-herself, who bore with an offensive pride her guilt, but translated 19 years through time. Orla, baton-majorette and cheer-leader for the Royals, Hinckley-Big Rock High School prom queen, Miss Illinois Photogenic Teen, and near-child bride, had borne Darla at 18 and Barb at 19, yet managed to bring up two academically and culturally spectacularly gifted girls. Once the girls were old enough to be in school the family moved across the border to McGill where with characteristic pre-eminence, having taken up curling as a hobby, she was selected for the McGill Women's Curling Team, and also served as a founder member on the first Olympic Curling Committee which later successfully got curling correctly recognised as an Olympic sport.

---'Too late for me, alas!' she would say, on the fact she never had the chance to go for a gold.

Except the successive swags and folds of fat, nothing marked the boundary between the upper slopes of her bust and her chin; and with nature's honesty or her own delusion she wore not turtle or even polo necks, but black velvet *décolletée* smocks or, as tonight, lacy *bustiers*. Of course her fatness was nothing to be ashamed of, was a misfortune to be played down, perhaps, like the one-leggedness of the chain-saw operative, or not even that: would have been happy, jolly, buxom, joyous, if it wasn't a dirty, honest echo of her monstrous soul. And this was the paradox: this bodily candour about its own soul's disgustingness, as if the impulse to honesty lurked in the kernel of evil. But it was the world that was honest, not her. And the world is honest, even about its Orlas and its Barbaras; this the miracle.

Unfortunately, it's also full of fools like me.

She'd perish, if she ever became thin, like a popped balloon. To be fair to her, perhaps I only saw what wasn't there: I projected her soul, if you like, onto her body; perhaps her body was not her soul, but only my model of it. And, like Schoenberg's paintings of the critics, I doubt she really looked like that. It wasn't possible. Humanly, I mean.

Don't get this wrong. It wasn't because she was fat; if she was thin I would have hated that too. It was just that my hatred had hooks in it. It needed things to hook at. And this was one. Or not even that perhaps. It needed words to say itself, and the same words, fat, thin, might be used of other things and be good words.

I hated her.

This rapid physical decline was not her fault, not something that even could be a fault. Something genetic, probably. The Ciamas still had picturesque poor relations living in the Maremma with scratching chickens and chortling pigs.

'Barb stayed with them when she did Italy, didn't you Barbara, she'll show you the piccys.'

'Sure did, Orla,' said Barb. 'Their powder-room was a hole in the garden with flies coming out.'

'I didn't know people like that still existed in this day and age.'

'The chickens kept coming in the kitchen and having to be chased out. The pigs didn't thank the stars.'

But it wasn't my fault either; and yet, ultra-subtly, she---they---made me pay for it: for the dishonesty, snobbery, 'style', 'charm', hipness. It wasn't my fault, and yet I had to pay. For her enormous thighs and buttocks, made small, almost laughably so, by the staggering girth of her trunk. And for that dank necessity which made her wear pointed yellow cowboy boots with chromed boot-tips along with her motorcycle leathers. And again, it wasn't my fault if I didn't like her, couldn't bear her, wanted to run when she spoke, and felt bitterly ashamed that I was even here in her downtown apartment drinking olive vodka and eating vegetable crisps listening to flute concerti on the phonogram. Mixed feelings about all this. An element of the immanent or universally permeating tension between the aesthetic and moral perhaps, that primary dualism.

---'How's Ryan?' asked Barb.

---'Pa's doing fine. He's in seventh heaven because he's handed in a draft of *Marx & Einstein* at last.'

Barb's ex-stepfather didn't really figure. Doubtless he had his own quiet agenda, involving books, libraries and the neon corridors of Washington---and this was harmless enough. I met him from time to time at the revolving doors of the Heinz Building. He would give me something of a sad, knowing smile before ducking by with more than the usual number of arms and legs. Self-effacing, spiderlike---some knew him as the World-Wide-Spider---though, strangely enough, not yet eaten by his ex. On some Washington greenhouse gas commission, a rancid climate change denier, and in acknowledgment of the spirit of eighteenth century jobbery, in receipt of a research stipend from some shadowy Big Oil think-tank setup. But with a high profile side-line in comparative biographies of 18th and 19th century philosophers with 20th century physicists---this seemed to be the pattern he was working through, for some reason---perhaps there are real parallels, I don't know. Also, I don't know whether he took the Big Oil money out of stupidity or malice. One of them it had to be. But this seemed one of those questions which are formally meaningless; there didn't seem to be an answer there. It was like the cat in the box, and there would be no way, ever, of opening the box, of looking in. An ambiguity not of expression, or knowledge, but of reality, truth.

Orla and Ryan had loved reading Barbar and Celeste on Sunday mornings over croissants and China tea with forest honey in bed, but the name Celeste wasn't butch enough for them. '

'I could have got Celeste but I got Barb', said Barb.

---'To tell you the honest truth', Orla was saying, 'it's a blessed relief to all of us. He's been tied up with that current book for at least a year now. Honestly, it's high time for him to get his ass into gear, get the next project into the pipeline and pass go'.

Her voice was almost identical to Barb's. Sometimes, on the 'phone, I couldn't tell them apart. Not so much husky, as squeaky-husky. Both she and Barb had smoked much until smoking became unacceptable. Orla, your true renaissance woman, also sang jazz fusion and jazz funk nights in the bars downtown, was an accomplished classical flautist who sometimes could be persuaded to sit in on master-classes at the *Conservatoire* and give her ten cents' worth. Quite apart from her Professorship of Critical Studies---she'd made her name with a deconstruction of the *Vita Nuova*, which gave the impression of someone skating with forced elegance over the thickened ice fields of the academic and intellectual establishments, whilst also revolving steadily as she did so, her arms arabesqued like someone on a mirror in a music box, and what with being a celebrated author in her own right *(Inside Every Woman* won a Pulitzer, as we all know) and, last but not least, acting Dean of Studies in the Humanities, with special responsibility for the school's ambitious programme of affirmative action. And also on some

Federal Commission which took her down to Washington Tuesday
afternoons. This is where Barb, a pianist and published poet on the side
in her own right, presumably gets it from, the renaissance woman tip I
mean.

And yet, in despite all of this giftedness and service and well deserved
recognition, you seemed to hear sprightly baddy music, on timps and
the bassoon, when Orla came in. Her coarse hair, done with the cropped
top and long stringy bangs of a skinhead moll, was bottle-black and as
drably refulgent as the broken wing of a crow. The blueish white skin of
her scalp glowed through it. A dulled bald patch on the crown, the size
of a gull's egg, was obscured by a comb-over but dusted as if with talc.
She affected those mauve and turquoise letter-box glasses which were so
fashionable then. Her eyes brown buttons puckering the unlikely facial
flesh. They swelled and slid within the constricting frames somehow
fearfully. The sense that she didn't like her eyes being looked at in case
you saw her. What was worse was that I didn't want to look either, and
for the same reason. In case I saw.

---'And Darla?' asked Barb.

---'Sissy's doing just fine, isn't she Deela. Have you seen Newsweek?'

---'She read it on my *Ansaphone*. Isn't it great?'

Deela Moore, Orla's partner, liberated years back from Ryan whose
amanuensis stroke mistress she had been, lay deep in a black-leather
sofa, taking it in. Deela was something in the university admin. Close
to President Krollheim---to the seat of the pants of power, so to speak.
Dried, whippet-like, with a sharp catty intellect. Brown hair, with
freckles on her withering cheeks of exactly the same brown shade.

---'Oh,' Orla said, 'and Norbert's here. He's addressing the regional triple-A
S tomorrow. So he's meeting us at Wully'z.'

---'It was he who asked if Orla could stage the dinner,' vouched Barb,
nodding with wide eyes.

Coming out of the basement apartment into the brittle night, the
buckles of Orla's *On the Waterfront* motor-cycle leathers jingling. This
freak weather. Orla's car well heated though---even the seats; but the
scent of kid-leather making me gag. Even now, even here, so many
years after, a shiver of distaste, despair, whenever I see a black B-series

Bimmer idling at the lights, or smell battleship-grey leather seating. Bellow reflects on the survival of a slave-labour era corporation into our supposedly moral age.

In a frosty urban playground, on the way from the parking lot to Wully'z, a small black kid sprayed Orla with bullets from a plastic Kalashnikov. She had this effect.

---'What on earth are you bringing him up to be?' she asked its father who, his teeth and eyes brilliant, and with the chain between his legs, was seated sideways on a swing.

---'Yes,' said Barb.

---'A man,' he replied.

Deela giggled. Orla farted.

We walked on. At Wully'z, a replica diner from the fifties, all chrome and soda and paper waitress caps, there was some confusion over our table.

---'Ciama,' said Orla, lordly; 'Ciama. Like glamour.'

---'Like clamour, more like,' said Deela, wheezing subversively.

A sense in which Barbara, or if not Barbara, then Darla at least, and Orla, were America.

Except that America is nothing like as bad as this.

Yet could it be so? Or the future, perhaps? Perhaps America is the future. For us. All of us. Either that or the past. It had to be one. Anyhow, why speculate. They were the Ciamas. The pushy, screaming, bestial Ciamas. But I don't know, maybe I needed them, maybe they woke me up. The world isn't roses and honey. There are also thorns and stingy things, and to know the world you must know these. And these days, thorns and stings have to be sophisticated to get you, to penetrate the stoic shield. They need to be flaky, tacky, cheesy, classless, base. This the role the bestial Ciamas filled. This their purpose, in the machinery of my own private tragedy.

A fawning waiter, misunderstanding rectified, led us our table. Orla controlled the faculty's hospitality budget. And this was big.

The plump linen cloth: as if even in here (dry heat, neon lighting), snow had fallen. Before sitting down, Barb and Orla went to the ladies' room.

---'He doesn't know how lucky he is. Don't worry, Barb, we'll stop this shit he's dumping on you. You don't need it, Barb. You don't need any of it.'

Their business-like voices, through the flimsy wall.

---'We're favouring him which he doesn't merit.' Orla's voice rising. 'After all, I got the place at the Setino Symposium, ungrateful turd. And I got *Canis lupus lupus's Classical Era Range* into *American Biologist*. He evidently doesn't know how to be authentically grateful.'

Deela Moore, left at the table with me, baring her teeth in irony yet squirming on her prat too.

Leicher was late. The air, when he finally arrived, of someone out of Lewis Carroll. His shoulders and his hat dusted with perfect snowflakes which slowly turned from white to grey, stopped sparkling, and began to twinkle. His eyes, too, twinkling behind gold-rimmed glasses; something in this of new life. And of affection for me. This is what I couldn't make out. Was this an essential goodness reasserting itself, after the megalomania and the tantrums of the month before? Or some stratagem to isolate Hella? Meanwhile:

---'Don't you love the parable of the cave, don't you love the myth of Er?' Orla was gushing. 'It's the real thing. Norbert! I can't believe you're here!'

---'Yes my dear Orlanda. Deela! Barb!'

From well-schooled, or even brilliant fools like her, not even Plato was safe. Hating her for what she had done: she had made Barb. Barb bore no responsibility for her own coarse, grasping self. All this was Orla's doing. And so I hated her. And yet, who made Orla? For some reason this was not my problem. But I knew I was out of order, too---impotent spite, the hatred of those on whom it is dawning that we were cast as losers, for the gifted and the successful, everywhere.

And as our forks clinked on tin (a Wully'z trademark) and dish followed dish---red-snapper soup, pan-fried camembert with mint sauce on a salty polenta, then tiramisu, and finally Congolese home roast coffees in tin mugs with home cooked chocolate truffles of course---I felt like when you see dying coming; a biting kind of misery, a bitter sadness, but

small, short-term, in the present; with no grandeur. You blame yourself
for the world's stink, and you may be right; it is the world's, but it is you
who so arranges it. I knew it couldn't last with Barb. I couldn't bear it to.
But some cross Goddess had hidden my destiny.

Next morning, opening the drift of mail which had built up while I was
over in Europe, and the telephone ...

---'Hey?'

---'Yes.'

---'It's me.'

---'Me?'

---'Hella.'

 Silence.

---'I'm here.'

---'Here?'

---'In New Cardiff.'

 Silence.

---'I want to see you.'

---'Why?'

 My stupidity.

---'I'll---explain ... that. When we meet?'

---'When?'

---'As soon ... as we can.'

Looking blindly at my diary.

---'It'll have to be Thursday.' Today was Monday. 'Five p.m.?'

---'Yes,' I heard her gasp. And then: 'Thursday?'

---'Thursday. Wilson Building, room 10-06?'

---'10-06?'

She didn't understand. This was the week of the New Cardiff Modern
Dance Festival. Barb and Orla, via Darla, had obtained NCMD comps
for every night except Thursday, when they were attending the $1500
a setting gala dinner in the presence of Governor O'Hanlon and the
Leader of the House. I forget his name.

---'Okay,' she said, winded.

---'Five o'clock.'

---'Okay, five. I'll come to the Wilson building. Room 10-06. On Thursday.
Fine. At five.' Talking for courage. 'I'll see you then ...,' she said.

---'Don't forget.' And at that, at last the cry of pain:

---'Hey---'

But before I could answer she rang off. My desk had become transparent,
expressed merely in tones of distortion, like one made specially of glass.

I was staring through it when the door opened and Barb came in,
carrying several shopping bags, her face bright red.

---'I've got this most amazing thing for Thursday night; it's claret silk, but
the hem slopes across to one side, with these panniers---... What are you
looking at?'

---'Nothing ...'

---'I said 'What are you looking at?' Answer me. I said answer ... It's her
again!'

---'Nothing.'

---'Don't you give me fucking nothing. Answer. What's she done, written
or 'phoned?'

Looking up at her, at least trying to. But I saw through her, too. Opaque,
brownish. A brownish stain.

---'I'll tell her where to get off, the bitch. What's her 'phone number.'

My address book, lying open on the desk.

---'What's her name again?'

---'Hella.'

---'Her second name fuck-face. Watergate or something.'

---'I don't know.'

Realising this; I didn't. How strange.

---'Like fuck you don't. Tell me.'

---'Don't scream.'

---'I said tell me.'

Oh yes I did. Skippergate. But I'd forgotten it. She was so real, she didn't need one.

---'It's Skippergate. Why.'

---'That's right, Skippergate.'

But Barb, drawing her finger down S. Mouthing to herself as, on a scrap of paper, she wrote the number. Then, gathering up her bags, without a word; opening the door. And putting them down outside to slam it as hard as she could.

Her voice, muffled, tearful, through the door:

---'I'll show you why.'

A few sheets of paper, drifting to the floor. The pages of the address book turning. A deafness in one ear, the nearer to the door. As the light sank outside, and the white lamps which limned the serpentine paths of campus came on, far beneath, under frosty fir trees, and in the room all white things---paper, the spines of books, my shirt---went slowly blue, then grey, then brown.

Those trees: remembering what Hella had called them once. Not coniferous but carnivorous. The girl with bare legs in a wood. And then a bloody bolt of fear.

The telephone rang. Looking at it. As if telephones shouldn't, didn't.

---'Where are you?' a voice screamed, so loud that it hurt.

Holding the receiver at a safe distance. She knew where I was; she'd just rung me. So why did she shout?

---'Orla and I have been waiting *fifteen* minutes. They've just rung the first bell. Are you coming or not?'

---'You go.'

---'Oh no you don't. You can't fuck us around like this. This has been settled for two fucking months. People are killing for these seats. Krollheim and Governor O'Hanlon are already here. Orla just saw them come in. You don't just drop out at the last minute. Orla and I will be waiting in the vestibule. Don't keep us hanging around. We've waited long enough, for Christ's sake.'

Then the blur of the disconnect tone.

So: placing the receiver back in its rest. And wearily, like someone with very little life and too much time, making my way across to the Hertz Auditorium where, Orla seated to one side and Barb the other, gravely, seriously, we watched the dance.

It didn't occur to me at first that Hella had come to see me---the momentous makes holy morons of us. But as soon as I could, after the show, I rang round the Four Seasons, the Hilton, the Holiday Inn.

Nothing.

She wasn't staying anywhere. She might have done it deliberately, only that wasn't her.

Barb, later, kept me up all night. I was supposed to be correcting the proofs of the wolf book, and trying to mark first year papers. It kept me occupied, but my soul felt liquid, nauseous. But these duties didn't get a look in with Barb's theatrics. In a way it was a battle between poetry and fact. The outcome being predictable.

On Thursday, seeing her tiny figure far beneath my window, dawdling in the park outside with an overdone scrupulosity which could have been sarcasm but was humility, waiting for five o'clock. I saw her look up suddenly, piercingly, straight at me, although on the tenth floor behind mirrored glass I must have been invisible, and then lean her hand heavily against a tree. The moving clouds, both in the sky itself and reflected in the building, had made her lose her balance and nearly fall. I too stepped back as from a drop I was usually too imaginative to see. She walked towards the building and disappeared.

I went round the room in circles, round my room. My heart beating. The colour of her eyes, the colour of her hair, and the colour of her skin (somehow she'd got in) struck me like new physical facts, new constants, new unknowns. But even while I was looking she lowered her head, ringed her arms around my neck, and tried to wedge her face into my armpit.

She was still. And after a time, as if this was as normal as shaking someone's hand, she lifted her face again, stepped back.

---'I came here to see you. You didn't realise that.'

---'After you'd rung off I figured that. I tried to find you.'

She glowed, swelled, her eyes shone. Black smudges under them like the smudges on the petals of pansies.

And her clothes were loose. She looked like someone in a camp. Not all there; when she moved her head her eyes moved, loose too, and in a different way. AWOL.

---'What have you done to your hair?'

---'I don't know. I needed to.'

It looked like a wheat field looks, after the combine harvester.

---'I don't know,' she said.

The fresh, weak gold of straw, yet with more warmth than straw: more humanity, more brown. You could see the marks the clippers had made. And even the brown, in its paleness, however rich, however womanly, contained grey.

---'But you looked for me? Oh shit. I was at *Prairie du Chien*.' *Chien* was pronounced 'she-an.' 'That's where I was all along. I've been waiting there.'

---'That's way outside of town. Why not the Four Seasons or the Holiday Inn?'

---'I liked the name. Especially the way it's said. Will you see me there? A motel, romantic, on a river ...'

---'I'll try ...'

---'He'll try! Why can't I make you understand. It's like speaking to the deaf. It's exhausting. You're wrong.'

Even her anger, or her stab at it, too gentle, too understanding to make fear.

She smiled again, weakly, reluctant, like a child you are trying to make smile through her tears. Her eye whites went pink. And her mouth puckered up into a shape I didn't know as water started dripping on the flower sprigs printed on her dress and she said something I couldn't understand.

---'Tell me, tell me?'

---'Sick. I feel sick.'

The glittering eyes, the see-through skin. Her tan was going already; her tone pallid now. Grey, almost. The tragedy of loving someone unworthy of you. The common tragedy, by definition. I can see that. But you are not made worthy by seeing that. And if you were she probably wouldn't love you anymore. It isn't about that.

---'It's fine,' she was saying. 'It's just seeing you again. I was so happy with you, hearing the bell strikes all night and all the gooses squawking ...'

As she turned up her face I felt the heat it radiated. Her blue, rayed irises, bald with emotion, wet.

---'It's okay,' she said again, looking at me. She drew the side of her finger down my cheek, which tickled in an unpleasant way. She seemed shorter than she used to be. Like those parachutists whose parachutes fail to open but who survive, just.

When we went out, a group of preppy fraternity men, half shocked, half longing, and saddened at their loss, turned to stare after her, like children with outstretched arms reaching after a meteorite which has already fallen someplace else. What was telling was that the sorority women also did. But that was later.

Her mouth moving, but no sound came, and then, as if the words like
sledge hammer strikes or thunder had taken a while to arrive:

---'Would you ever have a child with me?'

---'Hella!'

---'Tell me.'

This is what she had come to---not ask, just say.

---'It's not like that.'

Each word I spoke made her eyes drop a notch, from my eyes to nose,
to mouth, chin, chest---and made her mouth come wider open. As if
she wanted to hear my heart beating, her mouth as wide as it would
go, opened for some dentist to pierce a tooth, teeth protruding and lips
furled back, she pressed her ear against the centre of my ribcage.

My cheeks swelling up against my eyes.

We stood like that.

---'It hurts.'

---'It hurts.'

The tears clotting her voice.

---'I can't.'

---'I can't,' she said.

And with a moan, for the first time in my professional life, I began to cry.

She leant back and looked up at me closely, like someone observing a
test-tube.

---'Why?' she said, and wiped her nose with her hand, because a spool of
snot swinging there was bothering her. 'I don't understand it. Why.' And
forcing her open lips against my open mouth, she made us stagger. I
stumbled back against the hollow door, buckling it, slid down it to the
floor.

She kissed passionately, rolling her face about on my mouth, her tears
dripping hot onto my face.

---'I love you.'

Beneath her lips, warm teeth.

---'I love you,' she whispered. 'That's all there is. What the world is. Doesn't all the world is have to be enough?'

Later, we must have slept.

Then it was dark.

Again, we must have slept.

And I heard the door close again through an unknowing sleep, but then a sound of misery outside woke me suddenly.

She was walking down the corridor.

---'Stay, Hella. Stay.'

I was still half-asleep. The corridor dark, even though the lights were on.

---'Hoh!' she said, a sound expelled, as if I'd hit her in the back. And as if I'd hit her in the back, she began to run.

---'Hella.'

I heard her wail. She ran leaning far forwards with her arms in front. And kicking her feet out sideways, as if running over ice. The passage turned a corner towards the lifts, but she ran straight on, into the wall, bounced off, and lay down on her back.

Breathing softly, her lips parted in too toothy a smile, eyes shut, and in the centre of her forehead, visibly growing, white with a reddened tip, pointed like the horn of a unicorn or the sharp end of an egg ...

I thought she'd cracked her skull and the brains were pushing out.

But she was looking at me. Her marbled eyes stone blue, her canines showing.

---'Let me go,' she said. 'Don't do this.'

A difficult silence, whilst we waited for the lift.

Then the doors slowly closing over the vision of her reddening, lowered face, tears dripping off. Hella lifting her face enough for me to see, at the instant it was covered by the doors, a double spark of dark blue light.

Prairie du Chien was eleven miles east of New Cardiff, low on the side of a green bluff, two miles off the Interstate. It was really just an intersection amongst pastures filled with grubby dairy-cattle, but there was also a wooden church, a store. And a motel.

The rooms, in a long, flat wing at the back of the building, overlooked the empty parking lot and a brown river swollen with melt-water from the freak snows. The parking lot was new tarmac, with pukka white lines painted on together with the numbers of the corresponding rooms, but the brown water, shiny under the flooded grass of the lawn, had invaded its far end. She was leaning her head back against the doorpost of number seven, her hair mussed, her face damp, one leg cocked and revolving on the point of a trainer, a hand on her forehead and one on her hip as I drove up.

---'I wanted to see you', I said through the Chrysler's window.

She didn't move. But her lips did.

---'I knew you'd come.'

The brave words sagging, saturated. She spoke thickly, as if someone had hit her.

---'Cheer up. It may never happen.'

---'Are you coming in?'

She closed the door behind us. The television on, showing a blurred and unreal anchor-woman against an orange background, teasing, bantering.

---'I didn't expect you like this.'

---'What did you expect?'

Her voice monotonous.

---'It isn't the end of the world', I said.

The mask of her face shifted into a smile, but only a mask deep one.

---'Of someone's world it is.'

Grim.

And she wasn't concentrating. She'd come all this way for me, and wasn't concentrating. She was distracted by what the anchoress was doing, wedged as she now was up against a pillow at the head of the low double bed. Her scuffed damp scalp, her scuffed damp skin. She was uncomfortable, yet too lazy to shift. Her long legs stretched away from her, encased in a pair of glowing, barely faded blue-jeans. Her hands trapped between her thighs and her ankles crossed, one foot vibrating unhealthily. Her body light inside her cotton T-shirt, and as always too flimsy for the breasts.

But there was still mystery somewhere: there was still more to it than this. And as if to explore the mystery, to probe and irrigate it like a bloody gash, we did nothing that afternoon except watch adult cable-movies throughout a bout of sullen, abortive sex.

Without drawing back the counterpane of electric blue nylon, studded with the smudged brown melt-marks of cigarettes.

She kept her eyes on the screen. While I was fucking her.

Her face moving with my movement, but expressionless, impassively.

Her eyes to one side. Missing mine.

The light from the river, a steady greenish brown on the white gloss ceiling. And the screen-light, garish in its rhythms and its colours. Changing. On the white gloss ceiling too. Sometimes she moved her eyes to this. And down again to the eyes of the anchor-woman on the television set. Because its back had broken. She wasn't trying any more. What a fucking mess.

She vomited in the morning, revolted by it all. Her hair and skin damp again. But she still looked---was---beautiful, her wide forehead, a few spiked threads of sandy, gilded hair standing up above it, and the inflected, running outline of what right now were greenish, deadened, but still vaguely questing eyes.

So that when I reminded myself to look at her, to see her, my heart beat and I was scared.

In the evening we walked down the river towards New Cardiff. We could see the towers of the city, etched along the lower edge of the sun. The weather was warm, clammy, unhealthy and the last dirty bergs of snow had gone. The television advised us to stay indoors, forecasting flash-floods.

---'I didn't realise it was lovely here. I thought America was rich,' she said.

---'It's called the rust belt.'

We reached the interstate, walked along it a way, and found a diner. In the red, dark booth we were served by a sexy, self-sufficient waitress. One of those American girls who know what they're about. No nonsense, just honesty, coffee and apple-pie. And pretty. Hispanic blood. And a head of hair like Charles II. Only, her legs, like his, too thin.

Hella, seeing me watching her.

Through plate-glass windows, the remains of the smoky sun sank behind a jumble of rusty pylons, flared water towers, decaying elevated railways, fields of rubble blowing with a thinning hair of weeds. And dark green clouds.

She was shaking, as she detonated and poured our beers, a drunk in a train buffet booth. What I mean by this is her hand was going all over the place and so was beer. Not all of it found its way into the glasses. Some went into her lap, darkening a fold of her dress, and making her underpants and hair show through ...---she was speaking:

---"It may be over---but you can't take it back. Even if it has to end: it was worth it. Every little drop of agony. Don't worry your little head about that. Because it's a bit like money; once you've spent it there's nothing anyone can do---taxmen, creditors, litigants, boyfriends---to get it back. So: once you have drunk the happiness, and got drunk on it, no torturer, no executioner, no EC commissioner, no structuralist mathematician can ever get it back. Who was it who said: you can't call a man happy until he's dead. Because he was wrong. When it comes to the good ones at least. (I don't think the bad ones can be happy). So, our prime duty: to be happy. We're amongst the few who are in a position to do so. When the world ends, and it may not be very long, that's all that will be left. Beethoven and Chopin will burn, blacken and curl, Stendhal and Proust, Balbi, Claude, Radiguet, Ramsey; all gone. Only joy will live. With pain."

---"Because---" (her voice sounding stiff and artificial as she said this, and so it should:) "---I believe in love."

---'It's like sitting on a horse which till then has been tugging away at tufts of grass, its reins loose, and you with your legs hanging down, when suddenly, hardly even waiting to lift its head, it's away, galloping, and you trying to catch the flapping reins and get your feet in the stirrups and bouncing and twisting about on the saddle. It's like that. There's no mistaking it. And it happened. It happened to me. I don't know that I liked it. There was a side of me which said, *'Hey, whoa, stop, I want to get down.'* But of course, the horse took no notice and went on galloping all the same. Until I fell, and rolled across the hollow ground, and smelt the blood in my nose and tasted it on the roof of my leaking mouth ...'

Her awkwardness: it only came from the scientist's relative ignorance of cliché, and also her fearlessness of recycling cliché where it overlapped with truth.

---'And that's the last you see of me. That's ...---the last.'

When she looked up her corneas were bloodshot and there were tears on her cheeks, and her skin was blotchy and red.

---'They've been out here, you know.'

---'Who?'

---'The ugly sisters.'

---'And you're Cinderella?'

---'You are, prick. I'm the prince.'

The prince had to lose; which meant the world lost too. A reduction in the balance of goodness, an increase in that of evil, or pain, malice, a violation of the conservation laws; so that when it ends, something will be missing, will have gone astray; a quantum of happiness which could have, won't have been. Because Cinderella was foolish and weak.

---'What did they say.'

---'Who?'

---'The sisters.'

---'Pooper Scooper and Frumpy Grump? They said you wanted to marry her and I shouldn't confuse you.'

---'But I said I didn't ... !'

Hella was silent. Watching my face, with sadness. Then she went on:

---'I know they have it all, but they're not good people; you shouldn't be with them. Your generosity is misplaced, is enormous, an enormity, a bad thing: a sin. You take it too far; your duty is to breed with someone you love, not look after a selfish, pushy, exploitative cow. Because there's something wrong about the pair of them. Corrupt, shaking, stinking. I don't know why. And I hate saying this, I hate saying what it's in my interest to say. But I'm only trying to avert a tragedy. I can see it; why can't you. You don't have to be with me, but please don't be with them. It makes me mad; you can't see what is happening to you, what you are doing, and who is pulling the strings to make you dance ...'

Somehow Pooper Scooper (Orla, that was) must have got wind of Hella's visit, and come out with Barb in tow to have a frank word with her. Basically to warn her off.

---'As for Barb: she's totally faithless; I can see that, why can't you? Devious, calculating, and even---not malicious, but at the same time more than ruthless; more ruthless than she needs to be. Paying off old scores perhaps. If home is where they have to take you in, in Frost's words, then this is home for you. You're being taken in. You'll think this is special pleading. And it is: but for the truth. For all her beauty, I grant her that.'

It was strange to me, all this; Hella and Barb seemed from different worlds, it didn't seem possible they could meet. To look at them---well, they seemed different species. Different sexes, at least.

---'She is a phoney. A pushy, grasping phoney. You can see it in her eyes; they're like glass ones; if you tapped them they'd clink. The skin around them too looks dead. Everything---her smiles, her tears, generated by an effort of will. She's someone making faces in a mirror. Only---you are the mirror. And you fall for it. This is the weakness of the world. This its fracture, its poisonous snakes. Does it have to have this weakness. No. It isn't necessary. Not at all.'

---'She also said you were only after me for my money.'

---'You didn't believe her?'

---'It's what's called self-incrimination. People's suspicions tell you all
about them. She doesn't believe it, but even their lies say something.
Kant's method.'

---'And yet, she's prepared to lie to keep me.'

---'Honey attracts wasps,' she said simply. 'Please,' she said. 'This is for real.'

The genuine article, as we say in the States, rhyming genuine with
Clementine (as rhymed with brine.)

---'She reminds me of that cow Lorchen at the *Hôtel d'Europe*. She too
smiled a lot. And she too smiled wrong. It's like something's gone rotten
inside of her, Barb, a child perhaps. And so she smells. And for some
reason she's got it into her head that it's your fault. And you're going to
be made to pay for it. This is what you're being lined up for. To pay for it.'

---'She has a dirty, faithless soul. It isn't about you; I would have said that
anyway. It shows on her face. Her face says it all. Can't you see it? She's a
monster.'

---'She's not even faithful to you. I hate this, but I have to tell you. You
have to have your eyes opened. Don't get it wrong; please; because you're
about to. Get it wrong, I mean. You're about to do something stupid and
terrible, I know it ...'

---'What do you mean ... ?'

---'Muppet-face, the one who always looks as if he's shat his pants?'

---'Steve Krollheim? But he's gay.'

---'ACDC, apparently. Or so the story goes. And anyway, I don't know if
you have this concept over here, if it's even allowed any more, but she's a
bit of what used to be called a fag-hag.'

---'No, such concepts are not permitted here.'

---'I'm sorry, I'm sorry; but you have to know. She's a rat in the nettles,' she
said sadly. 'She is. I hate telling the truth when it is in my interest; I hate
it, it feels like I'm using it, dirtying it with my little sublunary desires; but
it is still the truth.'

She lifted some chilli to her lips---she hadn't tasted it yet. But by mistake she bit the fork which made her eyes water. She held the side of her face for a while, with tears flowing down out of one eye, before going on.

---'Your trouble is you have no trouble,' she said, mumbling slightly. 'And like the man who didn't know fear, you have to go in search of it. And so it's a bit like in the horror film: I am screaming: don't go in the cellar, don't go down there, no, wait for me, no, no; I'm screaming at you and you still go. Sudden darkness, and the sloppy crunching of gristle. Cut to her with a smile on her lips and blood on her greasy chin.'

---'You know the story around the campus, don't you. The story is that Professor Ciama's scared you stiff. You're scared to leave her daughter. You're scared she'll cut off your funding or something worse. I've asked, you see; I wish I hadn't; that's how they found me. They are saying that you're only with her because you're scared of her. Under the surface gloss; her ferocity. The new woman; yes; and you, scared, are the new man. You see, she's got what she wants now. With those dark-glasses which make her look like an insect. A stinging one. No nobility, no principle, simply straight personal advantage in a world without rules; that's how she operates. Of course, you have to appear to have rules, you have to appear to be noble. But you don't and you aren't. The reptile, the parasite. Are you listening to me?'

---'Or perhaps she can't help it, is not intending to destroy you, just as the wasp can't help stinging the hand which offers it marmalade, because stinging is so much more important than marmalade. Perhaps she is scheming for this alone: to be able to scheme. To be kind, noble, disinterested: these aren't options for her; or perhaps they are options, but not possible ones, just as it isn't possible to slide your knuckles under a circular saw. That's how she works, and I can see it, and you don't. That's the misery; all the misery, of a world which should be rich, miraculous, even scandalous, and isn't, and only because of you---and only because of me.'

---'She loves me,' I said. 'What would she ... if ...'

---'Forget it. She doesn't love you. She doesn't love anyone. You're the trophy date. But as soon as a better trophy comes along ...'

---'So much the better, if it's true.'

---'But where does that leave me?'

She wailed this.

---'Don't let me go. It's a disaster for me. We both know that. But it's a disaster for you too; and the tragedy is that that's something only I know. Why won't you understand. Understand what's happening. Why can't you see it, when I can see it so clearly. Please understand.'

---'I'll help you pack ...'

So: taking her to the airfield. On the way, heavy rain, swirling mist. In the seat beside me, biting her lips and sucking her cheeks. I could hear her even over the noise of the engine, the wipers and the rain.

---'Do you think they'll be flying?'

---'Don't know.'

She was silent.

---'What if you still kept her,' she said eventually, 'and I stayed on out here. You wouldn't have to come and see me very much. At least I'd be near.'

As your foot is diced by the toothed grooves of the escalator, you are too polished to cry out.

---'Accept what the world gives you,' she was saying. 'Don't fight its generosity. Don't fight God. It will make you unhappy.'

Because you lose if you don't fight. Too proud to sweat and grunt and scream with the bestial Ciamas. A higher, an older and a doomed humanity. Or rather, newer, but still doomed. Why didn't she take my hand and pull it? Pull me on the aeroplane. Pull me to Europe. It would have worked. But I could just as well ask, why didn't I walk. There are limits to our freedom, or to our strength. And my fetters chaffed. Beneath them, flesh stinks and rots. But they were invisible. As was the cage itself which, once shut, won't open any more until its sour mistress, while she may still have had further use for you, has still more urgent use for it.

---'Hey,' she said. We were crossing the runway. 'You didn't answer my question.'

Sinking feeling.

---'Yes?'

---'Would have a child with me?'

---'---.'

---'Would you?

---'Hella, I told you, it isn't like that.'

Silence.

---'Answer me', she said.

But when I started speaking she put her hands on her ears and shut her
eyes.

---'Hella; we've been through that.'

Tears leaked out.

Once, long before, killing a nest of rats. Lying in a row against their
mother's belly, suckling, under a bale of straw. With navy blue fur. Pink
feet, pink lips. Some with a little milk-froth on. Mushroom colours: at
least the colours of mushroom gills. I got a bucket, dipped it full, but
how did I get the rats in? I don't remember. Anyhow, I got them in, and
they swam round and round the bucket until I saw I'd have to push them
down. So pushing them under one by one, with an old bit of stick, only
it didn't work; holding an air bubble gently in sharp teeth each one
would come up beside the stick, gasping, it's mouth wide open. Killing
them all took half an hour. Even when dead they went on swimming for
a while. Sick work. What was it that made me think of it now?

---'Are you sure?'

---'Hella; don't go on about it.'

She stared a long time at the off-white concrete.

---'Why don't you answer me?'

Her mouth as she spoke was an ugly shape, her lips puckered, scalloped,
like the lips of the shell of a clam.

She slid her arms around my neck and kissed me. Her lips still knotted
and bunched. I could feel her breasts pressing hard against me. I could
even feel her nipples. One breast was thudding and juddering sharply.
Her heart. Resting your ear on wood into which a nail is hammered. Too
much. More than noise.

Her face a faint, strange pink. On her lips, a faint white froth. I could
smell metallic tears. When she reached her arm around my back and
laid her hand on my bare belly, under my clothes, it felt like a patch of
sunlight falling there. Even in this stenchy gloom of grey airs and brown
waters.

An odd silence beside the aeroplane. That delicate tail; something sexual
in its flexing, feminine. Especially where it met the root of the tail fin.

So, waving her off. When she climbed aboard that tiny machine, it
shifted under her weight, light thing that it was, with headlamps like a
car. Shining through the wet mist, gilding the bark of the dripping black
maples. Watching it bump along the concrete runway, set between two
dark lawns of grass, which were studded with painted yellow spot-lamps
stobing in blue, before getting up tentatively, as if scared, as if it wanted
to come down again, like a white kitten from the black fork of a wet tree.

And rocking in space, amongst the ghosting, wreathing mists. Was this
Hella, inside, flinging herself about? Her leaping-off trains trick? Or
was it just the wind? Frail and flimsy as her, its headlamps had seemed
to shed tears. You could also see tears spraying off the wings, even in
flight. The weather gone haywire: first snow, then warm wind, gutsy,
adolescent, strong but lacking purpose. And now this warm rising mist
and this hissing rain, each raindrop ready to burst: swollen, pregnant,
seed-like, ripe, shaken by the wind from the sky.

As if crashing, the Cessna sank beyond scraggy trees. Through the
branches, for a while, the sliding, startled pulsing of the navigation lights,
and the distorted mumble of its engines.

And, turning back to the terminal, a single gleam of steep sunlight
pierced the swirling clouds and shone---on Barb. So: all this cloud
was just a crust. That wasn't how it seemed. It had seemed everything.
Everything above at least. But no: you pierced it and the sun shone
through, and if you were lucky you even saw a fragment of blue. Which

in turn seemed everything. Above. Even on a day like this: a day of mist, various clear greys, and soggy trees.

---'I don't believe it,' Barb was saying. 'I really don't.'

She stood just outside of the great glass doors, her legs wide, her fists whitened against her hips.

Red face, white fists. Watching me.

And seeming unreal. The tufts of fluorescent grass around her feet. Going towards her, I was struck by an unexpected pang of diarrhoea which made me buckle with the effort of keeping it in. So: loping towards her grim lips with the grimness of struggle in mine:

---'Men's room,' I said in a clenched voice.

But shat myself before I made it there. Embarrassing. Deeply so.

Barb coming in and shouting me to hurry through the flimsy door. She turned the handle several times, like someone impatient to shit themselves. Then the sound of the urinals cutting in. Hiss, gurgle.

It must have been something we'd eaten at Prairie. The diner perhaps.

And in the men's room, no toilet tissue. All I had was my already soiled clothes to clean myself, but then nothing to wear.

The roller towel? Coming out the consul or the mummy, swathed around in it?

No.

But reminding myself that time, too, would roll on, that it would present, force some way out. This was like trying to reason with a lover. I don't know if it didn't make things worse.

Barb, tired of hammering on the door, went on. I was to follow in a taxicab. In the end I flushed my underwear away---alarming moment, when all the mess rose up to the white rim and swirled around, as if to rat on me. Because I thought it would spill over. Evenly. All around. Like a fringe. And floating on that filmy water---things I'd eaten, things I'd worn.

Suddenly, with a horrible sucking, the vision swirled away.

I scrubbed the leakings and splatterings from my blue linen trousers in the wash-hand basin, putting them on piebald and wet. Then I took them off again, and wet them thoroughly.

I'd been caught in the rain.

The driver wrinkling his nose as we whirled along the expressway.

'What's that stink?'

And I mean whirled. The sensation was of the car rotating steadily as it sped along.

He was speaking.

---'Sorry? I didn't quite catch ...'

---'Take a smell of that lake. Those fish lots. It sure ain't right.'

---'---?'

---'They've turned it rotten. It didn't ought to be like that.'

---'No.'

---'No?'

---'No, it didn't.'

In the apartment, Barb was wearing flesh-coloured suspenders, under a school-girl's uniform.

Gross.

Sex with her, without even the luxury of a shower. My heaving buttocks clammy, sticky. Meanwhile, a feeling of mortality, terror, as if I would very soon be dead.

Not only that: as if very soon the world would too.

Towards the end, in our joltings, my prick slipped out. And in her frenzy to get it back again, she unzipped it with a fingernail, so that a curl of flesh was stuck beneath her nail like a wood shaving or a minute snail shell, and the red meat glowed.

The moral pain of this, shaking my head about, biting my lips and my cheeks hard enough to make them, too, bleed while Barb, grunting, gasping, grabbed it roughly and thrust it back in.

Afterwards she lit up and said:

---'She's hungry for man, that girl. You can smell it. Very unattractive. Like feet. Or worse. Needy. And so stonking pretentious. What is she after all, but a silly goose with a taste for physics. A taste for bondage would be more interesting.'

---'Who?'

Barb stared me out.

---'You tell me. What a precious bitch, talking quantum mechanics and thinking that will make her attractive to men. Yes, Leicher's said all about her. He thought Orla ought to know. That's partly why he came. Yes, he had to address the regional triple-A-S too.'

The avenging angel, Leicher. Who had seemed so sweet. So nice.

Tender, even.

---'As if anyone really cared about it. Silly cunt, showing off her - genital knowledge! You get? General knowledge, genital knowledge. It's only stuff she's read in books. I know where she's coming from. There were plenty in the sorority. If she's your line I can find you plenty more. Oh yes. Oh yes.'

If it were only possible.

---'Barb ...'

---'She's been conning the encyclopaedia. The dictionary, even. And do you know why? Because no one will take her out. What else is she going to do, godammit?'

---'Barb ...'

---'Nobody asks her out. Trust you to get taken in. Wally. Who does she think she is? It makes me sick.'

She kept her eyes closed as she spoke. And an illusion, as the lenses moved about under their closed lids, that her eyes were open but

opaque, were of skin. Nasty, this looked. Even with open eyes, she looked
bad. Because even open, her eyes were the same colour as her skin. They
were yellowish, whitish, dry, flaky pink.

I realised this, and she revolted me. She revolted me. Her voice, her
cunt, her soul: they revolted me. And I was weary, sick, pierced and
aching, miserable. It was my fault that I was going to die. Sickeningly,
contagiously, painfully. This was how it felt. And all for nothing---and yet
I couldn't escape. I wasn't strong enough. Why? I don't know why. Is this
what determinism feels like? And was it worse than this, even? Because it
was as if just that arbitrary destiny had been chosen which would punish
Hella for her belief in freedom?

---'Little rich bitch. You're just itchy for her money. If she was poor you
wouldn't look at her. I know the way your mind works. Poor little rich
girl, thinks she can buy love. Got another think coming. I'll show her.'

---'You---you're full of crap.'

There. At last.

To escape from Barb and Orla I took room 7 out at Prairie.

Morbid.

I'd watch *Oprah Winfrey* and *Game for a Laugh* while the frost sugared the
tarmac outside, sugared my cooling windscreen and my cooling wheels.

When the door was open I could see lights reflected in the slowly
surging river, heaped up towards the middle just like the water in the
rocky bay in front of the *Pensione Otarí*. And also like the swelling mound
of the overgrown field near the cave. River, sea, field: swollen.

Dead leaves lay about, the trees so recently naked that it was still a
novelty. This was at the time our thing was falling apart. It had come
out about Steve Krollheim. I'd come round to her place as arranged and
there was no answer. I waited at one of the zinc tables of the *deli* over the
road. Eventually out they came. He goosed her when she was checking
her mailbox and I saw her smile. Thickened, rubbery lips, smiling. I
could see her breath. She wore a white knitted scarf with red ends and
a bobble cap: white cap, red bobble. Red cheeks, red nose. She fed the
brown envelopes back into the box and off they went, arm in arm, after

a brief snog. Barb was running the two of us. Couldn't choose; so, at least,
she made out: like someone's finger dawdling above a biscuit selection.

I had to fuck her in the bed he fucked her in.

The launch party for the paper-jacket edition of Ryan Eddy's *Hegel: Bohr*
clinched it. Although I, of course, was asked, she wanted to go with him.

At the motel, meanwhile, the sadness of the birds as the light grew dim.
And the river growing noisy at night. Wanking in the bed where I'd
fucked Hella. Same counterpane, a static electric blue, with its brittle
brown cigarette burns. Same scents of prickly detergents and cream
cleaners, plus the faintest ontological reek of those self-same cigarettes.
And same television anchoress, who I watched when I wasn't watching,
on my own internal television set, Hella's white bottom---one or two
small red spots---spread apart by the way she stretched apart her legs.
Cordlike tendons under the skin of her thighs, distorting the musical
geometry. And then, lying reddened and shiny under its hair, just as the
river water had lain, shiny, above the soil but beneath the grass outside
this door---. Glazed or varnished with something like the transparent
syrup that flows from figs which are ripe enough to split with one faint
poke … ⊠ and, but let's not go there. So, something she would have heavily
regretted, this preferring the artificial to the real. Yet even the artificial
is too much for most plants sensitive enough to detect it, which sadly
few are. Most of us take the world, and even those singularities which
are people, at face value, then fail to minutely examine even the most
valuable face, let alone its spirit and what that implies.

The music went on playing when the pianist stopped: this is how she
was. She'd say things which would evolve like a train of lost chords, silent,
affective. Her words didn't stop when they physically stopped. Sexually
too. When we fucked my body moved, juddered on its own likewise. My
brain jellying about in my skull. And when I came---such delight---but
violent. It felt I'd rip apart, leave genitals embedded in her, like a drone in
a queen.

The unaccountable charge to her looks---the faces she made, her
sprung stance. And then, even in someone into bald science, the charge
irreducible, upheld. At *Prairie du Chien*, I'd look at her, and still couldn't
work out how the charge was fired. The supernatural blended in with
the natural, obviously, like the naturalistic dream which transmits a
mystical, luminous message between its lines. Curiosity, a relentless

tendency, kindness, courage, battered lips ever pursed for a question which usually but didn't always arrive. Eyes glowing, sensuous, sparkly, and yet ⊠ the quality of making you restless, speedy, distressed, perhaps because you feared you'd lose her.

Waking from a bad dream to find I hadn't even been to sleep, but simply spent the night offending against goodness, sweetness, and what the past was for and the future would be. You must be a prisoner, but one final freedom you reserve, at least. The freedom to hate your warder. To be a prisoner and love the warder; even the warder's daughter: this idea revolts you. Everywhere you struggle to make yourself strong, but here you must struggle to make yourself weak. Christ asked this for everyone; I couldn't even bring it off for one. 'He didn't love her,' they will say. I did. But wasn't strong enough to give away my power. Raise a family. Yet. To be fair to me, it wasn't time. And so, rather than become a prisoner of love, I chose to be a prisoner of shame. To erase a family instead. At first. Later it became hate I was a prisoner of. And so: there is injustice here to darkness; darkness is evil, darkness is wrong, has all the hatred of the base for the beautiful, darkness lacks mystery, is limited, faithless; but darkness is also necessary, in the innocence of its hate. Some poor fool has to take that part. Was God using the Devil? So that 'I'm just the patsy,' he might have said. Or did the Devil, like the man who plays Captain Hook at least, if not Captain Hook himself, choose to be used. Why didn't I go with her back to Europe. Presented with someone who is not merely an answer but a dream in herself, you turn away from her. Because it's only a dream? Because it never happened? And you're scared it never will. Or, because of the thing about dreams which is you have to wake.

She had happened. I loved her as Pluto loved her, by which I mean she was better than me, and the better one is made to pay for that. I'd damaged her. Hurt her too much for it to be saved, not through her resentment, but my guilt. I thought things had to be perfect all the way through, that I had to be irreproachable, that there was no way of erasing shame or error. She was too young to diagnose this, and override my stupidity. And well, but do you really want to hear about calculus from a girl with her eyes shut and her mouth open? And her head bent backwards on her neck. Who lifts her head and opens her eyes, bewildered, but only to look down between her opened legs as a fleshy cylinder of prick slides in and out? Isn't there something wrong with that?

Lacking courage, I was victim too, of the delusions of induction. I thought she'd come back. And if not I imagined there would be more like her, not knowing a goddess come to stalk on earth and fuck with history when I saw one pursing her lips, readying her eyes, to kiss me. And that, even if there could be more like her, I could also love them. The world as full of shit, and the will to wade into it, to share *its* destiny. To get yourself crucified to see what that's like. The will to leave Hella for Barb. You do this even when you know your destiny is good. Even? Especially. Because after that it's settled, it *is* determined? Your happiness may start, but your freedom ends? Spiking determinism.

Because this spirit reunion was ordained, arranged. I didn't believe in arranged marriages. The room I was entering had no exit; and however sweet the nude was, arranged on a yellow chintz chaise, however blue and scared her eyes, as she dented her lower lip with her teeth, however fine the hands she laid, one across her breasts and one with honey smeared across its palm, flat between her legs, it was a *room*. It had no trees in. Because this is a death of a sort; the equation is solved, the answer pat. Nothing is left but the unwinding of the main theme, steady and predictable, with no variations and a deficit of suffering. The plot thickens to solidity. There is more to life than happiness.

If the holy grail is the Magdalene's vagina, so to speak, then drinking wine from this vessel, and eating bread. And yet, I pushed away the cup and spilled the wine. And underneath the soil I heard the asthmatic corpses of my forbears gasp.

Two strands; that nature is possible, and that our certainties, our one-plus-ones, are fallible. Nothing is true, everything approximate, indeterminate; hidden amongst leaves, and naked under clothes, and warm, and wet. She had one horrible failing which went right to her core like a stain of gritty rust in the flawed heart of a sea-green jewel. She loved me. She needed me. So: to have had everything, and destroyed it. Unless that's everyone's fate. Or perhaps not even that; perhaps most people get to destroy only what others had. I at least had something real, my own destiny, my own little scrap of the beauty of the eternity, my own equal of a star to smash. What is sweetest, having it; and how contingently it falls apart. The logic of decay in everything.

But necropsy not the answer because its precondition is death. Me, Barb were both violent to the universe. Lying on that electric counterpane, studded with its hard, shiny cigarette burns, shaped and coloured like

minute anuses, the whirring, self-assured lunacy of a game show on
the television screen, and a reluctance, a false laziness, a sudden hunger
or thirst: any kind of pretext not to think, not to ask such questions
as these, but to wank again, come again, across the complex band of
swollen, creased, hairy flesh which ran from front to back between her
imaginary legs, so as to mask the agonising realness hidden under all of
this and flashing like the light on an ambulance or in the armpits of her
aeroplane.

Amongst the junk mail that had gathered while I was at Prairie was a
letter from her.

Miraculous.

> *Did you get the letter we fought over when I posted it? It was for you. The man I
> loved as much as you was you. But you needed teasing, you needed waking up. I
> could see you didn't know what had happened, that you didn't value me enough.
> Because I am valuable. I know I am. And you don't.*

It must have been posted---written, at least, just when she got back to
Paris on the train.

> *What are you doing now? Not now, now you're on that horrid plane flying away
> from here, but now when you get this. Tell me your news. I'm very fond of you, you
> know, you mustn't hurt me, you mustn't let me down. By Ohm's law and Boyle's law
> and by all that is sacred, I love you.*

The US postal service, or the PTT, warping time, juggling chronology
with the ingenuity of a screenwriter.

> *This journey is a bitch. How's yours? I have a top couchette, and the man opposite
> snores long organic snores all night and the man---his feet smell!---underneath.*

I love you.

I'm not afraid. Of anything. I love you.

Hella.

My body wet with a film of flowing sweat.

On Wednesday, another letter came. Solving the mystery of their delay:
she had the zip code wrong.

This said nothing about coming to New Cardiff: chatty, cooler, more offhand, and brave, and drab.

> *And you remember the moth I couldn't identify. That was driving me nuts!(?) None of the entomologists here can either. May be a new variety. I found it because I love(d) you. Do you remember?*

I'm keen to hear from you; how you are getting on and so. Perhaps you've written already. I hope so.

Write something to me, even if it's something bad, even that.

Because I love(d) you, Hella. (Skippergate!)

Painful. Making me cringe.

The leap of the salmon into space; but it can't jump high enough. The waterfall bigger now. What was it that stopped me answering these? She herself had overtaken them, a larger, heavier parcel of bones, padded with flesh, wrapped in brown skin, rendering them obsolete?

A few days later, another envelope, addressed in her writing.

Inside was a compliments slip from the physics department at Blindern.

A rumbling as I opened it. How can a sheet of paper change the world?

> *It's hard to tell you this, but here goes.*

I was pregnant, and made a termination.

I lowered my face.

'Hell', I said, almost calmly, you might have said, to look at me. 'No.'

> *I thought it was my problem, but it is (was!) your problem also.*

'No.'

Meanwhile, a sense of watching myself; as if it was all a game, watched through glass.

Her English deteriorating. Or was it simply when she wrote? A mystery: she could speak but she couldn't write. One of the commonest mysteries, and I don't exclude myself.

I wanted to tell you. But I couldn't: you wouldn't have welcomed it. So I have had it done. I wasn't even going to tell you this, but I must. I feel BAD. And real bitter. I could kill. (I have!) God, it isn't good.

Outside: the sky the colour of meat.

The graal-legend as the story of each life. So, we hunt, and each thing we find uses up one life; we die that death. Or the foetus does. Until all there is for us to find is our own death: this is the last, true graal. This is all there is to hunt for now. And making Haakon happy(!).

And, rain, seen as a vibrating in this colour, and the window beaded with greasy streaks of water, white beneath, grey on top.

I've aged, I've aged. Enough to see that art is no more than the pleading of our ancestors for worship, science only the search for a way round death.

Her curly, girlish script. The paper crackling like onion skin.

I loved you: how could you understand that?

Like flames.

A man.

Her child had died because I wasn't up to scratch. The first instinct: get her pregnant again, placate that little ghost, make another beaker to decant it into, quickly, like replacing the broken fishbowl for the fish.

Bye-bye. Hella (Skippergate!!)

The will of the child in the way Hella had changed over that summer. She had grown plumper. In her happiness, over the summer, she had filled out. Her body had told her she was married. She could sit back, relax. And she was. Married. Only such developments as academic calendars, scheduled flights, the tatters of Judaeo-Christian morality had screwed this up.

Where was the soft tiny skeleton, the doll's bones and egg-skull, of our love? The crab-meat tutelary ghost. What had they done with it? Landfill? Or burned?

No love after abortion. The love flushed out with the baby. The couple who have killed their child don't want each other anymore. Except, I still wanted her.

In this case, not even my affair with Barb survived. She started making me wear condoms in case I'd picked up anything from that Norwegian cow. Then she definitively went over to Steve. But although it was over she kept her key to my apartment.

And I still didn't write to Hella. Or ring her. Or answer her letters. How must this have seemed? How could it be? Like a battery chicken in a factory farm, when Barb took away the cage I still couldn't go outside its shape.

---'Oh no you don't!' she advised. 'You don't go creepy-crawlying off to her right after you finish with me. It's utterly offensive.'

---'What?'

---'It's disgusting. That's what.'

---'And Steve?'

---'You stay out of me and Steve. Okay?'

A long pause for a rigid, sinister, humourless look. Then:

---'As for her ...'

---'What about her?'

---'She has a smelly cunt, that girl. You can smell it. I can smell it across the Atlantic Ocean. She's got a smelly cunt. I can tell you that for sure.'

A shitter-on-sweetness, was Barb. She'd go out and find some sweetness and shit on it. This was her mission. This was part of what had happened to Hella and me. But why? Why was it her mission? What was in it for her?

What was in it for Stalin? Hitler? Or for the devil, you might as well ask. An old mystery. But I'm being unfair.

I read Plato instead. Trying to comfort myself, by reading him in Greek, with a dictionary, back in room seven. As if Hella's finger was following mine across the page.

This was foolish. It didn't work. There was nothing in this I wanted, nothing here for me. There was nothing in the world, in fact, I wanted.

But her. And I was giving her up. For reasons invisible even to me. So: nothing left.

Bleak.

More letters. Not even opening these. The pain, the sweating, the cringing. Like being burned.

Barb moved to New York city soon after that, to help her step-sister Darla. Darla's latest kick was virtual art. It used to be that you failed as an artist and then turned critic. The cliché is that now it's the other way round: that now you succeed as critic and then turn artist.

Darla was using early ray-tracing techniques to create impossible, spatially self-contradictory forms. The Escher of virtual reality was how she sold herself. And she wanted---needed---Barb to help her. Far from being an artist now, she was becoming an industry.

---'Oh yes ...' said Barb on the telephone.

---'Yes?'

---'Darla wants to be put in touch with that girl.'

---'What girl.'

---'The floozy from the conference.'

---'Why?'

---'Darla knows Eugene Skippergate would love to sponsor her show. She's into virtual reality now you know.'

So, hating myself, losing my pride. I wasn't even interested in my career. Poisoning myself with my own dirty breath. And then, an e-mailed suggestion, mystifying, from Dr Ron Jones of Rothamstead, that I might be interested in applying for an honorary research fellowship on the basis of the paper in Soil Science. Which I hadn't written.

This mild disjunction in the function of the world, things no longer adding up so neatly as they once had, a sense of lurking mystery beneath the bald, bland stare of logic, was characteristic of the time.

When I checked the reference, I saw my name at the head of the paper, followed of course by hers. Not strictly ethical, this. She'd written it

there in the same way that a bewitching teenager spray-paints your
initials, interlocked with hers, on a tree. But it was no surprise that,
when the group photograph of the symposium arrived, glossy, large and
painfully coloured, neither of us was there. Kohlhaas, Cundy, Johnstone,
Sir Mel, Molinos, Waddington, and all the rest of them. Professor
Leicher in the renaissance ducal throne (the strawberry leaves); under an
escutcheon of seven gold balls on a silver ground. But not us. There was
no gap in the scrubbed or even burnished, smiling, creased and tightly
suited ranks, no indication, even that we weren't there.

Unless we were. Unless we were the virgin and the unicorn in folds of
flowery tapestry which formed the rich green backdrop behind their
heads.

This past was now meaningless to me. Unable even to understand it. Its
motives, its passions. The way in which you suddenly lose fragments of
your civilisation. A literature here, there a science. Even a cookery or a
pornography.

And taken to a morgue to identify her, I would have got it wrong.

Until, years later, like secret, unknown wings in the house of your
childhood, blinking foolishly, emergent from a personal dark-age, as
suddenly you rediscover them. The lost civilisations. The lost worlds. In
your very heart.

Late one night she rang.

Her deadened voice. Disoriented. It took me a moment to realise who it
was.

---'You?'

---'Yes.'

---'Why didn't you ask me?' I said.

---'I did.'

Silence.

---'How could you?'

---'I did.'

---'How do you know it was mine.'

---'No doubt.'

---'Why?'

---'With him I used contraception.'

---'And with me?'

I imagined her small white face on the far side of the whirling earth talking into the black instrument, heavy, heavy, almost too heavy to hold.

---'Not.'

---'Why not?'

Plaintive outrage.

---'Because I loved you.'

A pause.

---'You know I wasn't going to tell you,' she went on. 'But I did---I must have owed it to the ghost. I didn't tell for me or you, I told for it.'

Her voice wooden, as if she'd learned her words too thoroughly.

---'I wasn't even going to tell you that. It just came out.'

Another pause.

---'I wanted to sleep with you, even on that first walk we went together, under the castle, on the island, in the sandy woods. I wanted pregnant even then. But I knew it was foolish---foolish! Mad! I couldn't believe that buzzard and that snake. It's like someone being granted their wish by a fairy, and as it does with fairies, it went wrong. Now it's finished, over, the child got muddled and died before its own fucking birth.'

I sat there for a while, my eyes cold and shrunken in my head. The feeling that if I moved even slightly they would rattle. Outside it had grown dark.

I had forgotten she was still there.

Then I heard someone speak.

---'Why won't you leave me alone. Leave me alone. Leave me alone.'

---'Hella!'

---'Hey?' she said. And rang off.

In the end I rang her back. Trying to piece it together.

---'Hella?'

Patient, despairing, her voice coagulated:

---'Yes.'

But a lump of saliva got wedged in my throat. I couldn't speak. She
waited awhile while I choked and grunted, but then I heard her say:

---'I'm going now. It's all so fucking tragic. I didn't understand life was bad.'

I kept hearing, or thinking I heard, the rising wailing of the child.
Interrupted by furious little coughs. I kept hearing it.

---'Hella,' I asked, nervous, 'can you hear that?'

---'Yes,' she answered, and then: 'It's ours.'

Cruel. Chill. In my back; and a prickling.

---'What sex was it.'

---'Oh God, I don't know, they don't say, don't be so fucking wet.'

And cracking, abrupt, sudden:

---'I'm going now, it's hard for me ... you understand. Have a nice life. Bye-
bye. Bye my ...'

But her voice gave out.

---'Hella?'

---'No, leave me alone. I'm not strong enough. It hurts too much. I can't.
I'm not strong enough. Please leave me be. Please, for me ...'

---'For it ...'

She stopped speaking.

But there were still sounds.

What were the sounds?

The sounds of someone being drowned.

And other sounds: sounds coming up her throat from her belly: sounds from her insides. Down a wire, up into space and down again, and down another wire to me.

The wonders of science.

And later, even after putting the receiver down, inaudibly, just beyond the borders of sensation, a rising wailing, interrupted by small and furious, half-deliberate chokes and gasps of breath.

It went on all night.

If that was in the Technicolor past, this is sepia: yesterday.

The deserted carriageway somewhere in Europe, evening, and stopping for the hitcher.

His navy duffel-coat with fang-shaped buttons. His milky face and ruby spots. His wheedling, manipulative charm. And the man on a mule we passed, headed the other way. The alarming rate at which he bowled towards us down the bald new tarmac---illusion of our own speed---and sped away.

On either side, abrupt rocks rose hundreds of feet, torn and veined like meat. Beside us the relics of marshy pastures, orange in the closing rays of the sun. Then a village where we stopped for gas. Fine liquid gushing into my tank. And feeling like a man with a drink, a man who could go anywhere, a man who could do what he liked.

We drove on in third, Armance shouting and bouncing on his seat. Pulling at my sleeve. Trying to bat him off. The tyres shrieked mildly as we flung from side to side. I thought it safer to stop.

He alighted. Stared in through the car's open door and smiled. With one hand he was raising an invisible glass to his lips. With the other, pointing down.

Offering me a drink. Somewhere down there. The idea seemed harmless enough.

We left the car where it was, slewed over the empty carriageway. The bar was hidden right underneath us, half-engulfed by the embankment. Sliding down to it in a cloud of dust. The broom and gorse they'd planted to stabilise the soil already dead. The summer dry.

Lying on the cool concrete inside was an elderly mongrel. Wearing a grubby cone round its neck. This was to stop him scratching his many sores. A warning of the terrible future fate, in some way inevitable, of His Master's dog. It gave him a bathetic air, deepening his eyes. Astride him, legs hanging down on either side, was an irritating yellow puppy.

A swelling sense of---something. As Armance walked under the bar flap without raising it.

The elderly dog, lifting his cone like a heavy, astronomical device, pointed it wearily at me. His eyes bunged up with a dried yellow grease. Under the bleached fur, his knuckled tail and knobbed spine distinct. But already he was standing, wobbling on loose table legs. The puppy tumbled off and amused herself with trying to catch the slowly swinging tail in her teeth. While, nostrils flaring, feeling the air, tasting it, the dog shambled towards me. We have two nostrils, just as a snake has a forked tongue, so as to be able to smell in stereo, and the dog, clearly blind, was utilising this. On the way, a short rest. And on again, towing the puppy on splayed legs, until close enough to thrust his muzzle manfully between my legs, impeded only by the cone. Then he was bouncing and singing, turning slowly in the air as he rose and fell. Higher with each leap, his ears fluttering within the cone, his body twisting in space, his voice in time.

The puppy, amazed, lying on its back regarding him, all legs bent.

A bench against the wall. A few elderly men were there. All staring at the cobbled floor and, in uneven rhythms, gobbing on it. As now we waltzed to the dog's own music, his hind feet stomping, hopping, paddling, pedalling, his tongue flying back beside his head like a pink scarf. This went on for minutes, or so it seemed. Anyway, far too long. His brown eyes communing with mine as with those strange, stabbing gestures in his legs, we waltzed.

His pelvis trembling; it was too much. His limbs, creepering round mine, his chicken breast, dinting my soft thigh. Taking his warm skull between my hands, breasting the dirty, doggy breath (dog-shit from the wrong end) I smiled at him. As casting his eyes from side to side in an evasive shame, sliding his tongue between my lips and furling it inside, he juddered once or twice and came.

A little hairy pumping on my leg. Randy old thing.

Withdrawing, detaching; his pelvis weak and sinking, settling astern, heading back to the stove. Mouth wide with the screaming effort. Breasting time's gale. On the way he rested the weight of the cone on the concrete. And at last, grateful, by the hot red light he turned three times and sank.

Just under the bagged knee, on my trouser leg, a tiny misted slug of teeming sperm. Flattering.

On the bar; a *Pastis* waiting. Armance had fixed it for me. Misted, teeming. I needed it. Things, meanwhile, conspiring. The thundery floor, as if I was still on the carriageway. And my heart subtly misfiring. Armance had disappeared.

---'Yes; another. Thanks.'

---*'Mince alors!'*

The dog had reared himself up and was gnawing at his genitals. One hind leg kicked blindly. But then: down he sank again.

More *Pastis*. The barman handed me a teacup and a dish of olives balanced in a basket of bread.

Innocent enough.

Then he held a tin teapot out across the bar. I took it by the spout. A slug of liquid scorched the web of my thumb, making me drop it. It fell. Hit the floor. And squirted boiling water all up my leg.

All laughed. Some even rose to support their bellies as they did so. Even the barman raised his bar flap and came out to laugh.

With my olives, my teacup and my bread, limping away to the corner. Then, with the crack of an axe the first olive I took broke my tooth. I could feel it, taste it even, the tooth, sliding around in my mouth with fragments of olive stone.

Using the far side of my mouth I bit off some bread. Preserving--- scrabbling for---the normal. But when I looked at the loaf, it had tomato on it. This was blood. Were they going to laugh again? This was my fear. I wasn't so much bothered about the slicing pain, though I later came to be.

All had straight faces with innocence written on. All however still staring at me. Waiting on my next act. First another drink.

---'It's alright,' I mumbled.

Playing it down.

---'I get like this.'

And lying down on the floor. Because: the mood I was in: something
bubbling, molten, never known before, inside. As without warning,
caustic sick flowed up my nose, pooled in my eyes, tickled my ears,
made me choke.

Someone licking it off.

That dog. He lay down beside me, the better to lick, his eyes and
forehead bulging. And lying like this, not without courage, warding off
death, we slept a while.

---'*Un café. C'est qui?*'

Someone was speaking slowly; in a language I didn't understand. And
then I did:

---'Your name, what the devil is your name?'

---'Pluto,' I said.

But it was hard to speak. The broken tooth sawing at the roots of my
tongue. By now, of course, I knew very well where I was. Above me,
but upside down, lodged on the edge of the carriageway, my car, red.
Working my way towards it like someone doing the butterfly-stroke.
On my back. Had I been in an accident? In a sense. My varying limbs
discovered no purchase. Something squodgy in my pants. And that was
it. Nothing more.

Until the fumes, the geraniums, the latex, the mosquito-song. And I am
me, here. The smell, too, of diesel painted on bare wood. Once or twice
before I'd caught a whiff of these and felt the universe rumble underfoot.
And yet forgotten why.

Someone, evidently, had found me, sluiced me down and carried me to
bed. Armance perhaps?

Dabbing meanwhile with a scrap of bald white towel at the parched skin
beneath my mouth---either snot or a blood, I couldn't tell.

But on the towel: black. Blood. I could taste it too. The broken tooth. It
was like licking butter off a vegetable knife. I kept slicing off slivers of
tongue.

And here was the dog. By skilfully arranging his cone he managed another sniff at my balls. Then licked them. Tickled. Tapping sharply on the cone to stop that. To stop it at once. Not because it wasn't delightful. Because it wasn't done.

So what. He wrapped himself around my naked leg. Just as a gust of nausea got a grip on me. Dragging him with me to the basin I filled it with a shallow pool of sick. Running both taps to flush this away but of course, no water came. Only a phlegmy hissing and a spider.

I'd been here before.

The dog meanwhile, egging me on, giving me clues, still glued hot and hairy to my leg. The cone knocking on the waste pipe. I could feel his own balls, hard as golf-balls, parted by my ankle. And gently kissing the top of my foot, the moist hole at the root of his tail. Foamy brown liquid was leaking out. That tickled, too.

And a grinning ache in one of my shoulders; not a pain to be borne but something worse than that, something terminal, wrong. The dog humping and grunting quietly. Until, for the second time, he came.

Twice in one night. At his age. Not bad.

Meanwhile a problem to attend to. A spiritual one. That biting remorse. What had I done? What could I have done to make me sweat and retch, as I was retching now, over a sink? A stinking reed with liquids bubbling out. Who with mounting frenzy padded over to the shutters, each step a chord in delirious progression, and threw them open.

They clattered to the ground outside. The moon had gone and so had the mosquito. The sky turning brown in the East. As I leant---winded--- on the rusty railing of the balcony. Looking out through sinking, drying eyes, also gummed with yellow paste, at the night.

Not even Odysseus knows he's back. But it is coming to him. The message getting through at last.

Again, my body, tossing and heaving like something else. Inside---liquid and burning. Trying for the sink, raising myself up to sit on it. It came loose from the wall of course, and hung there nodding moodily. The only thing for it in the time available was to pull out a drawer and use that.

The dog stretching, yawning, then waiting patiently while I too frothed and bubbled.

Looking intently at the drawer, in a way usually reserved for stones. His head twisted, tongue out like a pink tab, ears hanging down.

It was already light when I rose. Nothing to clean myself. It had been a drawer of linen. But the trusty dog: slurping and gurgling as he sucked it up. His cone getting in the way. He squealed once or twice with the frustration of it.

The basin still nodding on its pipes. Meanwhile, a collapsing, a caving-in of my chest, and a bitter, drenching splash of fright---I'd seen a looking glass above it. Now, slowly, raising my face to it, braced for what else I might see.

Misty, foxed, but unmistakable---the bitter lips and crumpled eyes and something stinking in the mouth. Time making you do things no one else could, like dye your hair and pull a horrible face. Raising my hands to this vision: lifting it from its hook, taking it down, turning it over, as if to cancel it out.

And there, written in biro on the plywood backing, pierced by worms, ...

31 *Août* ☐ *Je suis ton Épouse* ☐ Hella

Because this of course was St Antonin, the dog Pluto. Hella had a habit of writing on the backs of mirrors in our hotel rooms. Even in the Palazzo Setino, the *Pensione Otari, Prairie de Chien*. Meanwhile---this hit me hard---something was very wrong indeed. I had grown old and Hella was gone.

Far away, finished, heat-sealed into the past. Until a gilled, crab-meat ghost, grieving for its parents, for their sadness, their loss, induced the blind man to drive this route, then led him down to the river and made him drink.

How had I forgotten her? If I hadn't forgotten the words, I had forgotten their meaning. I had lost the central event, the moral, the storyline of my life. The faint echoes of ancient civilisation, as viewed from ages now very dark. Being the first glimmerings of a renaissance, I hoped.

The aimless life, life lived on the surface, day-by-day, for its own sake, without religion, mystery, love, was dying now. Something new was on its way. I hoped. Amongst the nauseous drenching tides of misery, was a trickle, a pure, clean fount, of the fizzing excitement I felt with her.

And now I would find her out again. Make it right. Rising from emotional snows, suddenly calmed, soothed, as if by her, and filled with radiance, sweetness, a welling warmth: I knew what to do. Whether I failed or not was material, but out of my hands. What was important was that the world would---was, had---received a meaning at last.

Meanwhile the little gilled foetus, giving the impression of something naked, prized from its shell, was partying.

We might be holidaying here now, me, her, our tricky, amoral teenager.

A ratty family with the sun pressing hard on the golden crowns of our heads.

How the idea of killing it would seem to us!

Attractive, perhaps.

On the bedside table, under a tea-cup: Casino Royale. Waiting all these years. Which was weird. It looked like nobody had stayed here since us, nobody even washed the tea-cup. Were these even our sheets? But which was understandable, given the décor. To mark the page she'd reached she'd used a photocopied sheet:

> *'Phenomenal Trajectories'*
> *Towards a dynamic of SMM*
> *In the presence of Professor Emeritus*
> *Norbert Leicher, TDA, BRIGS*
> *Belisha Institute*
> *Palazzo Setino*
> *Sponsor: European Commission*

The air was of a treasure hunt. First clue.

> *Address list of participants:*

Running down the list until:

> *Skippergate, Dr Hella, Dept Physica, Blindern Universitett, Nordre Aker, 01272*
> *Oslo, +47 31 27 23*

The crab-meat, tutelary ghost being thorough, if nothing else. That came from her side. She too had her thoroughnesses. This was what I identified as lack of humour. She could see the structure of a task and got it done, even when that task was to love me. She got it done.

I found my clothes. Slid the stinking drawer in. And followed earnestly by Pluto, went to find a telephone.

Lorchen's wing had fallen in on a hollow space. What was left of the hotel looked like a roast chicken after lunch. But then, I couldn't talk.

And Lorchen ... Armance? The same melon rind smile and enormous forehead. The air outside was dark with jackdaws. Fluttering round the teetering chimneys in a thick black smoke, making their ejaculatory sounds. But also, bright green parakeets---this was new.

The barman washing glasses, looking grim. I was unwelcome. But too excited to worry. Elated, exalted, inflated with misery.

---'*Hôtel d'Europe?* What do you mean?'

---'*Non, c'est L'Hôtel François Mitterand.*'

---'Marise and Albert.'

---'You're mistaken.'

---'Marise and Albert---and Lorchen---where?'

---'Nowhere.'

He looked at me like a specimen. For me it was like coming back after your own death. Someone else in your house. Someone in your bed. But no one in your body yet.

---'And Pluto!'

---'*Vieux?* He'll peg out soon. We've got a new dog now. Minnie, as in Mickey Mouse. Tell me that's not neat?'

Remembering something she had said: freedom when things go right, and fatalism when wrong. Let yourself off the hook. Go easy by asking not 'why did I do it?' but saying 'it had to be'. The world is beautiful and this is it. It had to be.

Under glass, on the wall, was a montage of tattered photos of the old St Antonin. Amongst them, of course, Lorchen, pregnant, her enormous smile. And Albert and Marise, florid and cross. And the young Pluto, with a sharp shadow, gazing intently at a stone. And then a misty photograph of us ...

Standing by a ruined bridge, Hella with one raised hand tidying a strand of hair. My own hair all over the place. Our faces blank, featureless, too much for the film in the brilliant light.

So: my brain pressuring the inside of my skull. Tears falling on the counter like coins. The stuffed ptarmigan still on the wall. The ptarmigan, the wall, and us; it had to be. Seeing her beauty, even in the blank face in the photograph: abstract, eternal; so that as well as loving I could be proud of her. It had to be.

The river, mysteriously, was running now, having been dry in the night. Apparently, to save water, they ran it only by day. Pluto ploughing waist deep, snapping at waves. As I climbed into the car he crawled onto the bonnet and looked in through the windscreen, swinging his tail.

---'Down, Pluto.'

Ignoring me. Trying the windscreen wipers. His cone followed them but just too slow, so that his face was always moving the wrong way. Trying the squirter. Poor Pluto. That made him bark. So off we drove, Pluto on the bonnet brave, something of a mascot, showing the future his bottom, but something also of the stuffed animal going to the dump. When I stopped and opened the car-door for him, tenderly, turning back a quilt for a hairy lover, he jumped down from the bonnet and crawled in.

The road was like a runway and I wanted to take off. Hunting out our death; teasing it, like a bullfighter a bull. Faster, faster, until even Pluto, seeing the hills shoot by each side was moved to bark. And as he did so we performed a swirling arabesque and ended facing back the way we came. I opened the door, climbed out and looked down at a stream, flowing amongst huge boulders and under the dappled shadows of hazel trees. The engine ticking, slower than a clock. The meandering greasy marks we'd made. Trying to work out our trajectory, but it didn't make sense: like the slippery-road sign, you couldn't work it out. It broke geometry, violated the assumption of four relatively fixed points of a moving plane, made use of dimensions invisible to us.

Heat, making the mountains undulate. The road itself, up ahead, mirrored like glass.

Another pang of diarrhoea. Running to the lay-by, with its caged litterbin, and squirting and playing my bright jets way down the bank. At its foot, half buried in rubble, a low ruin. Three empty windows and an empty door with sunlight shining out. And one gable made from an enormous split stone. Something sexual there: the fuzz of ferns growing in it.

We'd thought we were so high.

It was as if this hot, gleaming road in tar and concrete with its neat white dots and stripes and lines had been burned across the cordillera by our footsteps. But why the destruction? Why was everything we'd touched destroyed? Or, but were the things we hadn't touched destroyed as well.

Pluto barked once or twice. Then climbed back in. We drove on. But what was this. A man in a suit. On the shimmering, mirrored road. Flagging us down.

---'Yes?'

Gesturing wildly, back at a concrete bunkhouse perched on the edge of a terrible drop.

---'What is it? What's wrong.'

---'You are our most visitor.'

Eternally accommodating, so as not to hurt him, leaving the car slewed on the empty road and going in.

---'You are our most visitor.'

---'Most visitor?'

---'Yes.'

It seemed they had built a tunnel. With EU Status One funds. This the museum of it. Everything had its museum; their tunnel too. Which, I now learned, performed a corkscrew inside the mountain. In a glass case were diamond tipped drills, brown with rust, heavy, round. And on the wall a photograph of that old waterfall, below the lake where she'd swum.

---'Ah,' he said, 'our waterfall.'

---'Where is it?'

He was flattening the wings of his moustache. Then drawing me to the window, opening it, leaning out. Behind the building, a deep dry pit. But deep. Scary. The sort of place the devil might hang out.

---'Is that it?'

---'Of course.'

---'But where's the waterfall.'

---'In those pipes. It gives us this.'

He was flicking the light switch, so the light came on and off. Exactly what I was never allowed to do.

---'Here, let me do that.'

---'Of course.'

---'Ahh.'

---'Electricity, yes?' he said. 'We now have refrigerator, television, hair-dryer, electric mixer---can you hear me?'

He must have thought me odd.

---'Excuse please, can you hear?'

I needed sick. Quick. Out.

---'Can you hear, excuse please?'

Pluto waiting on the drivers seat, wagging his tail tentatively, looking concerned, looking perplexed. Squeezing into the seat with him and driving on; it was like flying a plane through cloud; sudden bursts of light, and then into darkness again. The world and its cockeyed significances; nothing adds up, and yet it seems to, pretends to, even. To figure. It seems, all the time, as if suggestions are being made, cards proffered ...

The shattering pink flash ...

And the fat blue light shining under heaving clouds ...

Like an emotion which comes too late, the thunderstorm. At last. I
rested my elbows on the steering wheel and squeezed up my eyes while
outside, through glass awash with layered plates of water, the thunder
clamoured, lightening burst and flickered, the moving car rocked
stiffly like a boat, and Pluto, his voice amplified by his cone, barked.
Manoeuvring for shelter into the open mouth of the tunnel, where
shockingly enough, the rain stopped. Where lazy turbines turned.
The beauty of these propellers, turning, slowly, venting imaginary
accumulations of exhaust---imaginary because no cars came. Imaginary
carbon monoxide, nitrogen dioxide, sulphur dioxide. The poetry of the
gases.

Inside, the clean, dry road, gleaming the black of caviar, its neat dots and
lines white as underwear.

A human form was bolting on ahead. In the lights of the headlamps, his
large buttocks wobbled ludicrously. He wore the remains of a short
yellow cardigan and nothing else.

And as expected, the corkscrew, turning and falling. With this pale figure
lolloping on ahead. I was going slowly so as not to tire him out. Kneeling
on the floor now, operating the pedals with my hands, a squiffy glimpse
of his bottom between the radial struts of the steering wheel on the
lower curve of which I hooked my chin, boring mechanical, a man-mole
obsessed, through virgin rock. Sweating with the effort of aligning road
and car.

Somewhere, above all these tons of shattered, interstitial rock, an iron
cross. Moaning, farting, in the wind.

And a gleam, splash of brilliance, filling the tunnel. It came from a niche
in the wall. What could be there, pumping out light---the spirit of the
mountain? Its treasure? And climbing out of the car and walking up
to it as to a window, and waking up in wonder in a magic valley, dry
yet overgrown with trees---ilex, pine, a few cypresses. Here, under the
mountain, in a magic cavern, as it were, with its own sun and its own
universe. And the tiny figure, hairy, naked buttocks, stumbling and
running, towing a comet's-tail of dust.

We climbed into the light and slid, with some of the technique of surfers,
down scree. Pluto in paradise. Looking this way that; unsure which
of the many, many stones to stare at intently until someone, through

chance alone perhaps, or the strength of his, Pluto's, desire, or whatever, it didn't really matter, should pick it up.

At the hill's foot amongst the soft brown shapes: glittering, vibrating, a metallic blue singing at the sky: the waters of a reservoir. Rippling, sparked, etched, an artificial blue, as if dyed, amongst brown hills.

I knew where I was going. Crossing a zone of cracked mud carved with contours like a map, I walked straight in. Naked. Without so much as a pair of underpants.

Hot red plugs of clay oozed from my toes. Pluto, his tail sagging, a stone held softly in his blind mouth, waited expectant on the beach. The water warm. Like a bath. Feeling better after that.

The dam buildings; hardboard and corrugated tin. Old letters, lying about, some of which had been used as toilet paper. A place to live, a good place. To bring her to, should I find her again.

So: probing the wound. Irrigating it.

A concrete culvert, filled with streaming, sparkling, snow-white liquid. On a headland, stuccoed with mud---a few old piles of stones.

Usually under water.

Sprightly now, after my swim, identifying what was once a door, picking the mud off the centre of its lintel like the icing from a scab:

16 + 92

My flesh fish-cold; creeping like a pupating caterpillar, through mud.

Worming under it.

Wet under a deceptive crust.

Clothing my naked body, face, fine hair, in sludge.

Through that door we used to walk. Before the flood.

And the dumb witness of all of this. Looking up at me, four footed, politely expectant, tongue lolling, a lazy moving tail. Soft black ears, powdered with flakes of dandruff. Perhaps he thought I was taking it too hard. After all. the world was suddenly and miraculously filled with stones, some of which rolled down the slopes all on their very own.

But this, for me, was a serious moment. Critical. Or not for me, so much as for my body, squirting out each end in its limited yet still expressive corporeal misery. The burning in the throat and nostrils, liquidity in the bowels. Intent, perhaps, on giving me a reason to feel so bad---my body that is. And bad I felt. By my materialistic reckoning we had one chance and I had screwed the best half of that one chance up. It hits you when it comes, this news. The dark wood sudden, terrifying.

To make it right, she was my only chance.

There'll be others, the world would say. Fine, fair enough. That's what I thought too.

Only there weren't. She had become the dictionary, the store of meaning, in a universe of vacant structure, empty grammar, scaffolding. Without her, it had no point. Without her. Poor thing. Poor me, I mean. Most people have it screwed up for them. I had screwed it up for myself.

Pluto comforting me. Seated on a mud bank, cupping his lukewarm head between my hands, his grizzled body thrusting and sinking between my knees. Unstrapping his cone and allowing him, unencumbered now, to kiss me as much as he wanted on the lips; allowing him to drink my tears. Because, rendered good by misery, I didn't have it in me to deny another's happiness. And then again, I needed him. I kissed his open eyes as he licked the tears from my eyelids, mud from my cheeks, foam from my lips.

So many kisses! So many stones. He was barking. I didn't have it in me not to: throwing a stone for him; it skipped and splashed across the water.

Pluto jumped in. Swam in dogged circles, his head underwater.

Something was wrong.

The water heaving and tossing around him. Pluto himself undulating gently.

Going in after him; still enough life to bare his teeth. But then, stuff came out with enough force to form a fountain, and clouded it the water. Perhaps he wasn't growling after all.

He'd been waiting. Waiting, patience tried, for me to release him. He must have known that every life, not just his own, has a miraculous stone-filled beginning and a miraculous stone-filled end. With a long mundane central interlude. In front of the stove. While I, headed in the wrong direction, steadily, conscientiously, all my life, wanted to start again, be redeemed, freshened up, forgiven. Even released, like him.

In other words, to find her, where ever she was, and lead her away. And make her happy. And give the universe the purpose it craved.

Leaving Pluto floating, his head and legs hanging down towards the abyss like those of the irritating puppy who had rested on his back, I climbed back through the hole in the side of the mountain, entered my car and began the long slide down to sea-level.

You don't need war or gods or science or foreigners for such tragedies. You can do it by yourself.

Blindern had no record of her whereabouts but the head of department remembered her. His eyes sparkled when I said her name, his lips twitched, and he smiled tenderly. They had been students together.

The healthy glow of his skin, his fitness, the beauty even of the few sharp crows-feet at the ends of his eyes. His short blonde sticky-up hair. Perfect body, perfect English, perfect career.

As for me, several years his junior---falling apart. This must have struck him too. I couldn't even speak properly. The pain from my tooth was less savage, and I had learned to avoid it with my tongue, but it gave me a clumsy lisp. I often had to repeat myself.

In Wisconsin I found Kohlhaas.

These heroic flights, long enough to have a curvature. Perhaps I should have telephoned instead.

Kohlhaas---his hair was white. This I couldn't believe. It had glowed before---almost blue, almost red. Now it was white.

---'Your hair ...'

---'I know', he said wistfully. 'Can't be helped.'

His face, however, hadn't aged at all. It was as if he was wearing a white wig. Very odd.

We dined in an over-chilled restaurant, to the hum of the air-conditioning. I had grown good at eating only on one side.

---'Remember she'll be older if you find her', he said. 'She'll be a woman, in fact.'

---'I love her.'

---'Can't be helped. She studied for a while in Leningrad, but that was before the Symposium I believe. Also you could try Leicher. He's gaga you know. His daughter married a Parisian and put him in a home. Entente cordiale I think it's called. The marriage, not the home. She still writes me occasionally, asking me to visit him. Hella wrote too a few times after Setino. After that a few years I had Christmas Cards. Then these ceased. I lost her new address when Martha put my address book through the wash machine what, 10 years back? It's interesting how many friends were washed away. All for the best, perhaps. We age so rapidly, and that's so sad. She's no longer an academic, otherwise it would be easy to find her. But better to make new friends you never knew young. When they die, its less sad, perhaps. But I'm rambling.'

He took me to the airport. I was glad I hadn't telephoned. A sense the world was inhabited after all, that morality was absolute. That I was loved.

Leicher's old-folk's home when I looked it up, turned out to be only six or seven kilometres from my hotel across the centre of Paris.

The treasure, in the end, always turns up under your own bed.

I figured I could walk along the river.

Foolish idea. This was Paris, not St Antonin. The banks of the Seine had been made into an expressway. I escaped into a florid palace, which soon turned out to be the fabulous Louvre, in search of air and drink and food. A sickening glass pyramid, placed in the courtyard of what must already been a pretty sickening building, destroyed my appetite. And since I couldn't eat I ponied up to wander through dim galleries, gazing at tourists and not even aware of the canvases until one I'd already walked past wrenched at me. Balbi's *Lust*, of course. Portrait of a mistress rescued from a bawdy house. Key to the objects ranged symbolically round her long white feet lost irretrievably. Excerpt from Balbi's letter to Francis I challenging him to explain them. Excerpt from Cardinal Freschi's reply conveying at Francis's command his failure. And desire for hints. Excerpt from Cardinal Freschi's reminder. Excerpt from Francis's letter: give us a clue. Please. Excerpt from decree exiling Balbi from duchy. Translucent shift painted on in the reign of Paul. Removed at the command of Beria. Some damage resulting, particularly to left shoulder and breast. Catalogue No. 66. *State Museum Catalogue* Ba218p. Exhibited by kind permission. Etc. Etc. I read these manic words and numbers, stencilled on a Perspex plate screwed to the wall beside her, my eyes gleaming and my brain deliquescing. This how it felt. A headache, but not a sharp one, a gooey one, with soft upbeat zings in it here and there. It wasn't the body, which wasn't Hella's at all, but the face, which was. A gooey ache in my heart, too, playing a duet with my tooth. And yet, I was able to look at her coldly, if frenzied, sadly, if morbid. A gynophile ghost studies a woman, a dog, a star.

Reminding myself, further, that she once was mine. In the hope of stirring a prophylactic pride. It made it worse. This, once, had been. But I didn't believe it. It was gone. That she once loved me was dead. The sensual mask too good to be true, and what was even better, her sadness. I hadn't seen this before; it was as if, like Dorian's, this portrait grew sad only recently. The weight of the lips weighed down the outer ends of her eyes, which had a way of turning round the edges of the face to the side of the head. As did Hella's. With a tender sadness; a sadness for me, not her. But if she was good, if she was even the best thing that elaborate lined and padded jewel case the universe contained, she was useless to me. I was through with this. Past it. What I really mean, of course, is this: when she said the past lives for ever she was wrong. This past was gone.

My mechanical self had moved on. A *Perspex* plate with small black lettering announced Ottery's *Rocky Shore*, leant by the generous Tate. Nothing odd here. Until I looked at it. And saw the same swollen bay, pale over sand, but over seaweed the darkest, brimming blue, edged with brandy-snap rocks and a little creamy surf, and then the steep green walls of the basin, sometimes breaking into cliff, and climbing high enough to disappear under the gilt frame. Twilit rainfall inside my head, overflowing and running down my cheeks. Because I recognised this view as clearly as I recognised her.

This was where we had stayed, once, long ago, just after leaving the Palazzo Setino in disgrace. No miniature palaces, no esplanade, no dog shite, yet, but the orange cliffs and brandy snap rocks and the swollen sea were there. Weird, to find these two paintings brought together in some supernatural way. Weird enough to make me interrogate my sanity.

The exhibition was a travelling one. It had been to Italy. It was going to Spain and then America. And yet, we read too much into such things. That was Balbi's Lust, of course; and admittedly Lust resembled Hella. But, I now figured, only a misplaced sense of association made me see the Rocky Shore as our bay. And besides, we'd been unhappy there. Nothing was meant by this. Unless it was something sinister.

Was she dead? My tattered tongue---it tasted horrible.

The biologist loses his marbles. Once so brave and bright and now: see his fate.

Proud of his trade plates. Broke up with Barb, didn't get tenure. Delivering expensive cars around Europe in a lounge suit. Which made a change from delivering them around the States.

Let it go.

As, at last, I did. I'd looked for her, and found *Lust*. Not, of course, literally. But perhaps seeing Lust again was enough, was the better outcome after all. Because if *Lust* was older and perhaps sadder, she was no less lovely. Hella, as Kohlhaas had warned me, would be older too. And if not sadder, maybe less lovely. In a sensual way at least. Except my quest was not about the senses, of course, so much as the heart.

I let it go. Sniffing a little, seeing a faceted gallery through sticky tears which unlike the usual ones made it hard to open and close my eyes.

A sweet ache as I moved my limbs, far from the slicing, bitter ache in my tooth. But I nursed these aches, I wanted them. Because once the quantum of pain was paid off I would be freed to remember her, painlessly, guiltlessly. Not having lost her, but having turned her down. Having lost her was a crime against nature, but turning her down was a crime against us. Which, despite her looks, her nobility, her goodness, extreme to the point of provoking its own destruction, was undeserved.

Leicher's ward, too, like a gallery. A sense of polish. Of gleam. On the ward doors, the glister of a square of Perspex with a number printed on. And Leicher, just inside, with tears in his eyes.

And yet: the terrible smell. He was slumped in a chair.

---'Penny for the guy', involuntarily, I said. That was insensitive.

But he was muttering, muttering; then laughter. Throwing back his head, showing his teeth. Then, dark-faced: muttering, muttering. And suddenly throwing back his head and laughing.

---'We're so glad he's had a visitor at last. Apparently his fame is worldwide. It's sad when nobody comes. He waits for news of his Nobel prize. He's happied up no end since you rang. It's done him the world of good. He believes we conceal it from him but you've brought the news. You're staying for the Social?'

---'Professor Leicher, do you remember Hella?'

Leicher nodding his head slightly, an intensity on his face. Then opening his mouth:

---*'Ierrropp!'*

And closing it again. Then: muttering, muttering. And with the sudden Leicher charm, throwing back his head and laughing.

---'It's no good, his memory's gone. Are you staying for the Social?'

---'Hella, Hella Skippergate. Dr Skippergate. Do you remember her?'

His glasses, too, were gone. The skin beneath them soft and frilled and a bluish white like the skin of a shell-fish prized from its valves. Looking at me with sudden fear. His hot-needle pupils, scorched with brown. And his blue irises, misted, smudged, congealed; poached too hard.

The Social: rock and roll by wheel-chair. And it really was a happy spectacle, not too far from rock and roll by roller skate. As back, forth, back, forth, then round and round we rolled. Pushing Leicher steadily, revolving as we went; and him, meanwhile, muttering, muttering, then throwing back his head and laughing with the ancient Leicher charm.

Too late to go; I stayed the night. In a soft spare bed. On the ward, the soft moans and chokes and gabbling of dreams. It wasn't so bad. Was a valid choice. To end up here I mean. And in the bed beside me, in the dim blue light, the muttering, muttering, and sudden, charming laughter, infectious, full, in it a real happiness---until late into the night.

Then it stopped. His bed empty when I woke, and neatly made.

Bad news: he'd died. First Pluto, then Leicher. The trail of death. The angel of it, of dark and light. So that, if you asked the angel what it was like to be the angel, it would reply, like delivering expensive cars, with trade plates. Having broken up with Barb. And not got tenure.

Or was I, rather, the angel of meaning, of rounding, redemption; of release. And if so, why didn't the magic work on myself?

---'Know this, that it will not be the same thing without him. We will lack him on the ward, is it not so?'

---'*Aaarick.*'

---'*Glossoomap.*'

---'*Meep meep!*'

---'But what good lucky you came in time. He waited for you, waited. And when you came---we'd never seen him like this you know.'

---'Never!'

Such vehemence in a childish voice that I turned to her. A pretty nurse; with a cross pouting face. Bushy blonde hair above a creamy brow, bunched crushy lips and cross dark eyes. No, it wasn't so bad. Trying the words out myself:

---'*Meep meep!*' A valid future. '*Gloosomap.*' My tongue, as I dreamed, feeling the shattered contours of my tooth. Not even this would hurt any more if ...

If ...

Seeing me watching her, she half-smiled.

---'He carried us to Stockholm to the prize dinner, he said before his mind failed,' sister droned on. 'All of us. 'I owe you my profound debt of gratitude for never doubting me.' You see, it's all for the best,' she said.

---'Always is,' said my nurse, and burst out in a radiant smile. Shy, radiant.

---'What's your name?'

---'Berenice.' The crossness in her face very sweet, even when she smiled. A kind of fuming intensity, and slight misalignment in her dark eyes. Her teeth; so neat, so bright. And those pink gums, wet with spit. Is this where all the good girls go? Sister, too, looked cross.

Leaving with some reluctance. There was a yearning there. There were schemes, echoing those when I first saw *Lust* all those years ago. How to reach her. To be writing a life of Leicher and to want her memories? Discuss over lunch, or even dinner? Etc. Or be admitted after a psychotic episode in a bleak hotel room? Etc. These was the best I came up with, lying on my hotel bed exhausted, but not so exhausted that I couldn't wank.

Perhaps, after all, not yet dead. But then, Pluto, towards the end, I mean, too ...

And the hanged man in the Tarot pack. Yes, but something in the air of rebirth. The air had bite, and juicy bits. And the rasp of the rakes in the parks, raking up dried grass. But in me, rebirth was the theme. Cradling Berenice in my heart. Her cross face, her creamy forehead. Framing my plans. And letting Hella go. In the particular at least, but only so as the better to embrace her in Platonic form. Platonic breasts, platonic legs. Because it sometimes seemed that all the girls thronging these sexual boulevards were her in disguise, bouncing back and forth through time. That evil was no more than goodness with the time-signature reversed.

First the tooth. Because: enough of pain, expiation done; accepting this; having seen so much; having paid at last, going to the dentist. On the way, somehow, the stations got jumbled up. *Montparnasse*, then *Étoile*, then *Sacré Cœur*. How come?

The dental hygienist, battered, grim. Blocking the door.

---'Can't I come in?'

She looked at me and stuttered.

---'You've grown up!'

On the sill, the pigeons cooing. Cooing.

---'Put down your bag; give me your coat; and try not to look so scared. It isn't nice.'

She put me in a leather chair like the seat of a sports car. Battleship grey leather. Pumped a bit at the foot of its stem and said:

---'He doesn't remember me.'

And as she spoke she fitted dark glasses to my eyes, then she moved the light across and shone it in my face.

I felt its warmth.

Even before I had a chance to answer, something shifted inside of me; something crunched, made me sick. The same people who had built the dam, the tunnel, had been at work on her face.

---'Ah,' she said, smiling. 'Aha. We remember. Hello stranger. You do, don't you. You've grown up. I wondered when you'd pop up. Tell me. Fill me in. What have you done with your life?'

I removed the complimentary shades, chewed the bracket, waved them with vehemence.

---'I'm warning you,' she said. 'It better be good.'

I was silent.

---'I have high expectations.'

I'd grown up, yes.

Some might say too late. But so had she. Her face: it had both melted and grown coarse. Meanwhile she'd left her skin too long in the sun. Leathery and brown, tanned in the leather goods sense, and subsiding in hidden ways, and slipping in ways unhidden. And her long, full legs, which had asked so sweet and irresistibly: lie between me, were now thin. You could see too clearly the bones. She saw my face.

---'That was a very long time ago. I am older now---happier too. But a different sort of happiness.'

It had stopped. She had used it all up; it was so intense it hurt; and then it stopped.

---'Not the long, steady, unbearable exultation of being with you. That was too much for me, you know. I blew a fuse. Gave up physics. Even metaphysics.'

She leaned over to clip a bib on a chrome chain across my chest. Seeing very close, too close to focus on, a few inches from the rounded, gleaming surfaces of my eyes, under the blotched and parched brown skin, near the stiff yellow edge of a low-cut frock, and the stiff white edge of her lab-coat, her collar bone leap like a flying buttress almost clear of the skin, but discontinuous, sheared, as if broken and badly set, which made me cold.

A lump there, like a knot in a string. And near it a botched belly-button puckering the skin.

Raising a blind face, slowly and open mouthed, to hers; her lips pursed; but suddenly she pecked me on the forehead, and smiled. Her teeth yellowed, with veins of brown. Her eyes too; only the blue still as bright, as strange. Stranger, perhaps, by contrast with this new face.

It wasn't her. And yet it was.

She looked worried now. She pushed the light away and took my cheeks in her two hands.

---'What's wrong? Was it something I said?'

I struggled unwieldy out of the chair. Winded, gasping, gesturing with the shades in one hand, I pressed my forehead against the hard bit between her tits. Half through embarrassment: I couldn't look at her. And half through misery at what had been done. And then there was the loneliness. Sadness. The waste. So on.

---'Qu'est-ce que se passe ici?'

Perhaps every life wasted. Every single life, not just mine. That was the hope. Not out of malice, but simply so as not to have to regret what I could never anyway have done.

---'*Qu'est-ce que se passe ici?*'

But she had turned away. The dentist had come in, and understandably enough, perhaps, was I understood asking what was going on. Black hair, balding. Green eyes. Sad ones. Thick and glossy red rims. And obscenely big, so that you felt you shouldn't look at them in case they popped out.

---'Oh Haakon,' she said; 'he's crying. An old friend. Lover. The one I met at Setino years ago. Do you remember?'

---'What's he doing here.'

---'He's the broken tooth.'

Haakon, teasing.

---'Aha! Good. Into the chair.' Squeaking and snapping his latex gloves suggestively. 'We have little score to settle, no?'

The smell of condoms.

---'Don't worry; he's teasing you. Don't tease him Haakon. But he'll do a good job. You will, won't you Haakon. Do you feel ready yet?'

---'Revenge a dish best eaten cold,' said Haakon jovially, 'but we can't be waiting all day.' Holding up his drill-bit to the light, inspecting it closely and like a mosquito, making it whine.

On my forehead, a cold sweat. As if grease had been applied there. My clothes, too, were wet.

Lifting a corner of his theatre-mask, to disclose a smile; lifting, at the same time, a corner of one eyebrow. He had the dentist's intricate humour, Haakon. And then (was it malice? Could it be?) asking me questions even as he drilled.

---'Is that hurting?'

Not exactly. More like having builders in.

---'Am I in the gum?'

His accent: Clouseau; as if he wasn't really French at all; but putting it on.

---'It bloody well should be. Now. He is a brave one, is this. Not a squeak.'

What was I supposed to do? Nod and struggle, and feel the drill-bit skid, rip and spool through the lining of my cheek?

And meanwhile hoping he'd forgotten. Hoping he'd forgiven me. Hoping her moral judgement was precise.

Suddenly he looked alarmed, my head too cold, and my skin; '*Renversez lui, vite!*' he shouted; Hella jumped to it, her *Paris Flash* splashing to the ground. Still in the chair, they turned me upside down. Clammy. Sweating. My stomach bubbling and frothing, a small black sack tight with sick. And the surgery lined, packed with black fur, pressed against my eyes, cheeks, inside my mouth.

---'What is it?'

---'Psychogenic shock, leads to syncope. All the blood it drains from the extremities and even from the brain; then you risk entering the coma bloody damn fast. You must turn them upside down bloody damn quick. Can you hear me? Has it happened before?'

---'Don't make him speak,' she said.

---'I cannot do any more with him today. He will have to come back. Where are you staying?'

---'Don't make him speak.'

---'What have we got next?' And he spoke to me again, slowly, loudly: 'Is there anyone who can look after you tonight?'

---'Haakon, let him recover. Don't make him speak. I'll look after him.'

He looked at her a moment, distrustful, and above the surgical mask he winced. Then snapping and squeaking the used latex gloves as he changed them for clean.

---'Help him out then. Take him upstairs. And bring the next in. Not another lover. I can be forgiven for hope.'

---'Haakon, you old woman,' she said.

Her voice. She loved him.

Upstairs: the hot flat. The fluffy cat, lurking like a panther amongst cheese plants on the sunlit windowsill.

---'There; under the window.'

She filled the electric kettle by its spout. Stripped a frond of rosemary into a cup.

---'Here's *Paris Flash*. Don't worry about Haakon, he's a terrible tease. Dial 1 if you need anything, or if you feel faint again. I've got to help him now, but we'll talk later. Is no-one expecting you.'

A racing despair, shooting like clouds across my silver heart. Yes, nobody was.

Not even Berenice. Was she rubbing it in?

---'Stay the night. You can, can't you? You must. I'll make you a bed on the sofa. Or you could have Lally's room. Tomorrow's Saturday. Haakon plays Golf. We'll have a talk. You'll be alright.'

And she laid cool palms on my cheeks again, kissed me on the forehead, and closed the door behind her as she went out.

Face in my hands, I heard her on the stairs. Sobbing, breathlessly, like a child until she came back.

Later, we sat in silence round the dinner table. A white linen cloth, white napkins, and white china, printed with green sprigs. Haakon slurping his wine. Hella looking yearningly at me; but unnecessarily bright; trying to make us speak. Otherwise the only sound the clinking of our knives and forks against our plates.

Haakon, sucking his soup. He held his chin over the bowl, so that the droplets from his spoon would fall not on the napkin she had passed him, nor his trousers, but back into the soup. Which shone like a buttercup on the underside of his chin. Poorly shaved. For a dentist. It was carrot and orange with a few flecks of ultra-green parsley afloat. And a double-spiral of cream. The double spiral: this almost her emblem. Not a double-helix, a double spiral. Horned, like a galaxy. The fact that a double spiral is possible; in calling it her emblem, this is what I mean. Counter-intuitive. Because a spiral seems to close space; it has the quality of a closed curve. This is how it feels. It feels womanly. But it's only a line. A sorry, manly line. And consequently you can double it. But Haakon, sucking away, suddenly darkened. His nose and forehead, which had been white and shiny, went red and matt. And he stole a sudden glance at me and reddened more. And sucked more soup.

What was he thinking.

---'Who wants more?' asked Hella bravely, tipping the pot on one side and using the ladle to scrape the bottom.

Haakon stuttering:

---'I will save the appetite for the rest.'

Then: chops. Crackling like Rice Krispies. Charred with a tiny, white-bubbled froth.

The air heavy with tears. Saturated. Wet with weeping. Wondering who would start first. Haakon growling as he sawed away at his.

---'Haakon!' said Hella.

---'Pardon. I excuse myself.'

Out in the suburban street, lamp-lit under the rain, cars hissing past.

Hella brought in the cheese on a pink marble disk. Haakon, casting his eyes about in artificial glee:

---'Shall I tire the salad?'

The joke fell flat. But was appreciated. This was a gesture, a welcome. And with a bolt of fear, knowing it could never be put right. It was much too late.

---'And I'm glad,' she was saying; 'if I'd stayed in physics, well it would have been self-indulgent, I would, apart from my doubts, have had a good time, but I wouldn't have known the answer to the question, *What good have I done?* I wouldn't have known the answer to that. And I do know the answer now, I believe we are doing good, taking away people's pain, and preventing future pain. I believe that is good.'

Haakon, he grunted.

---'You see, I know what pain is. The collar bone I broke; it wasn't that it was so painful, but that getting help took so long. And then, needless to say, it was set wrongly. They had to snap it again, which hurt more than the first time, except that it was done not as a torture but a cure, and somehow that made it easier to bear. But they couldn't get it right, and had to give up in the end.'

It wasn't her. Anymore.

---'And then, Lally's birth. That hurt. You probably don't. Know I mean. Yet.'

Silence. Haakon, taking more bread. And Hella, speaking brave.

Her voice with a quaver in it; this was courage. But why go on about it?

It was better than silence, perhaps.

---'So, we're doing good---in the simplest possible way. People are in pain; we stop it. Perhaps there are ways of doing greater good---saving lives perhaps; but I'm not even sure of that. If you save people's lives, you save them to breed. That's not good. While we ... people bring their pain, and go away without it; they leave it with us. And people understand this, that is why they allow us to hurt them. What is that if not the purest form of doing good. Perhaps there is a purer: someone comes to you hungry, and you feed her; purer still: someone comes thirsty and you offer her a drink. Purer still: someone comes horny and you fuck him.'

Haakon, his knife half way to the butter dish, rucking up his forehead and staring at her in astonishment.

---'No, no---don't worry; I'm joking.'

She smiled sadly. Haakon's look: loving, impatient, bored. Contemptuous. He'd heard too much already. For many years he'd listened to this.

---'No, but seriously, this hungry business: you are not necessarily doing good by feeding people; or at least, good may be what you are doing, but good may no longer be good. Humanity has outlived its nobility, its animal grace, now we are vermin. Worse than rats, than rabbits, than foxes, however pretty, however cuddly, however white, however black, we are a menace to every species, and even to the clouds, the rivers, the seas; and if they were not so innocent, if they knew what they were doing, they would combine and swamp us, keeping only a few exemplars in our natural habitat---you, me, Haakon & Lally with luck. By a fire, in a cavern, in deer-skins, while outside the wind whirrs and the snowy forests stretch. Because as a species we are out of balance, are a wrong, a liability, and we have to go.'

I exchanged a sympathetic glance with Haakon, his face turned down, the features thrust upwards on it by an incipient burp.

---'Sometimes I think like this, and the world grows heavy, and I grow urgent and sad; and since this isn't a good state of mind, I give up; I give up thinking like a god, not being strong enough, and I accept my destiny, and with it the destiny of the world, and Haakon opens the front door of the surgery with his keys and we wash our heavy hands and roll on latex gloves and put on clean white coats. For after all, even if the world dies poisoned by us, it will spin on still through space, wrinkled, brown, dusty as bone, carrying with it our dead bone, embedded in its dead flesh like fragments of bone in soap. We aren't the only guilty ones; the logic of natural selection sees to that. What we are, as far as we know, is the only ones capable of understanding their guilt, the only guilty ones who don't have to be guilty; and that is a little worse. But then again, we are the only ones who see and admit their guilt, who have a chance of expiating it, who feel fear of justice and remorse, and that, if not better, is a necessary step on the road.'

Married to a dentist. Her daughter a dentist's daughter.

Haakon washed, I dried.

Hella made my bed.

---'Here's something for you to play with,' she said. 'My grandmother's godfather gave it her. He floated down the Tigris on a raft. This is from Nineveh.'

It was a lion, a tiny one, with an inscription on. Its wings open; one tip snapped off, and one forepaw and one hind leg, and with it the tail which had snaked down the thigh, but otherwise it was perfect, rounded, sharp. It even had a navel, and enormous balls. It had that quality small animals had: you wanted to hold it; round the waist, especially; you wanted to touch its head.

---'He kept it as a souvenir, it was not recorded or reported or whatever you did. No white number, painted on its base. The secret of twenty-five hundred years kept still. Very few eyes have seen this little flying lion; and so it has kept its mystery, its purity, its darkness.'

Why was she showing me this?

---'Science is not the only mystery,' she said. 'We haven't given up
everything in giving up science. And in giving up science, do you
know what I most regret. It's the people, not the science. The groups of
intelligent, curious friends. The academy.'

The lion felt far heavier than it should. It pulled my two hands towards
the earth, made my hair slide and shift on my head, and the sheet of
white fat beneath my skin went hot and seemed to fizz.

---'Strange,' I said.
---'You feel it, don't you. I wanted to see if you did. Here; give it back. I
don't want to use it up, this power.' She wrapped it up again in a square of
brittle striped silk, scorched by time, and put it to bed like a doll on its
bed of dried rushes in a tanned wooden box.

---'That was my mistake, you see. I used up my power, all at once.'

Haakon, hovering in the shadows, still with his napkin hanging down his
front. He cleared his throat. Then she tucked me in.

---'That marble was already lion, and probably already lost, before
Homer's lips within his beard said 'Odysseus' or 'Nausicaa,' she said.
'That's scary too, isn't it. Because it was a small world in time, not only in
space. The weird power of secrets; the way they stir you up. That's what
physics should have done; with the bomb I mean ... Mankind: it's Icarus
every time, all over again. The civilisation that made that Lion; that's
gone. And do you know why? Because they discovered irrigation, and
raised the salinity of their rich soil. It's desert now. In their luxury, they
forgot their children would starve. Or perhaps they didn't forget. Had
other priorities, perhaps. I'm going now. Read this. It'll put you to sleep.'

A back number of *Paris Flash*.

So, breathing in the darkness, lying on his sofa, a hysterical, ageing
Werther, almost ready for death

Several hours passed. Then the light came on.

Opening my damaged eyes to this vision: a blond girl with a blunt,
turned up nose, and pink upholstered lips, her face curved up and back.
And on her face a kind of smile, or smirk; but her eyes were shut; two

furry curves. And then with the timing or affectedness of a teenage chorus girl she opened them and looked at me, and her eyes were round.

Fine blonde hair, crushed lips. Crisp bum. Round face and blue inflected eyes. That double curve again. In the eyes.

---'*Bonsoir, Monsieur,*' she said, and shifted her chewing gum from one side to the other of her mouth.

When she spoke she closed her eyes.

I could imagine her sitting naked on a bed looking serious. With her legs apart. Was I delirious?

Her nipples and her belly button. Her mouth, her hair. Her wide eyes and serious face. And then, between her legs, wet creases and soft hair ...

Or mad.

Covered for now by a velvet halter-neck which had its own stiffness and formed itself reluctantly into planes and folds as she moved about. The colour not of claret but of a bottle of it. Not dark blue, but not green or red either. It was black, perhaps. And then her body, as living and liquid as the wine inside.

She was offering me something, in her flattened hand, as you offer an old horse sugar. What was it?

---'*Prenez-la.*'

A pill.

---'*Prenez-la.*'

I know I shouldn't have.

She put a record on the gramophone. Aretha Franklin, as it turned out.

Something angular about the way she sat, on the bed edge. Perched. The hardness of her pelvis showed despite the pretty-pretty clothes. It was hard too to work out what she was trying to say. With her clothes, I mean, and the way she sat, as much as with her voice.

She had a bottle of vodka and drew vodka into a syringe. Flicking the barrel, squirting up the bubbles. Doubling her leg against her chest on the edge of the bed, and turning her ankle outwards, she shot up. Then, changing the needle, she drew vodka up again for me.

I preferred to squirt it into my mouth. She smiled, shaking her head.

Then: drawing back the covers very slowly, so that they moved across my body. But stopping at my waist, so that the sheet trailed around it.

Powerless as Christ.

Squatting above me. Lifting the hem of her plum velvet halter-neck briefly, just a flash. She wore no underwear.

Etc.

Evidently the shape of the future, this, but actually a little horrific even so. She was chewing gum, but very fast, much faster than she needed to. The window open: the smells of the night. Honey-suckle, privet, grass. And her: strong, intoxicant, sweet. And even, as it rolled past, the brief fumes of a rumbling bus. Her long hair held back with a black velvet horseshoe. A white shirt with long, rounded points to the collar, under the short halter-neck.

No underwear.

Something very wrong here. With her I mean. She wasn't happy. I sat up. And, taking my shoulders, she pushed me down again. Squatting above me. How light.

But one of her father's latex gloves---she had one of her father's gloves.

She took her gum out while she did so and filled the glove with spit. Then she rolled it like a stocking down my prick, wetted it again with spit, and spat herself on it, rising and lowering, fingering herself.

The long floppy points to her collar moved when she did, down when she rose, up when she sank. And quiet, almost silent, from her lips, a cross between a sigh and a gasp.

Pointing her elbows at the ceiling, touching her chin to her chest, she took the halter-neck off by the scruff of its neck and hauled it over her head. A brief scuffle before she could get her arms out. Unpractised at this. Her white shirt now, the white of surf which can never be worn. Stiff too, forming into panes as she moved, only partly responding to her shape. She was moving, and then she stopped moving. She was someone who could only do one thing at a time. Looking down at intricate fingers, and still forked on my body, but at ease, relaxed, like someone sitting calmly on a horse, she undid the buttons one by one. Then she opened the shirt. And then with a smile at me which suddenly disclosed her shyness too, her hurt, pressing her ear to my ear and her face into the sofa-cushion, squeezing my hips with the undersides of her thighs, my ribs with her knees, she touched cold nipples against my chest.

Not for long. She soon sat up. Chewing faster and faster until she stopped and dropped her chin so her mouth came open and the gum fell out.

Then she climbed off. Recovered the gum. Slid off the latex glove, chucked it through the window, down onto the street. And the gum, tasteless now, chewed too much. That too; down onto the street. The long, little hands with which she did this. The nails sharp.

The new world. Harsh, if still sweet. Very sweet. But not loving at all. Unless, stranger in a foreign country, I simply didn't understand its own, new ways.

---'*Je vais nager. Vous venez?*'

Now? In the middle of the night?

---'What?'

---'*Je vais nager.*'

Still breathless, beneath the cool glamour, the gloss; still breathing too deep, she did a breast-stroke with her arms. And moved by this means slowly across the room. She pointed through the window.

---'*Là-bas, dans le Bois.*'

Out in the park, the twittering of birds. The cool air, black waters of a lake. Paved with petals and leaves.

Walking beside me: it was Hella of course. The same light, long body.

But a different soul, alas.

---'Hella says you want to be a writer,' I said.

Lally looked cross.

Unless it was the same soul, but the me and the world had changed.

She went in first. Her ideal body. Her breasts, their own weight; solid,
yet not attached too firmly to her chest. She was older than she looked.
Unless she just looked it. And the water, climbing her legs. And the
sound, a kind of plok, as she squatted in it. Or on it, perhaps.

---*'Venez. Fuck! C'est froide!'*

Back at the surgery, sitting me on her bed. The frond of creeper, feeling
in through the open window, and rocking in space. Lally, making herself
up. Getting herself dressed. Tights, and a tight white dress, creased and
wrinkled around her waist.

And on this, a blue sash. Tying the bow on her hip. Her form as she did
this. Its twist.

Her hair: a fine pony tail. But feathered, layered.

Like a new sunrise, just when all the world is white, from dew or snow,
and the sky is white too, with no blue, and the tip of the sun itself is
white, just sticking up above the rocks, like the star that it is, and has no
yellow or red in. Yet.

But: the victory of evil. Evil always wins; the passive evil of decay, pain,
death if not the active evil of the Ciamas. Evil always wins. And good is
always reborn.

Kissing me. She was kissing me. Closed eyes. Her cold, cold cheeks,
warm lips, and the heat inside her mouth.

---*'Monsieur?'*

---*'Yes?'*

---*'Vous pouvez rester ici.* In my bed. If you want to do it. What you have
done to your tooth?'

---'Broken it.'

Caressing her; the side of her cheek. Her eyes not all there. Clouded
over, and they didn't look at me. But she smiled, and pressed her cheek
against my hand like a cat. Then, rolling down her tights again, rolling

up her long tight dress. Pulling aside the strip of her underpants like a guitarist putting wow into a string. Drawing my hand to touch her there.

Teenage rebellion. Was I being used? Was I too just a patsy? I had to consider this.

But it gave me a hard-on. It had to.

Remembering some words of Hella's. 'Accept what the world gives', she had once said. 'Accept its generosity. Don't fight God.'

And by the hot wet strip between the opening legs, pulling the underpants off. And, lying between them, seeing this vision: her lips, her nose, her eyes, looking at me, enchanted, as wide and round as they can go, and scared; her mouth. Scared of the future.

---'What language are you speaking now?'

---'English?'

Because when she spoke, I didn't understand.

She gasped.

Her legs up, her knees on her shoulders, her wrists side by side above her head. Her long white dress rolled up above her solid breasts. She lifted her head a little from the pillow and looked at me hypnotically.

I am wide open and soaking wet. Slide inside.

And when I tried to speak: she put her finger to her lips, closed her eyes, and smiled.

Sweet girl, vision of beauty; lips pulsing in front of her face, a blunted nose. And swimming-pool eyes.

She had her mother's eyes.

Then, sun already risen and heating a square of carpet, she stood on this to robe herself in white again, readying herself for a club.

She raised her arms behind her head, rucked up her forehead, and while still staring at me turned her face down. Still chewing. She made (if this was possible) herself ugly. She was doing something behind her head. She was forming her fine blond hair---Hella's hair---back into a pony-tail.

---'*Vous venez?*'

And what was that strange colour, burning in her face, in the sunlight. Pink, but not a carnal one, more a chemical, a marshmallow, pushing up against each eye from the top of each cheek.

Make-up, perhaps.

---'No.'

Getting the hang of her English now. But a heavy French accent. Like a starlet.

---'No, I not believing you would.' And a lovely malicious gleam of teeth. A dentist's daughter's teeth. 'That is why I have asked.'

Witchy malice in her eyes.

---'*Daddy-o.*'

And slinging a suede haversack over one shoulder, unwrapping another slip of gum, she opened the door and went down the stairs and out into the street.

Sweating, I slept.

Now, late morning and the sun heating the leaves of the cheese plants, heating the fur of the cat. Hella moving about the room.

---'Where's Haakon?'

---'He's playing golf with Roger.'

She was making coffee, tipping a slug of cognac into it. The tinkling of a tea-spoon, then the slow clinking of cups. Then sitting down, and staring at me a bit.

---'There are singularities in our lives. Hot spots. Moments you remember---know---for ever. That morning, when you were in my room, looking down on me, and you kissed my forehead, when I was pretending to be sleeping?'

---'Pretending to?'

---'Yes. I was willing you to kiss my forehead, to slip your hands under the
sheet, to move them over my body until they came to the place between
my legs; because it felt red hot there, and yet good; but it felt like it was
going to blow; I don't know, it felt like you had to do that, that if you
didn't do that, I would rip up the sheets---with my teeth. So I was willing
you, and only pretending to be sleeping; and you bent down and kissed
my wet forehead, and went to the door, and opened it, as if to go out; but
looked back at me---that was when I knew you loved me; because my
eyes were open, though you couldn't see me in the dark; I saw you, your
shape at least, still, looking back at me; and I said your name. Sometimes
reality needs a little help; like a toy train which has fallen off, you have
to lift it back onto the tracks. Otherwise it just lies there with its wheels
going round, and no-one gets anywhere. I said your name, very softly,
and you came back. And we fucked; and it's never, ever been like that.
And never ever will be, while I live.'

I didn't remember it like that. I didn't remember it.

---'That was when I knew I was right; you were mine, my destiny; I'd
found you at last; and could even take the credit for finding you; it was
even my fault, my victory, because it was for you that I came to the
Symposium, you won't believe it, but I came in case you were there. You
would be there, though I couldn't tell myself that, in case you weren't;
and in case you were I certainly couldn't tell Haakon. And I don't mean
all this metaphorically, either; it was you I was looking for, you. It was
because of meeting you before and how you ran away from me. Very
clever that. Like the decoy running away from the ducks. What are
the ducks to do? Of course, they follow it. I was faithful; I'd promised
to be; I didn't come to fall in love with you; and anyway, I already was
that. I came to see you, to understand you, almost like a phenomenon
in relation to my heart. Because I'm too much of a metaphysical realist
to believe in love working out. But something happened which never
happened before, inside of me; and like a good scientist I had to repeat
the experiment to see if I could repeat the result.'

On her face, the same expression, the same drawing back of the turned
up corners of her lips, right back, into the body of her cheeks, and this
tightness, vibrancy, yet fullness to her lips, opening them slightly over
her teeth, and still with the power to make my heart beat. She was very
lovely; it was only the shock of seeing her aging so fast over the space
of a few seconds like a vampire who has blundered into the sun that

made me overlook this. And it took my heart some time to thaw too,
and remember to love. Lally's eldest sister, she could have been. A sense
still there of speed, of speed through time so that, just as on a motorway,
when you are going much faster than all the other cars, you can do what
you like, go where you like, it is almost as if they don't exist; you can
drive round them like poles in the road, through them like mist; so with
her. She made the world go the way she wanted, or so it seemed; at least
not the world but the world in time, the world as it slid into the future.
For instance, she got herself to that Symposium and she made me come.
So why did her power fail? Did her power fail? And 'before': what did she
mean?'

---'Petersburg?' I said.

---'No.'

On her face, the same, gleaming smile; she was happy and she was
teasing me.

---'Leningrad.'

And the joy seemed to whoosh in her heart because lights came on
behind her eyes as she spoke again.

---'And at last, you've noticed. You didn't notice me in that library
however hard I willed you to. I even loved you then, even when I didn't
know you. Not very flattering, is it, to be loved for your face, your body,
and not your spirit or your soul. I forgave you everything: your stupidity,
your faithless worldliness, your puppy horniness. My heart swinging
and bleating with a kind of plump delight; so that I was truly scared that
you would hear it bumping in the silence of the library. 'This is the one.
This one.' Pathetic really; you didn't even see me till my last day. I was
too young to make you. And then, at the symposium and after (it wasn't
just chance by the way: in Leningrad you were reading a reference of
Leicher's)---at the symposium and after, you still didn't recognise me.
Truly, for what I am. And perhaps you couldn't. Because at the limit, you
never get what you want. You don't do the work you meant to do, you
don't get the husband you meant to get, you don't live the life you meant
to live. You don't even read the books you wanted to read; something as
simple as that you screw up. I'll tell you something though: if you get a
child at all you get the child you meant to get. No problem about that.'

---'Lally,' I said.

---'Yes. So, rudderless in time, you take what you get, and I got a little, very little, of you. Thank goodness. Because how few in this world or even in its history are lucky enough to get what I got: eternity in form, in idea. Most put up with so much less. I am lucky, glad, and that has kept me living down the years. Of course I'm fond of Haakon; he's always been good to me, he loves me, serves me; he is kind; reliable; he's there for me; his name says it, after all. Like the world, you can rely on him. You go to sleep, and dream perhaps, but when you wake, the world is there, the bedroom walls, and so is Haakon; and that's what you were in my life; you were the dream that gave the thing its meaning; and maybe I misinterpreted you, and maybe I even used you, abandoning my science to give you more qualities than you had, for the purposes of my art, if you like, of my dream; ...'

I wasn't listening, but thinking. She turned away from science, I turned away from her. Strange parallel. But what did it mean? Was science, and through it reality, if everything, still not enough? Everything there was, under and over the sun, as not enough. It didn't seem right, or if right didn't seem good.

---'Do you remember the sheep?'

What sheep?

---'I didn't realise it then, but that was the happiest moment of my life. And the geese, honking like bells when the bells rang?'

What was interesting was how insubstantial it was. Three weeks, out of a life. Out of eternity, in fact. This was all she had asked. This made the whole thing worth it. The whole enterprise. You could say the whole of the universe. I too saw that.

---'Haakon was a physicist too. But he got thrown out in his first year for putting a cat in a box. It was a joke of course, though not for the cat. He's much older than us. This was 1968. The union, controlled at that time by the Trots, staged a riot and demanded---got---his scalp.'

---'I suppose they had a point.'

---'He was quietly transferred to the dental faculty. But over the years he completed his degree. So you see, Haakon, too, dreamed. My serious, old, steady Haakon, with his black, bushy eyebrows, his dark red cheeks. He knows how to love; in all the years I've known him, ever since he first

saw me pushing open the wired-glass door of a room where I was giving
a guest seminar, and fell silent, and opened his mouth, while all around
him people were bursting and roaring and crying with laughter, in that
exaggerated way students have, at the face he made, he's never wavered
in his love for me. And he's had what he wants. He got the girl. He's been
happy.'

Here, house music came on loud behind the wall of the kitchen; making
it hollow, making a space which had not seemed to exist, exist after all,
and with its own qualities, loud and stupid, at least for us. Her empty
coffee cup, stained with grounds, turned slowly in its saucer. It broke her
train of thought.

---'She's been up all night,' she said. A kind of burning, aggressive love; I
could see it in her eyes. She had ruffled up her forehead in the way Lally
had and, while staring at the driven coffee cup, lifted her hands behind
her head to adjust her hair. Then she turned her face up my way, and
filled it out in a smile.

---'Except, with dreams,' she was saying, 'you bring back nothing. I
brought Lally back.'

---'Brought?'

---'She's yours.'

---'But ...'

---'Didn't you guess?'

--- 'The ...'

---'No; I couldn't to do that. No way. Never any question. I knew you'd
realise in the end. I knew you'd come back. She was my way to have
you, too, forever, throughout the history of the world. Do you think
me foolish enough to give that up? When you look at her, as well. How
could I kill her. How could it be asked of me? That's what they call
sin. That would have been a sin against my whole history, against the
purpose, as it was intended, of my whole life, perhaps of the whole
cold universe. No way. But I couldn't tell you that. Could I? It wasn't fair
on you. It would have turned you from someone---well it would have
turned you into someone who had done me wrong.'

---'How do you know?'

---'With Haakon I used contraception.'

---'And with me?'

---'Of course not.'

---'You didn't know me.'

---'I know.'

---'Haakon?'

---'Of course I told Haakon. He was pleased.' She spoke without a hint
of irony. 'Tears ran down his face. Do you know why? Because now he
could do something for me, he could help me, I now needed him---or
not so much that; that's the wrong way to put it; not now I needed him,
but now he could be generous to me, now he could prove how much he
loved me. And he loves her, too, like he loved me; in a sense, he didn't get
a daughter, but a purer form of me, and a form more closely wrapped
in his own spiritual history; so he's right you know, and that is why, even
though she gives him a hard time, and even though he's distrustful of
you, he can't afford to hate you. You gave back me, and you gave her.
Happily ever after, just like in the fairy tale.'

---'And you? How about you? Have you been happy?' she asked.

Ugly question.

The man who came back with a scar on his leg, known by the nurse and
robed in ermine, but only by mistake, only because he just happened
to have a scar, just happened to be liked by the dog. It wasn't me
who deserved this, I was just a symbol, as she'd said, of someone else;
something that, in her richness, in her excess, in her art, she'd used
to twist her life into meaning. And meanwhile I, who'd been offered
everything, had turned it down, had sailed away again in search of
shipwreck, misery. I had been the one to end up with nothing, the one
on the outside. The rich become the poor; the weak are the powerful
ones.

---'No.'

My mouth, distorted, and my lips wet. And my cheeks. Her arms out; I leant the side of my face against her breast; the hard nipple through the cotton plugging my ear; and I heard myself moan and tasted salt. And had seen eternity. This was important and was so real, the world so light, so nominal, that I thought for a moment I would drop through the floor.

---'And Lally?'

The music had stopped. Silence in Lally's room. Could she be sleeping, at last?

---'Lally,' she said.

---'Did she know?'

---'She's always known.'

---'No---that it was me, I mean.'

---'I told her you were coming ...'

---'You didn't know ...'

---'You booked, remember. It was me you spoke to. She didn't seem excited though. And she didn't want to come back for dinner---I asked her.'

---'She came back in the night.'

---'And went out again? She often does that. Did you talk to her?'

Not exactly.

---'She's a funny girl. Even when very small, when people asked who she wanted to marry, she would say *Daddy-o.*'

---'Haakon?'

---'Haakon to her has always been Haakon.'

Oh.

---'I worry sometimes. She seems so quiet. She doesn't talk, you know. And she doesn't have friends. What did you think. Do you think she's alright?'

---'Well ...'

The world, which seemed so full, seeming small and empty now. But richer, more luminous. As if I understand it; as if there is nothing new, as if all the old mysteries are gone and the new mystery is simply this: that everything is something else, as if creation has been skimping again, as if there are differences in degree perhaps, such as that between dogs and girls, but no differences in kind, one kind only, stretched and pulled into the sea, the girls, the trees. And this one kind is good. But someone speaking.

---'Oh, yes, and she wants you to take her to Euro-Disney tomorrow. Like you never did.'

Men and women as merely tamed. Oaks as succulent as lettuce, red-black wheat, yellow barley, green oats: flying down a road as soft and grey as fur between the fences, trees, and cornfields, playing house-music loud, conscious of her profile beside me, chewing chewing-gum.

On the way to Euro-Disney. Guttering in the sky: rat sized moths. The crickets, sharpening their knives. And huge rooks, sprinkled like pepper on shorn barley. And the vibrating heads of grasses in the wind, making her eyes go wide?